Caeia March was born in the I[...]
up in industrial South Yorkshi[...]
in October 1980, and she has [...]
and 20. She lives in Cornwall. She is a countrywoman now
and is a very keen gardener. She has published poetry, short
stories and non-fiction articles and is widely known as a tutor
of women's studies and creative writing. She is also the
author of three other novels, *Three Ply Yarn* (The Women's
Press, 1986), *The Hide and Seek Files* (The Women's Press,
1988) and *Fire! Fire!* (The Women's Press, 1991). She is
currently working on a new novel in the form of a ballad.

Also by Caeia March from The Women's Press:

Three Ply Yarn (1986)
The Hide and Seek Files (1988)
Fire! Fire! (1991)

CAEIA MARCH
REFLECTIONS

First published by The Women's Press Ltd, 1995
A member of the Namara Group
34 Great Sutton Street, London EC1V 0DX

British Library Cataloguing-in-Publication Data
A catalogue record for this book is available from the British
Library

ISBN 0 7043 4419 X

Phototypeset in Times by Intype, London
Printed and bound in Great Britain by
BPC Paperbacks Ltd, Member of BPC Ltd

ACKNOWLEDGEMENTS

This book could not have come into being before I had come to live in the inspiring landscape of Cornwall: the moors; the coastline; the sky, which changes constantly; the weather, always unpredictable; the old valleys; the secret woodlands; and the highest proliferation of prehistoric sites in Europe. I wake every morning grateful to be alive, here.

Some of my friends have played particular roles as the manuscript has developed. Thanks to Christine Holden from Sennen Cove for her hospitality at Kyoto, where I did some of the early writing, and completed the penultimate draft.

To Ann Kerr for detailed and encouraging comments on the first draft, and for giving so much time to me on the phone, throughout. To Keri Wood, Peg Wiseman and Cynthia Morris for sustained support of my work. To Jan Crewe, Liz Clarke and Priscilla Doherty for sharing their experiences of work with women, girls and children, whilst I was researching the early drafts of this book. To Penny Holland for endless long-distance phone calls, and always just when I needed them. To Hannah Carbis for walks on the cliffs and listening to my new work in progress, which has been the context in which the final draft of this novel was created.

To both my sons, my nieces and my sister, for love and friendship, to my older son for our trek around Ireland where I did some of the early research, and to my younger son for our fascinating trip to the Scillies.

I have been exceptionally fortunate in having Kathy Gale as my in-house editor for *Reflections*. Her enthusiasm for and enjoyment of each draft and all the intricacies and changes, has made the development of this manuscript very exciting for me. I am grateful for this delightful opportunity of working together.

To all the readers who have written, and to all those friends who have talked about their own creativity at different times, I owe a deepening of the understanding of my own process as a woman writer.

I want to thank all the lesbians who live in Cornwall for doing so. There are many of us, some very scattered, some more or less visible in everyday life. We are part of a changing, complex network, which in its very existence is inspiring. We do live here. We live everywhere that women live.

Similarly, there are women here and all over the world, celebrating many versions of woman-centred spirituality. There is no one way to do this. I am grateful for everything I have learned with many different women here in Cornwall over the past few years.

It is important to affirm that this is a work of fiction. The women in *Reflections* are fictional characters and do not directly resemble anyone I know. But in a book called *Reflections*, and given what women's lives are like under patriarchy, we may expect some resonances, however indirect.

Finally, and especially, I thank Cheryl Straffon, my partner, for editing the second draft in the sunshine summer of 1993; for all our days of play and research all over Cornwall and through part of Ireland; for the gift of sharing all aspects of our lives and work, including our jointly written non-fiction; and for loving me.

Caeia March, July 1994

PUBLISHERS' ACKNOWLEDGEMENTS

The Women's Press and Caeia March wish to acknowledge that the Cornish names for the festivals are from the original research of Craig Weatherhill, author and Cornish bard, and are reproduced with his kind permission; and that where the words 'She changes everything she touches and everything she touches, changes' appear in the text, they are believed to have originated in a poem by Starhawk.

BOOK 1

Between the earth and outer space there is a part of the sky in which, above the cloud cover, the sunset spins deep blue, red and orange ribbons of shining satin, and you can watch them, thinks Vonn, from behind a glass window, from the safety of an airplane seat. This in itself is pure delight, good for the soul, but it is not all that there is.

You can also flow your spirit self through the glass and then there are no boundaries. You need no broomsticks but this is what the witches meant by flying. Before airports and tarmac runways, before air-conditioned hermetically sealed metal birds with engine wings, before high-tech, late twentieth-century woman with her knowledge of passports and boarding cards; before this time there were women who flew.

Perhaps, thinks Vonn, allowing herself the luxury of being waited on by charming air hostesses, the late Elizabeth Somerville would have been one such woman. Not an ordinary village wise woman, though there were many and Vonn herself would have been more than content to have been a rural herbalist, complete with a cottage, a besom broom, an earth floor, and sage branches on the fire to cleanse and protect her home, but not so Elizabeth Somerville. Elizabeth was from the aristocracy. Somerville is after all an aristocratic name, and she is likely to have wanted status and some form of hierarchy, perhaps seeing herself as high priestess surrounded by novices, nine of them, or thirteen, or nineteen.

Elizabeth was a powerful healer during her twentieth-century life, and her newly edited diaries, published five years posthumously, available only from the States in expensive hardback, are Vonn's unusual reading material for the return journey to England.

Vonn absorbs the sky colours through the glass window, smiling to herself. Elizabeth was not the kind of woman

Vonn would usually meet, so of course they were not friends whilst Elizabeth was the consultant neurosurgeon and Vonn was nursing sister in the operating team.

Hospital etiquette is tight; the organisation is highly structured. The two women colleagues liked and respected each other, but they didn't know each other outside of the work context. But then Elizabeth Somerville learned that she had cancer. That terrible, taboo disease. The very word cancer is frequently taboo. But, ironically, this particular cancer was the direct cause of one of the deepest friendships Vonn feels she could hope to find.

Wanting a change herself, Vonn took up work as Elizabeth Somerville's personal nurse, left the city behind her, returned again to a rural environment not dissimilar to the one in which she had grown up, and became Elizabeth's friend in her house on the dunes.

Elizabeth Somerville's diaries are a joyous example of the Celtic thread of life. There is no fear in these writings, though life and death flow through each and every myth and legend. The wheel of the year turns and the land, sea and sky patterns shape-shift themselves through the stories, via the exploits of the colourful Celtic heroines. There are heroes too, but Elizabeth Somerville was a tough Celt, a woman force to be reckoned with; she loved the Celtic women and accorded them their full authority.

On the thirteen-hour flight, Vonn reads. The sun gives up her power and sets, pulling the satin streamers down out of Vonn's view, dragging them over the horizon's edge. The airplane moves on across the time zones from North America towards Heathrow, and Vonn is reminded by Elizabeth's writings that for the Celts time was not linear. Past, present and future shifted into now and then, and here and beyond and back again. Days turned to nights turned to days as the solar and lunar festivals marked the transition times between the seasons, whilst the moon took nearly nineteen years to return to her specific alignment in the pattern of earth and sun and moon with land and sea and sky.

Vonn reads and thinks as the moon sea night closes around the airplane. Other passengers eat or sleep or watch the movies on the cabin video screen.

Elsewhere it is day, or becoming so. Indeed as Vonn reads

2

on, through Cerridwen and Rhiannon, Maeve and the Morrigan, Bride/Brigid and the internecine struggles at the interface of Paganism and Christianity, she absorbs the Celtic mythos: that what we think of as boundaries are not always so. What we think of as beyond the here and now is sometimes inside us and all around us. There is time between time and space between stones, and what we think of as real may need to be re-examined; for within the apparent real, there is the hidden real, the unspoken real, waiting for us to connect.

Below the airplane the Atlantic is deep. Pulled by the moon, the tides of the Atlantic ebb and flow on the shore beyond the dunes, where Vonn has made her home. The fact of Elizabeth's life and liveliness flows through Elizabeth's diaries, bringing a sense of continuity, a gift from Elizabeth to Vonn.

Here is a top neurosurgeon who says that the psychic surgeons of the Philippines are possible. That they are real. Here is a woman trusted by the medical establishment, who says that she goes to a hill thirteen times a year to gaze upon the full moon, which illuminates her whole mind and allows her to develop some of her most prestigious scientific work.

Here is a woman who writes about holidays where she meditates in total darkness in an iron-age fogou in the Cornish landscape. A straight high-status medic who goes on a television programme about past life experiences. Elizabeth Somerville comes across, through her diaries, as unashamed and unapologetic, a humorous person, a complex personality, whose life is itself an illumination, and who writes of the healing power of each of us, our reflective centre, our creative inner dark.

It is dark night now over the Atlantic. Engrossed in *The Diaries*, Vonn intends to read for most of the flight, for the words are calling up happy memories of Elizabeth, the house on the dunes, and Elizabeth's researches into Celtic legends.

However, Vonn is rather tired; presently, whilst in the middle of one of Elizabeth's favourite legends, that of Tristan and Iseult, Vonn's concentration wavers, and, in spite of herself, she falls asleep. The book lies open on her lap while she dreams.

3

The sea is calm, at dawn. A Norse-style ship lies broken, stranded, visible in the cove, her masts snapped like saplings, her prow torn and tilted, her stern submerged in slow blue water. Her crew, now scattered, float somewhere like jellyfish, arms and legs downwards. Lost and gone, invisible.

Gulls wheel and scream, passing over. They observe a woman asleep, sprawled high on a rocky ledge. Mist steams from the young woman's soaked skirt and riding jacket. Her cloak is strewn around her, greener than the grassy cliffs, bluer than the morning sky. Rich red and sumptuous purple patterns are embroidered around the hem, which makes dazzling contrast against greyish-green lichens on grey granite boulders.

The young shipwrecked woman stirs. Her clothes are soaked; her hands are salty. She stands, with difficulty, bruised and sore. The leather belt which holds her athame and her sword is chafing her around the waist. She unbuckles it, and drapes it over a tree branch.

She strips off, and spreads her clothes on warm rocks to dry. She removes her riding boots and underclothes. She stands naked, raises her arms to the sky.

'Oh blessed one,' she calls, 'I thank thee. Mother of mine, mother of the sea, mother of the sky, mother of the earth, the air, I thank thee. Thou who made a great storm to free me from my captors. Thou who cast me from them, high above the tide line, on to this strange land, this wild and forested place, whose trees are greener than my cloak, whose waters are bluer than my eyes. I thank thee.'

She assesses the four directions, north, south, east and west. Arms raised, she turns through a full circle, giving thanks, calling, calling.

Spiralling, she moves slowly, aware of pain and bruises. Aware of life and strength and future.

Then, suddenly, she stops. Her arms fall to her sides. She shivers. She sits down. She faces the wrecked ship.

She, the niece of the king of Dumnonia, daughter of Blancheflower, his sister, raised in Armorica, has returned. She is a pagan, a country dweller, and this is a dangerous place for her. Here there are powerful barons who will deny her, who will plot against her, vengeful of any who are close to the throne. She will have to be on her guard, with all the skills of self-defence attuned, and she is ready.

She lifts her gaze to the distance. The horizon is limitless, indigo deep. Nothing between herself and never, herself and forever. Distant water is a mirror through which earth and sky interchange. She searches the horizon, to meet herself reflected back, alone in the universe; for water is the element where land and air do merge, each dissolving, shape-shifting. Water always stands between the worlds. Water carries her to go beyond, to travel through to search the other side.

Rapidly the young woman returns to herself, journeys inwards, inside herself, to meet her spirit guide. It is true, reveals her spirit guide, that you are alone. It is also true that you are strong, alive and about to move on.

Tristanne, Tristanne, your abductors have not destroyed you. They are themselves dead. Shipwrecked. The warrior-ocean wreaked her vengeance upon them. Tristanne, Tristanne, today is the dark time of the moon. Understand this dark. It is your future. You are here, now, alive in this new land. It was meant to be. Remember Carnac. Recall your ceremony.

So, now Tristanne sits naked, waiting for her clothes to dry.

She faces seawards on a rocky promontory below the castle.

Think back, says a voice inside her, think back, Tristanne, to Carnac, in Armorica. To your ceremony. Recall it now, in its entirety.

You are thirteen, magical lunar thirteen. Your woman time has come.

Your foster parents Rual li Foitenant and his good wife, Floreate, are kind, attentive. Theirs is the role, to pass on to you the powers, to initiate you into becoming a warrior woman, to focus and centre you, to ground you and keep you safe as you begin your journey.

You are the daughter of Blancheflower and Rivalin. Your real mother died giving birth, passing all her life force through her womb, into you, her baby daughter.

So it is that Rual takes you in his arms, the baby daughter of his closest friend, Rivalin. So it is that Floreate, his good wife, feigns a pregnancy, feigns her labour pains, falsifies your birth, takes you, Tristanne, as her own child, passing you off to the neighbours. Only the midwife, paid to keep the secret, knows. She will never tell. Such is the power of the secret, the power of the money, and it must be said, the power of the loyalty that flourishes between herself and Floreate. No, the midwife will never tell.

Tristanne, you are thirteen. Rual and Floreate accompany you, love you, fuss over you, on the way to Carnac.

There in the old, old stones, the needles on the body of the earth, pulsing with energy, giving off warmth and wisdom, there do three people arrive for your ceremony.

Rual, Floreate, Tristanne.

Together you form a triangle. Together you construct a blessing. For the passing on of love, for the passing on of power, for the initiation of you, Tristanne.

You call for the spirits to attend you. Earth. Air. Fire. Water. You cast a circle of protection, calling to the spirits to attend these your rites.

Rual begins his chant.

Daughter, daughter, foster daughter, take my wife's right hand. Come to the centre of these stones. I, Rual, bless you, daughter, touch you on your forehead with this blessed water. I call the spirits of earth, air, fire and water to protect you. I call them to teach you. I call them to your side in your acts of self-defence. I call them to hold you safely. For you will travel far, to far-off lands, and danger will befall you. Travelling the earth, wearing this cloak, no one will overpower you. In these difficult times, these times of trouble, church and war, when men from the church in Rome, unholy soldiers, trample the earth, declaring Christendom, you will cling to the old ways, the known ways, the world of spirits, and ancestors, the world of the country dwellers, the farm and fishing folk.

Woman warrior, blessed one, you will be received as equal to any man, talented on the harp and lyre, speaking many tongues, skilled with sword in self-defence.

Thirteen years have passed since my wife, the faithful one, the good loved one, Floreate, your foster mother, faked your

6

birth to keep you safe. For you are the niece of a great and wonderful King. Mark of Dumnonia is your patron, you are his sister's child, his sister Blancheflower's child.

Tristanne – whose name means sadness – I respect you; hold you safely while you learn your warrior powers; reach with your tutor the heights of scholarship; and learn the skilled arts of self-defence.

You are loved by us both, Floreate and I, your foster father, your own dear father's closest friend.

Rual kisses Tristanne on the forehead and, taking an embroidered cloak whose every skein is needled so finely by Floreate, he places the cloak across Floreate's outstretched arms.

She walks towards you, Tristanne, chanting strongly: Tristanne, daughter, foster daughter, I place this cloak around you. Today you begin your training. Your woman warrior training. Today you receive this cloak, embroidered with the thread of life. You will be no one's chattel, no one's wife. You will be free, a woman of spirit. Free of body; free of mind. Tristanne, daughter, foster daughter, you will travel far away. But I will hold you in my heart, safely in my heart, always. Moons and seas and stars you'll know. Ships you'll sail and gladly. To the corners of the earth you'll go, and I will miss you sadly.

Sadly, sadly, Tristanne, sadly. I will miss you sadly.

On the mirrors of the oceans, I will watch you, gladly.

Floreate places the cloak around Tristanne's shoulders. She sings softly, composing a melody as the words come to her. Music flows between the spaces of the great stones at Carnac. Music fills the stones and flows up to sew the land to the sky, to join them. There are men from the church in Rome who will change the lives of women, sings Floreate, for centuries to come. Men from Rome called Christians will march and sail the earth, plundering, invading, wiping out the old ways, the country people's festivals. Rual, my husband, your foster father tells it true. Women who were respected will be derided; women whose blood was sacred will be defiled; mothers will lose their babies taken into churches; husbands will lose their wives and daughters, raped and vilified. We feel this is soon to begin. With this cloak you will be empowered. Defended by the thread of life. No one's chattel. No one's wife.

They may compose their songs about you; write their epics, tell their tales. A warrior woman, Tristanne, of noble birth. From a lost land across the water, known as Lyonesse, where the stones meet the land, their powers drawn deep out of the earth. We shall know you, Tristanne, for below the legend there is you, woman. Your sadness is our sadness. Your gladness is our gladness. Beyond the stones you are woman, Tristanne, woman.

In years to come, down the lines of descent, they will have your stories, Tristanne. Some time somewhere there will rise up a whole generation of new women, strong and whole and wanting freedom. Freedom from wifedom. Freedom from Christianity. Freedom from soldiers, rapists, plunderers. Freedom from kings. Demanding once again the respect for our femaleness, wrapped in fine cloaks, and acts of self-defence. Then, my daughter, Tristanne, daughter, they will come once again to know you. Their moonlight will be so sure, so powerful, cutting like a knife through the sky, on a journey to tomorrow.

Tristanne gathers up her dry underclothes and puts them on. She steps into her riding skirt and fastens it. Dons her riding jacket and her boots. Reaches to the branch of the tree for her heavy leather belt and buckles it around her waist, checking that her athame and her sword are firmly placed. She shakes her cloak in the fresh air, admiring again her foster mother's fine needlework – a brilliant display of Celtic knots, serpent trails and dragon tails.

Go forward now, says her guide, blessed be. Learn. Grow and be firm. Know yourself. Be unafraid.

Journey onwards, free and strong.

* * *

Vonn wakes up and does not open her eyes. She holds on to the dream that has been so vivid. The airplane cabin is quiet. Slowly, into her early wakening awareness, there comes the familiar feel of Elizabeth Somerville's book, as Vonn realises, still with her eyes closed, that she is returning to Heathrow, to stay in London with her friends, Ben and

David, and then home by train, home to the house on the dunes.

Half aware of the sounds of the engines outside the aircraft window, she lies back, eyes still closed, recognising, with a wry smile, that it is typical of her to turn all dream heroes into women.

Vonn begins to think about what this intense dream could mean. Slowly, carefully, she allows her mind to move at will, enjoying the freedom.

The young woman is dressed in royal clothes. Vonn recalls the original legend, in which Tristan was the lost heir to the throne of one of the sixth-century Kings of Dumnonia, an ancient name for Cornwall. The King, for whom there is some archaeological evidence, in the form of an inscribed stone, was perhaps King Mark, known as Marcus Cunomorous.

Resting in her airplane seat, Vonn is warm and comfortable in a holding place between sleep and full wakefulness. She identifies with the young woman of the dream, who was abducted by pirates and then shipwrecked. Perhaps the pirates were women as well.

Vonn reflects on the layers of her dream and its landscape. She contemplates the interaction of the gulls with the sleeping woman, the memories on the cliffs, the isolation, the willingness to jettison all that has gone before, in order to remake our lives, to travel through hard terrain, and face uncertain futures.

Are not all women in the present time shipwreck survivors of one kind or another, watching the waters for reflections, of each other and ourselves?

She thinks of her friend Nuala and the other women she has just been staying with in North America; of their courage and new ways of behaving. Of their determination, however burdened or damaged they are by the events of their past, to make a new politics that goes way beyond the here and now; their refusal to be stuck in endless searching within the self; or trapped in the idea of the individual.

Shipwrecked rather like Tristanne, women in landscape, like Tristanne, women on adventures, like Tristanne. Are not our dreams a reflection of reality? And if so, how?

Is it not a dream that we could reach out beyond boundary,

beyond one skin around one woman's body, beyond self, beyond couple, beyond triangle, to the edge of the universe and back, reaching out, communicating, passing the wholeness on? Dreams, after all, can become reality, or there would be no politics, no creativity, no new ways of being for women. Dreams moving women through non-linear time, to and fro out and in here and now, all at once create and make again. Time. Slip. Ship. Dream. Land. Woman.

Vonn opens her eyes, stirs and stretches. The plane arrives.

* * *

It has been a bleak day, the wind blowing from the north and bitterly cold, and tonight, unusually for her, Rachel cannot sleep. She lies awake, her mind far too active, aggravated by the fact that she *has* to get a good night's sleep, since there is a pile of word processing to get through tomorrow, on a deadline, and Melloney's* rent money is due.

At one o'clock she is pacing in front of the aga, making coffee. It's hopeless to try to work, or to go back to bed and try to sleep. It was like this sometimes during the Avalon crisis. In London Rachel would have been trapped indoors waiting for morning, but here, in the cottage in the cove, she now feels safe at night to go outside.

She dresses warmly and, taking a flashlight and her key, makes her way through the alleys behind the cottages that cluster in the curve of cliffs around the cove.

She treads carefully up the granite steps, remade recently, part of the heritage programme. Here, high above the cove, the dark night is very beautiful, like the best known of Melloney's photos from a recent exhibition. Rachel misses her close friend, whose father grew up in this cove, and who is away at present, travelling with her Nigerian mother, visiting their family in Lagos. Oda, Melloney's mother, is a poet: mother and daughter are known for their images of spectacular skyscapes, constellations held like fireworks, totally still, above dramatic dark landscapes, female in form.

Below Rachel is the fishing village at the end of the land. Here, when Melloney's father was young, they would say

---

*Melloney is the seventeenth century Cornish name for Melanie. Both versions have the same pronunciation.

10

'Cornwall, near England'. Now, the whole cove is waiting for daylight. Boats are pulled high above the tide; lobster pots are stacked; ropes lie slack; and rusted chains are resting, slumped in heavy heaps. Behind closed doors the people are asleep, dreaming, snoring. No solitary cat stalks the empty streets, nor scavenges the spooky alleys.

It is the night of dark moon. A cold, star-filled night with barely any cloud. Rachel loves it, grateful for this wild place, its gift of night safety, so rare in women's lives these days.

She absorbs the quiet night, where she can almost touch the sounds of the sea. In her mind she hears one of Oda's songs:

> Call me Libya, the old name for Africa
> Call me Mother, in the dark of the night
> Call me the origin, the night owl, the universe
> Mother of Europa, my daughter who is young.

Above Rachel is the dark sky; beyond her is the night ocean; beneath her feet, the woman-land, at rest.

Then, as if for the first time, Rachel begins to understand how it may have been that ancient peoples believed that the whole universe was female: for the ocean is now curled around the land as two women sleeping. They could be mother and daughter, like Oda and Melloney; or they could be two women lovers. For wherever there are women, there are also women lovers, however hidden, however open, and they are here, the sea and land, at night, this night, sleeping.

One is soundly dreaming, the other not quite so, her sensual fingers stroking the land skin gently with slow rhythmic waves as if to say, sleep on, woman lover, and in the morning when you lazily open your eyes and part your thighs I will be here also, my long wet fingers in your caves, to bring you slow sliding gladness, in the early hours of dawn.

Although very quiet, the sea surface is busy. Lighthouse beams sweep the ocean, each beam distinct and each with its own reliable pulse and pause, individual as a fingerprint. Ships' lights move across the scene, at irregular intervals. Like oceanic glow-worms, the blobs of light move along,

11

each one making a slow arc across the surface of a black obsidian mirror.

Rachel watches, aware that she is not the only human being in this expanse of sea and sky. Behind the lights are people, people linked with other people; next to them on the ships, away from them on the shores. People who love and hate one another; people who tell truth and lies.

On the cliffs, in the night of dark moon, Rachel is an adult woman, the powerlessness of childhood long, long behind her. Childhood: a ship with no lights, a ghost ship, passing along unilluminated by truth. Things died there, without voice. Death by lies on the sea of adults who called it family life.

What if she sorts through these ghost ships, and finds some truths, what then?

Rachel realises that she has come on this walk because she is disturbed by memories of her teens and earlier years. They are stopping her from going to sleep; and have picked a strange night to intrude.

If only she could look back on family life and shrug, remembering some good times, and let the rest pass by, then maybe she could move on. But somehow, somehow she can't.

She feels stuck, emotionally. She doesn't want to stay stuck. So here she is above a silent sea on a dark and starry night, watching the sky, across which the lights of an aeroplane are now curving in a knife-like arc. The plane is heading inland, perhaps towards Bristol or London, in from the dark Atlantic. Briefly she thinks about the passengers up there, and wonders if they are sleeping, watching the movie, eating and drinking, talking, thinking, or reading. Rachel watches the lights of the plane until it passes out of sight, taking the people onward, on journeys of their own.

She has a blurred memory of her flight to Amsterdam, last summer, with her sister, Mieke. Memory plays tricks. Rachel has always trusted her memory, but now childhood memories come and go with less certainty, causing bewilderment and confusion, and whole periods are like these cliffs shape-shifting in the mist, sometimes completely obscured by fog.

But with sharp clarity, she recalls that it was during *that* holiday that Mieke first broached the subject of their mother's anger towards Rachel.

'You see, I was the younger one. It was different for me. Easy. Don't you remember Mum hitting you?'

'Not really. I remember Dad hitting me, but not Mum. I only remember some rows, and the crying.'

'But she did hit you, Rae. I used to be so upset.'

'I don't really know what you mean.'

'I mean she was often angry with you. Very often.'

'Was she? That often?'

'Very.'

'Why? What had I ... what did I do?'

'Anything. It didn't take much. You really can't remember it, can you?'

'No. Like I said. Only the crying. Having some rows.'

'I remember because I couldn't bear it. I mean her always on at you. I couldn't bear her going for you. Couldn't bear what she was doing.'

'Mum hit me? Are you sure, Mieke?'

'Very sure. And she's still ... she's angry about you giving up a well-paid job. I can't make her see reason. I've tried.'

'Yes. I know.'

'She won't give an inch. She's furious. I tried so hard with her, but it's hopeless. I can't bear it ... I tried so hard for you, Rae.'

'I'm glad I've got you, in all this mess. I'm so glad I've got you.'

'I've always loved you, Rae. I couldn't bear her hitting you. I never accepted it, and I still don't. And I,' Mieke pauses, 'I thought if we came back to Holland together, maybe I'd find the right words.'

Rachel watches the constellations far above her. Nothing moves. The sky tonight is peaceful. Her mind drifts back. Her father was from a solid middle-class family. His mother, Virginia, Rachel's grandmother Markham, had been Cornish, but her mother had died when she was born. Thus orphaned, Gran was raised in dire poverty by her aunt and uncle near Launceston.

Was Gran deeply alone as a child? Did she need to block that pain? Is that how come after she married into money in England she never went back over the Tamar? Is that why she used to declare that women must be ready to make new lives and not dwell on the past?

No wonder, thinks Rachel, sadly recalling Grandmother Markham's very English voice which held no trace of her early life, that my father thought himself entirely English.

Rachel was sure, even as a very small girl, that she was her father's favourite. He always made that clear, and it was amazing looking back that Mieke loved her without resentment.

Rachel was also sure that she was special too, to her grandmother. Gran was Rachel's ally, buddy, and secret admirer. Rachel needed her – and was aware that because of her, life at home was a good bit softer than it would otherwise have been.

Rachel stands still on the cliff, her eyes held steady on a dark space between some stars, aware of time warp, and of the power of sky and sea to pull her like the tides.

She can hear the clocks, the many clocks, ticking and chiming in her father's clock workshop. Clocks by which her life was measured. Segments of time, beyond her control. Clocks in frames – time encapsulated – time was power over all the women of the family. Her Cornish grandmother with all those years before marriage denied and dismissed. A Dutch mother exiled from her homeland – her own past slipping inexorably away.

Even her mother's real name, Truus, had been denied her. Gran, who had never showed any warmth towards her, refused to use it. An unpronounceable name, she declared. She introduced Rachel's mother as 'John's wife, Tracey.'

Now Rachel asks herself why her father didn't challenge his mother. Why did he allow her gran to treat her mother like that?

Why did her mother stay with her father, unvoiced and unnamed?

Truus van der Putten married John Markham.

She became Mrs Tracey Markham.

Wife of . . . John.

Mother of . . . Rachel and Mieke.

Daughter-in-law of Virginia.

She became unheard; de-cultured; dispossessed.

She became sad; depressed; angry; bitter.

She became incapable of protecting her daughters.

She became helmswoman of a ghost ship. Silent people on a silent ship on a silent sea in the silent night.

Slowly, sadly, Rachel retraces her steps down into the cove, and up again through the alleys which lead to Melloney's cottage.

In bed, falling asleep, Rachel feels more distant from her father than she has ever felt before. The chemical bond is dissolving; Rachel is watching him from a long way away, but can see him alone in his clock workshop, self-possessed, self-assured, working at home where he can control her mother's actions, and monitor her comings and goings. Her day belongs to him. She did not even have those kinds of control over everyday life, within housetime, that some housewives have when their husbands go out to work.

For the first time Rachel recognises that her father was a silent and ominous controlling force. He did exactly what he wanted, when he wanted, including bringing her mother across the sea from her homeland to his homeland, which was not her choice. That they loved one another Rachel doesn't doubt. But now, in Melloney's cottage and in a process of connecting with all the components of her past, Rachel amazes herself at how slow she has been to study the actual dynamics of her family life, and that, as soon as she really does so, she finds a distinct structural situation with her father firmly in control and her mother fighting him for an equal place at the head of the household.

Mrs Tracey Markham. The woman who brings Rachel much anguish. Her mother. A woman in pain. Unable to protect Rachel, her child.

* * *

There's a strong north wind with snow in it. High tide was about seven in the morning. It's now twelve noon, as Rachel strides towards the shore. As fast as Rachel and 'the girls' make footprints, the wind covers them with sand. Theirs are the first on the beach.

'The girls' bound along, tails wagging, full of the morning, glad to see Rachel again. Grey and white clouds are full overhead and moving very fast. When blue patches break through, they colour the sea blue. Fragments of mirrors appear at the tide line, rough and turbulent, broken scattered mirrors reflecting blue. They remind Rachel of Clare's favourite ornament – a tiny Indian elephant covered in minute diamond-shaped pieces of mirror with gaps between, unjoined. Clare and Rachel are ex-lovers, close friends. There is company here in this faraway place, now that Clare lives in the next village, with 'the girls'. But Clare cannot walk in the wind.

The tide has a terrific struggle to flow out westwards. The wind buffets from the north, trying to force the waves to turn south. Wild waves are thrown head over heels. The splashing spray doesn't stay in the hard pushing air, for the wind smashes it back into the sea with great ferocity.

The waves are whisked to egg-white peaks, stiff and packed with bubbles, then the wind palette-knifes them flat. Whisk white palette knife whisk white palette knife. Rise and slice; rise and slice.

Clouds hurry overhead. Rachel feels the wind and water's elemental power. She breathes deeply in the pure clean air.

Colours change as sunlight cuts open the wind with casual certainty, creating a delicious but temporary theme; meringue clouds with cream and butter edges. Rachel is thrilled by the unexpected contrast. The sea catches yellow mirror diamonds which shift and vanish.

Only the grey is reflected now in an ocean marbled with blue as Rachel's work schedule forces her back to Clare's house with 'the girls', away from the call of the healing beach. After hurried goodbyes, she returns to Melloney's cottage, where she bribes herself to get on with her work with the promise of the beach tomorrow.

* * *

It is dark outside the train windows on the last stage of Vonn's journey to the house on the dunes. Having returned from her holiday with her North American friends, landed at Heathrow, stayed with Ben and David in London, and been waved off by them at Paddington station, Vonn feels that she is now a veteran traveller. She is alone in the carriage since a noisy family with over-tired children alighted at Truro, much to Vonn's relief. She likes children and felt sorry for them and their harassed mother.

There are no refreshments on this part of the London to Penzance line, as if British Rail research has proved that people who live in this part of the country don't suffer from hunger or thirst. Vonn stuffs herself with her last packet of chocolate chip cookies and drains the last of her flask. The cookies make her thirstier still.

She sorts her luggage, checks that she has her cab fare handy, then makes her way to the vestibule between the carriages, where she lets down the window and watches the dark countryside trundling past.

Over the sea, which is just coming into view, the moon is invisible. Two more nights of dark, before the moon's new phase can be seen. The night brings powerful dark, thinks Vonn, watching the reflections of the distant harbour in the water. The healing dark. In the dark of this night lies positive power, and ancient peoples knew this – until their ideas were superseded by cultures whose only value was the light, whose language reflected this value, and who redefined the dark as fearful, disempowering, wicked, evil and female.

Vonn is almost home, where the dark times of the moon hold promise, wholeness and good fortune. Home.

The stars are floating in a black sky above a black sea and the paths of light from the reflections of the quayside lights dip deep into the waters of the bay where once lay an ancient oak forest. Legend has it that from here to the Scillies was the lost land of Lyonesse. Some versions declare that Tristan the young hero came from here, instead of Armorica, the old name for Brittany.

The atmosphere of *The Diaries of Elizabeth Somerville* remains with Vonn. Now, on the last part of her homeward route to the house on the dunes, she senses a calling, a significance in the timing of publication of *The Diaries*, as if the land of Cornwall to which she is returning holds new or different meanings for her, but she doesn't yet know what they are.

Through her work with retired people in nursing homes here in Cornwall, and through the power of this very old landscape, she has come to trust her intuition, which she used to block or sidestep.

Besides, she is going to meet Clare again, Ben's younger sister, who has come to live here because she is allergic to benzene in the city air. Clare has been very ill and now experiences a level of disability that is hard when you've been so active, in the midst of a busy city life.

Almost home, thinks Vonn, as the train runs slowly on around the bay. Coming home on the train can be magical when it's a night journey. Vonn always stands, alone, by the open train window, gazing at the curve of the bay, the distant house lights, the reflections, the land and sea and sky.

This always affects her deeply. Its beauty, its meaning – she is nearly home – its welcome. She always cries.

* * * *

Next day is dull, grey and misty. Rachel stands by the wall of her two-strides-across garden, thoroughly let down by the weather, unable to see the sea over the rooftops, or any sign of the sun, which is hidden behind heavy cloud. She has no plans to meet Clare or walk 'the girls' today since Clare's neighbour, an elderly widow who misses her own dogs and adores Bernese mountain dogs like Suky and Floss, is more than keen to take them out.

More word processing awaits Rachel, which does nothing to ease her disappointment. So she returns indoors and settles to a heavy workload, hoping to overcome an uneasy echo of voices in her head from Gran and Mieke. She makes coffee, stokes the aga, switches on the word processor and types up an extremely tedious chapter from one of her few remaining customers. Some of them have found it cheaper to type their own work, and others, caught in recession with rejects from publishers, have stopped writing.

A dose of the grey greebies lurks, ready to engulf Rachel. Outside the cottage the monotonous misery of the weather is broken only by a shower. It is very cold. It costs a fortune to keep warm whilst sitting working like this. But Rachel is determined. In spite of herself, she shrugs off the sense of being overwhelmed and works on, stopping only for a brief lunch. The manuscript has had many alterations and the handwriting is spidery, confusing at times, but is familiar, and she feels better when the pages mount up and she knows she is making headway.

Suddenly, about three o'clock, the room seems lighter. Rachel realises that the memory voices have faded, and the grey mist is lifting, bringing a bright grey and white afternoon.

Again that pull towards the seashore. That come-to-me beckoning by the finger-curling waves. Despite her workload, Rachel cannot resist.

In warm clothes, wearing heavy boots, tucking her dark shoulder-length hair firmly inside her balaclava, she makes her way from the cottage, through the back alleys, across the car park and over the dunes to the ravine that runs directly down to the long beach.

* * *

Meanwhile Vonn's day is peaceful, busy and happy. She puts off going shopping, deciding instead to doss about, making flapjacks, kicking the wonderful storage heaters, lighting a fire for fun in the living room, and investigating the contents of the deep freeze.

It's a mundane stay-at-home day, which would include a long walk on the beach if it wasn't for grey mists, cold wind and the occasional shower. From time to time Vonn looks out of the door to test the skies, willing them to clear so that she can go and say hello to the sea, at close up, at first hand, instead of waving at it across the dunes.

She listens to Radio Four lunchtime news, same old stuff, just the patriarchy shifting its arena of discord. Behind the male voices and the male assessments, Vonn can imagine the women and children. She catches up on *The Archers*, with delight, revelling in the rich accents, noticing that this episode has a woman writer and the dialogue is real. Then, while the flapjacks are cooking, Vonn enters the music room, removes the dust cover from her piano and plays, filling the house with classical themes, blues favourites and rock and roll oldies, which she was too young to have heard first time round. Now she loves them, and sings along happily, making herself at home.

Presently she stretches her arms, links her fingers and

flexes her wrists and hands, and returns to the great outdoors to see what the weather is doing.

To her surprise, matching her happy mood, and as if called up by Vonn's own very individual brand of magic, she finds that the skies have lightened to a light, bright silvery grey, no longer heavy or dull, and the sun's warmth is beginning to disperse the cloud.

Without hesitation Vonn finds her all-weather gear and makes a flask of hot coffee, a big flask, Elizabeth's posh double-capped one, for Vonn intends to stay by the sea a good long while, and she knows from experience that the temperature plummets towards late afternoon. She also finds a thick piece of plastic which makes an excellent damp course when you're resting on spray-soaked boulders. She packs a canvas bag in case she finds some pretty shells and pebbles, and sets off.

She chooses a solitary route, for she wishes, this time, to be uninterrupted – just herself and the sea, a new beginning.

The scene changes every day, she remembers with deep homecoming pleasure, and appears different in each movement of light, as each hour becomes the next. During her absence, winds have blown extra sand on to the paths which lead down through the dunes to the beach.

Vonn loves the variety, the fluidity, like returning to an unfinished watercolour painting. But today, she experiences with a shock its lack of colour: white sand, grey and white water, grey and white rocks. As if no other colour has been available, like an old grey and white photograph, vaguely hand-tinted with green on the edges of the cliffs.

She leaves the dunes and runs, arms and legs joyfully unco-ordinated, aware that she must look absolutely crazy, laughing and running across the dry sand, over the rippled, rivuletted wet sand and down to the edge of the low, low tide.

'I'm home. I'm home.'

She flings her face up to the sky and shouts aloud, though there is no one about to hear her. Then she runs and runs the length of the beach, letting herself splash slightly, skipping like a child, free and wild. It's wonderful this connection, this returning, this thing called life. She reaches her favourite boulders, and climbs across them to the part of the beach only exposed at very low tide, where she knows she may find some colourful pebbles. A singing deep contentment fills this solitude.

* * *

Rachel stands for a while on a sandy path above the long white beach, aware that she is alone in the universe. The hours have passed; the sharp disappointment caused by the grey wet mists and amplified by memories on the cliff path the night before last has disappeared. She pauses, watching the sea from this distance away, quietly allowing its bright silver-grey bouncing light to surround her, to ground her. There are soft, white fluffy edges on flat low waves indicating a very low tide.

Rachel thinks of the number of times that she longed for this kind of experience when she used to work in London. She would have liked a little peace, then. But she was not yet ready to leave the project nor to depart the city for a remote beach such as this, where challenge ebbs and flows like the tides, wave upon wave of questions coming in off the Atlantic in the wide fetch of the wind.

Hands in pockets, feet firmly planted on the sandy path, Rachel now lets her gaze trawl from the cove and headland on her left slowly across the vast expanse of ocean, towards the cliffs and distant headlands up the coast.

Rachel sighs, pulls her shoulders up to her ears and lets her shoulders drop again as the tension flows away. The beach is silent, except for the slow waves. Today, the distant headlands face a calm low tide, storm and crisis free. She herself is living alone, coping with half a year without dole as a state punishment for daring to 'voluntarily leave work', and instead of being torn apart by an under-resourced community arts project, she is being recreated here in this lovely place, which seems always to provide her with the energy she needs to meet its particular kinds of confrontation.

In the distance to her left, towards Land's End, are the grey or white cottages and houses of the cove. She can make out a few rare splashes of colour, higgledy-piggledy up the steep hillside. Someone's garage doors are blue; someone's tiny cottage is pale pink; someone's garden shed is deep green; and there is one set of red doors. All the other buildings and dwellings are grey, white or cream.

Rachel turns away from them, from any contact with the people she might meet if she walked in that direction. She walks down from the sandy path, across the dry sand, over the flat, hard, corrugated wet sand exposed by the low tide, to the edge of the waves, glorying in the strange threads of silver light that stitch the waves to the thin satin sunshine. The sun itself is a silver disc, cool and distant through translucent clouds.

Rachel puts the toecaps of her heavy boots into the sea. The waves are so low they pose no threat today. Clare was right about the powerful properties of this place. Ebb and flow, give and take, challenge and deep comfort.

Immersed in her thoughts, Rachel follows the waves to the furthest reach of the long white beach.

She climbs over the rocks, calculating that the tide is not yet on the turn, and scrambles down to her favourite hollow which can only be reached at low tide.

To her surprise, someone is already there. A woman is sitting, passing sand through her hands. Rachel immediately feels invaded. But she is in a stubborn mood, so she sits down, hackles rising, staring out to sea, willing the woman to leave. Neither of them speaks.

From the edge of her view, Rachel notices that the woman begins to examine intently a collection of small pebbles and shells, dropping them one by one into an old canvas bag. Rachel focuses on the distant white waves which are now regrouping, reforming as the tide turns.

Rachel asks herself whether the woman might live locally; and whether she might know just how dangerous the beach and the rocks are; and how capricious and fast the incoming tide can be.

Rachel bores her questions silently into the other woman's space. Her own defences are so high that she expects a force field, so she is taken aback as the woman turns, still seated, asking if Rachel is a visitor.

Rachel nods.

'I live here,' says the other one and smiles.

Rachel smiles back, taking herself by surprise.

Vonn stands up and begins to gather up her things. Without planning to say anything, she hears herself saying, as if she knows this stranger, 'The tide will cut us off here.' She smiles, picks up her canvas bag, then intuitively she finds herself offering to share the flask of coffee, because the temperature is falling, just as she had expected.

'I've got a flask,' she says. 'Would you like some coffee?'

The other woman nods, saying, 'Thanks. It's cold now. I'm chilled to the bone.' She stands up and manages a friendly smile.

They find a huge light grey boulder, safe on the upper shore.

Meanwhile Rachel is amazed at herself for bothering with someone towards whom, only a few moments ago, she was aiming hostile, please-leave-the-area vibes. But in spite of herself she finds that she's responding with a casual, almost friendly manner, something that could never have happened while she was working in London. It's a weird feeling. She can't quite get her head around it.

'Where are you staying?' begins Vonn.

'Chynoweth, in the cove.'

'Melloney's cottage? Here, this'll warm you up.'

'Thanks.' Rachel sips the coffee. 'Lovely. You know Melloney?'

'Not closely. But we're friendly if we meet. I've been away since the end of October. Has she left the cove?'

'Not for ever. She's travelling with her mother. She'll be away for a year or two, and I needed a place.' Rachel sips the coffee again then adds, 'We were at college together. I love Melloney's cottage.'

Vonn smiles, waves her free hand at the ocean and says, 'And all this. I just arrived home.'

'Have you always lived here?'

'No. I used to work in London. I was nursing there.'

'What brought you here?'

'I came here to work. To nurse someone who had terminal cancer. She died five years ago. I work part-time now, and I feel I belong here.'

'I'm not surprised. I feel this place is home already, I still say I'm a visitor but . . .' Rachel searches for words, but can't find the right ones. She smiles and shrugs instead, concentrating on the coffee.

'Top-up? There's plenty.'

'Thanks. I'm Rachel, by the way.'

'Lovely name.' Vonn smiles. 'I'm Vonn.'

'Vonn?' Bells are ringing. 'I've heard that name before.' Recognition is dawning as Rachel runs on, 'I don't want to pry, but are you, er, a friend of a nurse called Ben Nolan?'

Vonn laughs. 'Rachel? Are you Rachel Markham? You were with Ben's sister Clare?'

'You're Vonn Smedley. This is ridiculous!' Rachel is laughing.

Vonn laughs again. An infectious laugh.

Rachel says, 'I have always wanted to meet you, Vonn. You were with Frankie Jones, yes?' Vonn nods, smiling. 'And you two and Ben and David went round as a foursome.'

'Those were the days. Last century. I've heard so much about you, Rachel.'

Rachel is grinning broadly. 'Do you keep in touch with Frankie?'

'Yes. Letters. We grew up together and when we split it was because we'd become adults and we weren't childhood friends, or teenage sweethearts. Not any longer. We all change, don't we?'

'I hope so.' Rachel chuckles.

'Exactly. Frankie's a good soul. She's got a good heart.'

'And lots and lots of money, I heard.'

'You heard right.' Vonn laughs. 'The difference between us.'

'Wages being what they are in these parts.'

'That's right. More coffee?'

'No thanks. That was lovely, but, just an idea, I've got some soup slow-cooking at home. And home-made bread. Would you like some?'

'Yummy. I'd love some. Thanks.'

That infectious laugh again. Rachel finds herself relaxing. She hasn't heard women's laughter for a while. They shiver, packing up the flask tops. It becomes really cold now. The mist begins to roll in.

'I was in another world entirely when I came to the beach today. I can hardly believe this. Today started off so badly. What a turn around.'

'Never underestimate the power of this place.'

'We seem to be the only two humans left in the world,' says Rachel.

They stand for a few moments, taking in the scenery. The cove in the distance shows no sign of habitation. Out to sea there seems to be nothing between them and America, except three thousand miles of empty ocean. Behind them there are the remote cliffs, awesome and isolated, as they have been for centuries, silently withstanding the onslaught of wind and water. There isn't a single black-headed gull, nor red-legged oyster catcher, nor insect, nor sandworm.

Vonn says, 'They say people are called here. I don't know if that's true, but I do love this place.'

Once upon a time, thinks Rachel to herself whilst they climb the ravine that leads to the path through the dunes, I used to be open and friendly like this.

During their first meal together in Melloney's cottage Rachel finds herself talking easily about her life and how she came here to the cottage in the cove.

She gestures at the piles of papers around the word processor. 'It's horrible work, but I used to do some in London now and again if I wanted extra cash.'

'It's better paid than bar work or cleaning.'

'There's no work here anyway in the winter. Seasonal only, they said. And I have to cover Melloney's mortgage or she can't let me stay here.'

'This is a lovely cottage,' says Vonn, taking in the beams and the deep window ledges, and what seems to be a clarinet case near a music stand, with sheets of music scattered around. She feels compelled to get to know Rachel, though she doesn't really understand why. What a joy it would be if Rachel was musical, like herself. But now she recalls Ben saying that Rachel was feeling solitary right now, after some terrible trouble in London, and Vonn doesn't want to invade this privacy, nor outstay the welcome, though it was a warm welcome. So, she doesn't ask about the music at this time.

'Was it very awful, in your last job? I don't want to pry, but is that what brought you here?'

'I was working with a woman called Myrtle. We were appointed to two administration jobs together. We became good friends. Four years.'

Rachel pauses, serves the soup and rolls, then, with a deep sigh, she continues: 'They wanted to cut one of the posts. Myrtle's.'

'Why hers?'

'Good question.' Rachel bites her lip. 'We threatened them with everything. Community relations, everything. We argued it would be racist to fire her and not me.'

There is a lot of hurt in Rachel's dark grey eyes as she looks at Vonn. 'Myrtle was my friend. And also a single parent. It was awful. I couldn't have stayed there without her and ever looked any of my Black friends in the face again. And I'd always had this,' she nods over in the direction of the word processor, 'as a cash back-up. So after a lot of thought, I resigned. Sold the car, came here. If I make it through to the end of March I can sign on. I don't want to. But there's not really enough work coming in. I'll see how I go.'

'Do you want to live here? Stay here?'

'Yes. Yes I do. Very much. But I've always worked. Always had a job.'

There is a short pause. The soup is delicious. The bread superb. Presently Vonn says, 'I suppose I have the best of both worlds. A part-time job and the rest of the week to myself. I work in a residential home, three nights a week. And I've just finished an OU degree. I promised myself the winter as a reward.'

'I do admire people who do that. OU, I mean. Takes true grit.'

'If I'd known that I mightn't have started.' They both laugh.

'A long reward then. Good for you. Where did you go?'

'With friends in Oregon. Lovely women.'

'I hear the scenery's beautiful.'

'Yes, the landscape's nice too. Trees and such.' Vonn winks. Their laughter is free and out and proud.

'You know, I really should be going.' Vonn sounds reluctant.

'Yes, and I should be working. Though I'd rather talk to you.'

'And me to you,' replies Vonn.

It is a warm moment, and they notice each other in a different way.

To Vonn, Rachel seems very lively, with soft, dark grey eyes and dark shoulder-length hair and a fine fair skin, almost perfect. Not a pretty woman in the traditional sense, but with a deep sense of caring and some pain showing through. Her eyes are clear and intelligent, her hands well kept.

Rachel thinks that Vonn has a lovely face. Vonn's eyes aren't brown or green or grey. And they certainly aren't blue. More greenish-blue than greenish-grey. Her hair is short, chestnut, with a slight wave, not curly. She has uneven features but they fit together to make Vonn's face, which they fit exactly right, and it is a very interesting face. At least, it is to Rachel. Vonn is about five feet five, medium build, with strong hands, not large but practical hands. She has a calming effect on Rachel, who can imagine Vonn with vulnerable patients, giving them confidence without fussing.

'I'm glad I met you today. I can't get over it. I really can't.'

Vonn smiles. 'Will you come for dinner tomorrow evening?'

'I'd love to,' says Rachel, surprised at the speed with which she accepts. The words are out of her mouth before she has even considered them. 'I mean,' she adds hastily, 'if it's not too much of a rush, if you're only just home from travelling.'

'I have to do a mega shop tomorrow anyway, and after that I shall be starting work again back at the nursing home. Do come. About seven?'

'Okay, great.' Rachel allows herself another smile. 'Do you like red wine? Clare gave me a bottle that she can't use. I've been saving it. I'll bring it, shall I?'

'That would be lovely. Thanks.'

They stand shyly for a moment, as if the old days of the women's movement, when you naturally hugged at the end of a meeting, were long, long gone. These days you hesitate, and there's a nostalgia sometimes for the old spontaneity. Then they grin and meet each other's eyes, and seem to recall that they're not exactly strangers, for they each know Clare, and have known about each other, and so they find themselves hugging, warmly, saying see you tomorrow.

* * *

Later, when Vonn has returned to the house on the dunes, Rachel prepares for an evening's work, asking herself how it was that she knew when they met on the shore that afternoon that something was happening. She knows that Vonn had felt it as well. Was it one of those chance meetings that people here in this part of the country don't seem surprised at? Had they been called to that moment?

* * *

I was called to Cornwall, certainly, says Vonn to herself as she prepares for bed, and then remembers how she used to deny such 'superstitious nonsense' as she used to call it when Elizabeth Somerville had been alive.

Elizabeth had laughed loudly, not unkindly. As a Celt, she had said, she knew there was no point in planning out the future. Plans are human beings' way of boxing up uncertain reality, framing it, trying to make it safe. But real life has an incredible way of refusing to go to plan. Hence the awful New Age cliché of going with the flow. You have to, according to Elizabeth, who had no time for New Age nonsense, because the flow is what there is. It *is* reality.

Vonn climbs into bed and opens *The Diaries*, looking for the story of Tristan and Iseult. She wants to know it, she feels suddenly, backwards, forwards and inside out:

During those times of the great legends, there were two phases of migration from Ireland to Dumnonia from the end of the fourth to the middle of the seventh centuries, current era. We can use the latter as our pagan term for anno domini, leaving out the star, the stable, the manger and boy child lying there.

One wave of Irish migration was from the north to the Camel River Valley. These immigrants were fine potters, bringing their designs, known as grassware, with them. The other was from the south across the Irish Sea to South Wales, and thence to Dumnonia. Both migrations took place during those times in which the story of Tristan and Iseult was first told.

28

Vonn pauses – Tristanne and Iseult. She finds herself lying in the dark, thinking about the meeting with Rachel. When Vonn thinks of Rachel's eyes, her face, the shape of her shoulders, a deep feeling stirs inside her. Not nostalgia for Frankie, her first lover; nor memories of Danielle, who has been back in France for eighteen months; nor, more recently, the lovely warmth of Joan – for Joan is in Oregon and they had both known that this warmth was real but temporary – instead there stirs in Vonn at the thought of Rachel, a surge of wanting which is tantalising and unexpected, touching a new kind of music. Vonn has nothing with which to compare this feeling. She has never felt so compellingly drawn towards a virtual stranger, known only by hearsay and experienced only for a couple of hours. Nevertheless she recognises this sparkle and, lying in the dark, thinking of Tristanne and Iseult, Vonn seeks only to know this sparkle more thoroughly and not to extinguish it at all.

* * *

Rachel works until two in the morning, mainly because she cannot settle to get ready for bed. She has a floating image of Vonn's face.

At three in the morning, Rachel stretches and yawns, goes to bed, puts out the light. She lies awake thinking about Vonn. She recalls her own free laughter, and her alacrity at accepting Vonn's invitation. She has never said yes so fast to anything, it seems. She smiles at the memory, then, becoming drowsy at last, she drifts off into sleep.

She dreams of Vonn but can't recall the dream itself.

Next morning Rachel works hard at her word processor, trying not to think about dinner with Vonn, whose face floats just above the screen all day.

When Rachel has to stop for food, drink or a pee, always Vonn's face is there, smiling, so that eventually Rachel says to herself, at the very least we could begin to get to know each other.

* * *

Meanwhile Vonn spends her second day back in the house on the dunes in contacting the nursing home, verifying the date she is to resume work, then taking the car to the supermarket, where she does a mega shop and browses over frozen raspberry pavlovas for tonight's dessert.

Rachel's soft grey eyes seem to dance just a little ahead of Vonn all day. Vonn remembers the touch of Danielle; the lovemaking with Frankie all those years ago; and the glory of a beautiful, sexual slow waltz in Oregon with Joan. But with Rachel? I have to see her.

She buys the pavlova.

* * *

Rachel arrives exactly on time with the bottle of fine red wine and a tiny kangaroo vine plant which she potted up specially, since without a car she couldn't get to the florist.

Vonn has prepared carrot soup with coriander, which they eat by the fire in the living room, whose wide windows face the dunes.

They talk of Clare, and 'the girls'; they talk of Melloney, Ben and David; they talk of Clare's mum, Eileen, whom they both know and love; they talk of Elizabeth Somerville and her *Diaries*; they talk of where they each lived and how they lived and how come they never met until now.

The main course is a spinach roulade with new potatoes, which Rachel finds delicious. Talk turns to food and travel, and Rachel notices that Vonn says almost nothing about her family.

Throughout the dinner, which they eat on trays on their laps, with their wine beside them and the fire leaping and dancing, Rachel is aware of a strong physical pull towards Vonn, and feels rather frightened. It is all so very, very fast.

The pavlova is exactly right.

After dinner, Vonn tends the fire then pulls a large cushion on to the hearth rug and sits there, putting logs on the fire from time to time.

Vonn is aware that Rachel fancies her; aware of Rachel's clear body language which can't easily be hidden; aware too that Rachel is pulling back. She begins to talk about music, hoping that this will interest Rachel and trying to put her at ease.

'I couldn't help but notice your clarinet back in Melloney's cottage,' she begins. 'It was lovely to see it there, with all your music lying around. But everything was so fast, we never talked about our music, did we?'

'Have you always loved music, Vonn?'

'I've been musical since I was small. When I was five I heard a violin on the television, for the first time. I asked Mum if she'd let me learn to play one. She said it would be too expensive but I could go to Mrs Jones, my friend Frankie's mum, for piano, and if I was any good she'd see about a violin later on. Of course she couldn't afford one anyway, but she didn't say that. I longed and longed for a violin. These days I love the piano as well, but when I was small I only played so that I could have a violin. Now I try anything that makes music.'

Rachel allows herself the luxury of sitting back while another musician talks, admitting to herself that Vonn is lovely to look at. They talk of favourite composers, and Ethel Smythe's centenary, and Rachel's love of the clarinet, which she learned to play in her teens at school.

Presently, Vonn goes out to fetch more logs and Rachel picks up a copy of a hardback book which is lying with a bookmark in it, on the low table. It's a very beautiful book with a picture of the author, Elizabeth Somerville, on the back cover. With an intake of breath, Rachel realises that she has heard of this book on the radio, and that this must be the woman whom Vonn nursed through terminal cancer.

The book falls open at page twenty:

This legend is my favourite, that of the triangular tragedy befalling Iseult, princess of Ireland, and King Mark of Dumnonia, to whom she was brought by a young envoy, Tristan, to be married. I imagine the young pair on the ship, the movement of the waves, the wine being drunk by both of them, wine which unknown to them held a love potion which was meant for Iseult and the King. I imagine them falling asleep, waking and recognising that they were fated to meet, to drink the potion, to begin a relationship with one another.

I imagine the unfolding of their shared experience, the delight in conversation, the language of music in which they both excelled.

Rachel drops the book as Vonn enters with the bucket of coal.

She gathers it up quickly. 'Sorry. Such a lovely book. So clumsy. Sorry.'

'Don't worry. Easily done. No harm done.' And, in answer to Rachel's visual question about the woman on the back cover, 'Yes. I nursed Elizabeth Somerville here in this house.' Vonn makes up the fire, then comes to sit by Rachel's armchair as they read the blurb on the cover together. Then Vonn says, 'I had a little flatlet in London. And I kept it when I first came here to work. The people who rented it from me absconded with some of my things and left me twelve hundred pounds of debts.'

'Bloody hell.'

'I know. Elizabeth said she couldn't allow me to be so insecure, so if I sold my flatlet she would sell me this place, which as you can see isn't very big – this floor at ground level and two rooms under this level built into the hillside. I used to have those and she this top bit, which is okay for a wheelchair. The price I got on my flatlet just about covered the price of this. We lived here until she died. A strange time, but very happy. She called this the sunset room.'

'Can I ask you something?'

'Of course.'

'Do you think we were meant to meet on the beach, yesterday?'

'It seems like that, doesn't it?'

'But I don't quite, can't quite . . .'

'Put your finger on it?'

'Something like that. I need a drink!'

'More wine?'

'Yes please.'

Vonn fills their glasses and they both drink the wine, slowly.

Vonn waits quietly by the fire. She has plenty of questions of her own, but she feels that they can wait. Her thoughts and feelings often come through to her as music, just as some artists she knows see everything, feel everything in light, colour and image.

She lets the space between her and Rachel float lightly, and she pushes away a remembered harmony from Wagner's opera on the Tristan and Isolde myth. She has her own compositions swirling in her mind, but most of all at this moment she wants a cadence for the experience of meeting Rachel and the sense that something is happening to them, something not quite in their control. Vonn breathes slowly, so as not to interrupt the silence.

Vonn's breasts feel soft and full, though she doesn't look at Rachel, whose nearness is making Vonn's body sing. She has only to think of Rachel's mouth, her lips, her tongue, to make her breasts firm and ready, her nipples waiting, wanting. She calms herself, slowing her breathing evenly, steadying herself. She turns her face, slightly smiling, with her eyes open, towards the warmth of the fire. Her hands are calm, not fidgeting. Slowly she begins to look into the shining holes in the fire, imagining the sounds of the sea as she and Rachel travel in a safe boat from Ireland to Cornwall. They are two women, in the boat, happy, seated beside each other, drinking the potion. The boat moves on, effortlessly.

Music fills Vonn's mind. She is working, listening intently now to her inner world of music, as she composes the phrases for her body's feelings being mirrored by Rachel's.

In the deep plumpy armchair Rachel leans back, observing Vonn's very quiet breathing, and the friendly minute noises coming from the open fire.

Rachel thinks of herself playing the clarinet, notices the tilt of Vonn's head, the intensity with which Vonn is listening to her own inner world. Vonn seems to be distant, self-contained and comfortable, sitting cross-legged on the hearth rug, her face in profile turned towards the fire, her eyes open. She has an unruffled presence, and a silent language, recognisable from one musician to another. Rachel can imagine Vonn's mental space as a vessel of multiple sliding liquids, all transposed into rhythm, tone, halftone, chord and pattern. There is something quite philosophical, definitely mathematical about it, the pure logic of how sounds fit together, and the sheer deviance of wilful notes that won't fit so that they tip the melody this way, the harmony that way.

From the corner of her eye, Rachel catches firelight glinting on the silver clips of Vonn's violin case, and on the edges of the music stand where some open music doesn't quite hide the metal.

Perhaps this is Vonn's way of giving me this space, thinks Rachel. Either it's a very clever turn-on; or it's simply the composer in her taking over, guiding her through. If in doubt, work. There's never a time without music for a woman who can work like this. Whatever her experience, she can make something. I don't operate creatively like this. I analyse, weigh and measure. Like now, the brain's on red alert. I want to shut this process down, to just be. Too much head stuff. For my body's opening, and I'm already moist where it matters, wanting her. If I let my body out of this brain box, I could be there, next to her, touching, lips, mouths, hands, thighs. Her jeans have soft, old blue material. They pull slightly where her hip bends as she sits cross-legged; they stretch slightly over the curve of her knee. She has wonderful thighs. Oh I'd like to smooth my hands on the soft material there along those thighs. This is too fast for me. I hardly know this woman. Who is she? Who could she be in my life? I wish I could stop analysing and just be: reach forward and begin. I know this is mutual. It's obvious. She's lovely. Does it matter that this is faster than I've ever known? Does it?

Is my body wiser than me today? I amaze myself. She is self-contained there. Complete. She's creating. I can see it, creating from the inside of herself. She is like a very quiet candle, alight from inside. If I want to touch her, I simply move from here and begin.

For many minutes they sit there. Vonn is listening to her inner world, searching into the gleaming fire. It seems cool inside the white and yellow spaces, where there seems to be not heat but water, and the fire becomes a mirror into the ocean.

Rachel is drinking her wine, thinking about the extract she has just read in *The Diaries*, noticing the lovely grandmother clock in the corner whose soft tick-tick has a very gentle, unhurried metronome quality. Time. Let it flow. Let the music fill the spaces, do not fear it, do not hurry it, it will compose itself, in its own rhythm, in its own time, if it is allowed the time it takes. Non-linear time. Circular and plentiful, unboundaried by the conscious mind, flowing from the inner spark, room time, womb time, woman time my time your time our time.

The sparkle that shifts and changes between them is so strong as to be almost tangible. There is a wanting, a needing, and a sense that this is so for both of them, mutually.

In spite of herself, though, Rachel hears herself whispering, and without intending to she discovers that the whisper is opened into the space between them, just audible, so that Vonn can catch the words, hold them, consider them.

'I'm frightened.'

Vonn turns slowly, as their eyes meet. Rachel's are filling with tears, though she is not crying.

'Tell me,' says Vonn very quietly.

'It's simple really. I'm very frightened.'

'Of us? Of this?'

'No. Just the speed of it. We only met yesterday. I can't catch up with myself.'

'Me neither. I can't quite understand it, can you?'

'No. But it is real, isn't it?'

'Yes. It's real. It's astonishingly real.'

'Are you frightened?'

'Not of the reality,' says Vonn. 'It just is. But I am shaken by the speed, yes. It's never happened to me like this, never in my life.'

'Nor to me. I've been so lucky – the lovely women, not many, just my fair share. But not like this. I don't cope very well like this.' Rachel swallows, rubs her nose, sniffs, then smiles. 'Oh, what a relief it is to talk.'

'I'm in no hurry, are you?'

'No, but I can't get you out of my mind.'

'Nor can I. It's very strong, isn't it?'

'Oh, yes. You know what I'd really like? If you'd play me something? I'd love it . . . then . . . would you mind if I went on home?'

'Sounds fine to me. I'd love to play something.'

'And will you come to lunch tomorrow? I know you're

working tomorrow night, and it'd be an awful long three days otherwise.'

'Perfect. Do you play the piano at all?'

'Bit rusty.'

'I've got a recorder?'

'That'll do. Where is it?'

'Downstairs. Come on.'

At the end of the evening, as they kiss good night, Rachel says, 'It's wonderful, isn't it? I can hear all kinds of music in my mind.'

'So can I. You were fantastic on the recorder.'

'Haven't played for a while. I enjoyed it. All of it. Beautiful piano. Superb. You're very good, you know.'

'I've had an idea. Can we have a day out, sometime soon?'

'Oh, yes. That sounds great. Let's go to the sea.'

They hold one another, then touch each other's faces, kissing each other's fingers, kissing each other's eyes. Presently Rachel sighs, a deep relaxing sigh. 'Thanks for offering to lend me *The Diaries*. I'll have so many questions, you know. Legends and places, and migrations and astronomy. What a book. I'll take good care of it.'

'I know you will. It's safe with you. That's why I offered it.'

'What time for lunch?'

'Twelve noon?'

'Brilliant. That's not long. A read and a sleep and I'll see you.'

'I'm going to miss you.'

'Me too.'

They hug again before Rachel leaves. Vonn watches the torchlight bobbing up and down in front of Rachel's retreating figure, delighted that Rachel turns to wave good night with the torch in her hand so the beam curves and bounces over the dunes. Vonn returns the wave, hoping that she is silhouetted with the house lights behind her, so that Rachel can see her. Then she hugs herself against the night air. The sky is dark, full of stars; the sea beats on the shore in the distance.

She locks the door, checks the windows and prepares for

bed, stacking the washing-up which she wouldn't let Rachel do, this time.

Then she sits in the dark by the embers of the fire for what seems a long time, thinking about the extraordinary events and pace of the past few days. Her thoughts turn to Oregon and the women whom she visited there; to her first lover Frankie, whose mother was Vonn's first piano teacher, beginning soon after Frankie came to live on their council estate in Brighton; and back to this evening and an amazing woman, Rachel, whose figure was last seen disappearing along a sandy path to the cove.

Sitting, thinking, Vonn doesn't notice the passing of time until Elizabeth's grandmother clock chimes midnight.

Vonn places the fireguard around the remains of the living-room fire, and goes into the music room, where she tries a tune that is beginning to haunt her, a tune which began whilst they were sitting by the fire earlier that evening. Two women in a boat, drinking wine.

Presently she closes the piano lid, and, needing to reconnect with Elizabeth, she carefully unwraps a brand-new copy of *The Diaries*, intended as a special gift for her close friends, Lou and Annie, who were fond of Elizabeth.

She hasn't meant to use this copy. Feeling a little guilty, Vonn takes the book to bed, and reads carefully, without damaging the spine, knowing that Rachel is at home doing the same thing.

As she reads *The Diaries*, Vonn recognises that winter is almost at an end here in Cornwall. Elizabeth seems so close as she reads her words on the page:

To the Celts the new year began in November. Winter was the period for fireside gatherings: storytelling.

Everything in threes; or three times three.

So it was that the crone, the maiden and the mother were the guardians of the seasons, in that order.

The wheel of the year began with the time of the creative inner dark. A time for positive creativity, for community, for warmth, for hearth.

In the dark was fire. The spark. The ember.

In the dark came the old woman, she who was wise, knowing, who would be the guide through the short days, when the sun lingered not long in the sky, and the nights were long.

She was the great one, Brigid, crone and maiden, for she emerged again in her new form as the young and vigorous woman of the end of winter, the beginning of regrowth.

She was the great one, the fire goddess who kept them warm all winter. She was the goddess of water; of the flowing, nurturing powers of the wells and curative properties of the rivers and springs. She was the goddess of poetry and prophecy, her crone wisdom encapsulating all other wisdom, her winter aspect being that of storytelling for her communities until the expansive days of summer. She was the goddess of science, one of the first great women scientists, who taught her people the art of smithcraft and metallurgy.

On the eve of the first of February she was welcomed with candles and songs, with drums, dances and feasts. Her bones were young again. She could fling her arms and legs with wild movements, shedding her winter wise self like a snake-skin, allowing her people to witness her wisdom outside herself in her end of winter growth. In Ireland they called this time Imbolc. The Cornish word for Imbolc was Corawis.

Vonn closes the book, falls asleep, and dreams of Rachel.

* * *

That night, in the cottage in the cove, Rachel reads Vonn's copy of *The Diaries* until, exhausted, she can't read any longer.

The photographs are stunning, the descriptions of the wheel of the year are new to her, and the sense of who the writer was is inspiring. More than that, though, there is something reaching to Rachel beyond the words on the page, integral to the connection with Vonn Smedley, through whom this book came to be loaned to Rachel; and beyond all of that, a feeling of identification, of coming home.

Something very old is touching Rachel now, in a way that nothing has ever touched her before. Something that takes her into her own past, through her parents, her Cornish grandmother, her Dutch grandmother, to a time when women were the focus of community and the earth was respected for her essential femaleness.

The sun, the moon, the stars; the ocean, the streams and rivers; the valleys, hills and fields; the forests, woods and glades. All were female, part of each other, belonging.

Woman. Woman in land. Woman as land. If you hurt the woman, you hurt the land. If you hurt the land, you hurt the woman.

Woman and land. Reflected. Integral. Whole.

Rachel is becoming aware that within the reflection – Woman and land – there lies the legend of Iseult.

A story that created poetry, passion, and music.

A story that lasted three or four hundred years in the oral tradition before the Norman French scribes wrote it down.

A story of a woman.

A young woman.

Sold by her father to the King of Dumnonia.

Against her will.

And her mother could not prevent it.

Wanting suddenly to leave the legend-world, Rachel puts down the book. Clicking off the light switch, she fades almost instantly into a dream-world of sleep.

* * *

Iseult is running from her father, but he must not know that, for if he does he will pursue her. Outwardly, Iseult appears to be finally accepting her father's plans that she shall go to Dumnonia to marry King Mark.

She packs her belongings. Her combs and brushes; her lovely embroidered undergarments; her handmade shoes; her warm winter cloak. Unhurriedly, she gathers together her favourite hand mirror, her small leather bottles of ointments and salves; her precious wooden box with compartments for dried herbs.

Jewellery she leaves behind, knowing that Mark will heap precious gifts upon her once she arrives on the distant shore where he has his castle.

Presently, Iseult is ready. Her mother holds her close, whispering to her that Brangane, her maid, has everything Iseult needs for the nuptial night. Iseult suppresses a shudder, deeply disturbed that her mother seems to approve of

Iseult's planned marriage to a king, an older man, a stranger whom Iseult has only heard of, never seen.

Thus, Iseult departs the coast of Ireland, travelling towards the sunrise, watching the black sky, the rising waxing moon, and the moon's path to the underworld, beneath the waves.

She is offered wine by Brangane. She wishes to drink heavily, to become oblivious for a while, and is glad of the spicy drink, which warms her as she sips it. The travellers are soon sound asleep.

All night the boat moves across the open sea. All night the waxing moon provides bright light to guide a pathway to an unknown future.

When Iseult wakes she finds that she has been dreaming – of a forest where she will find shelter. She has dreamed of running away from the King, who has pursued her in her dream as if he were her own father, with power over her life and her wishes.

As Iseult reflects on her dreams she is very angry at being turned into a victim by the two father figures: the one her real father, the other an older man, her husband-to-be. But Iseult knows that if she is to survive at all she must marry the King, go through with the ceremony, and lie under him in his bed and please him. Despite her fear, Iseult believes that King Mark's pursuit of her will be worse if she doesn't at first appear to succumb. For it is the tradition in her family that the daughter represents the land itself. The old ways linger on, she knows. She has been well educated by her parents and tutors. She is accomplished in music, languages and healing. She is female, of the land, and is the land.

The King of Dumnonia cannot have his power linked with the land of Ireland unless he marries that land, in the form of the Irish Princess, Iseult herself. In the past she would have been a descendant of the great Goddess Brigid, and though the rule of Kings has become the modern way in Ireland in Iseult's time, and though there are debates throughout the courts about the changes taking place in religion, the people still honour the old ways, and the lights never fade on the fires of Brigid in the temples at Kildare.

To marry the daughter of the land is to marry the land. She, the young Iseult, is the land. Her healing powers are from the land, and of the land. She grows the herbs that are the cures; she finds and blesses the waters that spring all over her beautiful homeland in the hills and from the sacred wells. The traditions are strong, the land provides. Mother Earth is the mother of the people, and has many names, and all of them are still sacred in Iseult's time.

She rises and goes on deck. She stands watching the waves. She is not the first woman of Ireland to make this journey. Irish potters and craftspeople have been trading with Wales and Dumnonia for years. How many women have travelled, young and vigorous, alongside their sweethearts? How many have been with child on departure, and birthed their children in the new lands? And have slept again with their men, and have become heavy again with child, and birthed again, a second, third and fourth time? There are Irish families now, in Iseult's time, in southern Wales, and some have travelled onwards to Dumnonia itself, taking with them their beliefs and goddesses. Along the Camel estuary, so Iseult's father has been told by traders, there are people who are originally from Ireland. The voices are known; the children are grown; the pottery is considered to be fine.

Iseult takes from her pocket a small obsidian mirror. Obsidian is very beautiful, shining, black, reflective. Her mirror is dainty, pocket-sized, and surrounded by a finely worked pewter edge, pewter so thin that it isn't heavy, and formed into a dragon, coiled around itself like a thread of life. There is no end and no beginning. There is self and reflected self. There is victim and survivor.

Iseult knows that she is both of these. She abhors her forthcoming unwanted marriage bed. But Iseult is very strong, aware that the survivor inside her – her determined inner self – will see her through the ordeal of the unknown future time. That self is capable of meeting and matching the King strength for strength. He may be older and very powerful, but Iseult has the healing power. She uses it whenever she can. The country people often hurt themselves on the land, for the land is not always easy, or willing, or kind, and Iseult can treat their wounds. The land is both victim and survivor. The land fights back.

She, Iseult, reflected in her small obsidian mirror, is both woman and land. This is her inherited strength, coming through the air, from the flames at Kildare. Coming through the water, from the springs and wells of Brigid, the great one; coming through the fire each time a hearth is kindled; coming through the earth each time a healing plant brings forth leaves, or whenever the land provides Iseult with food.

So she stands upon the deck, as the cliffs of Dumnonia come into view through the early morning mist, watching the colours of the sky and sea, noticing the patterns on the waves, and searches for herself in the obsidian mirror's depth.

* * *

Rachel doesn't wake until mid-morning. She lies in the dim room in the cottage in the cove, thinking of the intense dream, running and re-running the film of it until every part is coherent, clear, and can be recalled in detail.

Then she gets up and writes it down in its entirety, then takes pastels and draws some of the images that arise from the dream, finds fixative and sprays her drawings to set them. She writes the date on the back of each one.

The dream is so meaningful for her that it seems to exist all around her, and she tidies the cottage inside its ambience as if the dream is a hologram in whose energies she lives.

She washes herself, gets dressed and makes coffee, all inside the hologram. She stokes the aga and prepares lunch for Vonn, inside the hologram; she hears Vonn's knock on the door and opens it and lets Vonn into the cottage, still living inside the image power of the dream.

They hug and, taking one look at Rachel, Vonn says, 'Are you all right? What's the matter?'

'I read *The Diaries* until the early hours. Then I slept, till eleven. I had a dream and it's still all around me. Are you okay?'

'Yes, I'm fine. Want to talk about it?'

'Please.' Rachel nods vigorously. 'Tea or coffee?'

'Tea, thanks.'

Rachel begins to respond to the solid presence of someone else in the cottage. She says, 'I've written it down. It's on the table.'

'Is this it?' Vonn picks up the writing.

'Yes, and the drawings.'

While Vonn reads and the kettle boils, Rachel goes out

into her two-strides-across garden and watches the sea over the rooftops: a cold sea, grey and brittle, ready to break into pieces. The cracks on the surface where light slices the edges reflect a shining grey sky with glimpses of blue ice and some cream and yellow streaks of cloud. She returns indoors.

Vonn has read the dream, twice, and studied the drawings. She puts them down and moves towards Rachel. They hold one another warmly, then slowly their first long kiss begins. Rachel returns fully into herself and the here and now. The women slide soft faces against one another and then kiss again, slowly, and for many minutes they make no sound.

Then firmly, gently, they move apart and smile into each other's eyes. They have begun to name what is happening for them. But they do not name it aloud, not yet.

Over a delicious lunch of salad and new bread, they talk about the dream and of the importance of dreams in each of their lives.

Vonn tells Rachel of her Tristanne dream; and they talk of how it might have been for Iseult, in Rachel's dream, if the warrior woman, Tristanne, had been there with her.

Then Rachel says, 'I know that one aspect of the meaning of my dream is that my mother is angry with me. She is part of Iseult, because she was herself exiled from her homeland, which is Holland. My father insisted that I and my sister Mieke were brought home to Salisbury to live, near Grandmother Markham, so that we could go to school there.'

'Didn't your mother want to leave Holland?'

'No. Not at all. I don't think she ever recovered, not really.'

'Must've been awful for her.' Vonn pauses, and takes hold of Rachel's hand. 'And for you. Did she hold you responsible somehow?'

'I think so. But I'm only just starting to sort it out. Later on, she exiled me from Salisbury with a whole series of rejections. She's very angry at my life, all of it, in lots of ways. It's my stuff and I don't want to burden you with it, especially since we've only just met. But *The Diaries* opened parts of my mind that have been shut down. Mieke says there are things I've forgotten from childhood, but I don't know what they are, not really.'

'Exile runs through all that writing . . .' says Vonn, glancing along the table to the papers and drawings at the other end.

'It's very painful.'

'You can see that from all these images in the drawings. They're very vivid, Rachel. How can I help?'

'You are. Lending me *The Diaries* to start with. Being here. I'm beginning to be close to you, you know?'

'Yes, I do. Me too.'

'I'm glad.'

Vonn thinks of Iseult, the details of Rachel's dream, the father figures. She wonders whether to talk more about it and decides against. Instead, she tells Rachel her image of two women in the boat from Ireland whilst watching the shining holes in the fire yesterday evening, and composing a melody afterwards.

'That's beautiful,' replies Rachel. 'Dreams and daydreams. I dream a lot here compared to London.'

'Oh, yes. And I had some wonderful dreams in Oregon, too. I hadn't been dreaming for a while. I really started again there.'

'I don't always understand my dreams,' says Rachel. 'But I'm sure that, somehow, this place is bringing me face to face with myself. That's why I've been solitary, except for my friendship with Clare, of course.'

'How is she?'

'Not good. She can't walk much. Her legs won't hold her up.'

'It's a monster, isn't it?'

'They still don't know that much about it. At least people have stopped calling it yuppie flu. It's so unpredictable – that's what she finds hardest. She can't plan anything. But she's better than she was in London. She looks less drained, slightly pinker, d'you know what I mean?'

'She was so grey-looking last time we met. It'll be good to see her.'

'I walk Floss and Suky for her. I love dogs, but I don't want my own, so it's perfect. Clare says she's dreaming a lot now she's here. She was telling me about it. Much more powerful, she says.'

'Interesting.' Vonn pauses. 'It was actually a dream that started my leaving London. To live here.'

'Was it really? I like to discuss dreams, always have. It must have been very intense, to have that effect?'

'It was.'

'I'd love to hear it, Vonn, if you've time. More salad?'

'No, it was lovely, thanks. But I'd love a refill, please?'

'Sure. I'll just set the kettle on.'

Presently, when Rachel is seated again, Vonn says, 'It'll make more sense if I start with real life. In the operating theatre. It was neurosurgery – and the NHS shortages were appalling. We were always short-staffed, but this particular time we were left without a runner . . .'

'What's a runner?'

'Literally someone who runs – runs around fetching and carrying equipment, essential if the operation is to go smoothly.'

'But you didn't have one?'

'No, we didn't. It was terrible. But we did fine, all of us. The patient survived. It was one of those rare times that we had thank-you letters, which was nice. But after that, the dream started: night after night the same dream – of a tidal wave about to get me. Like the Aberfan pit disaster, only a wall of water instead of the slag heap sliding down.'

'God, how terrifying.'

'Yes. I'd wake shaking. I began to be afraid to go to sleep. The whole place was going to be engulfed, everyone was running, running. Huge wall of water. Very high. Each time I woke up I knew I was at a turning point.'

'What did you do?'

'I had to talk to someone. I started with Ben and David. They were marvellous. Couldn't talk to Frankie, we'd not long split up. Then I found this woman who gave her time free . . . I mean, I was needy but I didn't have the money . . .'

They are both quiet for a while.

Vonn is thinking back to those times and that dream. Rachel is topping up the coffee mugs and nodding slowly to herself, deep in thought about the dream and its significance for Vonn.

Vonn says, 'She was called Carol Belvedere, the woman I talked to. To cut a very long story short, she knew Elizabeth personally. They'd been medical students together, way back. So she was aware that Elizabeth was diagnosed with terminal cancer and . . .'

'So she sort of linked you both? Oh, I see. Then you both left London – and came here – you and Elizabeth?'

'Yes. In a nutshell. I loved nursing but I couldn't carry on as I was. The dream told me that.'

'Was Elizabeth a lesbian?'

'Absolutely not. But Carol Belvedere was and they were close friends, so I was confident, safe to be myself, living here.'

'Yes, it would have been important, wouldn't it?'

'Yes, because I can't bear not to be out.'

'Oh, yes. I have to be myself, too, and myself is out. I mean, you take your time about it, don't you, you pick your moments and you take care of yourself, but you have to know that coming out is possible, don't you?'

'That's right. Elizabeth was fine about all that.'

'And do you still have tidal wave dreams?'

'Not since I lived in the house on the dunes.'

'It's a good story, Vonn.'

'Good to share it, too.' Vonn smiles than adds, 'I was just wondering if you'd like a short walk.' She looks at her watch. 'Mustn't be late for work, but I've got time left.'

'I'd love to. I was just thinking that.'

'By the sea?'

'Sounds good. I'll just stoke the aga then I'll be ready.'

In the distant isolation of the long white beach they kiss again. The inner naming has begun and will continue. The sharing of dreams enhances their sense that this pull they both feel is incredibly powerful. The legends, the meetings, seem beyond coincidence, and it feels fascinating and dangerous at the same time.

They both feel the need to be cautious about the speed, yet they are propelled onwards into each other's lives, inevitably. And so they kiss each other by the sea, with a passionate tenderness that doesn't want to hold itself back.

Presently Rachel asks gently, 'When shall we meet?'

'I'm on night duty tonight, and then tomorrow I have to sleep. But the day after that's free.'

46

'Yes. That's ages away but I've also got to work. I must finish the manuscript, and I'll be done with it by then. And I'll go and see Clare tonight, or she'll think I've abandoned her. What time?'

'Eleven? Come up to the corner, and I'll have the car ready. Shall we go to Megiliggar, d'you know it?'

'Heard of it, but never been. It's perfect. What if it's bad weather?'

'We'll go anyway. We'll think of something.'

'A day out together!'

'I'm glad.'

'Me too, very glad.'

* * *

Vonn arrives at the nursing home, ready for night rota, where the residents have missed her. They want to hear how it was. She tells them of the places and some of the people she has met. She doesn't mention a slow waltz in Oregon with Joan, nor returning home and meeting Rachel. They say she is looking wonderful, that the trip has done her a power of good. She doesn't tell them that she has spent today's lunch time kissing Rachel and talking about dreams; nor that Rachel doesn't seem to be a stranger, for they have mutual friends whom they both trust; nor that her body longs to linger with Rachel again.

* * *

'Vonn,' says Rachel aloud into the night air in a Cornish lane, on the way to Clare's place, 'this is incredible. I am supposed to be in a solitary phase, talking to the sea, walking with "the girls": not distracted by the fascinating face of someone new. I just can't stop thinking about you.'

* * *

'D'you believe in magic?' she says over dinner with Clare.

'How do you mean?'

'Meetings that aren't coincidence, that kind of thing.'

'A bit like fate, d'you mean?'

'*Do* you?'

'I'm sceptical. You know I am. Why?'

'I've just met someone and I feel compelled to meet her again.'

'Compelled? Strong stuff. Who is she?'

'I'm not imagining it, honestly. She says it's mutual.'

'Oh Rae, you're hopeless. For sure, didn't you just say you were happy on your own?'

'I know but . . . she is magical. *We're* magical.'

'Sure. I'm Danu, Mother of all Ireland.' Clare laughs. 'Who is this spellweaver anyway?'

'Your brother's friend, Vonn.'

'You're not serious. You can't be serious. Didn't she only arrive home yesterday?'

'We met on the beach.'

'She's the mermaid of Zennor, is she?'

'She's magical.'

'And she's your fate or something?'

'I knew you'd mock me. I didn't want to tell you yet, but then you'd think I'd been devious and I'm hopeless at being devious. I don't know how.'

'That's true. Hopeless you may be but devious you're not.' Clare sighs. She shakes her head in wonderment. 'So how far's this thing gone?'

'It hasn't.'

'But it's magic already? You are making no sense at all, you know.'

'I'm trying to make sense of it myself. We were both in the same spot, you know, my favourite part of the beach. And we both knew of each other. And now we're both reading *The Diaries* and dreaming about the legend of Iseult.'

Clare says nothing. Her expression says it all. Rachel continues: 'Maybe it's my Irish ancestry. I just feel that this legend – you know – is being reflected somehow in the here and now. In me and Vonn. I'm trying to sort it out. But it all happened so fast.'

'Reflections, Rae? Two women making love are reflections, same only different . . . But that's not what you mean, is it?'

'Not only that.'

'More?'

'It's something to do with the legends.'

Clare doesn't answer immediately. She gets up, lets Floss

and Suky out into the garden, then turns to Rachel looking rather grey and tired, weary with the shifts of reality.

Instead of returning to the table, where there is a disarray of dishes, Clare flops in the armchair by the fire, like a rag doll whose limbs adopt the shape of the chair. Then slowly, choosing her words with care, she says, 'Vonn's a good woman. I trust her. You're my ex and I love and trust you. But you were right about me the first time, Rae. I'm not into this magic stuff.'

Rachel had intended to stay at Clare's, sleeping in the living room and walking 'the girls' next day. Instead she takes them out onto the moors in the night, under a sky of stars and with the moon not yet visible. There's a strong wind pushing thin clouds fast across the milky way. Distant house lights illuminate the black hills which lie quietly asleep, their round female forms under black duvets, soft cotton, you could reach out and touch them, black soft pillows askew, ripples of bedding, surprise of occasional shoulder.

Shifting sounds of night surround her: squeak of a bat, high and supersonic. Bark of a fox, on its way home. Crunch of old heather underfoot. Floss and Suky lolloping and panting. Small scurries in the grassy places.

She follows deserted tracks up and over Sancreed beacon, the sky bright satin black: Orion and the Pleiades at crazy end-of-winter angles.

Rachel walks and walks, keeping to the paths in the dark, using a strong torch, on routes she now knows well, aware that Vonn is also awake all this night working, and wanting to stay awake with her, tuning into her, keeping time with her.

After pausing a while on a granite outcrop at the height of Sancreed beacon, absorbing the full circle of night around her, Rachel's footsteps take her downhill to the east, towards a cluster of houses around Sancreed church.

St Creda, she remembers from one of the guide books, was a swineherd. In Celtic mythology, pigs were totem animals of the underworld goddess, the old one, the wise one, the Cailleach, the winter one, the one who cared for those who needed to rest while the land itself was resting.

Rest was active, not passive. Inner wisdom, from the inner

world, was work of profound change, taking place in the deepest parts of the land, ready for re-emergence in the spring.

Approaching the old village church, with its strange and mysterious dedication, Rachel recalls that the guide books corroborated what Elizabeth Somerville wrote about the church, that it was built on a much more ancient site, which had been understood to be a gateway between the worlds.

But it is so difficult for us in the twentieth century to come to terms with the complexity of ancient beliefs and ways of life. We oversimplify, always. We seem incapable, these days, of getting inside the ancient minds which could hold together, much more easily than we can, the dimensions of time, and the interrelationships between the celestial round of the sun, moon, planets and stars, and with the agricultural round. The underworld existed all year round, but also represented both winter time in the season's turn and the unconscious mind of the individual and the group.

Why is it so hard for us to grasp that reason and intuition flowed for ancient peoples? Their astronomical observations were so accurate that they still work today; and their personification of deity was unproblematic to them. Theirs are the monuments which became ancestral to the Celts, and were incorporated therefore into the mythology of the Celts. Churches, much later, were the Christian overlay.

The Cailleach was present all year round, in the names of the hills and the appearance of the land, but she was also specific to winter, and the Celts prepared to say goodbye to her as the end of January approached, ready to welcome her transformation into the young woman who energised the wells once more in the outpourings of the spring. But the young woman who matured into the corn mother was present all winter too: in the corn figure made from the last sheaf of harvest, she sat upon a high shelf not far from the fireside and rested there, her gentle presence presiding over the storytelling around the fireside hearths. Present and not present. Ubiquitous and yet specific. General and yet particular to certain seasons. One and the same, yet differently named and variously invoked or revered.

Rachel recalls these images as she calls Floss and Suky to her then holds open a swing gate for them, which leads from the road opposite the church onto a silent path away from the village.

But many ancient sites, dating back into or beyond the neolithic, were too powerful to be built on directly. A site such as Sancreed well would remain half a mile to a mile away from the later Christian building.

So, a silent path through a turn gate and over a stone stile leads Rachel and 'the girls' to a long secluded lane which, in turn, becomes a long narrow curving track to the distant Sancreed well.

She has no real idea why she is being led along this route, though with Floss and Suky she feels completely safe, and the remote well, which is hard to find the first time you try, is one of her favourite familiar places.

She climbs over another stile and curves past a low building with a water tank inside it, finding that its trickle and splashing noise are recognisable and satisfying. She wades through a muddy area, along a narrow and overgrown path, leading to another tumbledown stile of stones pale against the surrounding trees in the torchlight beam.

Then she pauses. She listens to the sounds of the night: slow breath of cows chewing and munching on the other side of a Cornish hedge; creak of branches overhead; crackle of twigs and swish of foliage where 'the girls' are bounding on. An aeroplane overhead, high, distant, reminding her of the plane she saw on the cliffs near Melloney's cottage. Again the pull towards Vonn. An all embracing closeness, inexplicable, but strong.

She lets out a deep sigh.

Calling to 'the girls' who immediately lollop back towards her, reassuringly, she continues on, bending a little through some overhanging rhododendron branches until she turns a corner and there, opening into the ground ahead of her, is Sancreed well.

Three thousand years old.
Stone steps into the earth.
Night of dark moon. Womb. Room.

Silent. Overhanging hawthorn, arching.
Protecting. Entrance. Stone.
I am a woman made of Blood and Bone.
What can I learn here?
Dark, dark of the moon.
New woman. Newly met. What do I need to know?
Why do I call this magic?

Rachel calls to Floss and Suky. They come to her; she hugs them warm and close. They settle by the entrance to the old well. Protection. They know something. Wisdom. I am going down in there, she tells them. Stay.

She begins her descent, thinking of *The Diaries*, thinking of Vonn, thinking of Vonn's dream character, Tristanne.

The woman warrior. What if she really had been in that boat with Iseult? What if? What if?

This is one of the most beautiful old wells in the world, thinks Rachel. There are probably other places on the earth, in the earth, as beautiful, but it isn't possible for anywhere to be *more* beautiful, only differently beautiful. She shines her torch around the small deep chamber and standing, turning, lights up the steep granite steps out into the night sky, staring up through the opening, up into the sky, from deep in here, looking up and out.

She turns again, illuminates the quiet water, the phosphorescent ferns and lichens, the overhead stones and curving symmetry, the niches and nooks where someone left a candle.

Peace. Silence. Floss and Suky for safety. Deep breaths. She clicks off the torch. Plummets into warm sensuality. Womb. Room. Her own heartbeat. Dark beat. Heartbeat. She can hear Floss and Suky breathing. Outside. Beyond.

In here. Self. Inside. Outside. Shift. Change.

She pulls her waterproof down over her bottom and sits on the stone beside the well water.

The still, dark surface of the water is the space between the stars, the same space into which she stared on the cliffs above the cove on the night of dark moon. Move towards the same dark space. Pass through the silent surface.

Through an obsidian mirror's face. Into an obsidian mirror's depth.

Afterwards, she will not be able to tell if she fell asleep and dreamed what happened; or if she slid into a deep meditation and experienced it semi-conscious. It doesn't matter.

Afterwards she will not need to question the reasons that led to the images, the storytelling, the re-storytelling, the reinterpretation. It doesn't matter.

Afterwards, she will allow that these are her images. She owns them, they came from her into the enclosing dark, from the creative inner dark. What we think of as boundaries are not always so; what we think of as time is not linear.

Beforehand, she sits, anorak pulled down, safe in the depth of the female space, three thousand years old, built by people who knew how to blur the boundaries, touch the inner fear, shift it into making something.

Beforehand, she sits. She doesn't know why she sits there, but is clear that she is here to do this, to be, to know, to allow.

She brought herself here. Did she?
How do we know the things that we know?
How do we find the places we need?
What does it mean to carry a forgotten child
inside a solitary woman
and hold her in such a space?

In the foetal position, Rachel sits, allowing this. Dark. She can hear Floss and Suky breathing.

She can hear her own heartbeat.
She has her eyes open.
The dark is total. Infinite. There are no walls.
The space is, she knows, small, beautiful, safe, enclosing.
It is dark. Time slips. Flows. Water. Deep. Dark.

An image forms of a boat. An ocean. It is night.
Two women are on the boat. On the ocean. Deep. Dark.
The boat slides over the waves. It is night. Deep.
The waves slide and slip. Ocean. Ocean. The surface is

an obsidian mirror. Dark. Deep. The boat moves from one land to another land. Time. Slip. Boats upon the dark night ocean.

Mirror. Waves. Ocean. Obsidian. Mirror dark.
Movement. Rocking. Ocean movement waves slip across the waves from one land to another land. Slip.

Angry mother. Sharp edges. Time words. Wear away. Can we? Can we? Over the sea to another land. The sea the sea can the sea carry me? Sharp words sharp anger carry me carry me. Short words. Maybe. Perhaps. Time gaps. Crash the waves. If only. If only.
Two women mother and child two women daughter daughter give you away.
Away.
Exile you across the sea: daughter daughter leave leave go away away from me angry angry carry me child woman exile me me.

Two women? Who can they be? Ocean ocean potion carry me carry me. Slip time slip move waves carry carry me.

Here is a boat. A boat from Ireland to Dumnonia. A woman stands on deck now. She is Iseult. Daughter of Ireland. She is on deck, watching the dark ocean, facing her worst fears of impending marriage to King Mark. She appears so still as she quietly prepares herself to endure the terror of opening to the King.

Woman is land, she thinks. The land is cut open, like a woman is cut open, when the seeds are planted.

She speaks aloud, but softly, her voice clear in the dark night air. Above her the sky is black, below her the water is black, and these are her own mirrors, into her self, and she must reflect herself back, from the knowledge of her inner dark, if she is to use her inner strength.

I will not bear the fruit of the King. I have the knowledge to prevent myself bearing his child. I have the power to decide what kind of harvest I will choose to bear: there will be fruits in the orchards and wheat in the fields; there will be vegetables in season; there will be berries and seeds. But there will be no child for the King of Dumnonia.

I, Iseult, will be true to my love of Tristanne, beloved woman, woman warrior, whose arrival at the court of King Mark caused such sensation among the barons.

Iseult lifts her arms to the sky, raises her voice to the night:

Woman warrior, do not the ancestral powers shine over you? Woman warrior, are not your ancestors cousins to Maeve and the Morrigan? Woman warrior from Armorica, is not your language the cousin of the voice of Ireland? You are skilled on horseback like Maeve; fleet of foot like Maeve, victorious in battle like the Morrigan, warm and nurturing with your nearest and dearest, my lover, my lover.

Am I not reflected equally, I, Iseult, daughter of Ireland, in my physical desire for you, Tristanne, to whom I will turn for healing? I will open myself willingly, gladly, wet and wanting to you, Tristanne. This is a gladness. Land with land.

Iseult drops her arms, but goes on speaking, speaking to all women lovers, across all time:

Woman with woman. Land with land. Our love will be the bringing forth, the fruitfulness, the harvest. Our cries that will fill a night sky with desire will be the harvest. The moans that come from our deepest places when our gladness flows from us in our blending and needing will be a song of the land that will nourish our woman love that grows. There will be growth, and seasons, and sunlight and moonlight. There will be fire because we have passion; and air because our breathing is free and we women lovers are voiced when our union cries out in a wild wind; and water because our thighs are soaked with our spring-flowing wet needing, our breasts wet and full from the touch of our tongues; and earth because we are earth, we are land, we are women born from and out of land and loving together upon land.

We will run from the castle, as soon as it is possible to do so; we will be sheltered in bowers in woodlands; we will be protected by the waters of the wells; we will hide in caves; we will be fed from the orchards and fields; we will search for home as have all women lovers everywhere, for as long as there have been women on earth, in-land, who loved each other.

Iseult stands for a long time on the deck, watching the hills and valleys, the cliffs and shores of Dumnonia arise out of the mist, as women from Ireland have by now been doing for many years. She is comforted by the knowledge that she is not the first. Neither the first one to travel, nor the first one to leave her homeland, nor the first one to endure exile, nor the first to survive a nuptial bed, nor the first to be a powerful healer, nor the first to love a woman friend.

It is almost dawn now. Iseult gazes at the sky and begins to realise how much she now knows.

She will survive her unknown future. But more that that: when she has completed her life span and died, she will not end. Death of her physical being will not be all. For her, Iseult, daughter of earth, representing land itself, her female-ness will remain through spirit, and will be available in the form of her healing power.

It comes to her there on the deck of the boat, just before dawn, that she will return to women elsewhere, in times to come, especially in Dumnonia and Ireland, to women who are hurt, women who as daughters of earth are suffering.

Iseult reflects, self understands self, as she herself stands there on the deck. Her voice will be heard; her spirit will be freed; her travelling will be over water, over land, and over time. Iseult will be there in the elements – earth, air, fire, water – part of her connection, her reflection across the centuries.

She, Iseult, will connect with the inner healing power of future women, the force of life of the land. She will be willingly open to this calling, this thread, this connection. Such is her power, in the tradition of her people, to join, to empower, to reflect.

She doesn't know whether in any other time she has had this healing power, but she knows that she has it now; and that now she knows it, she cannot ignore it. It is there like breath-ing. Its purpose is huge, but she understands the tradition from which it arises, and why it happens to have come down the line to her, daughter of the land of Ireland. She is about to connect this power to the land of Dumnonia. Somehow it will be passed on. It is not the kind of power that will fade. Over the centuries it will remain, and will be there whenever it is called upon. Iseult is certain that this is so.

On the deck of the boat, she raises both her arms to the sky once more, feels the strength inside her, and imagines centuries ahead when women and children abandoned and frightened on a cold hillside will need it; when women who have lost their nearest and dearest will need it; when women call in the dark of the night and need it; when women face aloneness and loneliness and need it; when women face exile from their homeland and need it; when daughters face exile and estrangement from their mothers.

Meanwhile, the boat makes headway; the land ahead becomes larger, with tall cliffs which are grand and awe-inspiring. Iseult can see gorse and bracken, with flowers growing in the crevices.

She returns to their quarters and wakes Tristanne.

Together they prepare for the shores of Dumnonia.

* * *

Back home again at Melloney's cottage, not having slept at all at Clare's place, exhausted but pressurised by her workload, Rachel works frantically to make up for her time off. It's a clear day, with cool bright sunshine.

* * *

When Vonn returns from her night shift, the memory of sitting watching the fire with Rachel in the armchair behind her dazzles the house with light, amplifying the morning sunshine as if the house on the dunes is filled with fireflies, and each one of them on the wing and shining.

Before she falls asleep, Vonn lies quietly thinking, letting a surge of joyfulness flow through her body, remembering her kisses with Rachel only yesterday: I'm overwhelmed but I also feel marvellous, my whole body is talking about her to me.

She'd walked into relationships before, with good friends, or danced forwards, delightedly. But this was quite different. This was an instant attraction, like water catching sunlight, without waiting, being open there, wet and shining. It felt right, breathtaking. As she falls asleep she thinks: a new old story. Rachel, I want to go on holding you.

Rachel takes her tea break in the garden, watching the seagulls in their committee meeting on her roof and finds herself laughing out loud. No more meetings, plots or subterfuge. She watches the gulls strutting, some of them standing on one leg, heads to one side, listening, others locked in a vocal power struggle, and is content to let them do it for her. She is free from Avalon, the community arts project; the future awaits her here by the ocean.

She talks to herself as if her small garden is a stage, watching herself, half-mocking and half-jesting: I can meet anyone I like, feel what I like, and I damn well will. I will be true to whatever is true for me. Not as a play on a legend, with somebody else's lines. I speak my own, and I know this is real life, not an act. It's not a sham, or a mockery, or a lie. Vonn, you are real; real to me.

Rachel stands in splendid isolation, in her tiny garden, by the wall that looks over the rooftops of the cove to the open sea. She knows she's performing, self the audience for self, and she throws up her arms and does a full-circle turn, delighted with the ocean, the sky, the cottage, and the amazing circumstances of the last two days.

> Woman into whose eyes I'd dive
> to swim with dolphins
> Woman into whose breasts I'd breathe
> with healing celebration
> Woman into whose mind I'd call
> with detailed questions
> Woman into whose spirit I'd blend.

* * *

After her night shift Vonn sleeps till the afternoon. In the evening she practises a new composition on her violin. She tape records it, then copies the tape to accompany a letter to her friends in Oregon. That night she isn't on rota at the nursing home, so she is happily tired when she turns in reasonably early. She sleeps soundly, without dreaming of Iseult or Tristanne.

Next morning she wakes to the muffled beat of the sea

softened by a damp, low mist. After breakfast she takes a quick stroll over the dunes to the beach, with the intention of checking at first hand the state of the weather. At sea level visibility isn't bad. From the vantage point of the upper shore, Vonn can make out the edge of the waves, where the surf is flat and steady, green and white.

She considers the damp grey daylight, hoping that the sun will be powerful enough to dispel the mist during the morning. Satisfied that her plans for the day can go ahead, she returns to the house on the dunes, where she sorts out her wet weather gear, packs some lunch, kicks the storage heaters and drives to the appointed meeting place.

The dunes are otherworldly in this light. Where Vonn parks the car, the mist swirls tantalisingly. But between the land and the sky some luminous layers of brightness slide in sideways, slipping silently between the mist and the sea. Entranced, Vonn stands beside the parked car, so that she can listen to the sounds of shush-shushing slow waves which lap the far-off shore. Elizabeth Somerville's voice comes to her: This is where I want to be.

Memories. Vonn is a little girl. She is on the beach with her sister, Jenny. The waves go shush a bye. Shush shush shush a bye. Jenny and Vonn make an enormous castle. They dance around it, then stand on it, letting the slow waves wash right up to them.

Safe. A safe childhood. Vonn and Jenny. Nothing to fear. Hush a bye baby on the tree top. When the wind blows, the cradle will rock.

Vonn is not a little girl now. A deep sigh rises from inside her. The innocence of childhood is gone. When the bough breaks the cradle will fall. As a nurse Vonn has seen so many broken boughs, fallen cradles.

The waves say shush shush shush a bye. Shush shush shush a bye.

Vonn listens. She shakes herself. She thinks of Jenny, closes her eyes for a moment and sends love and warmth towards Jenny.

Reminded of Jenny, Vonn feels temporarily disturbed. She speaks to herself to ground herself once more. Once I was a little girl, playing by the sea. The same little girl hears a shush shushing sound today. She is inside me now, integrated into my adult self, now.

Rachel's figure comes into view, stepping up the path through the dunes towards the car. She appears to be soaked in fine mist, enveloped in waterproofs. Vonn feels a surge of warmth, thinking to herself that at this moment in time she's exactly where she wants to be, doing exactly what she wants to do. She runs with open arms towards Rachel who also runs forwards, so that they meet, kiss and hug, dancing a hop-toe dance, laughing like children who are going out to play.

'You made it. I'm glad. Let me look at you.'

'I look soggy.' Rachel laughs.

'You look wonderful,' says Vonn, as they kiss again. Minutes pass as they respond to each other, kissing and reconnecting, unwilling to get in the car.

Laughing they break apart, as Vonn says, 'Come on, let's go.'

'Can I put my backpack upright? I brought a flask of soup and some rolls. Oh, and fruit.'

'Sounds good. Here, wedge it behind the seat.'

'I wondered if we might not go, if it was this bad.'

'I think we'll be all right. Forecast's okay. Maybe when we get over the moors it'll clear. This side's usually worse.'

'Don't start the car yet. Kiss me again first.'

More minutes pass, until they break apart, wonderfully in love, searching each other's faces, swimming in each other's eyes, like lovers-to-be everywhere, amazed at each other, the heat, the wanting, the newness.

But in a little while they are on their way, with Vonn driving and Rachel, unable to stop touching Vonn, resting her hand lightly on Vonn's left thigh, where the heat between them is so strong that Vonn wonders if her jeans will singe and Rachel thinks her hand may melt, and they say so, laughing and thrilled with the whole simple scenario: one woman driver, another woman next to her, equally in love.

* * *

They talk of Vonn's night shift and chuckle over the things she didn't say. They talk of Clare's reaction to the startling fact of their new relationship. Vonn comments that she has a couple of friends who will be more than surprised, and she's working up to telling them as she hasn't seen them yet since her return. Then she asks after Clare and they talk of ME and how long it takes.

'Doesn't Clare get lonely here? I really must get my act together and go and visit.'

'She is lonely, but she was lonely in London too, and she'd rather live here. At least I can stay over, keep her company sometimes. How about you? Do you get lonely, Vonn?'

'No. I like to choose my crowds. I don't want crowds at the moment.'

'Nor me. It's very different here from the city. Bleak and wild. Just what I need.'

Vonn nods as she drives. She slows behind a tractor, taking extra care as the tractor signals to turn right. Beside her Rachel relaxes silently while Vonn waits for the tractor then changes gear and accelerates on towards a tiny village. Hedgerows roll past, wet with mist and hung with cobwebs strung along brambles.

Vonn tries to concentrate on her driving but is intensely aware of Rachel, who brings the gift of silence. Rachel doesn't babble, but appears to be delighted with the wet winter hedgerows which boast many different shades of green. Windswept hawthorns stick up at crazy angles, and there are scattered flowers even now – early gorse in droplets of yellow, rare winter-flowing pink campions, some purple hebe and winter-flowering periwinkles, an extraordinary bright blue here and there, set off by scarlet and crimson leaves on some varieties of brambles.

To Vonn who composes music in much of her spare time, the gift of a companion who knows silence is as unexpected as is the surface of the sea sometimes when it shines and swirls with silent gold and white, though it is said to be blue, as everyone knows. The colours, the silence and the gaps between the sounds; those are the richness of Vonn's inner music. Through the gaps in the sounds she can travel very fast without appearing to move at all.

Vonn bites her lip as she brakes for tail lights ahead: a car pulling a caravan, a rare sight at this time of year. Rachel smiles but stays silent. In profile Vonn has uneven features, which Rachel finds wonderful to look at. She is becoming tuned to Vonn's changes of expression. Vonn, meanwhile, is aware that Rachel is watching her, and it sends a pleasant quiver across her shoulders. She releases the handbrake, changes gear and drives slowly, following the caravan that is wobbling from side to side.

'You're an excellent passenger. Sorry about that. Where were we?'

'City and country. Crowds and making choices.'

'Yes. I think that meetings happen organically. That they don't work if they're contrived.'

'Yes.'

As Vonn drives through the towns and villages, with Rachel's hand on her thigh, she explains that she knows this route very well. She has friends in places along the route, and on the Lizard. Grinning, she says that she and Danielle had been known to do this trip at seventy, flat out, at one in the morning. But that seems a long time ago. She explains that her two good years with Danielle came to an end over eighteen months ago when Danielle went back to France. She asked Vonn to go with her, to make a new life, but Vonn didn't want to leave the house on the dunes, nor give up her OU course. She takes her left hand off the wheel, presses Rachel's hand and replaces her hand on the wheel again, since the lanes are winding, so driving isn't easy.

Then, with a sideways smile from one dyke to another, Vonn adds that she and Danielle are still friends, and friendships last longer.

'Like me and Clare,' says Rachel. 'We're good friends. And me and Petra. She's still in Amsterdam. She was a lovely woman. I was very lucky.'

'Is she with anyone now?'

'Yes, she's called Esme. She was Mieke's friend – my sister.

Esme went over there, and met Petra. Well, like I did. The difference is that Esme met Petra and stayed. They got married. Rings and everything.'

'Strewth. Do they use the dreaded word itself?'

'So Petra says. They've got cats and she actually says "Happily Married, Three Kids." '

'Don't!!'

Their laughter is free and safe.

Soon, after a signpost to a hamlet, Vonn parks in a grassy lay-by.

'We have to walk from here,' she says.

But first they reach for one another, kissing, touching each other's faces. Eventually they break loose, reluctantly.

'No mist. You were right. We left it behind.'

'Strange, but it's often like this. It'll wait for us, though. I think the forecast's wrong. It isn't going to lift completely.'

Shouldering the small rucksacks which are packed with food, they start along a farm track towards the sea. The sun is struggling through as if it wants to be user friendly but can't quite make it.

In companionable quietness, they stay with their own thoughts, but Vonn freezes as two huge dogs dash out from a farm-yard. Rachel, however, walks firmly towards them.

'Hello, you lovelies. Hello there. Good dogs. What a lot of noise. It's all right. We're not going to your house. We're going this way.'

The women are over a stile and along a path like greased lightning. When they're a distance away in a wide sloping field which stretches right to the cliff edges, they flop on a dryish bit of stone, out of breath, laughing and holding each other.

'I was terrified. You were wonderful.'

'It's my only party trick.'

'It'll do. Can you repeat it on the way back?'

Laughing together, they scramble up and make their way towards a stream which runs from a boggy area on the dip of the sloping field. Down the cliff, where the stream drops to the beach, slippery wet steps have been hewn in the cliff side and formed in concrete behind wooden holding barriers. They clamber down to a rocky beach, where it is low tide, leaving a wide stretch of quartz pebbles above the water line.

Winking at the play on words, Vonn says, 'Let's make a snow-woman marker. I forgot my tide timetable.'

At the water margin they place two large white ovals for a body and head. Rachel laughs. 'Very PC. Isn't she lovely?' Looking around, she finds a small piece of seaweed and ties it on. 'She needs a scarf in this weather.'

They sit on dry pebbles to have some coffee. One or two excessive waves reach the snow-woman marker, but the rest fail to make it as the tide recedes, giving them plenty of time for the day's excursion.

Vonn examines a beautiful quartz pebble. She passes the pebble to Rachel, who holds it carefully, then gets up and takes it to the ocean and wets it. She returns with it, smiling, pointing out the veins which appear varnished, lacquered, shining now.

'I was just sitting there, that day we met,' says Vonn, referring to her first day back from Oregon, 'minding my own business, looking at pebbles, and suddenly, there you were, shining.'

'And if you notice a pebble,' says Rachel, 'it's not just any old pebble, is it? It's *the* pebble – one that's unique, you know?' She turns the pebble in her hand, gives it a rub, and continues: 'You can drop it, avoid it, place it back into the matrix of other pebbles,' she smiles into Vonn's eyes, 'or you can take a breath, look at it again and call it Treasure, can't you?'

She hands the pebble to Vonn. 'For safekeeping.'

While they unpack their lunch, Rachel says that she's never been to the west coast of the States. She's seen New York but not San Francisco or Portland, but has heard of the women's music there.

'It's all around you,' says Vonn. 'It's wonderful!'

'And the women are wonderful too?'

'Magnificent!! Truly!!'

They both laugh. Vonn adds, 'Best of all was the singing – my friends there love to sing.'

'Oh, yes. Melloney's mother, Oda, writes songs. I do miss them both so much. They sing together – it's something else, it really is.' She sighs, remembering. 'What's your friend's name?'

'Nuala.'

'Oh. Is Nuala Irish?'

'Her grandmother was from County Cork.'

'That's interesting – have you known her a long time?'

'Years and years. She's a good woman . . . we can really talk. We help one another to name things. Always have. It's harder to make something or someone disappear if the naming is very strong.'

Vonn pauses, looks at the sea for a moment then adds: 'Like you, I have a difficult situation with my family. My mother's called Vera . . . She's still alive and is also very angry . . . I can't talk about it yet . . . but one day soon I'd like to.'

Reaching for Vonn's hand which she holds, Rachel says quietly, 'You don't have to speak. And anyway, there's no hurry.'

'I want to,' Vonn says. She repeats, 'One day soon.'

'There are times I don't want to speak, either. It'd be awful if you thought you had to.'

'Thanks. That's a comfort.'

'You mentioned naming things – to stop them disappearing . . .'

'Yes . . .'

'Well, my father tried to make my mother disappear. Truus van der Putten got married. Van der Putten became Markham. Bumph. In one stroke of a pen. But I'm beginning to realise that Truus was once whole and visible, where she wanted to be, in her home town, with her extended family. Then they came to this country, where she was unvoiced. But I don't know how it is for others in exile. And of course exile means many different things. Do you know Isabel Allende's *Of Love and Shadows?*'

'Yes, I do. She's one of my favourite authors.'

Rachel says, 'Me too. I'm understanding more and more about how the woman who started off as Truus van der

65

Putten became my mother, and disappeared. I think my father stopped having to speak Dutch. I think he unvoiced her into *his* first language. Not just "telling it slant", as a woman, as Emily Dickinson says, but worse than that, because my mother was also forced into denying her native tongue. No one spoke Dutch here.'

'You don't speak Dutch?'

'No. They called me clogs if I lapsed at school. I couldn't bear it. Mieke couldn't either. She hated being teased at school. Both of us refused to speak Dutch at all once we'd come to England. If my mother called to us in Dutch we didn't answer.'

'How awful for you all; you must have gone through hell.'

'Yes. I think we did. But I didn't realise my father's role in it until very recently. I had him on a pedestal. I adored him. Now I think that we became my father's donkeys. Saddled with his language. It's good to talk to you. I haven't felt so safe with someone for a very long time. Work was a kind of war zone. When women are at war they can be very cruel. That goes for our mothers too.'

'That's right. It takes a long time to sort it out.'

They hold one another, kissing long and slowly. They are aware of the ebbing ocean, the quartz beach which is being revealed, the thin sunlight trying to struggle through. Their bodies cling closely, fully clothed, as each of them thinks ahead to the evening, wanting to make love long into the night.

They are quiet again, watching the sea retreating. Listening to the pull and suck of the small waves on the pebbles.

After a little while, sitting snuggled up close, they notice a disturbance a few hundred yards out to sea: shapes in the water, indistinct at first. The women lean forward, watching intently. Then silently they both leap to their feet, not speaking but pointing, and nudging each other, and pointing again. Sleek grey surf-boards are now skimming the crests, between them and the horizon. Vonn knows what they are. Rachel has never seen them in a shoal before. She jumps up and down, without making any noise. But inside her she is laughing and squealing with delight: the dolphins are back, the dolphins are back. With life, energy and graceful beauty they cross the bay, disappearing off to the right.

The sheer power of their bodies curving effortlessly through the ocean will stay with Rachel as a memory of sharing this place with Vonn. The women hug and laugh, wordlessly, eyes alight. At first they can find no words for this experience, but as they sit for a while, watching the space that the dolphins have left behind, Rachel feels Vonn's nearness, feels her own womb lurch, feels her cunt heat rising with sexual energy, erotic need. A sensuous curving of dolphins over the crests of the waves is echoed through Rachel's body in a warm surge of wanting. She imagines her body and Vonn's body flowing together, arching together, and asks herself whether this is what she means by life force, this energy, this knowing.

'I love their beauty, their sensuality,' says Rachel.

'So do I. They're superb.'

'So full of life.'

'Yes. They belong exactly where we see them, in their element.'

'They're doing work on Dolphin language in the States, did you come across it?'

'Computer research, squeaks and blips and things?'

'Yes. And the first sentence they translated was: stop killing our species.'

'Strewth. That makes sense. But the dolphins are being used here as a symbol of New Age nonsense and I can't bear that, can you?'

'No, I can't. I don't think of dolphins as reincarnated star children. Not my thing at all.'

'Oh good.'

'Elizabeth was into reincarnation in general, wasn't she?'

'That's different.'

'Well, the only person I ever knew who was into reincarnation was a woman who was trying to seduce me.' Rachel giggles. 'She said I'd rejected her in a former life so I should get into bed with her now.'

'Brilliant. Nice one.'

'She didn't get anywhere. She terrified me. Anyway, she ran off to the hills with another woman who said she was once a shamanka. I breathed a sigh of relief, I can tell you.'

Both women are now laughing.

'Come here,' says Vonn.

Their kissing makes slow shush shushing sounds like the sea. They take their time – today there is plenty of time.

'There's something I was going to tell you in relation to *The Diaries*,' says Rachel.

'Are you still enjoying them?'

'Very much. I walked all night while you were on night duty, and went to Sancreed well. I found myself replaying – or it might have been dreaming, I don't really know – my Iseult dream with Tristanne alongside Iseult. It was amazing. And it followed on from dinner with Clare, who thought I was off the wall, going on about the Tristan and Iseult legend. But I feel something links us – you and me – to *The Diaries* and to the past. Something tells me to let it unfold. But anyway ... what I wanted to say was that my great-great-grandmother was Irish, on my mother's side.'

'This is very odd,' says Vonn, recalling Ben's joking statement in London about Rachel's Irish great-great-grandmother.

'Why?'

'Ben said he thought your great-great-grandmother was called Iseult.'

'Didn't you believe him?'

'In a word, no.'

They both laugh. Rachel says, 'That was wise. He's a terrible wind-up merchant.'

'Exactly. But he was also confused, because your people are Dutch.'

'Three-way chain, actually. And it might be fabulous coincidence.'

'Or not,' says Vonn.

'Dunno. My great-great-grandmother was Kathleen. She was from the Aran Islands off the coast of County Connemara. I've been there. It's an astonishingly rugged landscape. No romantic silliness about the sea being kind.'

'What, no pretty blue sea and tourist tales?'

'No. It's dangerous and cruel.'

'So what happened to your great-great-grandmother?'

'When she was young, and very strong, she and her brother

emigrated in one of the coffin ships to America. As you know, thousands went but didn't survive. The ships were so overloaded, or badly repaired, they sank in North Atlantic storms. Others died of starvation, thirst or disease.' Rachel pauses, then says: 'Kathleen was a healer, a powerful healer. A very strong young woman.

'She was used to long hours in the fields. On Aran they made their own soil. Can you imagine that? They ground up stones and mixed them with composted seaweed and burnt seaweed. When I first heard of it it seemed unbelievable. That kind of labour.'

'She sounds very brave, too,' says Vonn.

'She does, doesn't she? She had different kinds of work in the New World. Significantly, she went as a domestic servant in the home of a Dutch merchant.'

'Diamonds in the New World?'

'I don't know. Maybe. Trade is trade.'

'It's very interesting, go on.'

'She became mistress of the son of the house. He couldn't marry her. Wrong class. Wrong race. Wrong religion. His people were not pleased. But he loved her. He took her back to Amsterdam. She gave birth on the boat. They never married. But he worked hard and they had hardly any money.'

'Cut off without a guilder?'

'Cast out in the cold. Love, love changes everything.'

'Ireland to America to Holland. What a journey.'

'Yes. It's pure Virginia Woolf really: a woman has no country. National boundaries make nonsense of women's lives. Take someone like me – what meaning has nationalism for me?'

'Your great-great-grandmother crossed the Atlantic twice.'

'Yes, she did.'

'In those conditions.'

'There are Irish great-great-grandmothers all over the planet.'

'Taking their legends with them.'

'Exactly.'

'Strange that your great-great-grandmother – Kathleen – also had to leave her homeland; and that she had to keep moving to find somewhere to settle.'

'I was thinking about that yesterday – to me the story of Iseult is very much about homelessness. A contemporary version would be a girl in London running away from her father and sleeping rough. I think that when Iseult's story was first being told, in the six hundreds, it would catch the imagination of anyone who had to find somewhere to live. It's got a Gretna Green quality to it – young lovers running away together, but it's much more than that, because Iseult keeps on trying to make a home – in bowers in the forest, on the cliffs, everywhere.'

'You mean she and Kathleen are reflections, in a way?'

'Yes. But more than that. Both are reflections of homeless women now. Now it's benders on the cliffs, railway arches and cardboard boxes in the cities. Iseult is still searching for a home. I think that's one of the reflections of the legend now. Nowadays we've got repossessions, a high and rising homeless population, and people still need shelter – a roof over their heads, and in Iseult's case, shelter from being emotionally pursued.'

Rachel stops talking as Vonn takes a sharp intake of breath.

'What's the matter, Vonn?'

'I was just thinking of my sister, Jenny.'

'Are you all right?'

'No. Give me a minute. That's better. It was to do with her boyfriend.'

'I didn't mean to upset you.'

'I know. I didn't mean to interrupt your story.'

'Shall I hold you a minute?'

'Please.'

Presently, when Vonn is much calmer, they pack up the remains of lunch and, holding hands, they clamber along the stony beach towards dramatic rock formations to their right. Turning a corner, Rachel realises that this is the origin of all the beige swirling wallpaper patterns of the seventies and eighties in places like Heals and Habitat. All kinds of minerals are streaked and washed into the rock formations. Some resemble batik – as if wax droplets have blobbed the colour in some places; others have split patterns as if the material has been moved whilst printing; others are blends and swirls of green, splashes and trickles of creams and salmon shades, beiges and browns. The natural washed-out look. Somebody came here on leave whilst working for the design centre, thinks Rachel. They copied all the ideas, went home and reproduced them and then walls and work-tops all over the country boasted the so-called originals.

Vonn climbs across huge rocks to the water's edge and then leans back, thinking of Jenny, and appreciative of Rachel's sensitivity. She turns to wave to Rachel, who is now pottering about further along the rocks, peering into rock pools which have been left by the retreating tide. Vonn is aware that her assumption that she would have time for a slow reconnection with this landscape, sea and sky scape, has been completely overwhelmed by the incredible process of falling in love. An all-consuming process, which has its own speed, pattern and rhythm. Now Vonn needs to readjust, taking into account that she is no longer a lone figure in the landscape. She wants this chance with Rachel, a chance to open up, which is exhilarating but also quite frightening, because there are deep sources of vulnerability, so that panic can arise unex-pectedly. There is deep healing work still to be done.

She leans back thankfully against the giant rock strength, allowing herself to stay open, to not close off, to let herself be.

Meanwhile Rachel is watching the rock pools, which hold complete underwater gardens of anemones and weeds, with minute fishes and small mussels. The pools are not shining because it is still cloudy overhead, but in each pool there is a reflection of the rocks above. Rachel takes her time, realis-ing that Vonn was very shaken by her recollection about her sister Jenny's boyfriend. Rachel doesn't know what this might be, so she can only hope that by giving Vonn some space, Vonn will be able to come through the hurt, whatever it is. It seems to Rachel that if she wants Vonn, which she certainly does, she must face, and quickly, the fact that there are no undamaged women in the world. There is no new lover that could possibly arrive free from past hurts. Such is the level of damage done to women.

Searching contentedly among the rock pools, Rachel tells herself that she can either stay alone, be celibate, continue her own healing work by herself; or she can try to run her life, for as long as is real, in parallel with Vonn, having recognised that this compounds the vulnerability. It's not just that there are two lots of periods and PMS, that old lesbian chestnut, it's much more serious and also celebratory than that. If it can be done – and Rachel, having fallen in love, very much hopes that it can – there is the possibility of double healing, of empowering one another, supporting one another, giving one another space.

Rachel doesn't know if they can succeed, and it is early days, very early days. But she wants to, there on Megiliggar rocks.

Back home they cannot wait to make love. In Melloney's cottage they hurry upstairs, undressing quickly and falling on each other, diving under the duvet laughing and holding one another since the room is not yet warm.

Rachel becomes Vonn's head-to-toe lover, scrigging her fingers gently in Vonn's hair, running the pads of her fingers smoothly over Vonn's face, bending down to kiss Vonn's eyelids, her fingers finding Vonn's mouth, parting her lips, feeling Vonn's tongue licking her fingertips.

There is no hurry, now that they are here making love, so they take their time, touching kissing stroking exploring with hands and fingers, mouths and tongues, as if their bodies are the ocean, and each rise and fall, curve crest and flow can be glided and floated upon, swirled and rested upon.

Rachel loves being Vonn's new lover, arching over her – dolphins on the curve of the waves – her mouth on Vonn's nipples, waves and waves of feelings rising wet and wanting. Now Rachel is the sea washing on round boulder breasts of woman shore and her hand curves so firmly over Vonn's mound, feeling a fire rising cunt heat body heat as Vonn's clit leaps in the warm dark sea cave in the palm of the hand of the sea.

They opt for all the many possibilities of sex with hands and fingers. Vonn's fingers find Rachel's inner thighs with long wise slow slow strokes deliberate and easy that send shivers from Rachel's skin into her womb when desire moves inside her and she, finding a voice, makes welcoming sounds that slip out from her soul into the open air calling for Vonn's fingers to slide inside, to explore her sea cave warm and dark and wanting. Rachel's body has been waiting, without knowing, for a surprise new lover – and she suspends all disbelief that this wonderful woman can be here in her bed, making hot wet love in a deep sea cave inside her, with a pulsing exhilarating thoroughness, so the bowl of Rachel's pelvis is shaking with pleasure and the waves of it reach down her thighs down her legs over the arch of her feet flowing off somewhere into infinity.

Vonn's mouth is on Rachel's breast and Vonn's fingers are miming love stories to her clit, with a women body knowledge that reaches back to ancient times when women were birthed to be lovers for one another, women lovers brought forth from the primordial womb of the sea. A new woman lover who is warm, sexy, sensuous and is found by the sea. A funny warm and sexy woman lover. Fun-loving lover whose fingers find your centre, a fine woman lover who is found by the shore. She comes from the sea. She makes you laugh, she makes you weep, she makes you cry her name. A good woman lover who is a good woman. A good woman lover is found from the treasure of the earth.

Rachel calls Vonn's name many times into the air, the safe air of her bedroom in the cottage in the cove.

Vonn likes to be a head-to-toe lover too, shifting position, now her mouth kissing Rachel's thighs down behind her knees, long slow sliding kisses down to her ankles across the tops of her feet.

So they are each other's want and gladness, arching and diving, curving the crests of the waves, hands inside each other, wet and warm and bringing pleasure gifts with pleasure sounds woman sounds from an ocean floor, where dolphins dive and surface swim and glide, swimming now around each other – mouths and breasts and fingers. Smooth bodies curving bodies sliding gliding dolphin women lovers diving delighted dolphin lively on the waves rising and surfing wet with love and joy and wanting.

BOOK 2

You think the windows are in the wrong place; you don't know why the door and the chest of drawers have moved; then you remember where you are. You have a new lover; you're in her bed; you surface from deep sleep; you turn your head; your soft face touches the curve of her breast. Is there any awakening quite so magical?

* * *

Beside Vonn, Rachel is murmuring in her sleep. Her dark eyelashes and fine dark eyebrows complement her peaches and cream complexion; her mouth is soft and pink in repose; her dark hair is tousled on the pillowcase; her eyelids are making rapid eye movements. Despite being sound asleep, Rachel is perhaps subliminally aware of Vonn's scrutiny, because she stirs and snuggles closer, still murmuring, apparently dreaming.

* * *

There is an old woman whose name is Warning.

Warning lives over the next headland in a house remote and inaccessible. Sometimes, early in the morning, Warning dons her heavy gumboots and her old green coat, and, taking up her walking stick – a staff made from seasoned hawthorn – she stomps up her hill to the crest, a flat area on stony ground, from whence to look down towards the place where Clare now lives.

Warning calls from the stony summit, calling to Clare to take more care, give her credit where credit's due – show some respect for her wisdom.

Warning is a healing kind of woman.

Warning lights a bonfire. But the winds are strong. Gale force six, increasing. Storm warnings on the forecasts in the region. The fire doesn't take at first. The storms die down. Clare doesn't receive the signals from the smoke or flames.

Warning returns home.

Next day Warning looks from her cottage window and sees a bright blue sky the colour of friendship. She imagines Clare in her new home and notices with deep intuition that Clare is heading for a downfall.

She speaks aloud. 'It's not that you are bad, dear, nor that you lead your friends a merry dance, though you'd like to be able to dance all day and all night too, with your friends in a circle, dancing with you. Nor that you are foolish, dear, you have the best of intentions, I am sure. But you must heed me, I must send a message to you.'

That day Warning dons her heavy gumboots again and her old green coat. Takes up her walking stick – the same staff made of seasoned hawthorn – and despite the bright blue summer skies she stomps determinedly to the top of her hill. She looks down towards the place where Clare lives. There is a woman weeping there. Her legs have buckled under her. She is afraid; she does not know what to do.

Above the old woman on the crest of her hill the sky is blue, bright friendship blue.

The old woman builds a fire, a good fire, she lights it and it takes very well. Light breeze. The kindling catches and sparks, the dry wood soars with flames, the smoke begins.

The flames leap high; the smoke spirals and curls until Clare can see it, rising there from the top of Warning's hill.

* * *

The dream stays with Rachel when she wakes. The images won't move, the voice of Warning continues in her head. She and Vonn don't want to hurry out of bed nor to be so abruptly shaken out of last night's loving into today's reality. They had wanted a slow morning together. They need to touch each other. They find it hard to close down, close off suddenly. But when Rachel recounts her strange dream they both know they must act, and quickly. So they breakfast rapidly and then leap into Vonn's car.

It is a lovely day, with very bright blue skies, and a high, wide dome of mackerel cloud. Vonn drives fast but with care. Rachel is tense and silent.

Clare's door is locked but Rachel uses her key. Immediately they can hear Clare crying despairingly upstairs. Downstairs, the two visitors exchange anxious glances as Rachel calls out, 'Clare? It's only me. It's me, Rachel. I've got Vonn with me. It's only us.'

Rachel ascends the narrow stairs but Vonn hesitates a little way behind her in case Clare feels invaded.

What Rachel finds in the bed is a sobbing, crumpled figure with tousled light brown hair and grey skin. Her eyes are red and swollen, though set in dark-rimmed sockets, which give the impression of a grey and white panda, like a photo negative with the grey circles where the white ones would be. Clare looks a mess; the bed is half made and the duvet is hanging off; there's the spilt remains of a glass of juice on a tray on the bedside cabinet; there is a stench of urine; the curtains are half drawn; and 'the girls' are lying on guard at the foot of the bed, because they won't leave Clare's side while she is distressed.

Clare is wearing an old T-shirt that has seen better days, and she is too thin around the arms, with fatigue lines around her mouth and tired lines down her neck.

She has obviously been crying a long time. The girls are alert to Rachel's footsteps; they jump up to greet Rachel but won't stay away from Clare for any length of time.

Rachel goes to the bed, sits and leans over to put her arms around Clare. 'Clare, you should've phoned Mrs Trembath. She's only next door to me. She wouldn't have minded taking a message. I told you never to let this happen.'

'I couldn't. It was your first night at your place.' Clare turns to look over Rachel's shoulder to where Vonn is standing waiting in the doorway. 'Vonn, I'm sorry. I didn't mean you both to be interrupted.'

Vonn walks around the bed, steps over 'the girls', and, taking Clare's hand, she perches on the bed opposite Rachel. 'It's me that's sorry. I'm the sorry one. I should've got my act together. It's been a long time. Hello again.'

'Hello, Vonn. I don't usually entertain in the bedroom, like this.'

Clare's feeble laugh breaks the mood, and they all relax.

'You should've rung for us. We'd have come to you.'

'It's not fair, Rae. Not fair on you. I'm a wreck, I'm sorry.'

'It's okay, it's you we're concerned about.'

'I peed the bed, my legs won't work, I couldn't get there in time. It smells. It smells terrible.'

'It happens,' says Vonn matter of factly. 'Now don't you worry,' she adds kindly, 'we'll have you sorted out in a jiffy.'

'Hell, I'm sorry. It was a shock. I've been doing so well.'

'Overdoing so well,' says Rachel.

'Yes, I know. I hate it. I can't stand any more of it. Years and years. I'm only thirty, for Christ's sake. I'm only thirty and my legs don't work. I can't do any more of it. I just can't. I just can't.' Clare starts crying again. The tears are very hot and wet, and they come from somewhere that Clare can't control. Clare has always found that the crying helps but is itself a very frightening symptom. This time the crying has an element of terror, because Clare is facing long-term disability and they all know this.

She came to the rural area by the ocean to get well; she isn't making progress in the way that she had hoped, nor as fast as she had hoped. She has been dealing with this, as Rachel knows, as if it were an illness from which she will recover. Now she is facing a long and very hard adjustment to disability, and she has no way of knowing how much of the current problem with her body, and especially her legs, she is going to have to deal with, nor for how long. The gap between next week and forever could be any length at all. No wonder that Clare is frightened.

'Never mind. We'll soon have hot water for a bath for you,' says Rachel, giving Clare another hug.

'We can take the sheets to my place and put them through the machine. It's no problem,' says Vonn.

'Thank you. I'm sorry. I feel ghastly. Wiped out and no hope. I know what did it, and I feel stupid and hopeless. It's hopeless. I'm so fucking fed up with it all. I'm sorry.' More tears.

'What happened?'

'I spent yesterday weeding the garden. Well, not very long, but about a couple of hours. It was such a lovely day, and when I can't walk too far my garden's my delight. Being outside. Well, I was going to just sit there but it needed doing and I got going, and didn't I just have plenty of energy?

Energy? Bloody stupid joke. Then in the early hours I woke up and I couldn't move. Like somebody pulled out the plug.'

'It must have been very frightening,' says Vonn.

'I didn't know what to do. I'm so glad to see you, but how come you're here?'

'I had a dream about an old woman called Warning who was trying to send messages to you,' says Rachel.

'You what?'

'A dream. One of my better pieces of timing, wouldn't you say?'

'So glad to see you. Both of you. Thank you.'

'Right now, what shall we do first? What would you like, Clare?'

'A cup of tea, please. Then would you give me a bath? For sure do I want to get clean.'

When Clare is comfortable again and comforted, with food and a flask beside her for later on, Rachel and Vonn take a break under an old pine in her secluded garden. The tree grows beside a garden pond which has been carefully tended by the previous owners and has been landscaped into the contours so that it appears quite natural.

There are drifts of snowdrops and splashes of bright colour from the first daffodils, which are early this year. Primrose leaves are apple-green, though there are no buds yet; and the old pine tree overhanging the pond has blue-tinted dark green needles and luscious upright pine cones of a warm russet-brown. A beautiful tree, it leans over in the direction of the winter winds, for its trunk is high above the protective Cornish hedge that borders this garden on all sides, and in which early bright green campion leaves are just beginning to emerge.

Some overhead branches are reflected in the pond, so that anyone who might try to hide in the welcoming pine tree would be clearly visible to someone looking into the water.

To Vonn *and* Rachel the significance of this overhanging tree lies in its origin in the legend, because King Mark of Dumnonia hid in just such a manner when he was trying to catch out Iseult who was accused by the court barons of taking a lover into the King's own bed. The lovers planned a meeting in the forest by a river. But, betrayed, they found their meeting was being overheard, for they saw the King's reflection. Thus they spoke to one another as if they were only friends, so innocently that King Mark believed that his wife was true to him. Thus the barons' hopes for Iseult's demise were foiled. In a tryst beneath the branches, their passion once more delayed, the legendary lovers pretended to be friends.

Tristan and Iseult's passion and its interruption by a third party has an uncanny resemblance now to Vonn and Rachel's story, though Clare is not King Mark nor even behaving in a patriarchal style, and is at this moment resting safely in her freshly made bed indoors.

Sadly, Clare is not capable even of weeding this garden today, let alone climbing the old pine tree and swinging in its branches. Vonn and Rachel sit talking quietly, aware that Tristan and Iseult's love was tested over and over from the very beginning, and wondering just what kind of testing times are now awaiting them here in the twentieth century.

Since Vonn is at work tonight and 'the girls' need a long walk, the women replan and reschedule their time, trying to arrange when next to meet. Rachel suggests borrowing Clare's unused mountain bike to return home later to work on her word processing in the evening.

'How d'you feel about my Warning dream?' she asks.

'About the dream – fine,' begins Vonn. 'I'm glad we rushed over here. It was real – I've dreamed into reality like that myself. That bit's not a problem. But the rest – whew! I am so bewildered by it all. The speed of it. The interruption. I feel guilty for not coming to see Clare before; angry at myself for not caring before . . .'

'At yourself? You're a better person than me, then. I'm angry at Clare.'

'That's honest. I love your honesty. Yes, I'm angry at her. The timing. I could've done without it. I wanted a slow morning waking up with you. I was just thinking how lovely you looked, lying there asleep, when you must've been having the dream . . . then suddenly we're here, you know?'

'I know. I want to kiss you, hold you.'

'Don't see why not, d'you?'

They look around, quickly checking where Clare's neighbour's windows are. But, just as they'd thought, there are none overlooking this part of Clare's garden. It truly is secluded. So they stop talking for a while and kiss slowly, thankful for the mild weather and weak sunshine.

Presently Rachel says, 'Clare can't help having ME. I feel mean and horrible inside myself when the situation makes me angry. But the trouble is that she didn't ask me if I wanted her to live in the next village. I do like her being here, but I knew it'd be a problem. Part of me wants to help, take it on board, because we're friends and I love her and heaven knows she needs help; but part of me just wants more separation, more independence.'

'That's understandable.'

'I do feel angry sometimes, though. Clare knows that. There's nothing you can do to stop the anger. It wells up in you. You just have to go through it and out the other side of it. If you pretend it's not there it gets worse and worse, then it explodes, and that's much more damaging. For everyone.'

'Clare wouldn't want pretence. She'd see through it.'

'Yes, she would. We know one another very well.'

'Besides,' adds Vonn, 'Clare herself is angry. She'd have to pretend if you did. That'd be worse for her too.'

Vonn drops Rachel and 'the girls' near to the coast path. The women hug goodbye, feeling empty and disorientated by the suddenness of the turnaround that morning – the intensity of Rachel's dream, the hurry over breakfast, the dash to Clare's, the teamwork with the inevitable ending – disconnection. So, although they are pulling together in the process of rearranging everything, they both feel bleak at the prospect of sudden separation.

They hold each other, kissing slowly, searching each other's eyes and faces, and reassuring one another of their next meeting, which will be the following evening, at Clare's place.

Vonn is disappointed that she can't accompany Rachel with 'the girls', but there simply isn't time before work. Rachel waves goodbye as Vonn's tail lights disappear, calls to 'the girls' who hated the short car ride, and sets off with thundering steps, pounding her feet into the coast path. In spite of herself, she thinks, bloody Clare, couldn't she wait just one week? Why now?

Then remorse overcomes her. At least your legs work, don't be a horrible person, get on with it, she scolds herself.

The coast path is scattered with early gorse and new green rosettes, indicating future primroses. Noddings of sparse wild narcissi shine above old bracken tops, whose brittle beige branches are cracked and bent low by the wind. It's a mild bright day, with a soft blue sky and a light greenish-blue sea, under thin skimming clouds in wisps.

Rachel's mood changes as the miracle of health and the beauty all around her reach into her, touching her deeply. Being able to walk is itself a blessing; and although it has taken her a while to realise that the coast path is a safe place for her, especially with 'the girls' for company, she now takes a deep breath as the reality of health and the spirit of place reach into her.

She can walk safely here, with or without dogs. She is alone, and she feels safe. She *is* safe. A buzzard appears, hovers, swoops, dives, catches something and sweeps away, as Rachel and 'the girls' clamber down to a cove to which tourists hardly ever come. The beach is empty, indented by only a few footprints in wet sand, and some paw prints.

From this angle, the sea appears eau de nil, deepening now to a bright bluey green, a cold colour. The ocean has a sort of fickle humour, very much the practical joker, cartoonist extraordinaire; it can make things happen. Rachel shrugs sadly, thinking that not even this ocean, wise and so creative, can make Clare's dis-ease disappear. The sea is capable of changing many things. But Clare is in relapse, beyond the sea's jurisdiction.

However, the sea has great healing powers, perhaps for Clare too. Rachel decides to talk this through with Vonn. Maybe they can give Clare time by the sea this summer. Maybe they can find coves where they can park near enough for her to walk by the sea, though she cannot manage inclines at all.

It's good to be alive and in love. Around Rachel there curves a beautiful deep beach, with clean beige sand and grass-covered cliffs like a half pudding bowl holding the beach safely. An offshore wind meets the incoming waves, lifting up their white hairs and streaming them back towards the horizon. To Rachel's left the sea is beige and bronze, catching and holding light like moving molten alloy, but further away the water is now kingfisher blue, rolling towards the rocks with white hair flying. Splashing, the waves fall and part, running back to meet the others in semicircles of silver and white.

A wonderful sound explodes from Rachel, coming from some uncensored spring of delight, spontaneous and happy. She has forgotten the source of such sounds, but now seems to open her voice box, and there is her own voice rising up, surprising her, making her joyful.

She is invigorated by the clean air, the open movement of water and air on land, by the presence of only three other living creatures – Floss and Suky, who are bounding on ahead, and the buzzard, who is now hovering again in the arc of the cliffs, playing the thermals, maintaining a steady position. The experience of isolation with two animals and one bird feels like being in on the start of the universe.

Rachel runs with 'the girls' along the beach, which is terraced into wide, sharp-edged scoops by the receding tide. Channels of fast water have carved deep treelike trunks and branches into the wet sand running to the water's edge.

Some light brown rocks are draped in black bobble seaweed: a huddle of sleeping spaniels, dreaming in the sunshine, their floppy seaweed ears over their faces.

Rachel is alone, except for the dogs, the buzzard, who is still hovering, and her magical companions of earth, sea and sky, who provide glory and energy. They don't interrupt Rachel's thoughts, but they influence them instantly and integrally because images arrive, blend and blur continuously through changes of light and sound and the movement of the waves.

Following the edge of the waves, Rachel walks the full length of the beach, to the rocks and rock pools at the far end. Here where the sea had appeared kingfisher blue, it now changes to pale green, the colour of Grandmother van der Putten's walls in Amsterdam. Eau de nil. Rachel remembers the walls, and the Dutch lace window hangings, framed, flat against the glass. She liked to look out through the lace pictures at the street and canal.

Last year, in a splurge of nostalgia for Holland, for the bulb fields, the countryside and culture, she took up a long-standing invitation to spend some time with Mieke at Petra and Esme's place, in Amsterdam.

It was during this visit that Mieke had wanted to talk about their past, and Rachel has already begun to face the first part of that conversation. Later on in the holiday, Mieke had wanted to talk again. With much care, and clearly much anxiety, she had said, 'There is more to say to you, Rachel. Do you think we could talk about it?'

'I don't know, Mieke. We can try.'

'This is difficult.' Mieke swallows, then says, 'When I started all this you said you did remember being hit by Dad, yes?'

'Now and then, yes. I mainly remember rows with Mum and terrible crying.'

'He did hit you. I think that I must tell you . . . everything. I'm your sister and I think you've a right to know.' Mieke pauses, holds Rachel's hand, then says, 'Mum slapped you, quite often. Dad, he was different, but when you rowed with Mum, then he was unmerciful. Not like he'd hit me – I got the odd swipe, but – well, I used to think you were his favourite – and when he hit you after a row with Mum it was over the top. I mean, he had real anger in him. I used to hide behind the armchair, and you'd be howling, Rae. I remember . . . because it was awful hearing you crying.'

Mieke cannot look at Rachel. They both look down at the floor, trying to come to terms with what Mieke is saying.

Mieke is finding this very painful. She has come to realise that Rachel really does need access to this hidden, forgotten part of childhood, if she's to understand the background to her situation now and to Truus's anger with her. Mieke remembers it all so visibly, but Rachel has obviously blocked it out. They hold hands and sit together.

Rachel whispers, with some difficulty, 'I'm glad you told me. I need to know.'

'I'm sure that you should know. I realised, a while ago, that you'd forgotten. I wish . . . I wish that our childhood didn't hold these things.'

Rachel enjoys Holland as an adult. Her visit to Petra and

closeness to her own sister, Mieke, make it wonderful. But the visit is over all too soon. The sisters return to England, one to her husband and children, the other to havoc at the Avalon Community Project and a crisis that with each waking hour seems deeper, until the agonising splits and schisms become irretrievable.

Now Rachel walks by the sea, her life full of complexities and unsolicited gifts: Clare living nearby – wonderful but not straightforward – and a new lover who excites every inch of Rachel's skin, the gift of passion when she least expected it.

She walks by the sea, today, watching its changes, aware of its surging strength and infinite energy, and asks herself how to move on through these complexities, how to hold them all together.

As Rachel watches, she feels a desire to be taken over by the sea's rhythm, for it seems that the sea knows everything. She feels her muscles loosen along her shoulders, which had tightened at her memory of Mieke's remark, 'I wish ... I wish that our childhood didn't hold these things.'

Rachel calls to Floss and Suky. 'Here, girls. Come. Come.' As they lollop together, tails wagging, across the beach towards her, she has a strong sense that the sea's energies cannot change the past – but they can illuminate the here and now. Can it be possible to find peace of mind, to understand, and to go forward?

* * *

During the next couple of weeks, Vonn and Rachel do not have easy flowing time to nurture their new relationship. They get through their separations by focusing on work and caring for Clare, who makes steady progress towards being up and about and semi-independent.

While Vonn is on duty Rachel sweats over a hot word processor; when Vonn is sleeping after work, Rachel shops, cooks and cleans for Clare, putting in more hours of word processing when Vonn offers to take Clare to the sea.

They watch the moon become full and then begin to wane. They make love sometimes in the afternoons and reach for each other in the early hours, when, waking in Rachel's bedroom, their body need overcomes their unfulfilled desire for sleep.

Days become nights become days while they juggle Vonn's shift work, Rachel's typing deadlines, and Clare's healing process.

Eventually Clare says that she feels the relapse is receding; her energy is returning, her crisis is passing. She can walk to the village shop, make the bed, prepare her own food and tend the fire. Sometimes, though, when she is about to fall asleep, Clare thinks of her ex-lover, Rachel, who seems to be changing so much these days, then dreams sometimes of an old woman, who lives on a hillside, wearing an old green coat and carrying a staff made of seasoned hawthorn.

The daffodils open in early March, heralds of springtime. In pagan Dumnonia, which had been barely touched by the Roman occupation of Britain, and which in the fourth to eight centuries was densely forested, there the wild daffodils would carpet the woods with yellow, cream and white. Long before Dorothy Wordsworth and her brother were delighted by the daffodils along the margins of the Cumbrian lakes; long before Rachel and Vonn fall in love in the nineteen nineties.

At night, before sleep, Rachel reads *The Diaries*. They give her a sense of connection with Vonn and bridge over the inevitable separations when Vonn is working. Vonn's copy of the precious hardback rests carefully beside Rachel's bed.

In pagan Cornwall this time of year would be the season of the Goddess of Spring. So powerful was she, with her sacred animal the hare, that early Christian Saints arriving in Dumnonia from Wales and Ireland simply did not know what to do with her.

They could not deny or diminish her; they could not delete her. Nor could they turn her into a folk heroine. For she was the season and was the land.

Where hares bounded across the fields at night, they were her, and she was they. There was no boundary between goddess and land; there was no vilifying of her animals nor desanctifying of her fields and flowers.

In Ireland this continued to be the time of Brigid. She and the Spring Goddess were celebrated separately and together,

with flowers and feasting, and the maidens visited Brigid's
wells with the Spring Goddess's daffodils, placing them there
as thanksgiving, dropping pins into the wells for divination:
Will my sweetheart come to me? Will my love stay true?

Like all new lovers everywhere, Rachel and Vonn are
entranced with one another. Yet, unlike some, they are aware
of struggles and difficulties ahead, for their memories are
hurtful and are bound to affect their relationship. As Rachel
reads, at night, alone in Melloney's cottage, she feels that
the connection is on every level, or as some might say, in
every chakra. The bonding has been very fast, and with a
knowledge of need and potential alongside a blurring of
past, present and future. Where this knowledge comes from,
Rachel is not sure. Somehow it comes with a big neon sign
over it which says, 'Let this unfold, let it happen.' Like one
of the maidens of pagan Dumnonia, Rachel watches herself
at this season, as the land around her opens in clichéd springtime performance. The land seems to know how Rachel feels
about this new love; the land flowers especially for her.

One day during this time when Rachel has finished word
processing, she feels strong enough to deal with the contents
of her Avalon files and she starts to sort and refile the
boxes of papers which she brought from London. All the old
Avalon files are there; and there are also files from a women's
studies course that she attended. There was one particularly
significant evening during the course when the women had
been discussing the Gulf War, and the relationship between
the superpowers and women as war refugees. Rachel was
deeply affected, as were all the women in the group, by
pictures of Kurdish people on stark hillsides fleeing from
Saddam Hussein. The cuttings slide from their transparent
plastic wallet and lie scattered on the carpet in the cottage,
their headlines KURDS PLEA FOR HELP shrieking up at
Rachel from crooked chaos there on the floor. She gathers
them up and cannot throw them away. She places the wallet
back in the box.

Later that night, thinking about her own amazing good
fortune, of this safe haven when she most needs it, she reads
The Diaries, focusing on the Tristan and Iseult legend, which
seems to be infiltrating her everyday life. The legend won't

leave her alone; nor the sense that Iseult, in exile, young and fleeing from soldiers, is desperately needing a safe haven with her partner.

Rachel does not visualise Tristanne so openly as Vonn does, which seems logical enough, because Tristanne has been dreamed up as *Vonn's* dream character, but the two women lovers have become psychically close, so that if the one is upset the other catches it and 'knows', and if the other is 'calling' then the one intuits this very urgently. This is not new or unusual. But the power that this generates for Rachel and Vonn is deepening and simultaneously there is a blurring of the boundaries between self and other. This is dangerous because to be so open is to be very vulnerable; but it is also very exhilarating because of the sense of unification with each other and with the landscape and world beyond them.

Mark is the older man, the husband, the King. Tristan is the travelling minstrel, young and brave, sent to fetch the beautiful daughter of the King of Ireland, for King Mark's hand in marriage.

Not Romeo and Juliet. The families are no longer at war, thanks to Tristan's slaying of Morold, the Irish warlord who has been plaguing King Mark on the shores of Dumnonia. Tristan's courage and skill endeared him to King Mark, who then bestowed the honour upon him of becoming the envoy to go and fetch Iseult. No more war: on the contrary, the marriage of Iseult and Mark is to unite the families – it is not against their wishes.

Rachel reads for a while, considering Elizabeth's interpretation of the centuries-old legend, which first came into being in the six hundreds and had such an impact that it was retold for decade after decade, before the Norman-French arrived in Cornwall and their scribes transferred the story on to illuminated manuscript, adding things and removing things according to their own inclinations, as is the case with all scribes. If they thought something would offend their patrons, then the scribes would adjust it a little. If they thought their patrons would like lurid details, they embellished them a little. They also made writing errors, copying some lines twice and leaping across others.

Tired scribes fell asleep on the job. Lively scribes sought a bit of extra cash. Romantic scribes wrote of courtly love; and courtly scribes penned of maidens in distress. Timid scribes wrote of brave knights; and brave scribes opened up well-kept secrets.

And in every case, the manuscript shifted a little this way, leant a little that way.

Rachel recalls Vonn saying, recently, 'Tristanne could well have been a warrior woman in the fifth and sixth centuries. To the pagan Celts this wasn't unusual. They had many warrior women in their legends. Elizabeth, bless her, was straight. She didn't need Tristanne as I do.'

What Vonn and Rachel have in common with *The Diaries of Elizabeth Somerville*, is a deep disgust at the level of abuse meted out to Iseult by her father, who in effect is selling his own daughter to another King. He is not severely challenged by the Queen, who appears to agree with her husband about the impending marriage of her daughter, despite the fact, which comes through strongly in every story, of the Tristan-Mark-Iseult triangle, that Iseult does not want to leave Ireland, can't at first stand the sight of the young male envoy, Tristan, and dreads the thought of bedding with a stranger, an old one at that.

Following their day at Megiliggar, Rachel and Vonn have begun to share some of the implications of this story of abuse, which touches deeply on the inner pain in each of them but in different ways. For Vonn the time is drawing near for her to reveal some of her family life to Rachel. For Rachel, who is about to go to bed having just been rereading news cuttings on the Kurdish people, there is a sense that Iseult is here inside her. How can this feeling arise? she asks herself. Has this story survived to tell women today about women's ancient powers, powers of connection, power of reflection?

Reflections? Rachel goes upstairs to the landing window from where, looking westwards, she sees the shimmering crescent of the four-day-old moon setting over the huge dark cliffs. Feeling connected to Vonn, who is now working on the night shift, Rachel stands by the window transfixed by the dazzling silver moon.

Memories: she is eight. The sun is pouring through one of the side windows of the Cathedral where she is bored silly, sitting with Truus and Mieke during a particularly long sermon.

But the light is beautiful and calls to her. Promises. They say that beyond this Cathedral is God and he will be good if she is good. But she is not good enough. She has done something wrong. They are hitting her. Truus is slapping her hard. She is running, running away from Truus. Truus is calling, calling after her. Rachel runs to her father, into his workshop. He turns. She is sobbing. His hand reaches out and a stinging slap catches the top of her leg. There is light in the workshop, coming through the window. Light like the Cathedral. If she is good, God will be kind. She cannot be good enough. Her leg stings from the hard slap. Her mother's voice echoes from the kitchen. Her father's hand reaches out again but she ducks and runs.

She runs away. Fast. Her legs going as fast as she can.

The sunlight is very bright. She is outside running, running. Her father's voice is calling, falling on her head like gunshots.

She runs and runs until she gets to her friend's house. It has a huge garden. She runs into the bushes and hides there. She is shaking all over. Her leg hurts. Sunlight is bright, bright like Cathedral light. But inside the bushes she curls in a shaking little ball and hides there until after dark. Her sister Mieke knows that Rachel likes these bushes. They play there sometimes, making swings for fairies. It is Mieke who gets her rescued.

Rachel returns from her memories.

She draws them, to show Vonn later on.

She makes herbal tea and hot toast, and then sits in a rocking chair, warming herself by the aga, aware that the news cutting, the reconnection with the Avalon files, the recognition of her mother's anger, the memory of her father's voice like gunshots on the Kurdish women and children, the trick of the light from the sea, and her readings about Iseult from *The Diaries* this night, are all combined in the changes happening to her.

Now she feels that during the past few weeks, walking up and down the shore, meditating at the edge of the sea, she has learnt of something beyond her as well as inside her, a connection with life force, a connection with times past. She doesn't want religion, formally. Wouldn't it be ironic to replace her childhood oppression with a sort of born-again spirituality, this time based on women? No, she doesn't want such an oppression, never again to be controlled from outside. She doesn't want rules or rigidity, nor structures nor deity.

But she rocks to and fro, to and fro, warm by the aga, her belly comforted by the hot food, and she is aware that something very old and ancient is reaching her from the darkness, from those times when the moon appears to vanish altogether from the sky, here, in this peninsula. This magical, mysterious place. There is female help here, from inside and outside her.

The fourth to eighth centuries in Dumnonia cannot properly be called post-Roman, even if they can in the rest of Britain. People still call them the Dark Ages and use that as a derogatory term – but dark was not negative to pagan peoples. Dark, as in dark phase of the moon, means hidden, available power and help, that is about to be revealed.

Vonn has called this the creative inner dark. Dark as empowering; dark as in womb; dark as the caves in the floor of the ocean. Birth places; so that the places of the deepest vulnerability become also the very places where the creative spark first happens. The start; the beginning; the centre.

Places of magic. Call this womanspirit. Rachel is slow to understand, to dare to name, but this does not cause any cosmic disturbance, this slowness. She is just a tiny blip on the universal timescale. She matters and she doesn't at the same time. She is both matter and ... something else.

Stronger wiser older more intuitive than simply matter.

She does simply matter. She is not simply matter. She matters.

Play on the seashore. Play as adult. Play with words, ideas, and seaside. She is by her own side. Inside. Outside. Play and work ... this is a serious matter. Life. Splash and play. Laugh with water. Dolphins like to leap high and dive deep. Break the surface. Be aware. Dare. To break the lies. Play is a serious matter. Simply matter.

She can reach out, tell the truth. Reach across. How it is for her. Rachel. One woman. Significant. Insignificant. She can walk here at low tide, feeling, thinking. She has muttered here at high tide, along the edge of the ocean, wording her knowledge, naming herself.

Cunning, cunnit, cunt, knowing, knower.

She has lived, walked, moving, musing. Muse.

Dive in and swim with dolphins. Ride the waves. Watch the sunshine on the sea. Dive in and swim to the deep parts. Journey to the centre of the self. Poetry smithcraft wordsmith fusing. Walking chanting feeling musing.

Muse. Wise old woman giving the Irish their legends. Wise old woman spider grandmother. Wise old woman young woman new woman. Woman muse musing cunt cunnit Kennet Stones Avebury. Her song rises from inside her not outside her. Her images swirl and blur and blend. She is a window on her own self. Naming herself. She is becoming her own reflection.

Rachel yawns and stretches. She has been deep in thought, rocking to and fro much longer than she had intended. She is ready for a long sleep. She sleeps with her curtains open, letting in the dark.

* * *

Snowy mountains, deep gulleys, stony, inhospitable. Thousands and thousands of people on cold hillsides, camped without food, medical supplies or tents. It is winter: nights are bitter.

KURDS PLEAD FOR HELP.

Headlines in the west notice the call. Bounce it off satellites, beam it to outer space. Lose it.

Nothing grows on the mountains. Not bandages; nor food; nor trees. There is nothing the Americans want. Not oil; not gold; not diamonds. Only snow.

The Americans advise the Brits to do nothing. Most of the Brits do as they are asked. Their war is over. Their sons are home.

People starve on the mountains. In the distance Iraqi helicopter gunships fire on deserted cities. On the mountains the snow is red with brightly woven scarves, blankets, hurriedly packed. In the cities, the streets are red with blood. In the west, many people watch passively. Snow has no market value.

Iseult stands alone in the moonlight. In Ireland.

She feels the earth dying. Negative energy swirls around the planet. She must do something. She touches the four points of the compass. She creates a circle to link them. She plants her feet firmly, turning her body to face the waning crescent moon. Silver light falls on her forehead. She lets it flow through her torso, and all her limbs. She raises her arms, surrounded by silver light.

Keeping vigil, she steadily chants every Kurdish name she knows.

Over and over. Naming. Calling each name to respect, to honour. Alone, how can she save a thousand thousand women and children? Alone how can she feed, house, or supply them?

Calling, calling, chanting, calling: a challenge to the death energy being aimed at the Kurds.

Iseult reflects her powers into the cosmos.

* * *

While Rachel is asleep, dreaming Iseult, Vonn is at work. She stands on the balcony of the nursing home watching the dawn sky, waiting for the first slim crescent of the moon to appear. Crescent moon rises just after sunrise and sets just after sunset. As the moon waxes, she rises a little later each day until, halfway through her twenty-nine day cycle the full moon rises at sunset and sets at dawn. Sometimes it is impossible to see the crescent moon rising because the sky is so bright at sunrise, and this morning is no exception.

It has been a busy and social night shift so far and has seemed to go on a long time. Consuela had a row with Emily – they are best friends who get on each other's nerves. Afterwards, Consuela wanted to be comforted. Her sister had written from Madrid, which always disturbs her. She takes it out on Emily, whose bad shoulder is worse if stress decreases her pain threshold.

Consuela's bed had to be remade because she is inconti-nent. Joe couldn't settle, needed to be turned and is heavy.

George needs help now in the bath; and later on, after Consuela was asleep, Emily wanted to talk.

Vonn is weary. Her knuckles are tight, hard white, gripping the balustrade. She takes deep breaths of clean air to calm and ground herself, and he is asleep at last, the old man in whose eyes she has seen once again the terror of the clarity of his knowledge that he is losing his mind. He is in the early stages of dementia. She has cleaned him up and washed the vinyl floor where he, in a moment of unco-ordination, knocked the bottle off his bedside cabinet. He knows that he doesn't have carpet because it would rapidly start to stink. Vinyl protects him from that tragic reminder of his progressive clumsiness.

She holds him while he cries and asks her to finish it for him. To finish it once and for all. He knows she can't do that. Won't do that. He knows she'll see him through to the end. This is his home now; she works here; he trusts her. He does not trust himself. His body and his mind are betraying him, every day. Relentlessly.

So she rocks him to sleep, then she checks the other residents, and now she has a short break, here in the first minutes of dawn. She is drained, tired, and it is hours until her turn to rest.

Behind her the closed and curtained windows of her workplace are quiet now. Unusually, everyone is asleep. Even Consuela and Emily have finally dropped off, and this despite Emily's left shoulder, which burns with arthritis and gives her trouble at night.

Vonn watches the sky but there is no sign of the new moon, though it is four days old now. She longs to go home to sleep. Several hours yet in a twelve-hour shift. But tonight, until midnight, the moon may be visible, a thin knife in the sky, cutting a route to tomorrow.

As she stands there, strong and calm again, ready to resume work, it seems that the sky is a bowl turned upside down, and look, it cannot possibly contain this surge of light which begins to flow down over that grey hill there. It seems that the sky may not hold the sunrise. It will spill, it will flood, it is happening now, rose-tinted liquid light, and Vonn loosens her grip on the balustrade but she's transfixed there on the balcony, surrounded by everything that is beginning today.

When sunrise fills the sky with liquid light suffusing pink and gold to the sky's brim and pouring over, it bathes the blue-green juniper trees, and their curving branches, and pours down on to leafy shrubs, dripping from spiders' webs pink and gold on to the lawn which surrounds the nursing home. Sunrise envelops Vonn, coming towards her. Carmine and saffron, rose-pink and grey-gold. It flows down from the bowl of the sky; it gathers, down the hills, streams of light into the trees and woods. The sky is rose-pink and grey, she hasn't seen it like this for a long time. Surging light, curving light, a rolling wave of rose colour billows now towards her, across the moors, down the sides of the valleys, over the hedgerows, into the lanes, fields and pathways, as if the earth is Rachel curled there, relaxed, sleeping, maybe dreaming, and the wave of light is Vonn who is awake early, leaning on one elbow very quietly, watching while her lover sleeps, leaning above her waiting, breathing, longing for her lover to wake up, open her arms, stretch and yawn, her breasts like hills reaching, rising towards the warmth of sunshine.

But Rachel is somewhere else, breasts rising and falling, limbs heavy with sleep, her hair on the pillow tumbled like the bushes in this garden, and the hair between her thighs soft and moist like the trees in this valley, while Vonn stands alone here, at work at dawn.

It is around her now; she is part of a hologram of light, molten sunrise on day four of new moon. She knows that the moon has risen too, by now. A new moon is up there somewhere, shining, but is obscured by all this pink light. She has to trust that it is there this morning.

Now the sky reflects from an ocean of light, too much for the sky, spilling on to the land, clarifying everything that is there to be clarified, everything that Vonn now knows.

She knows that she is in love. That her hip bones are a bowl of desire, that her breasts are rounds of want and hope. That eroticism is all around her, even while she is thinking of work, being at work, it is still there, like a rose quartz sunrise, its warmth flowing on to the body of the earth, making love to the land herself.

Around Vonn now is rose quartz light, an inverted sky

pulsing waves and waves of rose light from over that hill, and now condensing there, as the sun climbs up above the hill when the sky, which before could hardly contain that light, flips back into place, holding the pockets of sunlight safe between the clouds, so the sun doesn't fall out of the bowl on to the hilltop, but floats upwards, rising up beyond this hologram until it is up in the sky where it is meant to be at the top left-hand side of the picture – where, when Vonn and her sister, Jenny, were children, they said that the sun belonged.

Thinking of Jenny, Vonn shivers involuntarily. She returns indoors, where most of the residents are asleep, including Emily Pengelly, whose arthritic pain is muffled with pain-killers; but not George Constantinidou, who is writing his memoirs of a Cypriot childhood. He likes to write in the early hours, in a spiral notebook, with the light of his torch so that he doesn't wake Joe Eddy. George and Joe have been sharing a room in this council-run nursing home for four years. Joe was one of the first municipal dustmen of Penzance. Grandchildren visit them on Saturdays.

But now there is no sound from the nursing home. There are three more hours to go before Vonn's relief arrives. She checks all the residents, goes to the office, writes her reports and tunes into the world service for a while.

By the time that Vonn's shift is over, her back is tired, her arms are aching. She drives home to sleep, through morning lanes wet with sunlight, past fields where mist hangs low, and hedgerows steaming as they emerge into the day. Vonn catches glimpses of hills, grey-blue and shadowy, appearing and disappearing through the mist, and despite being tired she can't help noticing that some hills are freshly focused, whilst others are veiled, shape-shifting in classic Celtic style. She thinks of mist from legends, as the character of the countryside changes with the shape of the road and the angle of the light.

Vonn watches the colours of the morning sky, thinking of Jenny, her sister, and of Rachel with whom she is now ready to share her family's story.

At home, Vonn's ansaphone is bleeping. A message from Rachel says, Love you, sleep well, see you soon.

Tristanne wakes while Iscult is sleeping soundly beside her in the forest. Day four of new moon. Moon shining there, silver blade in the sky.

She has been dreaming of her battle with Iseult's uncle, the Morholt, and can hear in her mind the cries of the spectators on the cliffs as she and the warlord fight with skilled determination on a small offshore island designated for the purpose by King Mark of Dumnonia.

Before Tristanne's arrival in Dumnonia, the Irish warlord had been plaguing the shores of Dumnonia with raiding parties from across the Irish Sea. None of the men at the court of King Mark could slay the Morholt.

Tristanne well remembers the disbelief at her fighting prowess when first she arrived at the court. To all assembled there the notion of a woman warrior was purely a myth. Of course, they were only too happy for Tristanne to be skilled in languages and accomplished on the harp and lyre. They were amused by her ballads and entertained by her appearance and her singing voice. But they did not understand that her sword was a real sword nor that she could really use it.

Perhaps they did not take seriously her riding boots, her riding skirt nor for that matter her cloak of protection, which perhaps to them signified only that she was a woman of royal descent, so beautifully was it cut and embroidered.

So she settled into the court, performing her music, smiling and entertaining everyone, enjoying her acceptance by King Mark, the brother of her real mother, Blancheflowcr.

And still the raids came from across the sea, until one day, that fateful day, Tristanne offered to take up the challenge and defeat the Morholt. Great merriment was raised at court at this suggestion. If some royal wench from Armorica chose to lose her life so easily, who were they, said the barons, to stand in her way?

Laughter was loud and long.

Until she won.

Were it not for that battle the raids would not have ceased and a peaceful settlement between Ireland and Dumnonia could not have been negotiated; were it not for that battle, I would never have met you, thinks Tristannc, gazing at the sleeping form of Iseult curled in blankets by the remains of a good fire.

As if remembering the sword fight in her body, Tristanne's old wound aches in her thigh and she reaches down to rub it absent-mindedly.

Beside her on the ground is her leather belt from which her fine sword always hangs as she walks and rides. She is used to its weight, and wears it like an old friend, her means of defence against any who might challenge her.

Leaving the belt on the ground, and the sword lying there, she quietly removes her athame and holds it in her hands with reverence.

Athame, Athame, sacred knife. I will be no one's chattel, no one's wife.

Holding the knife in her right hand, she lifts the blade to the sky where it reflects the silver crescent moon, though its blade is straighter than the blade of the moon in the night sky.

Mother moon, she calls, mother of mine, pour down your strength upon me, I call to you.

Have I not used this blade to cut the herbs in my foster mother's kitchen?

Have I not used this blade to cut the branches from the trees in this forest to make our shelter?

Have I not used this blade to call to you, in times of need?

Did not the great Brigid teach all our ancestors the craft of metal work, our art of smithcraft? Did not her fires bend this very metal into shape?

Mother moon, crone, mother and maiden, in all your phases, are you not the night sister of the sun, the daytime one, Brigid herself?

> Come to me now, mother moon, I need you.
> I am young of blood and bone.
> I dance tonight for you, mother moon.
> I am the maiden dancing your tune.
> Pour your strength into this knife.
> I will be no one's chattel, no one's wife.

Were it not for your strength I would not have been able to sustain my battle against the warlord, he who was plaguing this shore. I am a woman, young and strong, but he was mighty: the warrior onc.

> Your strength did sustain me, mother moon.
> Pour down, pour down your lunar tune.
> Into this knife, from the knife in the sky.
> Give me your strength, as night passes by.
> Come to me, mother, mother moon.
> I need your mother-warrior might.
> I need your blessing this new moon night.
> Athame Athame, sacred knife.
> Sustain me, bless me, save my life.

She kisses the athame and places it back quietly in its holder in her leather belt.

She wraps herself in her cloak, needled so finely by her foster mother Floreate and, standing under the new moon, she lets the image of the knife in the sky blur and blend into that of a thin serpent, who lies around the lower half of a dark shadow egg.

She breathes deeply, letting the serpent energy flow down into her body from the shining one in the sky.

Then, as Floreate has taught her, she lets her spirit flow up to the serpent in the sky and blend with it and there grow arms and legs slowly. Now the serpent takes on the form of a dragon and she lets the back of the dragon grow silver wings until the serpent becomes the dragon and the dragon can leave the moon and fly.

Wrapped in her cloak with its beautifully embroidered border of threads and serpent trails and dragon tails, her spirit flies the dragon around the moon and circles there freely at will for a long time, breathing and flying, unboundaried by earth or time.

I, Tristanne (she chants softly), I am a warrior woman.
I, Tristanne, I am a warrior woman. Fly high, woman warrior.
Fly high, woman warrior, know thyself and be unafraid.
Know thyself and be unafraid.
Know thyself and be unafraid.

Wrapped in the cloak, the luxurious cloak of protection, Tristanne stands under the curve of the four-day-old moon and allows her spirit to dance through the skies and pass around the rings of stones throughout Dumnonia.

There are new tales being told of these stones, she hears, in the courts of Dumnonia. Minstrels sing for the barons and the King, who is beginning to listen to the missionaries who travel here from Ireland and from Wales.

They tell new tales of the rings of stones. It is now being said that the stones were once women, young dancing women, who dared to disobey the Lord, he whom the missionaries call the Christ. These young women, so sing the minstrels, they dared to dance on the Sabbath day, which should be the day of the Lord, and for their sins they have been turned to stone.

Tristanne draws upon her memories of her foster parents. They warned her that these men would come, though they could not know exactly what these men would say: no dancing on the seventh day.

Young women will be punished for dancing.
Especially if they dance for the moon.
Mother moon in the sky: crone – mother – maiden.
Shape-shifter: triple wise one.

Spirit, my spirit, return to me now, chants Tristanne softly, wrapped in her cloak of protection.

From the dragon flight in the sky her spirit returns and re-enters her body until she is whole, at one with herself, standing firmly upon the earth from which she draws her dragon power, on this the fourth night of new moon.

When the moon is maiden I shall dance.
When the moon is full, my mother moon, I shall dance.
When the moon is waning, the old one, the crone, I shall dance.
When the moon is dark, she rests, I shall dance to bring her back.
I will be maiden-warrior young.
I will be maiden-warrior strong.

The mother my mother is the moon. She is me and I am
she.
We are one. We are one.
The serpent shines above me. The dragon sleeps below
me.
I am they and they are me. I am young and I am strong.
Warrior woman, under the moon.
I am woman of blood and bone.
They will not turn me into stone.
Not any part of me shall they have.
I am woman and woman I love.

Tristanne raises her arms and hands to the sky as Floreate
taught her to do. She feels the light from the thin serpent
moon on her open palms and imagines it flowing right down
through her arms into her body and down her thighs and
legs into her feet and through her feet into the earth.

Then she kneels, as Floreate instructed her, and places her
hands palms downwards on to the earth and imagines the
dragon in the earth sending up warrior strength into her
hands. She waits until she can feel the strength flowing right
up inside her.

Then she stands, arms by her side, breathing very slowly,
aware of the huge trees, the young trees, the undergrowth,
the sky and the night around her.

She returns to the fireside, and sleeps curled beside
her lover, her woman lover, in the forest, on the fourth night
of new moon.

* * *

Vonn and Rachel drive to Lesingey Round, an old iron-age
settlement, now overgrown with tall trees. On the way there,
they talk of the fact that they've both been dreaming about
Iseult or Tristanne, and that perhaps as the spring becomes
summer they may be able to take time off together to visit
some of the legendary places which neither of them has had
reason to explore until now.

With Vonn behind the wheel, Rachel watches as the car
passes along country lanes. Presently Vonn says that she has
heard from her friends in Oregon.

'How did they take it?'

'Surprised and very pleased. I didn't leave them much room for anything else. I raved about you.'

'That's good. So you should!'

'Exactly. They sent some photos – I'll show them to you later – there's one of me working on the shed I was doing up.'

'You worked? I didn't realise that.'

'Everyone works. They love you if you roll up your sleeves and get grafting. There's a great deal to do. Minimum money to do it with. So they afford the materials, just, and do all the labour themselves. I had a wonderful time.'

'A working holiday.'

'Yes, and talking. And some laughing, and dancing, and singing, and circle dancing, and some more talking, and some crying.'

Rachel stays silent. She looks at Vonn, who parks the car off the roadside, and smiles as Vonn returns her look.

'Yes. There's quite a lot I want to tell you.'

'I had a feeling about it, when I woke up this morning. I was getting ready to come up to the corner to meet you, and you seemed so close, but I sort of felt you were sad, and you wanted to talk. Let me hug you a minute.'

Hand in hand, they make their way up a track, then turn uphill through fields. There are a few wild violets in the hedgerows, and an occasional patch of wild thyme. The daffodils that rib the curving slopes with yellow and cream every springtime are in full flower, so that the ribs are fluffy, flamboyant stripes, edged with green.

The earth looks so tactile, thinks Rachel, who loves sewing, as if made of corduroy cloth. You could make lovely children's clothes with this thick soft corduroy, and you could have yellow patch pockets, and thick little trousers tucked into green wellies with yellow frog eyes on.

She hasn't been to Lesingey Round till now and it feels so old and peaceful here, as if there was never any war at this settlement, no use for weapons, a safe haven for women and children; a place of continuity and equilibrium.

They clamber up a steep incline and enter the round via a green ivy archway, near a rambling holly tree. Rachel imagines coming here in mid-winter to gather the evergreens.

They scramble up over the first high ditch, under the trees, where now in the shelter of the branches there are thick clumps of daffodils, not enough to call a carpet, but plenty to give yellow haloes to patches of green.

'It's wonderful. Vonn, thank you, it's just wonderful. Look, look at the pools of light. Makes me want to hold you.'

'Me too. Hoped you'd like it. Not a tourist place. I love old trees, knotted and gnarled. They are timeless.'

They sit kissing under the overhead canopy, on thick waterproof mats, then set up their soup kitchen around them, laughing.

To Vonn, it seems that there is no hurry; that Rachel realises the significance of their being in the open air, together, in this peaceful place, which is secluded and protected, so that she can reveal a story that she rarely shares with anyone.

'What I'm about to tell you is the background of why my mother is angry with me. I think you'll find it disturbing.'

'You don't have to tell me, you know.'

'I know. But no one can get to know me without this background. It's completely woven into my life and who I am now.'

Vonn pauses as they share out the food they have brought.

'It *is* disturbing and it's something that didn't happen to me directly. It happened to someone very close to me. If this, well, some of this, had happened to me directly, then my life'd be different, not worse or better, just different. I'd be speaking from the inside. It's not very often I want to share this. It's not often I meet anyone I'd want to talk to about it. It happened to my sister, Jenny. She was just over two and a half years younger than me.'

Vonn pauses again, watches the trees for a moment, exchanges a smile with Rachel, and then continues:

'I left home when I was eighteen. I'd been away about three weeks when my grandmother died. I didn't know her very well. My mother's mother.'

'I lived in a flat with Frankie, and I used to go home now and then. Frankie and I had a put-you-up in the living room, so we could have someone to stay and I loved it when Jenny used to visit. We were very, very close. She'd known Frankie, as I had, since we were little. We all grew up on a council estate behind the town of Brighton. Sort of rural in a way – we sometimes used to walk up on to the Downs. We were from quite a poor family – there are plenty of low-waged folks in Brighton, my folks included. Dad was a fork-lift truck driver and Mum was a hotel cleaner at that time.

'My parents didn't know that Frankie and I were lovers. If they had I don't suppose they'd have let Jenny anywhere near us. They thought we were flatmates and so they felt Jenny was safe with us, which of course she was.

'Jenny came to stay, and one night she woke me up, crying in her sleep. We shared a room for years at home and I'd never known her do that in all those years. Now that my grandmother had died, my mother had taken it into her head that it was her responsibility to make a home for Grandad. My dad wasn't at all pleased. He hardly knew Grandad, none of us did, not really. Barely knew each other. I don't really know why Mum got it into her head to take Grandad in, but anyway, there was Grandad at home and Jenny crying in her sleep.'

Vonn looks at Rachel, then at the daffodils, and out into the distance between the trees, through which the daffodil fields can be seen sloping away.

Rachel waits.

Vonn begins again, talking very quietly:

'I didn't wake Jenny up. She was quite deeply asleep. She stopped sniffing and I thought it best to let her sleep through. If she was having a nightmare or something I thought maybe it was a short one, or surely she'd have woken herself up.

'I had the next day off. That was why she was there. She woke up pale and appeared quite drained. I was sorry I hadn't woken her out of whatever she'd been dreaming.

'We went out, shopping in Oxford Street. She wasn't her usual self at all. I asked her if she was all right. She said she was just tired.

'I went home a couple of weekends later. I couldn't work out what was wrong. Mum was her usual self. Not very talkative. Not warm. She wasn't a warm kind of person.

'Jenny was a bit pale, off colour. I took her out to the cinema. Then we went for a burger. I asked her if anything was wrong. She nearly bit my head off. Why should there be? I said she was a bit pale. She said her mocks were coming up. That was true, it was November. She was in the fifth year.

'Mum wouldn't let her come and stay until the Christmas hols. I couldn't get any time off. I phoned Jenny when I could, and you know what it's like with the phone in the hall and everything. Like talking at Clapham Junction. Frankie was a student and our flat was one of five grotty ones in an old house with one phone between us.

'So it was just after New Year when I saw Jenny again, and she looked pale but defiant. I was home and we shared a room. Like we always did. Frankie had gone home for New Year. Jenny and I walked by the sea. It was good weather, I remember. Not that the sea at Brighton is like the Atlantic – of course not, but we always liked a walk watching the waves, and there's such a steep undertow there, it makes a good rattle on the pebbles. We were quite a stretch from the sea. It was a long walk right the way down through the town.

'Jenny'd found herself a boyfriend. She'd wanted to be a lawyer until then. She'd had big ideas of university, all of that. Then the boyfriend came along. Suddenly there were rows and she wanted to go to his house. Mum wouldn't let her.

'Then she came to stay with me and Frankie. It was February. She said she was pregnant. She was going to marry the boyfriend at Easter, when she was sixteen, and go and live with him at his mother's place.'

'Did your mum agree to that?' asks Rachel.

'No. Mum was frantic. She threatened to make her a ward of court, and have him done for rape, the lot, because Jenny was, strictly speaking, under age when she got pregnant.'

'But she was determined to marry this boy, was she?'

'Jenny was very determined. She said that she missed me and she wished I was still at home.'

'Oh Vonn, didn't you find it heavy, her saying that?'

'Yes, but it was true, and I missed her terribly too. She hated having Grandad live there. She said that she couldn't study with him around. Didn't like the household. Couldn't stand the school scene, a whole jumble of things.

'Anyway, she talked Mum and Dad into letting her marry

him, just after her birthday. She was Pisces. She was sixteen at the beginning of March.

'She miscarried at six months. So she was married to a chap she didn't love, just to get away from home, with her studies down the drain. She got a job as a telephonist, temporary from an agency.'

Rachel offers Vonn the sandwich box. Vonn helps herself to cheese and onion, while Rachel, who feels sure that this is just the start of Vonn's story, waits, taking in the peaceful atmosphere of Lesingey: the bluey-green daffodil leaves, the fan-shaped clumps, the bright green stars of new ivy, the quiet light.

Vonn thinks back to the sequence of events in which Jenny was trapped, and sighs involuntarily. Then she continues:

'I was busy with work and studies, doing all my own coming-out stuff, making friends with Ben and David. I was happy nursing, working very hard. Frankie and I were in our dream come true phase, very happy together. Jenny rang me from a call box, one Thursday evening, when she knew I was off duty. I met her up in London, we went to a pizza place. She was sixteen and a bit, pregnant again and her husband was beating her up. I took her to Women's Aid.

'She was there a few weeks, then she went back to her bloke.'

'Women do. They quite often go back,' says Rachel.

'Yes. So I gather. It was terrible. Then suddenly, Grandad had a heart attack. He went into hospital and I went to see him. Just once. He didn't mean much to me, but he was family, so I went.

'Then Mum rang and she said she didn't know what to do with Jenny. Jenny wanted to come home. Mum thought she was over-reacting. Mum didn't want her back. She said she'd had enough trouble. I couldn't put her up. I didn't have the space. We had a tiny bedroom and a living room which was the kitchen as well. Okay for a night or two, but not permanently.

'Mum said Jenny wouldn't even go and see Grandad in the hospital. Something clicked inside me. I knew this was crucial.'

Vonn looks sideways at Rachel, who reaches out and holds

her hand. Vonn says, 'You know how you sometimes just know things?'

Rachel nods, and her eyes are kind.

'Jenny rang and she was in a call box again, he'd beaten her up. She was spotting. I told her to get on the train, I'd meet her. I went and got her. I brought her into casualty. They admitted her. They said she was very lucky. He was a big fellow, her bloke, and so his fist didn't fit in her eye socket. If he'd had a smaller fist he'd have done more damage.'

Vonn bites her lip. Rachel swallows hard. Lucky. Jenny was lucky. They said that Jenny was lucky?

'Then Grandad died. Everything at once, all hell let loose. Jenny in hospital, bleeding, losing the new baby. Grandad in the morgue, Mum going crackers. Dad trying to calm Mum down.

'I spent every minute I was free with Jenny. She said she would go back to Women's Aid. They said they could help her get a place. She was in the sixteen-to-eighteen category, that should help.

'We talked and talked. She would not go to Grandad's funeral. She got herself the boyfriend the year before, to hide from everyone the fact she was already pregnant. By her own grandfather. He'd been in her room several times while she was supposed to be on study leave. He said no one would believe her. He said it would make her mother ill if she ever told her. Her mother would say she was lying and throw her out.

'He made all kinds of threats. He wouldn't leave her alone. It was half term in the autumn when it started. She was at home all day. Mum was working. Dad was working. Grandad said he was lonely now that Grandma had died. He was very strong; a wiry, thin man with enormous strength. She said that his age didn't seem to make him weak or anything. He'd been a navvy all his life, she just couldn't stop him. She was terrified that she'd be thrown out. She didn't have anywhere to go.

'Then when she got pregnant she rustled up a boyfriend, because she couldn't see any way out of it.

'Anyway, she asked me to go to the funeral, so that Mum wouldn't find out. Mum still wouldn't have her back.

'I went to the funeral. I took Ben. He pretended to be my boyfriend. There was no way I could come out to Mum with all that going on. I pretended I was straight. It was all one removed. I was very close to Jenny, and it was her it was happening to. I didn't want it to be me. I don't mean that at all. But I had all this anger, anger at Mum, because I knew in my heart that Grandad was right. Mum wouldn't have believed Jenny. I knew that deep down.

'It wasn't Mum's fault. It was Grandad who did it. But Mum wouldn't have recognised the truth. I don't know how I knew that then, but I did know it.

'Jenny took out an injunction against the bloke, and eventually she was rehoused. Meanwhile Frankie and I were in our second year, and times were hard but we were happy. We knew each other very well. There was a lot of love.

'The next thing was that Jenny's bloke turned up in her neighbourhood. I don't know how he got to know where she was. I never found out. He started hanging around her flat. She lived near Tower Bridge. It was a fairly hairy place at night. She was living in fear: afraid of him and also depressed with the whole situation.

'She came to stay with us for a little while, but we were very crowded. One day she decided she would go back to her flat. I went with her, saw her in. I had misgivings.

'She had a job, she was still working as a telephonist. The injunction was there, but they're not all that easy to enforce. The area was badly lit and she was more depressed, sometimes suicidal. She went on to tranks.

'One day I was supposed to meet her at the pizza place and she wasn't there. I knew. I just knew. I hailed a cab. To hell with the cost.

'I got there and they were putting her in the ambulance. That was the first time. She'd taken a lot of paracets. Not enough. She tried twice more. The third time, she succeeded. She did it with alcohol, paracets and tranks.'

Vonn's voice cracks. She begins to shake. But regaining her composure, she continues:

'If you do it with paracets it doesn't work instantly. Takes time for it to become toxic. Your liver packs up. Very slow. Very painful. She learned that the first time. So she added the alcohol and tranks.

'And that's when I told Mum. I told her that it all began with Grandad.

'She was furious. How dare I make such an accusation? She'd had enough trouble all these years with Jenny. She thought she could rely on me. If that was all true, why had I gone to Grandad's funeral? I tried to talk and talk; the more I tried the more distressed she became. Then she went to live with my aunty Molly, her sister. Dad accused me of siding with Jenny and breaking up the home. Everything fell apart.

'Mum lived at Aunty Molly's for a long time.'

Vonn takes a deep breath, closes her eyes for a moment. In a while, she opens her eyes, reaches for Rachel's hand, squeezes it and continues: 'Then one day, after I'd come to the house on the dunes, I had a letter from my aunty Molly. Mum had gone into a very deep depression and had stopped speaking completely. She was having all kinds of therapy. Aunty Molly loved her like I had loved Jenny. She'd been seeing a counsellor herself. She was ten years younger than Mum. She said that Grandad had been abusing her and my mother. That my mother had repressed it completely, and the truth about Jenny overwhelmed her.

'I went up to London to meet Aunty Molly. I didn't know her very well. She hadn't known about Grandad and my mother before because of the huge age gap. Aunty Molly said she felt she was very lucky, because she had been helped for years to have the courage to heal. She said there was now a book by that title, and she gave it to me.

'I cried all over her. It was the first time somebody believed me, what I was saying about Jenny's life.'

Rachel fishes in her pocket for a tissue. She hands it to Vonn who blows her nose and wipes her eyes.

'Now my mother is seriously ill. It wasn't my fault, it was Grandad. All the years of repression. She had so little memory of it herself, that she even had him come to live with her, and it wasn't her fault, but she couldn't protect Jenny.

'And that's what I've been working on.'

Rachel holds Vonn's hand, firmly, steadily, without saying a word, hoping that Vonn can feel the warmth, the connection, the depth of caring. She says, 'Thank you for telling me. For trusting me.'

Vonn speaks softly, 'It's true that because I told Mum the truth about Jenny, that I was the catalyst for her distress. I'm not responsible for my mother's life, I know that, but this has had devastating effects throughout our family. I don't want my mother blamed. But at the same time I don't want to have to carry the blame for her anger, or the weight of it.'

'Will you be able to communicate with her, d'you think?'

'I don't know. It may take years. Maybe never. I don't know. That's what I've got to learn to live with. There's no certainty that Mum will ever be able to come through this. To help herself, or me.'

'Vonn, listen to me, please. I think you are wonderful. I want to be there for you, when you need me.'

'You are. In many ways. Not least because you understand how painful the unblocking process is.'

'I'm not very experienced with all this. I'm at my own beginning. I wish I knew more, could help more.'

Vonn says, 'You remember talking about Isabel Allende's book?'

'Yes. Yes I do.'

'Well, it seems to me that it's not only governments that make people disappear. Junta. Terrible crimes. The book had a profound effect on me ... I waited to say this to you ... My grandfather, by his actions when my mother was a child, made her disappear. As if he excavated into her mind, buried terrible things there, dead things, then walled it all up again. Inadvertently, I was the one who unblocked it. But she couldn't face what was brought out – the dismembered body of her childhood self – so the rest of her mind has now disappeared as well. You can do it to a whole nation, which is what the book is about, or you can do it to one child, which is what my mother's life has been about.

'Politically, it seems to me it is part of the same process. The abuse of power. The denial and disrespect of other human beings. The unvoicing. The killings. The maiming and making of madness. I find this so frightening, whichever level we're talking about.'

'So do I, Vonn, so do I.'

'I know. But we are also reflections of one another, aren't

we, and we can listen and sustain one another through the opening up of the mines. If we can't do that, then what does love mean, for us, for women?'

'I don't disagree with that. There are some mothers like yours who withdraw, hide in madness, whatever, and that's very frightening; and others like my mother, who deny their own reality and squeeze themselves into a frame, even when they know the frame is too small, they can't fit inside, and their anger seeps out through every corner, cold or hot, every version of anger, because the frame hurts them so much. As daughters we feel such compassion about this, but as ourselves, we need self-defence. Then we hurt so much that it is hard to hold all the parts of the self . . .

'And then,' says Rachel, trying to control her voice which is wobbly, 'it makes unblocking so hard that we can lose hope. But you and me . . . that brings back the hope.'

* * *

In the music room in the house on the dunes, Vonn is setting a poem to music, trying to follow Debussy's invention of the full tonic scale. Mysterious and haunting harmonies hang in the air around the room as Vonn tries to transform the colours and sounds of the rose quartz dawn at the nursing home into music, somewhat unsuccessfully.

Repeatedly, Vonn moves between her tape recorder and piano, improvising, remaining dissatisfied with the result.

Three hours pass quickly until midday. Vonn pulls on her anorak and drives over the moors along the bypass, past Long Rock and Helston across the Lizard to Porthallow, where she is to spend the day with Lou and Annie, who run a nursery garden there.

Entering one of the huge polytunnels, Vonn calls out: 'It's me. Anyone home?'

Annie comes forward, trowel in hand. 'Vonn, Vonn my precious. It's been so long. You're a naughty one to neglect us so.'

'I know, I know, but I'm in love. Like I said on the phone, I just don't know whether I'm on my head or my heels.'

'We'll forgive you, thousands wouldn't. Hey, any luck with the composition?'

'Slow.' Vonn smiles and shrugs. 'It's hard work. Is the piano free tomorrow morning? I might just have another go.'

'You're staying over? Oh good. We hoped you would. Anyway, why didn't you bring her?'

'Because I want you to meet her on home ground, for starters; and because she's looking after a sick friend tonight.'

'You don't trust us.'

'Too right I don't. Not with my new love life. I need more time till she gets the Lou and Annie interview.'

'What it is not to be trusted.' Annie sighs theatrically, but she's smirking nonetheless. 'Well, I hope you've brought some photos of her. Iseult the fair, am I right?'

Vonn hugs her good friend. 'Don't wind me up. I just said we'd got a bit of a reflection in the legend. That's all. You ex-journalists are such fibbers.'

'Always a nose for a new story, Vonn, darling. My, it's good to see you.' Annie puts down the trowel and hugs Vonn thoroughly. 'Come on, Lou's got cream teas for three in the new conservatory.'

Annie checks the air vents, closes up the polytunnel, and the two walk companionably together to the back of the house as Vonn says, 'It's so good to be here. The last time was October, you know. Just before Lou's op.'

'And so much has gone on, darling, since then. We don't talk operations any more – she's sculpting again morn till night. Oh, the sweet sound of hammer on stone is music to my ears. I never thought I'd say that. They say Lou's the next Barbara H, you know. Her exhibition was a dazzling success.'

At that moment, Lou comes to meet them. Arm in arm, laughing, the three women make their way indoors, happily aware of time stretching into the evening and all day tomorrow.

* * *

Next morning, whilst cycling towards Boscawen-Un stone circle, Rachel finds the road completely blocked by a farm vehicle which is trying to turn into a tight gateway.

A young, slight woman cycles alongside Rachel, stops, and holds herself steady, one foot down to the ground.

'Hi. Seems we're going to be a while,' she says, in a friendly manner, nodding towards the obstruction.

'Hello. Luckily I'm in no hurry. Are you?'

'Yeah, I am as it happens. Going to a place called the house on the dunes.'

'Oh? Vonn's place? You know Vonn?'

'Not yet. My family had a . . . a connection with Elizabeth Somerville.'

'Oh, really? Oh, I see. Vonn's gone out today. I'll see her tonight. I could give her a message?'

'No, ta. S'not urgent. You an artist?'

'Just a hobby. I like to draw, a bit. I was going to draw some stones. Boscawen-Un.'

'A truly legendary famous place.'

'Yes. I'm looking forward to it. I'm Rachel, by the way.'

'Rachel?' says the other woman, then, 'We haven't met, have we? I didn't see you daffodil picking, did I?'

'No. Though I might go picking next week. Why? Do I know you?'

The other woman then startles Rachel by saying, 'Maybe we did meet, once before. I think so. Yes, I think so. Do you live nearby?'

In spite of herself, Rachel finds herself drawn to the stranger and answering her questions, though she wonders if she ought to be offhand, or at least more wary, as she would have been in the city. But she feels no sense of unease, just a lightweight, friendly curiosity. A weird sensation comes over her of *déjà vu*, then a mocking awareness that she is about to give away some more personal details to a woman she doesn't know. Rachel thinks, In a minute I'll be singing like the proverbial canary. She says, 'I rent a place at Sennen. How about you?'

'Had a caravan up by Zennor. Got blown out of it in the gales. Now I'm homeless.'

'What will you do? Are you camping?'

'On a friend's floor. Till the summer. Then I'll camp outdoors. Not too bad – when it's sunny.'

'Did you know the quarry people?'

'Had a friend there. Why? Did you? Bloody bailiffs.' Sharp, staccato anger rings in the voice of the woman cyclist.

Softly, Rachel says, 'It was a scandal.' Quoting from a local dignitary, Rachel adds, ' "Got to set an example. We cannot have the rural homeless creating an eyesore for the summer tourists." '

'No, we can't. But we're short on railway arches, in the country.'

Rachel is on the point of asking the other woman more about herself but at that moment the farm vehicle finishes manoeuvring, and the other woman says, 'Here we go. He's done it. The road's clear.'

Rachel cycles slowly, careful of the ruts, thinking about the cyclist in front of her. Who is she? Why so open yet mysterious? So many questions. Yet she can identify with the woman cycling on ahead: the restlessness, never being settled, always moving. She herself has felt emotionally homeless for years. And, like the woman, she has also been physically homeless. Rachel thinks of Chynoweth, her new home, with deep affection. Safe and dark and warm. A womb with a view.

They stop by the small wooden gate that leads to Boscawen-Un.

The other woman smiles. Then she speaks quietly, as if steadying herself and choosing her words with the utmost care. 'You must think me very odd, or very rude, but please, I want to tell you about my name, and I want to talk to you, properly. Will you meet me after you've drawn your stones, if I cycle back to meet you?'

She reaches out and touches Rachel briefly on the arm, saying, 'Then I can tell you where I think I first met you, and you might understand me.'

Rachel swallows, unable to find her voice. She smiles, as the sense of *déja vu* dissolves, and then, as if compelled to take this further, she hears herself saying: 'All right, I'll wait here until one o'clock. Then I shall start cycling home.'

'I'll be here,' says the other woman. With that she flicks the pedal to the correct position, waves and cycles away from Rachel.

It is a peaceful morning as Rachel walks around and around Boscawen-Un, stopping at each of the nineteen stones, holding them, deciding on the angle and composition of her drawings. No one comes to disturb her. She leans against the quartz stone, thinking about its appearance, which is so different from the eighteen granite stones, and pondering over the meeting with the woman cyclist earlier. Who was she? Why the strange sense of *déjà vu*? And why did she, Rachel, feel confident and interested enough to say that she'd wait? She doesn't usually behave in such a manner. Her sense of reality seemed to float away while she was talking to the woman cyclist. But the floating was itself pleasant, and seemed to feel safe enough, despite the fact that the other woman didn't say who she was. Why? They talked together for a good eighteen minutes – why did the nineteenth minute bring a suggestion and a response? *Will you wait? Yes, I will.*

Rachel Markham, says Rachel to herself strictly, this isn't like you. You'd better take control of yourself. If this was London you'd not be so open.

But, replies Rachel also to herself, this isn't London. That's exactly what is different. This is one of the oldest, strangest and eeriest parts of the old country. It's a place of ancestors, unknown phenomena. A place of sacred sites, like Boscawen-Un, and of earth mysteries.

She looks at her watch. Almost one o'clock. She makes her way from the stone circle, through the rough gorse areas, along a well-trodden, though secluded path, back to the small wooden gate where she has left her bicycle and where, as she arrives, she finds the woman with the unknown name, waiting.

As she unlocks Chynoweth's front door, Rachel turns to her guest saying, 'Would you like to bring your bike in and stand it there by the front window, in case it rains later? I must have a quick shower. I can't think or talk while I'm this sweaty and dirty, and I won't be long. Teabags are right by the kettle, you can't miss them. S'that okay?'

'Fine by me. What a lovely, lovely cottage.'

Rachel answers from the bathroom. 'I love it. I was so lucky to get it and the rent's really fair – it's home already.'

Five minutes later, Rachel emerges dried and changed, to find steaming mugs of tea on the table and the stranger watching the sea.

Rachel sits back in Melloney's rocking chair, takes a very deep breath, and says, 'All right. Who are you, and why do you want to talk to me "properly" as you put it?'

'I hardly know how to start. It's so important to me to get it right. We may have met before. But I'm not quite sure about that. I imagined how we might really meet, for months. Ever since I was told to look for someone called Rachel.'

'Go on,' says Rachel, listening intently, unafraid. There has been so much mystery about this all morning that she wants the truth. She thinks of Vonn, who is probably talking at this very moment to Lou and Annie about falling in love and the speed and entrancement of it. She feels that Vonn is sending love at this moment.

Somehow, the stranger in Melloney's cottage now seems to be part of the total connection: Rachel wonders how this can possibly be, but is sure that it is so, in some way.

'My mother is Spanish, my father, Cornish. My father named me – my mother agreed. I'm named after two of her sisters who fought in the Spanish Civil War, Patricia and Anne. I'm known as Triss, which is short for Patricia Anne.'

Rachel's sharp intake of breath startles Triss, who asks what the matter is.

'My mother's name is Truus,' says Rachel. 'She is from Holland. It seems very similar.'

'Yes,' says Triss simply. She pauses, then says, 'I have a very close connection with this part of the country. My father's people are from St Ives. But I was brought up in London.

'I need to meet Vonn Smedley, and I heard from a friend of mine that she now lives in a house called the house on the dunes. You see, I am very psychic. It's not a thing I say to everyone, but my old friend who is a clairvoyant, who lives in St Ives, has told me that Vonn Smedley is close to a woman called Rachel. That this woman called Rachel is important to me somehow, but I don't know how, yet, and that this Rachel has Irish ancestry. It's very difficult to explain, because, well, it just is, but some of my ancestors went to County Cork, as Spanish immigrants there, with the lace industry. Somehow I have to meet Rachel. But this morning it was a surprise to me, I couldn't quite face up to it right there and then. I was told by my clairvoyant that I met your Irish ancestors when I was myself living a former life in Ireland. I went to a hypnotist to see what I could remember, but I couldn't remember much. But I was told it for real.'

'Triss, it's not that I don't believe you, but . . .'

'But you don't?'

'Hold on a minute. I didn't say I didn't believe you. But why Rachel – why that name?'

'I don't know. I was told I'd had a past life in Ireland. And I'd known your ancestors. And something else – something very odd. But I don't understand it at all.'

'What was it?'

'That they made their own soil. That's all. I don't have a clue what that's about.'

Rachel watches the sea beyond the rooftops below the cottage for a moment, before answering. 'Back in London, I'd have been very wary of all this, very slow to take it all in, wouldn't have felt like trusting you. Frankly, I simply wouldn't have believed you. But here, living in Melloney's cottage, Melloney being a friend of mine who loves this place, things are happening to me that are very unusual, strange and unexpected. Something's changing me. Even now, only a few months after I've come to live here, I find I'm listening to you, interested, not immediately rejecting your story.'

'I'm glad you want to listen.'

'Things have different meanings here in Cornwall, don't they?'

Triss nods.

Rachel continues, 'I felt it at the stones this morning. A sense of mystery.'

Triss asks, 'Do I make any sense to you at all?'

'I'm not sure . . . But . . . yes, they did make their own soil. They lived on a rugged island off the coast of County Connemara and they burned the seaweed and composted the seaweed, and ground the rocks up by hand and mixed them to make soil. That detail's real.'

'Thank you. But I don't know anything else.'

'What's the connection with Vonn?'

'She saved my mother's life.'

Again Rachel is silent, trying to absorb the information. A sixth sense tells her not to ask about it at present but to take Triss to meet Vonn, who will be home by early evening and isn't working tonight.

Rachel glances at her word processor, where there is not, unfortunately, a pile of manuscripts waiting. The recession is biting hard. Not enough work is coming in.

'We could have something to eat, and a walk by the sea, then Vonn will be back. We could walk up there later. Can I ask you something? Do you mind?'

Triss shakes her head and so Rachel says, 'Okay, I'm not usually so blunt, but does that double axe mean what I think it means?'

'That I'm a dyke, yes, of course it does. I left home when I was sixteen – I'm not out to my parents – and I went to Greenham. I was there until about a year ago, then I made my way here, because I was in love with a woman who lived in Hayle. Anyway, that didn't work out, but here I am. Then *The Diaries of Elizabeth Somerville* were published and I kept hearing about them on the radio. I had to find the house on the dunes, see the place for myself, talk to Vonn Smedley. I gather she's a friend of yours?'

'More than a friend.'

'You and Vonn?'

'Yes. Very much so.'

'I don't really understand what's going on, do you, Rachel?'

'There are questions. That's all I know. I don't have any answers. Not yet, anyway. Look, I'm really hungry. Would you like a toasted sandwich? Cottage cheese? Tomato? Onion?'

'Thanks. Anything without meat, thanks.'

When they've eaten they go to the sea. Rachel is beyond thought, beyond speech. What she wants most is one of Vonn's wonderful warm hugs.

They are quiet as they walk. For a good while they share the silence of the beach, and the noise of the tide, which is flowing out fast and only an hour or so from low tide. It's not warm today though there is some sunshine; patches of blue can be seen in a grey and white marbled sky. The sea is swirled grey-blue and white; the surf is flat and steady. Its sounds fold up towards them as they sit on the rocks at the far end of the bay.

'You're brave, you know,' says Rachel.

'We're all brave.'

'You don't know anything about me except my name. You meet me as you're out cycling. You don't tell me who you are at that time. You want to meet me afterwards, and . . .'

'And you were curious, and brave too, to invite me here. You knew, when we met in the road this morning, you knew that something was going on. You felt it as well, didn't you?'

'I suppose so. I don't feel safe around all this past lives stuff. Sounds very sort of new-agey to me. It unsteadies me.'

'Do you believe in fate?'

'No.'

'I do,' says Triss. 'My clairvoyant told me to find Rachel.'

'There are many women called Rachel. It's a very ancient name.'

'There aren't that many with Irish ancestors who made their own soil.'

'I give in. I'll just give myself a cliché and tell myself to go with the flow, okay?'

'Okay.' They are laughing together as they make their way back to Chynoweth, to collect Triss's bike. Then they walk along the sandy paths through the dunes until eventually they turn towards Vonn's drive, where her car can be seen.

'I'd feel better if I could wait in the garden, and listen to the sea. You could come and get me when you're ready.'

'Yes, why not. It'll give me time to fill Vonn in a bit on today's events. I won't be long.'

Indoors, Vonn and Rachel hug and hold close, as Vonn mutters, 'I missed you. Been raving about you. They want to meet you soon.'

'I missed you too. Sit down, I've got someone with me. She's in the garden. I've got some fast talking to do.'

Just a few minutes later, Vonn and Rachel emerge from the house to find Triss sitting at the picnic table, her mountain bike propped against the other side. They all go inside and Triss offers to take them through the next part of her story.

Rachel swallows. 'My Dutch grandmother had a female ancestor from Ireland. I'm feeling very shaky right now. It's all a bit unreal.'

'Don't be frightened, Rachel,' says Triss, who is relaxed and warm by a good fire. 'These things are magical, not frightening. They happen here in this land. Just allow it.'

'I can't stop shaking. I'm sorry. I thought I was okay. But I really don't feel okay. It's all very fast. Too much.'

Vonn moves over and perches on Rachel's armchair with her arm around her. Triss in the other armchair seems fine. Vonn has a sense of Elizabeth Somerville, of a strong, caring energy coming towards her. She has felt it before and trusts it, because Elizabeth would never do anything to hurt her. So she holds Rachel warmly, with her arm round her, and turns to Triss saying, 'How about if you begin with your mother, Triss? She's still alive, and Rachel says I had something to do with that?'

'You saved her life, Vonn. You and Elizabeth Somerville.'

'I'm glad that we did. How so?'

Triss takes her time. She says, 'It could have been the end of everything.' She takes a slow breath. 'But it wasn't. Everything in my life that is important began that day.'

Rachel reaches for Vonn's spare hand and holds it tight. Triss continues, 'It was seven years ago this summer. We'd been on holiday to St Ives, and we were all tired. Dad was driving, and we'd just come off the M4 coming back into London. There was a terrible pile-up. The car turned on its side. We were all very badly injured, arms and legs broken. They had to cut us out. Blood everywhere. I heard one of the ambulance men saying she's gone she's nearly gone. I was screaming because that was my mum. She had very bad head injuries. But there was a crisis in the hospital. You were short of staff. You were left without a runner.'

'Oh my God. Mrs Martin. Your mother was Mrs Martin.'

'Yes, she was. Is. You saved her life.'

'Full circle. It's come full circle.'

'My family were so grateful they wrote to the hospital. And all I knew was that it was Elizabeth Somerville who was the surgeon. I didn't know anything more about her until *The Diaries* were published and there's that paragraph in it where she describes that operation and they thought they'd lost my mother.'

'She stopped breathing under the anaesthetic.'

'I didn't know your name at the time, but in *The Diaries*, it says who the team were. Maybe Elizabeth Somerville mightn't have put it in *The Diaries* if my mother's experience of it hadn't been so important. That's what linked your name with it. It said that Vonn Smedley was the nurse who got her heart beating again. Then it said that Elizabeth Somerville got cancer and moved to the house on the dunes, and none of us ever would have known that if it hadn't been for *The Diaries*, would we?'

'Probably not, go on.'

'When my mother's heart stopped beating she had an out-of-body experience. She's been to see ever so many people about it. It changed us all. She was never one to make things up like that. She's ever so down to earth, is Mum. A very ordinary, very solid, practical woman.

'She said that she left her body and went and floated right up and it was very bright and light, and there was a long tunnel and lights at the end of it and no pain and no fear. She was safe. She knew her body was in pain, and they were cutting into her, and she was near to death. Then suddenly she flipped back. She was back in her body again, and she knew she would be alive after the operation. She would recover and not be brain-damaged.'

'Mrs Martin. You are Mrs Martin's daughter.' Vonn is staring at Triss with a fixed smile, while her mind is moving to and fro between the operating table where this is going on, with Mrs Martin's life in balance, and the room in the house on the dunes where she is solid, next to Rachel's warm presence, with a strong physical bonding in the here and now, and a fire giving heat and security, and Triss's light soft voice with a touch of London accent, telling this history and bringing Vonn up to date.

'If it hadn't have happened to my mum,' Triss is saying, 'it'd have been just another of those tales in the Sunday papers. But my mum is sure this happened to her and we've been living with it ever since. It was a teaching hospital. Elizabeth went on her rounds with her students, and she heard my mum's story direct – from Mum. But we didn't know she was into that sort of thing. It didn't go any further till I read it in *The Diaries*.

'When the accident happened, I was only fourteen, and I got every book I could and I read lots all about these things. Then, later on, I went to live at camp, and I met this woman who was into Goddess and women's spirituality. I came to Hayle to live. Then I met Consuela Brett in the nursing home. I speak Spanish, you see, and the Age Concern people wanted a volunteer to talk to Consuela. So I started to go there in the daytime.'

'Which is why we never met,' says Vonn. 'I do nights.'

'But you've been away as well, haven't you?' Vonn nods and Triss continues: 'I love going to talk to her. There I am, telling her about *The Diaries* and she says she knows you. So, here I am. I came to say thank you.'

* * *

In the days following this conversation, the three women meet often, filling in many details of their lives and finding a rapport together. Triss is also a musician. She plays the guitar and has a lovely singing voice. Together they go to see Lou and Annie, both of whom take to Triss immediately, especially as they were also friends with Elizabeth Somerville, and are as enthusiastic about *The Diaries* as Triss.

However, amidst all this sociability, Vonn and Rachel long for some private space. One weekend, Vonn offers to treat Rachel to a trip north to Rocky Valley to see the maze carvings and the river.

'I'd love to come. But I'll pay for myself.'

'Can you afford it? B & Bs cost more up there.'

'I've got a little bit of savings left. Besides, I'm desperate for some real time with you. One night'll be okay.'

'I love you, Rae.'

'I love you too.'

By a ruined mill, not far from the carvings in the rockface, Vonn and Rachel stand on a wooden bridge, looking down into the shallow, fast-flowing currents that fall and swirl over the flat beds of rock. Here there are beautiful old gnarled trees coming into leaf; and new ferns scattered in nooks and crannies. It is bright sunshine as the two women walk with mini backpacks across the bridge and along the track which leads slowly up and down the side of the river valley towards the sea. The powerful meeting of the river and the ocean in sharp, steep gulleys is audible in the distance.

Trees cling to the river's edge as the waters pour rapidly down the valley. Rocky outcrops fringe the path and tower above the trees on either side. An unpredictable landscape, dominated by water-in-land, thinks Vonn, knowing now that it was right to take this special time for her and Rachel.

Over the years their mutual friends have been bridges between them, but now they are walking along the same path in the same valley as if they were always meant to meet, sometime; the seasons turning, bringing them to this time, this place.

In the tradition of Celtic shamanism, thinks Vonn – recognising that the river flows from the east to the west – west represents water, the emotions and love. So it is that the river beside which they are both now walking represents part of a new cycle in the emotional flow of their relationship. The river is part of a continuous flow. The emotions themselves will shift, thinks Vonn, from the early weeks like this to greater closeness, everyday lived reality. From high ground, down valleys to the sea. Then disappearing, but re-emerging in the air above the seas, moving across skies, falling on high ground, returning to the source.

We have a new chance here, thinks Vonn, different in meaning from other relationships, but part of a whole, upon which perspective can be gained. We can understand this now, having met without being strangers to one another, as part of a gift of continuity.

They turn a corner to be confronted with the mighty power of the incoming tide in the narrow valley.

'Once when we were little,' says Rachel, 'Mieke and I were brought here by Mieke's godmother. Did I already tell you?'

Vonn shakes her head.

'I thought not. I'd only be about ten. It was before I knew that my grandmother Markham was born and raised in Cornwall. She didn't come. Just me and Mieke and our Aunty Doreen. She told me the Cornish heritage part of the family, but it was a sort of secret between us. She wanted us to know because she loved this place. I was so grateful to her afterwards. She had a tiny cairn terrier who hurled himself headlong at these rugged pathways, wagging his tail and twizzling his ears, working up to vertical take-off. He was a small white hearth-rug on legs. I thought this was the Victoria Falls, me being so small.'

They laugh together, relaxing and enjoying the newness of their togetherness, safe in the everyday knowledge that they are lovers with a sense of future.

Presently they sit facing the waters, each quiet with her own thoughts, whilst behind them the heather buds are fat and filling out in the sunshine.

It is the greening of the year, thinks Vonn, remembering a phrase from Elizabeth Somerville.

Introspective, she watches the deep chasm far below, churning and swirling. She feels strangely calm, unusually tranquil. Down the valley, far below her, she can see steep, rushing waters, swollen with recent rains.

Along the valley, where water pours down in rivulets that catch the light, there are rock formations, their outlines etched, clear at the edges. Clear, like the edges of memory, thinks Vonn.

Vonn feels drawn to the falling water, and gazes down towards a chasm of questions. She experiences a remarkable curiosity about the exchange between the river and the ocean. She is pulled to the chasm, not repelled. Her mind prepares itself for the changes that may happen to her, her senses heightened by the power of the landscape, as if her mind is a butterfly, the first of this year, leaving the chrysalis of her body for an independent life. To fly over the river, down across the mirror there, however thrilling, is also dangerous.

She is aware that Rachel is silently enjoying the landscape, connecting with it. They do not speak. There are no words. There is only the deep exchange of water, which forms the chasm, receiving the river, receiving the ocean and splashing up volumes of spray mist, through which the light is brightly filtered.

Light becomes dark becomes light. So it is with the cycles of the moon; so it is with the cycles of the waters. Light on dark. A mirror at Vonn's face and the land behind her back. Her spirit moves into the mirror and her eyes look back at her from years behind and beyond her. She is inside outside. All ages. Seeing and not seeing. Feeling young and not young. Being afraid and not afraid. Being wise and total. There is no past time nor future time. No glass in this mirror. The spirit of place is without time. Flowers rest and wait in the sunlight. Vonn's spirit moves between her eyes and the eyes in the legendary chasm. Call this awareness, or knowledge. Call this ancestral time warp. Beyond words.

* * *

During the following week Rachel secretly exists on the remains of her store cupboard, without dumping all her anxieties about money on Vonn, watches each day for the post, which doesn't come, and now faces the reality that her word processing work has dried up.

She spends Thursday evening alone in Melloney's cottage, while Vonn is working, and is aware of a vulnerability that until now she has not experienced quite so intensely.

It is also strange to hold time in the present when she feels drawn inwards to Iseult's era and outwards to an undetermined future, which does not hold pattern and schedule in the same way as the tightly timetabled work at the Avalon project would have done.

She can hear her mother saying, 'I told you so. You should've stayed at Avalon. All that university education, and all you can do is squander it on a community project. As if that's not bad enough, Rachel, you give it up of your own free will. I'm not surprised this government won't give you any dole money. I certainly wouldn't. Why should they? You have to learn to take responsibility for your actions – like the rest of us.'

Rachel thinks of the number of times that she longed for this kind of unscheduled time whilst dashing from meeting to meeting during her work at Avalon; constantly accumulating pieces of paper to be filed, articles to be read, memos to be attended to, agendas to respond to, demands to be met.

Walking on the cliffs at sunset, she considers the time it takes for the sea to perform its smoothing process on the boulders which crash down when a cliff splits open. Other rock falls can occur, with unpredictable timing. They might be ready to split at any moment. Perhaps some sudden storm will be the catalyst, like the catalytic effect the Avalon crisis created: the final, unpredictable rift between herself and her mother.

To Truus, Rachel's resignation was a searing rejection. It hurled itself at the cliff face, containing tons of compressed air, just as a massive wave does, gathering strength from the whole Atlantic. The air is forced at tremendous pressure into fissures in the rocks. When it explodes, it casts pillars of spray high into the air, in an upsurge of release, and splits the rocks along the existing lines of fracture. Such a wave falls away again back into the sea but the cliff is no longer the same cliff. Its structures are blown apart. So it was with Rachel's relationship with Truus, whose whole wifedom and motherhood was flung into the air by Rachel's resignation.

To Truus it seemed as if Rachel could throw away with one crisis the entire basis on which Truus had made her decision to leave her homeland – that Rachel and Mieke should be educated in Salisbury in accordance with John's wishes, in order to give them a strong foundation on which to build their future lives.

In Melloney's cottage after sunset, alone, because Vonn is working, Rachel recalls that Vonn recently said, 'I think we were meant to meet. I feel sure of it. I'm so glad you came to live here. Do you still dream of the crisis at Avalon?'

'Sometimes. My resignation blew my relationship with my mother. My father's dead. I think I was called here too. To deal with the past – childhood stuff – the dreams seem to be bringing up events and feelings from way back before Avalon.' She adds, 'When Grandmother Markham pressurised my father into returning to live near her, so that me and Mieke could go to school here, it ripped my mother's life apart. I can't quite put the pieces together, but I know I have to work this through.'

Tonight, in the cottage in the cove, Rachel's father seems near to her in an ominous way. Clockmaker and timekeeper, he was in control of his wife's daily routines while he himself was governed by the Cathedral clock which ticked away the

125

hours of the Cathedral calendar. Each Sunday of the prayer book had its own name and specific identity: one didn't deviate from its demands. John planned his own life and that of his wife and daughters: and perhaps Truus took some grateful comfort in the relentless predictability. Her new life in and around Salisbury became liveable and familiar, despite being second-best to the traditions of the extended family in the Protestant faith in Holland.

Rachel, by contrast, chooses to watch the moon's orbit, which is visibly female, integral to a much older rhythm, sometimes revealed, sometimes hidden, as if opening and closing to the fingers of the sky. There are many nights now when Rachel has dreams of Iseult, as if her mind becomes the ocean ebbing and flowing freely through her night world, her unconscious world, the world of her creative inner dark.

* * *

Iseult. In a large bed with a canopy, in a castle. A wooden floor. Scattered with white flour by the barons who are trying to catch Tristanne.

A lover's leap. Tristanne springs with athletic ease from the windowsill to Iseult's bed. Catches her shin on the bedpost. Swears under her breath. Blood drips from a gash in her skin. Droplets on the flour upon the floor. Next morning Tristanne is gone. Iseult lies awake alone, dreading the return of King Mark. Deceitful servants tell the barons of the blood on the floor.

There are no footsteps. But someone has visited the beautiful Iseult. She is in danger, in trouble. Once again she will have to flee from Mark. She is so insecure. There is nowhere to stay except the forest. Will it shelter her? With her lover? Does she truly represent the Vegetation Goddess here in Dumnonia? Daughter of Ireland. Daughter of the great Mother Brigid whom local people call Bride. She who births the universe. She who creates the fields, woods and orchards. She who provides and nourishes.

Iseult, Iseult, says a voice in the castle bedroom, you must go from here. Face up to your insecurity. Go where you feel your heart should take you. Daughter of earth, the orchards will nourish you; the hedgerows will provide for you. Leave this castle, depart from this place.

126

Iseult raises herself up in the large bed. Alone. Vulnerable but determined. Her skin longs for her lover. She leaves the castle, and goes to meet Tristanne.

* * *

Friday begins badly. The weather is filthy – it matches Rachel's mood. She wakes on her own, missing Vonn, who has come off night duty and is asleep at the house on the dunes.

Melloney's cottage is cold and unloving. The aga has gone out because Rachel has run out of coal.

A soaking mizzle drenches her while she waits at the cove's only bus stop for the early bus to Penzance. This is followed by a long wait in the dole office while she makes her first claim for benefit. She thinks of Vonn, and it seems ages since they held one another as she makes her way disconsolately up through town to the council offices and eats her sandwiches 'on the hoof', though it is still raining, then waits in a queue to see the housing people. They tell her she must return with a letter from Melloney stating how much the rent is, and they can't do anything without it. Rachel knew this but hadn't really wanted to deal with it so has made it harder for herself, for which she feels irritable and self-condemning.

Rain turns to summer thunder and she is soaked again on the walk back to Penzance post office. She has to buy pen and paper to write to Melloney, when she could easily have brought some with her and saved the money.

Self-mocking she tells herself, 'All in all, I am making a pig's ear of this whole thing.'

She posts the letter and suddenly the day brightens when she bumps into Triss on the way to the bus station. Triss is cycling, as usual.

'Why didn't you bring your friend's bike, for heaven's sake?'

'I dunno. I couldn't face the wet and wind I s'pose.'

'You look awful. Come and tell me all about it over a cup of hot chocolate. It's on me.'

The café by the harbour car park is the cheapest in the town. Thunder is rolling around above the moorings where halliards are clattering and boats bobbing about, buffeted this way and that by heavy rain. The café, whose windows are half steamed up and streaming with rivulets, has neon lights and formica tables with no cloths on and reminds Rachel of her favourite café near the Avalon Community Arts Project, but on entering she realises that nearly everyone is white here and that doesn't feel right at all.

There are many different nationalities making up the contemporary Cornish population, and a number of Black people have lived here for centuries. It is changing fast these days, but it isn't London and it is still very white; and in this moment Rachel misses lunch breaks with Myrtle, and all the familiar faces from the life and times of the multi-racial Avalon project in its heyday.

She outlines her housing and unemployment situation to Triss.

'I know you feel badly, but is it really a matter of life and death? Last day on earth? It's not a Cape Cornwall job, is it?'

'Fishing me out? No, course not. I'm sorry. I really must pull myself together. I'm always bad when I'm due. Vesuvius in waiting. Everything heaps on top of me and I just don't cope. I stopped the Evening Primrose oil – it used to help – simply can't afford it.'

'Drink up. You look like you've gone all cold inside.'

'I have. I've been dreading the dole. And I spent my last penny on that weekend away with Vonn. Stupid.'

'You've got to have a treat sometimes. Besides, you need relief after being chained to that computer. They don't pay much on the dole but at least you'll be free of that machine!'

'I hope you're right, Triss. You're a tonic, honestly.'

'The only thing you've got to watch out for is the fraud squad. You going broccoli picking?'

'I was going to, but my next-door-neighbour's son got done – they bullied him ever so nicely. Sort of pleasantly ruthless. They scare me shitless.'

'They're bastards. You've got to learn the system. They know no one can make it here without cash on the side, and I know it's no comfort, but you've got to cover your back. Everybody shops everybody these days. I'll help you.'

'The guy next door, they got his number plates. His dole was cut – wiped out. Nothing.'

'They're bastards,' repeats Triss. 'Fraud squad's red-hot – like I said, I'll help you. If you're new to it, don't work and sign.'

'I'm so scared about money. I'm waking up at night, pacing about. Then finally today I admitted it, there's no work coming in – zilch – so here I am.'

'You know, I woke up last night, thinking about you. You were meant to bump into me today. You'll get used to the dole. There's no money but there's a lot of time. Free-flowing time. Enjoy it. I do. You've got Clare's bike, haven't you, and you're a good cyclist, yeah?'

'Yes. Go on.'

'Get yourself out and about on it. Take the chance – think of it as an opportunity. There's women back in London hammered into the ground with work and pressure. They'd give their eyeteeth to live here, dole or no dole. Am I right or am I right?'

'You're right. I'll get another chocolate, d'you want one?'

'Yeah, why not? Ta.'

Returning with steaming, full mugs, Rachel considers Triss – how well she knows the system, how she is grinning and bright-eyed, unaffected it seems by the weather or Rachel's doom and gloom approach to unemployment.

'I feel so sorry for the visitors. It's not good weather for viewing the flowers, is it?'

'Not really. Listen, I was thinking while you were at the counter, I'd like to meet your friend, Clare. My clairvoyant says I need earthing.'

'You do?' Rachel is smiling, wondering what this has to do with Clare, and realises that she is feeling much better about everything.

'She's got ME, I think you said?'

''Fraid so. She's sick as a parrot.'

'Two things then. One is I need to dig – and I could help her with her garden; the other is she probably gets lonely and I like to meet strangers, so it'd suit me.'

'You go for action, Triss. I like it. I really do.'

'Well, I'm not backward in coming forward, it's true. Life's too short – I learned that at Greenham. So what about it?'

'Sounds good to me.'

'Right, drink up. Are we off then?'

'Where to?'

'Clare's, of course.'

'What, now?'

'Why not?'

'No reason. I never met anyone like you before in my entire life.'

'Come on then. It'll take you right out of yourself, do you good. Somebody's got to sort you out.' Triss is laughing, and her unstoppable joy of life is infectious. She says, 'Got any paper on you? Oh good. Draw me a map and I'll meet you there. How long'd it take you on the bus?'

They sort out bus routes so that Rachel can use her return ticket. As Rachel boards the bus Triss waves the map at her, calling out, 'It's stopped raining! See you there then!'

* * *

Late that same night, while she's getting ready for bed in Melloney's cottage, Rachel thinks back over a day which began badly but brought friendship, laughter and a great sense of fun.

Memories swirl: Triss in Clare's garden, a larger than life garden gnome, cross-legged by the pond, with heavy droplets dripping on her from the overhanging pine tree; Clare laughing like a grey and white panda, with the big circles still under her eyes, who has just been given an unexpected gift of bamboo; herself telling dyke tales; Triss and Clare getting on well, swopping dyke gossip; Clare suddenly doing one of her famous fade-outs and having to be helped back indoors, but saying that she hasn't laughed so much in months.

When Rachel arrives home for a hot shower she discovers a red reminder for the electricity bill waiting. It isn't as frightening as it would have been this morning. She is not actually homeless, and Clare gives her a bag of coal, which they strap on to the mountain bike, and lends her a tenner for food. Rachel is skin-shavingly aware, from her previous work at Avalon Community Project, of how accountable people are who live on the dole and have to get the state to pay the rent. She is used to form-filling on their behalf, and she knows how quickly dignity is undermined. By the end of Friday, Rachel is another statistic – one of the increasing number of out-of-work people in the south-west.

Meanwhile, Triss's perception – that despite the accountability, signing on is a relief – comes true for Rachel as she sits by the aga that night going over the day's events. No more word processing. She has hardly any money, no idea how she is expected to keep warm next winter on this level of income, and she will have to save up if she wants to buy a toothbrush, like the rest of the unemployed, but she is not controlled on an hour-to-hour basis, as she was when she did all that work in front of the screen.

Meanwhile, she lives in paradise, she is in love, she is fit and well, and summer is coming. Vonn loves her, the world is the right way up on its axis. She has no idea how to move through her days without an external schedule of word processing. Time flows openly behind and ahead of her, all around her, above and beneath her, as it never has before.

Tonight Rachel reassesses her decision to leave Avalon, asking herself what she wants now, and what kind of life may be possible. She doesn't want to become materialistic again like she was in London. She likes to be surrounded by her books and music, but she doesn't have to dress for work any longer, doesn't go anywhere that demands style, and finds that she doesn't miss spending or eating out which she did do a lot when she was on London wages full time. Fundamental changes are happening to her, and despite her financial vulnerability, she wants these changes to take place.

Tonight, late evening while Vonn is at work, Rachel rocks to and fro for a long time in Melloney's cottage, listening to the sounds of the sea, trying to imagine what life must have been like from her mother's point of view.

Truus was a woman embedded in her extended family, running the guesthouse for her mother who was in a wheelchair, and had almost given up hope of conceiving when she fell for Rachel at the age of thirty-five. They spoke Dutch in the household and Truus taught Rachel and Mieke to speak it too. Her English husband, who had read Modern Languages at Oxford, picked up Dutch easily, and spoke it fluently, with apparent enjoyment.

Rachel feels overwhelmed with memories sometimes,

recalling her mother, sister and father laughing together in Amsterdam. Now he is dead, and her mother carries such bitter anger in paniers slung across her back. How do people get tamed? Rachel asks. When does the saddle stop being an intrusion, a thing to be thrown off? How does acceptance of the saddle begin? How does a burden become hidden inside someone's body, while the actions of everyday life go on from day to day and the paniers appear to be being carried and the saddle worn, without question?

Her father, thinks Rachel to herself, coped with the language. He was not a very social man. Perhaps she derived her need for solitude from him. But why the sudden about-turn, why bring his reluctant wife and family away from all that was dear and familiar? Had he been unhappy in his wife's country? If so, why had he stayed so long?

A memory stirs. They are living in England. Rachel is seven. Something happens and her mother hits her. Rachel yells, I hate you. I hate you. When I grow up I'm going to get my own house. I'm going away where you can't hit me.

Her mother crumbles. She sits and sobs. John is in his workshop, as usual. He hears the commotion. He comes in. Rachel runs to him for comfort. She can't recall the whole row that ensues, but her mother is very distressed, sobbing that she would never say such a thing to *her* mother, she loved *her* mother. She wouldn't leave *her* mother.

John puts Rachel down firmly and goes to his wife. Rachel backs away, on the outside, further and further towards the living-room door. Her parents barely notice her. There is no way in for her. As she flees the room, she hears her father's voice: That's right, Truus. That's the whole point. You couldn't leave her. It's all right. It's all right.

Rachel starts to shiver. The aga needs attention. She is chilled through. She tops it up with some of Clare's coal. In her mind she hears a tape loop of Mieke's voice: I wish, I wish that our childhood didn't hold these things.

Tonight, as she falls asleep, Rachel has a swift mental image of herself as her father's favourite, in the house in Salisbury. She is seven. He invites her into his workshop. He sits her on his knee. He tells her what a clever girl she is.

He says that her grandmother Markham wants her to do well at school here in England. It will be best for her. Better than Amsterdam. She is such a clever girl.

The image of her sitting on his knee fades. She falls asleep.

* * *

He is hitting her. He is hitting her very hard. She is screaming. He does not stop. He is slapping her hard. Slapping her hard.

They are living in England. There has been a terrible row. She is now semi-naked. She is face down across her father's knee. She has no knickers on. He is slapping her. He is slapping her very hard.

Her skin is sore. She is howling. He is slapping her. She is a bad girl. He is slapping her very hard. Her skin is red and very hot. He is slapping and slapping her. He is very angry with her. She is wrong. She is a bad girl. A bad girl. She is a bad girl.

* * *

Rachel wakes up feeling the stinging slaps on her upper thighs. She is in deep shock. This is her father in her dream. A dream of absolute clarity. A memory dream. She is shaking. She puts her hand down to her thighs. Her skin is sore.

Betrayed. He picked her as his favourite. He slapped her, naked.

She lies awake in the bright bedroom, with the sounds of the sea beyond the window, and she knows that her dream is a memory dream. She knows that it is true.

She is safe here.

Growing, becoming, cunning, knowing.

Learning, connecting, warp threads, joining.

The moon sea sky is her magical friend.

Her father is dead; she does not have to confront him with this. Her mother could not challenge Rachel's role in her father's life. She could only be angry. Rachel was his first-born child, his daughter, to have and to hold, to choose and to control. He was not complete for himself. He had to have her mother. He had to have Rachel.

Rachel versus Truus. No wonder Truus was angry.

He set it up that way. Maybe it was subliminal. He was the head of the household, incomplete. An incomplete person. He was not enough for himself, by himself. He had Rachel seated on his lap. She was a clever girl. He had her face down, semi-naked across his lap. She was a bad girl. She was his girl.

Rachel now lies in her bed whole and alone, enough for herself, by herself. She asks herself what was going on for him when she was semi-naked, sprawled, hurting, face down across his knee.

Shaking, she realises she cannot reach for the phone.

This cottage doesn't have a phone.

She curls under the duvet.

She gets up, pulls on her thick dressing gown, pads down into the living room. Clare's bike is propped against the table. There's a half bag of fuel by the aga. She stokes the thing, mechanically, glad the place is warm again. Makes tea. Bad girl you're a bad girl. Memory dream. She opens the curtains and finds that it is a bright morning. The sea beckons. Come to me. I am the cool water to take the sting from your burning skin.

She dresses quickly, pulls on her wellingtons and warm anorak.

She grabs her key and runs.

Down the back lanes, through the cove, along the road and down the ramp to the long white beach. Then on, down to the hard wet sand of the water's edge. Come to me. Come to me.

She is alone on the shore. There are no footprints. A seagull wheels overhead and screams, its throat open wide, its power voiced across the sky. She joins it, opens her throat, and screams. The slight wind carries the sound away out to sea. She screams again, again, again. You hit me. I was seven years old. You hit me, you bastard, you betrayed me.

She runs and runs along the edge of the waves. It is low tide, the sea is blue and cream, silver and grey in the morning light. Above her, the sky is bright white and light, with blue patches and some light clouds, the wind not strong but blowing off the shore out to the open sea. Seagulls scream and dive into the low tide, fishing. The woman on the shore screams and runs, soaking up the bird sounds, filling herself with them, letting them mix and blend with the screams inside her. Naked. She was naked. She was seven years old. He was bigger than her. Face down across his knee. Why? Why?

Everything she has read on abuse of women and girls comes to her now, by the sea, in the early morning.

Pictures wash in her mind. The why screams out of her into the vast seascape. She was brought here to heal. The courage to heal.

Do it, woman. Start it now. Give it to the ocean. Give it to the sky. They are vast. They can carry this for you.

She runs. Her boots splash and splodge at the water's edge.

Life. There is life here. This is bad and there may be worse to come, but there is life here. Courage here. Run, girl, run. Run by the water's edge. Call up this life force, woman. Scream until the child inside you is heard. Until the child is part of the woman, held safely now. You were seven. You are not seven now. He is not hitting you now. He is gone. You are still alive. You matter. You can heal this out of you. His power over you is his no longer.

Hold this child and let her scream. She is a wild seagull. Trying to fly with oil on her wings. Rescue her. Clean her. Nurture and care for her. Hold her.

She stands at the water's edge, feet on the sand firmly placed.

She flings her arms to the air and lets her voice rise up inside her, gathering strength, up through her body, up from her womb, through her heart, into her throat and through her open mouth into the wild, free air.

In the village in the cove Rachel tries the call box.

Vonn.

'We are sorry there is no one here to take your call. Please leave your name, number and any message after you hear the long tone. Please don't leave a blank. Bye.'

Shaking, Rachel whispers into the ansaphone. 'It's me. I need you. I'll ring when you wake up.'

Next, Rachel dials Clare's number, because, whatever the news, Clare is always one of the first to know. Clare answers the phone. She hears. She listens.

You are safe now. Alive. Whole and enough. To heal. You have survived. You have come through, whole and enough. You are not to blame. The child is never to blame.

Rachel returns to the cottage in the cove, but cannot rest.

Memories. She is sitting at her English grandmother's table. She sits in misery, unable to look at any of the soft white oval baps that are displayed in a basket next to a dish of best butter. She tugs at her mother's arm, softly at first, then more determined. She slides down from the table, pulling her mother out of the room, through the back kitchen, out of the garden door, to the back yard to share a horrible discovery made whilst playing that morning.

She lifts a fallen slate. There in the cool, dark dampness they lie, like bread baps, six or seven of the longest, whitest oval slugs in the world. Her mother cries out in disgust, and recognises Rachel's horror. Her mother is gentle, not angry. Rachel doesn't have to eat the bread baps. Her mother kneels beside Rachel, and hugs her. The hug has no anger in it.

Rachel runs a hot bath, never mind the cost, and lies in the deep hot water, thankful for Melloney's immersion heater.

Memories. There is no lock on the bathroom door. She and Mieke are naked. At home. She is on the loo, her sister, Mieke, is washing at the sink, her father is in the bath, her mother is rushing around in her knickers, yelling and laughing, anyone for tennis. They think nothing of this till later. They think that this is a happy time. They are not allowed to lock the bathroom door. They are told that it is God's will that people are free to take off their clothes in front of each other. There is no lock on the bathroom door and they think that this is how everyone lives.

Memories. She is fourteen. She tries to fix the bathroom

door tightly shut. She wants to experiment with tampons. But she can't manage it properly and passes out on the floor. John is knocking loudly to find out if Rachel is all right. She daren't try tampons again till she leaves to go to university, where she can lock the door, leave it locked, and experiment in peace.

Rachel takes her time, has a long, slow bath, then when dressed, she has breakfast, thinking through many aspects of her childhood. At the front of Chynoweth cottage there is a small conservatory from which she can see over the cluster of houses to the open sea. Today it's a blue vista. Sometimes there is so much sea to look at that it seems – as does the future – too wide open, too many unknowns. Other days, like today, it becomes the unbounded, limitless horizon, blue on blue, nothing to interfere with her clearest thoughts, her most hidden memories.

During the day, slowly, but with intense clarity, Rachel remembers that when she was little she had years of crying. Now she feels it was no bad thing. She was fighting to keep her spirit. So, as the red-hot slappings were taking place, she was healing some of it out of her. But at the same time she was splitting off parts of herself, wrapping the memories around with thick insulation, for she was very small, with nowhere to go.

Perhaps that is how it began – her major fantasy that drove nearly all her friends and lovers crazy. The cottage at the end of the lane. Throw in a duck pond with calmly swimming ducks, a small green lawn, roses, leafy trees for protection in glaring sunshine, and small white-painted wooden fences, and the images were complete. A safe place to live and play.

Perhaps the memories wait until now to reveal themselves to her because now, having left the Avalon Project and in need of a place to rent, her close friend, Melloney, comes up with this cottage.

The cottage at the end of the lane.

The duck pond is three thousand miles wide; the grass extends for ever along the margins of these magnificent cliffs; leafy trees are the other side of the peninsula, away from the wind; and she doesn't need white-painted fences to make boundaries around the pain any longer. Here she can sleep and play. Here she can come face to face with the little girl child inside her who needs her love and understanding.

Memories. She is eight, perhaps nine. A fire burns in the old fireplace in the kitchen. The kitchen is also the living room. Two upright padded armchairs with wooden legs and arms are huge in the space. John has re-upholstered them with thick black tapestry cotton. Vertical stripes of yellow, blue, red and green cotton, thicker thread than the black, run in and out, up and down in parallel lines and lumps.

She has done something wrong. She can't remember what. She is wearing a frock and a pink apron with a bib and a heart-shaped pocket. She is being shouted at. She is naughty. She is a naughty girl. She is making trouble. Making a fuss. She is protesting innocence.

She is also wanting her sweets money. It's Saturday. Every Saturday she gets some pence for sweets. She is waiting so that she can put it in her heart-shaped pocket. Mieke is next to her. She can't remember whether she is in trouble too. Mieke has a pink apron too, with a heart-shaped pocket.

There's a row going on over their heads. Someone is deciding that Rachel is not going to get her money this week. Someone's saying that she doesn't deserve it. She's a bad girl. A naughty girl. She's trying not to cry. Her cheeks are flaming hot and red because she's not wrong. Whatever it was, she didn't do it. She is red with the effort of not crying. She is not very tall. She is watching the fire. The anger is going on and on. Above her. They must be standing up, rowing. The armchairs are empty.

She is wrong. She is a bad girl. A naughty girl. She is starting to cry. Maybe she will be slapped for yelling – she can't remember if they do slap her. They have decided she can't have her sweets money.

She is eight, maybe nine. Knows nothing of the world of work; of the wider world beyond home and the Cathedral; of the workers who toil all week for a weekly wage; of employers' federations; of unions; of negotiations or settlements. But already she knows about fairness and justice and abuse of power.

If she is good she is acceptable. If she does as she is told she's called good. If they tell her – if she does as they tell her – she is worthy. If they change the rules, and she doesn't know of the changes, if she gets it wrong, then she's a bad girl, unacceptable. If she plays by the new rules, it will be all right. If she plays by the new rules, which get changed again, by them, it won't be all right.

She wants her money, but she has to earn it. She has to do as they say. She has to be obedient. She has it on their terms. Their terms might change. If she is sorry it might be all right. If she won't say sorry, it won't be all right. If she's not wrong, why should she say sorry? Who says she's wrong? She didn't do it whatever it was. She didn't do it but they aren't listening. They think she's wrong. She's a naughty girl. She's a bad girl. They aren't going to give her her money. She will have to wait seven days. Seven days is a lot of chance to get it wrong. It isn't going to be all right. There isn't any sweets money to put in her pocket. They shouldn't be in charge like this. It isn't fair to make her wait. She is trying to be good. She is trying to get it right. It isn't a happy place. Living here makes her very unhappy. She wishes she was adopted. Then she could go and find her real mum and dad. That would explain it. They just said she was bad. She wasn't being good. She was a bad girl. Their first-born was naughty. She was a naughty girl. She didn't do as she was told. She got it wrong. She does not deserve her money.

She was wearing a pink apron with a heart-shaped pocket. Her cheeks were flaming red. It was her first experience of political awareness.

The boundaries between the conscious and the unconscious are blurred. Now her body tells her to prepare for a huge grief release. Crying for the lost Mother. The one she has said No to.

The training in feminism and compassion, which begins while she is lovers with Clare at Cambridge and sharing a flat with Clare and Melloney, becomes blurred with the sense of guilt around feelings about Truus, her mother. It is over-laid with the Cathedral stuff – a nickname to help her come to terms with the duty instilled into her through her mother, whose sense of duty overwhelms and threatens everyone, including Truus herself.

So although Rachel leaves religion when she meets Clare and Melloney, she thinks that she may have adopted feminism as a substitute religion. It tells her that she isn't supposed to give up on her mother. Her father – yes. But she didn't want to give up her father because of a chemical bonding. But since being fourteen or so, she has longed to set herself free from Truus. She would dream of tight lassoes and ropes fastening mother and daughter for ever – and longs for her to die. The guilt of such a terrible thought is a burden, and frightening. Rachel is pulled back into an emotional masochism with Truus, through the fear of such guilt. It goes on and on, and she doesn't know what to do.

At university they study some theories of patriarchy. Clare, Melloney and Rachel may talk for hours. But as to mothers, there's not much to help them set themselves free of them. They are to understand, empathise and intuit. Mothers are supposedly 'on their side' and vice versa.

This doesn't fit Rachel's experience. Despite rare childhood memories of warm hugs, she doesn't feel that Truus is on her side and never has, whatever feminism may say. She, Rachel, does not have approval. She is not enough. Was not enough. But needs to be enough. Enough for herself as she is now. She needs to be one hundred per cent real. All of her. Not living her life in boxes of silence.

Beyond the triangle of herself, Clare and Melloney, she keeps quiet about the control, domination, disapproval and emotional angst from Truus, in order to protect her. Years of trying to negotiate; and always being wrong. Finally the relationship explodes. She leaves Salisbury feeling that she never wants to return. Then, working with a healer, whilst living in the cottage in the cove, she's encouraged to read other women's accounts of their processes of healing from negative childhood experiences. For the first time, she finds a word to help her make the final detachment. The word – Abuse.

Perhaps this word, more than any other word, will catalyse her liberation. Perhaps it has, for her, the same power as the word sexism seems to have had for the women of the seventies; the same power as the word homophobia had for the lesbians and gay men of the eighties.

This word – Abuse – tells her that it's okay to want it stopped. Beyond this word, she has yet to find all that she is dealing with. She is facing the memories of her father – herself small, bruised, her skin red and sore from his hand slapping, slapping her hard.

This is new. Grief wells up in her. Did not Iseult watch as her mother, Queen Iseult, appeared to agree with her father's betrayal of her? There are mothers who have risked their own lives to prevent their husbands beating their daughters. Why did Truus not intervene? Why was Truus unable to protect her? Why? Why?

This is not a simple case for feminism, thinks Rachel. It is not that Truus was the cause, nor that she was to blame. That is the simple media and misogynist way out. Never mind what the father is doing, focus the blame on the mother – too weak, too strong, too near, too far. It simply will not do.

There is nothing simple about this at all. For it is truly John who is beating his semi-naked child; and it is Truus who is angry with that same child. A child who, as an adult, turns around and says:

Mum, I have something to tell you. I am a lesbian.

No, Rachel. You cannot be. It is simply not the norm.

Memories are going to rise up like stones from shifting sand. Childhood is unnamed. But the word – Abuse – has a powerful feel, because she knows that abuse is wrong. If abuse has been taking place then she has the right for self-defence. It doesn't take away her compassion. It doesn't make her unaware of the unfulfilment of her mother's life. But it tells her that she is dealing with an imbalance of power, which has made her smaller than she needs to be, and kept her emotionally immature for longer than she would have chosen.

To oscillate, at this time, would be to give it all away again. She wants to avoid that. By herself, and with a little help from her friends, she has opened up a space in the memories and lies. The lies that they call normal in everyday family life.

141

Like the sudden sliver of light across the sea, when after a cloudy day the sun breaks through for a momentary sunset, there's a glimpse of liberation now. This is her, here. All of her. Living with her arms around a little girl, who lives inside, who didn't have anywhere to go.

She dresses warmly and stands outside by the wall, listening to the sounds of the sea.

The sea is grey-slate dark towards the horizon. High tide at the turn of the tide. The sea pulls back, draining at varied speed from great berms of sand waving like hills across the shore. Comforted, Rachel watches and listens.

I am always here for you, Rachel.

No, Mum. You are not.

I am always here for you, Rachel.

No, Mum. You are always there for you. Not for me.

I have always been here for you. I am your loving mother.

No, Mum. You love who you'd like me to be. She is not me.

Now the wind blows the grey clouds, loading them up against one another, shoving them inland.

At four-thirty the surprise of turquoise at the edge of the about-turning tide is a gift. The waves begin to leave this part of the upper beach, rattling over the high-water pebble line.

An exceptionally strong tide. Rachel walks at the edge of the waves, underestimating the steep run up and the fast undertow sucking back. A sudden insurge catches her, flooding over the tops of her boots.

Memories move like waves.

The moon comes up, with bright reflective silver light. It rises very quickly, as Rachel takes a winding path across the beach towards the dunes. Fast-moving, curved mirrors of urgent water challenge one another on this stretch of the sand. Over the cove, some dark grey clouds gather, matt grey and unreflecting above the hills, giving way to light from behind, a bright light which bounces in crazy complex patterns in the molten mirror movement of the tide.

Every piece of available light is snatched and exaggerated by the foam at the edges of the waves. An echo, in her mind, says, 'So Iseult leaves the castle and goes to meet Tristanne.' An unexpected surge of happiness warms her. Her love for Vonn has awakened physical and emotional need which was unrecognised or repressed since leaving Avalon. She wants to build on this openness.

She leaves the water's edge and, making her way up the shore towards the dunes, she goes to meet Vonn.

* * *

In the house on the dunes Rachel breaks apart.

The story pours. Waves of words surge and curve, rising breaking splashing falling through air.

Rachel breaks apart in grief and anger. Like a Frieda Kahlo painting, she is exposed, her skin opened, her raw wounds bleeding.

Betrayal.

They sit in front of Vonn's fire, very close together. Rachel looks vulnerable, and is trembling while she is talking. She cries from time to time; sometimes she shouts, borrowing Triss's phrase.

'Bastard,' she says, 'my skin hurts when I remember. He hit me, Vonn. He hit me. I was so small. He was big. Why? Why, do they do it?'

Vonn listens. She asks, 'How can I best help you?'

'You are, just loving me. I need someone to hold me.'

'How about a bath and a massage?'

'Would it help me?'

'It might. We can try.'

The massage takes an hour. It calms Rachel's skin. The pictures of herself face down on her father's knee loom in the front of her mind. She shudders at the intensity.

'A man's lap is not the same as a woman's. It doesn't have the same meaning as if I were face down across my mother's lap,' she says. She cries then, and Vonn puts her to bed with a bath towel for a handkerchief, and a cup of tea beside the bed, then sits with her hand on Rachel's shoulder while Rachel sobs. She cries for a long time. She is hungry. Vonn brings her food. Then, unplugging the phone so that not even the answer machine can disturb them, Vonn undresses and climbs into bed beside Rachel, who is protected now, childlike with her pyjama top tucked into her pyjama bottoms and unable to be an adult woman in this time warp.

Vonn wears a nightshirt and curls around Rachel. It is early evening and Vonn wouldn't usually need to sleep, having slept during the day. But Rachel seems washed out, vulnerable as a pair of pyjamas crumpled in a corner looking for a pyjama case to be zipped into. The layers of protection have been peeled away by the upsurge of memories. It takes time to reprotect. Time to find the inner strength to heal this awareness out.

Vonn lies curled around Rachel as Rachel relaxes and drifts into sleep, and Vonn is thinking of Jenny and beyond Jenny to Iseult.

Young girl. Nights naked in the bed of a man she is told to accept. Exposed. Vulnerable. Irish Woman. Cornish King. Not of her choosing. Against her will. Against her will. Touched where she doesn't want to be touched. Pressed against a bed. Against her will.

Vonn swallows and keeps her arm curved softly around Rachel, who is curled in the foetal position, eyes closed, slow and regular breathing. Being held. Vonn zipped around her like the pyjama case. Cocooned. Vonn is the exterior casing, this night. Rachel sleeping, healing whilst asleep. Caterpillar in a chrysalis. Protected. Self-nourishing. Changing from the inside. Taking the time she needs. These things take time. There is no past, present and future. There is only time. The time it takes. It takes the time. Time is not linear. Time is two women curled, one healing, the other holding.

Vonn is wide awake, thinking. She knows the figures for child abuse in this county. They are some of the highest in the country. Iseult is not historical, in that sense. She is every girl lying tonight under the weight of her father, her uncle, or her trusted older male friend of the family. She is every girl face down naked over her father's knee. She is every child whose mother does know and doesn't acknowledge that she knows. She is every girl who longs for a girl friend, but lives with an unwanted man in her life, man in her bed. She is every homeless woman, every homeless young woman, every homeless girl child. She is every girl whose father has too much time on his hands because he is unemployed. She is every girl whose father believes in the discipline of his daughters, she is every girl whose mother wants her married off quickly. She is every girl who is beaten, unloved, persecuted, terrorised, invalidated; not allowed to be whole, enough for herself, but a complement to some man's ego.

Rachel sighs in her sleep. Vonn lets out a deep sigh. It circles the late evening air in the room then departs by the window to join the sighs of the tide, ebbing and flowing on the shore, the sounds pushing, pushing, pushing up against the beach. Not simple sounds. A grandfather pushing, pushing, pushing at his granddaughter. An unwanted husband pushing, pushing, pushing at his lesbian wife.

Not simple sounds, the sounds of the sea. They carry the muffled screams of drowned witches and beaten children, distraught women and battered girls. It is not easy sometimes to listen to the sounds of the sea. Not on a night like this.

While Rachel sleeps soundly, Vonn lies awake reliving the years since Frankie, years during which she tried to heal from the trauma of her sister Jenny's story. There were days when she was so angry she feared she would explode, nights when she was so vulnerable that she lay, curled like Rachel, needing a friend, only a friend, not wanting Frankie's touch, nights when Frankie burned with lust and Vonn dared not give or receive because the intensity of orgasm would blow her psyche to pieces. Break-up with Frankie was followed by therapy work with Carol Belvedere and arrival at the house on the dunes.

There comes a time when Vonn falls in love again, this time with Danielle. Theirs is red-hot passion, rolling around the bed, hands inside and all over one another, wild and wonderful sex for hours, the laughter, the rollicking, rumbustious hell of it. It was wonderful and it was just what they needed.

When I'm an older woman, thinks Vonn, I want to be one of those lusty luscious ones who still like hot sex with a good woman. I don't want to glide hand in hand to a soft sunset, unable to be moist for a woman, forgetting how my womb lurches and my thighs go weak when I want a woman. Not any woman. This woman. This woman who lies, curled, sleeping, needing a friend tonight. I've been there, where she is, in

145

that space where touch must mean comfort, not exhilaration. Where skin contact means security, not passion; where thrill is too much and aloneness too little.

This reminds me, thinks Vonn, of a Tristanne and Iseult scene where, exhausted, the lovers arrive in the woods, fleeing Mark. They lie fully clothed and Tristanne places her sword between them, so that when Mark discovers them he thinks they are friends, not lovers, and forgives them both. How strange, this resonance. Obviously, she tells herself, I can search for parallels and falsely construct them. But it's as if I don't have to, because the scenes unfold both into my life and my mind's eye with such ease, such clarity. Besides, I enjoy the reflection, even when I don't fully understand it. How exciting it is for me to consider the story as if Tristan were Tristanne. I wonder if I could write my own opera, based on this theme. Would Rachel help me? What about Triss, too? She plays the guitar and has tried her hand at percussion.

Vonn meditates for a good while, because she doesn't need to sleep and is conscious of the fact that if she leaves the bed, Rachel may wake and feel abandoned. They'll talk about this tomorrow. It wouldn't be possible to lie here night after night in this way, but one night in what Vonn hopes will be a long relationship doesn't seem too much to offer, nor too much for Rachel to ask for.

Let's suppose, thinks Vonn, that the legend really *is* significant in our lives, beyond what we may know or understand already. Elizabeth would not have discounted such a thing. She understood far better than we do the concepts of magical reality and non-linear time.

So far we have been dabbling with the impact of the legend in our lives. What if there really were some cosmic plan, some kind of fate or destiny? That's the sort of thing Triss Martin believes, whose mother's life I helped to save. But, Vonn reasons, I myself have usually been sceptical, more like Rachel, needing to control my own destiny and make my own decisions. How can I put this together in a way that makes sense for me, Vonn? And how can Rachel and I come through this together, whole, loving and passionate? The last thing I want to happen is that Rachel and I become non-sexual friends. I love to make love with her.

146

I feel about her as passionately as any young lovers have felt in any legend anywhere in the world.

At this moment, Rachel stirs in her sleep so Vonn squeezes her gently. Rachel murmurs, Vonn waits quietly. Presently, Rachel's breathing steadies once more, and soon she appears to sink back down into sleep again.

Vonn's reasoning continues: we have talked safe sex with each other and now that we both feel there is zero chance of risk we are so free with our bodies. I only have to think of her clitoris nestling pink in its shell-like surround, moist and wet, to want my mouth there feeling her insatiate need, wanting me. Then likewise, she with her mouth on my clitoris, her tongue so knowing, finding the tiny pleasure places where I most want her to make me dance. This passionate need. Her nipple in my mouth, likewise mine in hers. The palms of my hands tingle for want of her round breasts. The joy and power of us.

I want us, thinks Vonn, smiling into the cool air of the bedroom, where the sound of Rachel's breathing is steady, sane and reliable. I want this sleeping and waking. A life together. What I don't want is any reflection or resonance in our lives of the tragic ending of the Tristanne and Iseult story.

No. No. Please not a tragic ending. I don't want Tristanne banished from King Mark's kingdom of Dumnonia, sent to Brittany. I don't want her to meet another Iseult and make do with someone else as a substitute for the real Iseult, the lust and the passion. I don't want Tristanne to fall ill, nor the real Iseult to be sent for. I don't want the new Iseult to tell a lie and say that the sails of the ship on which the real Iseult may be arriving are black to signal that the real Iseult has not come. I don't want Tristanne to die of a broken heart. I don't want the real Iseult to arrive to find her lover dead nor to die in sympathy, nor the whole relationship to remain a passionate affair that ends in tragedy.

Vonn sighs and Rachel, as if hearing this subliminally, snuggles closer, unconsciously reaching for the reassurance of Vonn's warmth next to her.

What do I want? Vonn silently asks herself. I want a way for women lovers who have had terrible childhood pain to be able to heal out of that pain, to succeed in transcending that experience and be able to integrate the child and adult within into a new whole woman. I want love lust and hot wet passion. I want us to be able to sustain a sexy, well relationship, and laugh and hold one another wet with wanting and crying out glad sounds at the height of passion. I want this to be possible.

Are there any women who aren't hurt because of life experiences, with pain inside that threatens their emotional stability more or less? Are there any lesbians who have ever-so-easy lives, with joy and abundance and love and ease and a wholly pain-free existence? Would it be a good thing? Would it be real?

If healing is all that's on offer, thinks Vonn, we are right to be dubious about it. If all it does is start and finish with the individual it would be just another trap for us. But we have to start. We have things inside that cause us pain. Those who would doubt this right to heal – don't they have things inside that cause them pain? Don't they understand that there are times in a woman's life when she has to concentrate on healing herself? She's no good to anyone if she doesn't do that inner work. Her anger and grief will seep out sideways in bitterness and sabotage, won't it? How can you love if you are in that much pain? How can you go on giving and never invoke your right to receive? You can do a lot of inner work by yourself, but if a friend or woman lover won't help you, how can you move on? I think, Vonn tells herself, I think that all of us have an inalienable right to heal. To curl up like an animal in a box or a hole somewhere and let our inner healing power work its way through.

Hippocrates said that the greatest healing power is the one we carry inside each of us. It's not that healing is the end, the purpose. Now that's where some of the New Age stuff is so inadequate. Healing ourselves as women is the means to an end. The starting point. The prerequisite for each of us before we can move out into the wider world, reach out, on and beyond the individual.

Vonn visualises a woodland, the path into the woods, the light dappling down through an overhead canopy of green.

She takes herself along the path, following Tristanne and Iseult. She finds them there in a glade, protected under some arching branches. They lie sleeping side by side, clothed.

She lets herself imagine that Rachel is the sleeping Iseult. She listens for a while to Tristanne's regular breathing, for Tristanne is also sleeping.

Vonn adjusts her own breathing, slow and slower. Music fills her mind as she meditates on the two sleeping women and the potential for reconstructing an opera based on the rewritten legend. A legend of passion and friendship. A legend whose ending must not become a tragedy, not this time around. A legend of very strong women, who are vulnerable but determined. This time the women are not going to be slain, not if they have half a chance to turn this around.

Time. Turn the time around, play it backwards. Listen to the sounds. Three four; four three. Four five; five four. Two Two Two. Melody and harmony. Sounds of resistance to age-old themes. New women. Strong women. Song women.

In a green glade there are two women, curled, sleeping. Friends and lovers. Healing hands; the power of woman touch. The kind of touch. Kind. Friends and lovers. Sleeping. Dreaming into strong time. Time. Time. Flowing time. Inside a chrysalis a woman is healing. A child who was hurting is being held in the arms of a woman who is herself.

Rachel is dreaming. She is herself taking care of herself. I will hold you, myself, little girl, hold you. Inside me, in my arms. Rock you. You can tell me all of your story. I will be the mother who could not hear you. I am yourself myself strong enough to listen to you screaming. You are safe now here inside me rocking you, ready to let you voice yourself inside me. Say what you need to say to me – what I can hear from you. You who were not heard screaming child afraid I will hold you, rock you myself yourself. Safe now. Safe now. Me in you in me. Child and woman blending.

BOOK 3

On the last day of April, Vonn arrives home from night shift, makes breakfast, plays her piano for a while, new tunes which have come to her in the quietness of early morning, and then goes to bed.

In bed, she reads for a while, relaxing herself though the day is bright and she finds it strange to be preparing for sleep.

There are wooded valleys in the Kingdom of Dumnonia, valleys which lie on the trade routes inland from the Camel estuary to the powerful ritual centres of Dartmoor.

The valleys are cool in summer and sheltered in winter, and green, always green, overhead. Here grow the evergreens, sacred to the country people, yew and holly, mistletoe and ivy. At this the time of Beltane – 30 April/1st May – deciduous trees, hazel, alder, hawthorn and oak, create a canopy under which the young lovers fleeing from King Mark can find protection. There are mushrooms to eat and wild watercress; there are dandelion leaves, wild burnett, land cress and the flowers and leaves of wild marigolds. There is rosemary for clarity of memory and sage for cleansing. There are nettle tops which are delicious when boiled over a small fire, and wild leeks and sorrel in the undergrowth.

There are markers all along this route, some of which may remain to point the way for future generations; although some may be lost, covered in and grown over. People may break and remove the stones that surround the wells along this route, but others who come may carefully restore them. Some wells may be hidden, remote and undefiled, reminding people in the future that once, here, there were those to whom these woods gave shelter, and those who visited the wells for blessing and refreshment.

Later on in Christian times monks like St Clether will arrive in this land, and may choose to live on the slopes of these valleys, renaming the wells and springs, building on pagan foundations, and then rededicating the sites for Christian use. Centuries later, devout parishioners may build shrines or chapels over the sanctified waters and the pagan roots may be denied or suppressed.

But through folklore there may be hints at the origins, through stories told and retold. In the twentieth century some country people recall that once, along this route, many of the wells were dedicated to Bridget, and in recording this, folklorists may perhaps not be aware that St Bridget was the great triple goddess Brigid or Bride. They may have forgotten that Irish settlers brought her here.

Vonn is tired. She closes the book, places it on her bedside table, and moves through sleep into another world.

* * *

It is the eve of summer, in the Kingdom of Dumnonia. There stands a quiet figure in a woodland glade, looking into the brown waters a foot or so deep in a small enclosed well, in the evening.

The place is Landue, just south of the trade route.

The scene is contemplative, reflective. There are very tall oak trees and beech trees, whose leaves are spread flat against the sun on the last day of April, soaking up the daylight, breathing and growing. The sounds are those of birds' wings and scurrying things.

The woman at the well is Iseult, daughter of Ireland. She is very young. She has raven-black hair. They call her Iseult the fair because she is beautiful, not because her hair is flaxen. Indeed, as with so many of the Irish, descended from the Celtic races who are both light- and dark-skinned, this woman has not the skin colour of cream or rose. Her lovely complexion is much darker than that and to be celebrated for itself.

That she is desirable to men is a problem for her. In particular she is wanted by one man, the King of Dumnonia, from whom she is fleeing with her lover, Tristanne, who now stands a little way off, in the trees, witnessing and paying attention.

Spirits of the east, calls Iseult, I ask you to attend me. Come to me with your powers of the air and hear my voice today. I ask you to protect this sacred place.

Spirits of the south, she calls, I ask you to attend me. Come to me this day with your powers of fire, I ask you to guard this space.

Spirits of the west, she calls, come to me now. I ask you to bring your powers of water, I ask you to protect this sacred place.

Spirits of the north, she calls, I ask you to attend me this day. Come to me now and bring your gifts of earth power. Spirits of the north, protect this place and witness here these words.

Spirits of the east, south, west and north, spin a circle of protection around me and Tristanne as we stand here at this sacred place. Come to us. Surround us. Attend us. Protect us.

Iseult breathes deeply, slowly, then, facing the well with her back to the evening, so that her shadow falls now over the well, she raises both hands to the sky and makes her invocation.

Oh Brigid, great one, mother of mine, mother of earth, great goddess of fire, I call upon you.

Oh great Mother, wise one, triple mother of smiths, poets and healers, I ask for your help this day.

I stand here in front of your well, your holy place, your place of healing. I ask your triple blessing now, wise one, mother of earth, triple mother.

Mother of fire and smithcraft, bless the fire inside me, your daughter. I am cast from my homeland here in this new land where I am hunted and in flight from barons and soldiers. Do not deny me my anger as a woman, as your daughter. Cleanse the fire of my anger so that it does not destroy me. May I channel your fire, your sacred fire through all my body so that everything I make is made with its power and beauty. I ask to use my fire in this way and for the strengthening of women, now and in the future.

Oh Brigid, wise one, blessed one, mother of Ireland, mother of all poetry and storytelling, bless my voice. Bless the words of love and passion I share with my loved one, Tristanne, and the words of divination I use for prophecy.

Oh Mother, powerful one, you who heal through the mountain streams, which flow into rivers and wells in my homeland, you whose power is in the water in this well, you who come with the rain and whose love lies across every ocean wave, connect me to my homeland. Do not abandon me here in this new place, cast your healing power upon this water here in your sacred well and wash away from me all the pain and brutal actions of the King of this land who pushes himself on me against my will. Oh Brigid, goddess of healing, help me to find within myself the power to heal myself and don't let his desires devour me. I come to you. I am Iseult your daughter. You are mother of Ireland, wise mother, she who has the healing power, she who can help me find within myself the power to heal myself.

Help me. Help me. Help me now.

Find the power, inside myself to heal myself.

The power inside myself to heal myself. To heal myself.

Myself.

Iseult bends down and cups her hand into the water of the well. She throws it over her face, her hair, her shoulders, her breasts. She repeats this several times. Then she cups her hands once again and, turning, she steps towards Tristanne.

Sister woman sister lover I bless you with this water. Brigid will help us find within ourselves the power to heal.

Sister woman sister lover. Blessed be.

Then Iseult stands while Tristanne bends to cup her own hands and touching Iseult's face with the well water she says:

Sister woman sister lover. Have strength and courage. Blessed be.

Then Tristanne raises her arms to the sky and turning slowly calls upon the spirits.

Spirits of the east, the south, the west and the north, hear me. This night is the eve of summer, the festival of lovers. This night is a festival of fire, the fire of passion, the fire of love, the fire of summer and the fire of hearth.

Spirits of the east, the south, the west and the north, come dance with me tonight, here in this woodland by this sacred well.

Oh, where are the women lovers gone? Come dance with

153

us and show the way. We dance alone here, Iseult and I, we dance a dance for the summer to come. Show us the lovers here in this land, show us the women who will us befriend, show us a dance for the summer to come.

Tristanne raises her arms to the sky and she turns and turns, calling forth the spirits of summer to hear her voice.

We have travelled from far to meet in this land, we will journey the cliffs and the sea. We have no home save in this wood, we dance our dance for summer to be. Come summer, come summer to me.

Holding hands they circle round and round the green glade, chanting and dancing, until they feel their dance is complete.

Tristanne says: Spirits of the east, powers of air, we thank you for being with us this day. We bid you a safe journey to your own realms. Hail and farewell.

Spirits of the south, powers of fire, thank you for being here today. May your fire long stay within us. May you journey on to your own realms. Hail and farewell.

Spirits of the west, powers of water, thank you for attending us this day. May the healing power of this well stay with us this summer. We bid you a safe journey to your own realms. Hail and farewell.

Spirits of the north, powers of the earth, we thank you for this lovely place, the safety of this woodland, and the fruits of the forest. We bid you a safe journey to your own realms. Hail and farewell.

They sleep together that night in the glade by the well.

* * *

In twentieth century Cornwall, it is the first day of summer. Outside the town of Padstow, where local people have been preparing for the May Day festival, a queue of cars waits to turn into a large field. Vonn is waved into the field and directed to a parking place.

'Lovely day for it,' she says to the attendant, who looks at the blue sky, which is dotted with clouds, and crosses his fingers.

Rachel and Vonn sort the lunch packs while Triss and Clare fix the wheelchair. Vonn recalls the last time she was here with a woman in a wheelchair, in the midst of a singing, chanting throng. Today the wheelchair belongs to Clare, who can't yet walk all day.

Presently they are all ready, and they set off together, laughing and chatting, on a long, curving route downhill towards the fishing port.

Gradually they become aware of the sound of drumming and they follow the sound down towards the centre of the town. But then their way is blocked by a crowd of accordionists and drummers, dressed entirely in white and followed by a woman dancing backwards, waving a sort of wand with ribbons on it.

The four friends press back with other visitors, against a garden wall, as the sound of drumming increases and the musicians step steadily past.

Then above the heads of this procession, they see a huge horse-mask dipping and rising like a great horse on the waves of the ocean. Rachel immediately thinks of Rhiannon arriving from the ocean on the back of the white mare of the sea; but Vonn imagines a black horse, Epona, the horse goddess, the sea-mare herself, because she has been taught to think of this by Elizabeth Somerville.

Meanwhile, Triss is bending to whisper to Clare in the wheelchair to describe what they can see but she cannot, and someone hands them a printed paper with the words of the May Day song:

> Unite and Unite; and let us all unite
> for summer is a come-un today;
> and whither we are going we will all unite
> in the merry morning of May.

Soon, Clare too can see past the last of the musicians, who is drumming with exuberance, to the woman dancing backwards and then to the great Oss himself, lured onwards by the dancing woman. He is incredibly splendid, and ominous at the same time. His horse's face is a huge surreal mask of black streaked with red, and his 'body' is a five-foot steel hoop draped in black vinyl and suspended over the shoulders of a male dancer, before dropping almost to the ground.

The Oss dances to the drum beat, his body dipping and

swooping, his tail flying in the air, as the accordionists play the tune of the May Day song, over and over again.

* * *

This is not a tourist festival. The sea is not romantic and Cornwall is not a tidy sweet tourist place. This is a local carnival, representing the pride and resilience of those who live and work by the sea, whose knowledge of and respect for the power of Mare, the ocean, goes back as long as this tradition, and who can say how long that is?

Later, when this part of the Obby Oss procession has passed, the four women go down into the main square where a very tall maypole tree is adorned with leaves and flowers, symbolising the tree of life, the flowering to come for the summer, and the hopes of the people for a good yield from the land and the sea. Women who are pregnant at Beltane hope for safe delivery of their new child, and young lovers traditionally plight their troth.

Under the maypole tree the four visitors pose for photographs, arms around each other, smiling hugely.

* * * *

After lunch, Rachel and Vonn sit by the quayside. Vonn looks up as a plane passes overhead. Its white vapour trail arches inland across a blue summer sky.

Rachel catches Vonn's eye, looks up through the flags and streamers that flutter on the boats in the harbour, up to the passing plane, and in one of those split-second time warps that the imagination can perform, follows Vonn's mind to her journey back from the USA.

'Thinking of your journey home?'

'Yes, how did you know?'

'Just a feeling, and a sense that Elizabeth Somerville is watching. Am I right?'

Vonn nods. 'She loved the Obby Oss, because the Christians have never been able to suppress it.'

'The drumbeat gets you right here in the chest,' says Rachel.

'Yes, like a heartbeat.'

'Mmm. It's very ancient, isn't it? Older than the Celts, I

think. *The Diaries* name it pagan music. And aren't the accordions awesome!'

'Magic. I want one – well, a small one maybe, like the children's.'

'I like their white jumpers with OBBY OSS knitted in. Makes me think of Mieke's kiddies. She knits like that. Words and stuff. It's clever.'

Vonn smiles and says, 'Should we catch up with Triss and Clare? Give Triss a rest from pushing the wheelchair?'

'In a while. But first I'd like to just sit here in the sun and watch the boats and the crowds. It reminds me of Chania with people parading by the quay at night, walking about in their finery, bumping into friends, chatting. I loved it. You went to Crete with Frankie, didn't you?'

'We did. Backpacking.' Remembering, Vonn begins to laugh. 'Years ago. She wanted to live halfway up the Samaria Gorge, till I pointed out the endless stream of feet going past the door.'

'Heavens, yes. There was a little ruined mill or something. A single track with a million tourists.' Rachel chuckles. 'Worse'n the M1. You must've put her off. She came back with you.'

'Right, but we loved Crete. The sites; the olive groves; the mountains; and the museums, the figures, glowing there in their own homeland.'

'Can we go together when we've got some cash?'

'You bet.' Vonn pauses, watching the crowds. 'Elizabeth seems so close today. As if the plane is flying backwards through time, to when she was alive, and across the time zones. She did that a lot in her career. I suppose we take it for granted.'

'Flying?'

'Well ... backwards through time. I was thinking about it when I woke this morning, when I told you my dream of the well at Landue. So vivid; like I was back in that time. In that green glade. I could smell the forest.'

'I wonder what it all means, really, for us, Vonn. Tristanne and Iseult, I mean. They wander through the woods and through our psyches, and they join us together. You and me. We're blending.'

Vonn replies, 'We're certainly tuned into one another.

Even in sleep. I can feel it if you're not sleeping or if you're dreaming.'

'Ever since I met you, Vonn, and you gave me *The Diaries* to read, Iseult has come alive for me. She doesn't seem to be in the past. She seems to be here. She's real to me. Then I think of Elizabeth, whom I didn't know. I'd have liked to have known her.'

'She didn't think of past, present and future as separate, of course. She understood linear time. Something happens and causes something else. That's one definition. Or the wheel of the year turning in only one direction. Anything with a concept of an event and its effect embodies linear time. But to Elizabeth there was more to it: things happening simultaneously; wheels with no end and no beginning; things being transformed in both directions or being completely unobservable. She'd say: Is it real? How can we know? It was all so exciting!'

* * *

Late that night, back in Melloney's cottage, Rachel cannot sleep. She creeps from the bed trying not to wake Vonn, and makes her way downstairs in the dark. She pulls on warm clothes and goes out into the tiny garden, where she stands looking over the rooftops of the cove out to sea and up into a dark and starry sky.

Naturally, it would come to you, if you were one of the great stone circle builders, to align your stones to a May Day sunrise or a midsummer sunset; to use your maths to predict the eclipses; to use precision to chart the passage of the moon.

Rachel cannot see the moon, but she watches a star move fast and fall and disappear over the sea. She wonders if it would feel strange to you, if you lived in neolithic times, that your descendants might not understand such things. If you live in a cave in a cove by the sea, and your era is before the Garden of Eden, you will take it for granted that every part of the earth is female, and so is every part of the sky. Within the sky herself, the sun and moon are both aspects of the female; and this will be as familiar as if two women side by side were kneeling looking into the same water, two parts of one reflection, same only different. Moon and sun, two females, not identical, each with her own power and patterns.

It is interesting in itself, thinks Rachel, hugging her warm clothes closer to her, for the night is not cloudy and the air is therefore chilled, interesting in itself just what kinds of things we look for in reflections, what kinds of samenesses and what kinds of difference. What if you are not interested in the polarity of yin and yang, nor the balancing act of male and female so popular in New Age writings? What if you are one hundred per cent female, and it is this reality that you need to have reflected back at you?

Elizabeth interpreted the Obby Oss as a fertility festival, thinks Rachel, and made it sound very straight. But actually the Mare was female – originally it was the celebration of Mother Earth's fertility and of the produce of the ocean. Anyway there are research works which show plenty of festivals of lesbian lovers. There have been festivals of lovers all over the world where the unions celebrated are those of the same sex, and they may be for a fortnight until the second half of the lunar cycle, at which time straight unions take place, or they may be for a year and a day.

There's new evidence nowadays that gives us glimpses of the women's rites of earlier times. There are women doing research in many places, including Maria Gimbutas's work on Old Europe. So, if we go back beyond Celtic times to the older societies, they seem to be matrifocal, gynocentric. Temples of Malta, and Gozo, temples of Catal Huyuk and many more, seem to have had rooms set aside for women's rites and rituals, including those of same-sex loving. From Sappho backwards through time, dare we say that the festivals of lovers were female?

Let's imagine those times, thinks Rachel. You may live with your country-dwelling friends and family; and may build the stone circles and align the great henges to show your trust in the patterns of the cosmos. And, if you are the ancestors of what later comes to be called Dumnonia, you trust that summertime is the time of the summer goddess, she who is the light of *both* the sun and the moon. And if you are in Ireland you may call the sun 'tethin', which is a woman word, a female word, like teine, the word for fire. And you may celebrate with sun loving, and you may light fearsome fires on hilltops and feast with all your friends. And you may call it Bel-teine, meaning festival of a fire dance for summer.

You may dance and dance, chanting and singing, encouraging the sun to come and dance with you, and you, woman, may feel bright and lusty and slip away in the night and find another good woman to lie with. Then her breasts will be warm as the fires on the hills and your tongue will be the cooling rain. And every year, again.

But at present you are merely a twentieth-century high-tech jumbo jet traveller. You are flying perhaps over the Atlantic from New York to Heathrow, and far below you, there are women in a Cornish village, dancing with the Obby Oss, watching your plane in a blue summer sky. At night together, they talk to the moon, in wild and lonely places, where reason and intuition blend. Reason is the mirror into which they search, to check out what their intuition tells them. The moon is the mirror into which they gaze, to check what they feel that their reason is saying.

And where has the dancing gone?

It has gone to a hillside where women take drums. Calling and calling the power of the moon. It has gone to Carfury where women take flowers, dancing and dancing an ancient tune. Bring back the dancing, bring back the sun. Bring back the heart and soul. Reason is with us, and our minds have begun to challenge a New Age goal. Gone is the yin and gone is the yang. Gone is the need for duality. Bring back the moonlight, bring back the sun, blend them in woman, blend into one. Chanting and drumming the summer is come.

At this moment Rachel's thoughts are interrupted, but also validated, by the tail-lights of an aeroplane passing overhead on its way out over the Atlantic. It's as if the plane that initiated the talk between Vonn and Rachel this morning at Padstow is now going back home. Rachel, being in a particular train of thought, goes ahead of the plane towards New York and thence passes over a sun goddess whose statue wears a crown of flames and who holds high above her head a flaming torch. When the statue was first created in the very early days of settlement of the 'new' country, which was not a new country to the indigenous Indians, it was hoped that the flaming torch and crown of flames would symbolise a new dawn to the immigrants as they approached from Europe by sea.

Once again, Rachel's thoughts are taking her down paths already explored by Elizabeth Somerville in *The Diaries.*

The sculptor who created the image was inspired by the great Etruscan sun goddess, Lusna.

To the Romans, Lusna was known as Lucina, goddess of light, representing both the moon as Diana Lucina and the sun as Juno Lucina, who was the midwife of the heavens, bringing the light of day to the eyes of the newborn.

The statue itself was a gift of friendship from France for the new America.

To the early Christians, Lusna was too powerful. They could not sustain the idea that the trinity of sun, moon and earth was female. Lusna became Lucina. Lucina, who was thus Lusna in disguise, was so popular that the early church could not entirely obliterate her.

Lucina became St Lucy, a maiden known to be of great virtue. However, in order to retain her name and her independent identity, St Lucy was martyred in a terrible manner. She refused to submit to the patriarch who wanted her, who admired her lovely eyes. She told him that she would rather die, so she cut out her own two eyes, which were handed to the patriarch on a plate.

Rachel shivers at the image of St Lucy which has come uninvited into her head. There are so many women who do not keep their own names. She feels it deeply, and thinks of one women in particular. Her own mother. Truus van der Putten. Mrs Tracey Markham. Then into her mind comes her Grandmother Markham, who not only gave up her Cornish maiden name, but the whole of her Cornish identity as well. Grandmother Markham became so involved with her married life as an Englishman's wife, living in Salisbury, that she could find no sympathy or kindness for her daughter-in-law who grieved for her Dutch identity if not her Dutch maiden name.

In a war-torn Europe, and a violence-covered earth, where men soldiers are threatened with being shot by other men soldiers if they refuse to commit rape on the local women, can it be possible to imagine and create a kind community where women can keep their names without forfeiting their bodies or their lives? There are many variations on the theme of mutilation of women. Rachel shudders. Women who forfeit parts of themselves. Women whose lives and identities, minds and bodies are being torn apart still do not get to name themselves. And yet Rachel can understand that many women do not want to keep their fathers' names.

Markham. Is it a name worth keeping? Does it not signify loss of child, face down, semi-naked over a man's lap? Was there a hard penis in that lap?

Oh help me, says Rachel, to the sky, to the distant sea, which can be heard above the house tops in the cove. Help me. Help me find within myself the strength to heal myself. Myself. To heal myself.

She repeats this like a mantra for many minutes.

Help me. Help me find inside myself the power to heal myself.

Help me. Help me find inside myself the power to heal myself.

Me. Myself. The power to heal myself.

Presently, she goes inside, undresses quietly in the dark, and creeps upstairs to snuggle into bed beside Vonn, and sleep, in safety, till morning.

* * *

It would be so simple if that were all there was to the healing process. Memory. Recognition. Separation. Sleep.

There are those women, Rachel supposes, looking back later on that summer, for whom the process of separating memory from anguish is speedier than her own. Perhaps it is possible for them to call up a memory and split it from its emotional charge in a single workshop. She has heard of such things. However, it does not happen like that for her. Her healing is longer and harder and gets in the way of what she wants with Vonn.

Neither of them is lacking in courage or they wouldn't have survived as out lesbians this long; but it is not easy when you're only a few weeks into a new relationship to anticipate exactly how the acts of sabotage are going to manifest themselves.

Next day Rachel and Vonn set out to visit Hyrt Yseult – the ford called Iseult's Ford which is listed in the Saxon documents pertaining to Cornwall lodged in the County Records Office in Truro.

The day begins well with further sunshine, and they find themselves in the rolling countryside, which is inland from Lou and Annie's place near Porthallow, just before lunch time.

Afterwards they cannot remember exactly what it was that started them off, nor how it was that, seated on a picnic rug, miles from the route they were supposed to have taken, they spiralled downwards into uncontrollable anger, which became aimed destructively at each other.

'Well, I don't think she did take out her eyes and give them on a plate,' says Vonn, who doesn't agree with *The Diaries'* interpretation of the martyrdom of St Lucy.

'You're putting me off my lunch. Can't we leave this till later?'

'You raised it, Rae, and I don't want to be left holding this any longer. I want to talk it through. There's far too much writing about woman as victim, surely you must agree with that.'

'I do agree with that. Why can't we leave this till later?'

'Because the whole purpose of this trip is to find Iseult's Ford; and I thought we were agreed on our thoughts on women as victims and women as self-determining.'

'Well, it seems we're not. I was only going by what the book said.'

'You don't have to believe what the books say.' Vonn notices that her own voice is quite abrasive but she immediately tells herself that this is justified given how strongly she feels.

'I don't,' says Rachel, with more than a hint of annoyance.

'That's all right then.'

'I don't know why you're taking that tone,' retorts Rachel.

'What tone?'

'Don't play games with me, you know what I mean.'

'I don't know what you're talking about.'

163

'That's because you're not listening. You haven't been listening properly since we first got in the car this morning.'

'That's a hurtful thing to say. You've got a terrible tongue in your head sometimes.'

'Equal in all things – you give as good as you get.'

'I was trying to drive and we were on the wrong road.'

'Not my fault. I said go the other way.'

'Okay, if you don't like my driving *you* take over.'

'I didn't say I don't like your driving. I just said it wasn't my fault that we took the wrong route and ended up here.'

'Nothing's ever your fault.'

'What's that supposed to mean?'

'Nothing.'

'Look, can't we just stop this?'

Rachel doesn't realise that the reason she is getting very upset is that this is how she and Truus used to do things. At this moment, without knowing it, she is bonding Vonn with Truus. She is beginning to feel incredibly angry with Vonn, and the depth of this frightens her. From the well of fear into which she is falling, she attacks.

She spits the words, 'After all, *I* didn't start it. You did.'

'You seem determined to apportion blame.' The abrasion in Vonn's voice is hard-edged now.

'And you seem hellbent on goading me. Why couldn't you just let it go? I didn't want this discussion in the first place.'

'With you yelling fit to be heard in Porthallow, this is hardly a discussion, is it?'

'I don't like being told where we are going. I'd like to have some say in it.'

'You were perfectly happy about it when I suggested it.'

'So, I'm not now, okay?'

'No, it isn't okay. This is terrible.'

Instead of replying, Rachel leaps to her feet and makes off into the woodland. Over her shoulder at full blast she yells, 'I'm getting out of here. You're behaving like you've got to be in charge.' Under her breath, furious as she runs away, she mutters, 'Stupid controlling bitch. That's what she is.'

Vonn shouts top range after her, 'You're impossible, Rae. What am I supposed to do now?'

Rachel hears this, turns and screams back at her, 'Go

home. Just go away. Drive off. It's your bloody car. I don't care.'

Rachel stumbles on and on, down a country path wide enough for horses. She runs, fuelled by angry energy and takes a right-hand turn along another track, sobbing like a six-year-old.

Back on the picnic rug Vonn is shaking. She hates herself for pushing the argument, since she is fairly certain that they had both agreed on the interpretation of the whole bloody Lucy affair anyway. Rachel was no more likely to see women as victims than she was herself, so why had she felt the need to push and push at Rachel, especially as they could easily have left it till later as Rachel herself had asked? Besides, it *was* a horrible thing to be talking about whilst eating, and obviously it wasn't what the distress was really about anyway.

Vonn finds that she herself is crying quietly now, sitting in a clearing in the woodland, but without any of the companionship and support that Tristanne, her dream character, gave to Iseult at the well at Landue.

Vonn argues to herself that dreams are all very well, informative, revealing and healing, but the reality is here and now, twentieth century.

Vonn lies on her back and closes her eyes, trying to calm down and sort out her feelings. A great well of grief and loneliness now comes to engulf her. She rolls over on to her belly and, cradling her head in her folded arms, she cries heavily, wetly, for herself and Rachel, and for the discontinuity, which is so frightening when the love between them is profound, as they both know.

She remembers trying to talk to her mother about Jenny. She can recall how frightening was the recognition at that time that some*thing* she cared about very deeply was going to be disregarded by some*one* she cared about deeply.

She remembers pushing and pushing with the need to talk about Jenny, and the wall of resistance put up by her mother. Vonn needed and needed to be believed; to have her knowledge validated; to have her feelings confirmed and supported. Not since that time has she felt this particular pressure from inside her. She has studied so much about healing, and in particular enjoyed Billie Potts's book, *Witches*

Heal – a Guide to Lesbian Herbal Self-sufficiency, in which Billie Potts rejects the New Age ideas that women are responsible for creating their own realities – not that we can't change things and influence our own lives, of course we can, thinks Vonn, that's what healing seems to be all about, but that so many of the current philosophies in so-called alternative medicine put an implicit blame on women for their own dis-ease. Vonn wants none of it – and how very relevant this seems to her and Rachel, now that deep stuff is emerging into the relationship from the past of each of them to be understood, named, confronted, dealt with.

So it was essential, argues Vonn to herself, that she and Rae felt the same about St Lucy and what had happened to her or had been done to her. If she was a virgin from choice and would rather die than submit to marriage then she might be a martyr, but at least she was taking a stand and making an act of resistance, taking action, not being passive or simply letting things happen.

Yet Vonn herself had let this row happen. Worse, she had initiated it and sustained it up to the point at which Rachel, refusing to be bullied, had started to fight back.

And Rachel was well trained to fight back. Trained by her own parents when, as a little girl, she was fighting to keep her spirit against heavy adult pressure to make her compliant and apologetic. No wonder Rachel spat words out.

Vonn cries into her own arms lying on the rug until her jumper is soaked and she is a snotty mess with bloated eyes and swollen face. She cries for the lost innocence of her own childhood. Safe. A safe place for her and Jenny. When the bough breaks; the heart breaks. Now Vonn lies face down on a rug, and has only her own arms in which to cradle her own head. She is separated by angry words from the arms of a lover. Rachel.

It is their first real row, and though short it feels bitter and significant. To Vonn, at this moment, it is very frightening, because it could happen again. Neither of them can pretend to inhabit an unreal space between the worlds where they live saintly lives, always getting the process right, always able to take good care of each other, always able to suspend judgement, be reasonable and calm.

In the real world where we live, thinks Vonn, rolling over

on to her back and looking up to the sky through the overhead leafy branches, we behave badly sometimes. We're not inherently bad. We are simply imperfect, not saintly.

But I do love her so much. I'm so sorry that I hurt her. And I'm not even premenstrual! I haven't got an excuse. I hope she comes back soon.

Why do I behave so badly? she asks herself. Why do I hurt the ones I love best? Why this desperate attempt to make Rachel know something that I felt I had to voice, right then, about St Lucy?

She rolls back over on to her belly, head on arms again but not crying any longer. Why this need to impose her voice on someone?

She has a sudden vivid picture of herself trying to make her mother hear about Jenny. Her mother could not hear. Vonn has never come to terms with this, but in this moment she knows that this picture is one root of sabotage which must be recognised.

Cognito. To know. Recognito. To know again; to know differently. To take cognisance of. To place this in the forefront of the psyche; to work with it until the memory of it and the emotion associated with it are separated. To separate the hurt of it from the power to hurt someone with it. Many separations. A lot of work.

The search for Iseult's Ford, thinks Vonn, is also an inner search for the place where the road we wish to take now, Rachel and I, crosses our emotional streams from the past. The place where we can wade through, where the water is not too deep.

It is not Rachel's fault that my mother would not/could not hear my hurt about Jenny. It is not Rachel's need to be on the receiving end of this need to be heard, this need to impose. Yet, strangely, it was she who said I wasn't listening when we were driving here. And it's true that I was not. The irony of that should not escape us.

She realises she has done this before and now, shocked, she sees that this is a repeating pattern which she has not healed out of herself, because she has not wanted to until now. She has held on to this. This need to impose something. This need, as Rachel uncannily pinpoints, this need to control. For years she hasn't let anyone powerful enough, near enough or for long enough to really make a challenge to this pattern. Now, if she doesn't change it, she will lose a woman who came into her arms like a gift from the cosmos and whom she does not want to hurt or lose. As she sits up on the rug Vonn hears the first drops of rain falling. Shit, she thinks, what on earth am I to do now? She gathers up the picnic things, and makes a couple of trips with them to the parked car.

It is raining steadily now, a proper cloudburst, and shows no sign of stopping. Vonn sits in the car, covering herself with the picnic rug, and prepares for a longish wait.

Rachel stumbles along a farm track, her face hot with anger, her shoulder-length hair tangled and her armpits sweaty from the body heat that has built up with her outbursts.

High Cornish hedges protect the fields on either side. She's still running, running with hard, pounding strides; her breath forms in uneven gasps, half sobs with choking sounds. She veers left, following the track into a thin copse which separates one farm from the next; and runs through the copse on a wide track with deep ruts, rough and uneven underfoot, until the way is blocked by a five-barred gate. Driven by angry energy, she swiftly shins over the gate, into a wide sloping field where many sheep are grazing with two Jersey cows and a donkey.

The animals barely glance up from their dinner as Rachel runs down over the field and exits over a granite stile next to another five-barred gate. Now she is on a woodland path running alongside a rivulet of water that passes under a granite slab bridge. Unaware of brambles that have begun to invade the path, she catches her foot, trips and falls spread-eagled, on to tufts of grass and gravel, grazing her hands and bruising her knees. She lands face down, getting a mouthful of grass and dirt, thus adding insult to injury.

'Blast. Damn and blast.'

She is nine, flying downhill on her scooter. It is new and red. It's Saturday, summertime, and there is no school. She is flying down the hill, escaping a furious row with Truus. She has fled the house, grabbing the scooter, her mother's voice echoing behind her, 'You come back here, my girl.

168

Come back here this minute. You come back here. Rachel, can you hear me?'

Of course she can hear, but she is escaping. Flying away. The wind in her hair, flying past her face. She is nine, flying downhill on her scooter. The wind is in her face, her breath coming in uneven gasps, half sobs, with some choking sounds. Now the exhilaration of the movement; the speed; the escape; the freedom. The wind in her hair, in her face.

The wall at the bottom looms up fast, so fast. She swerves, takes the corner. Fails the bend. She flies one way, the scooter the other.

Red fire shoots up through her hands. Splat. She is spread-eagled on the tarmac road near her school-friend's house, her new scooter flung far away. There is red fire in her brain. Fail. Fail. Fall. Fall. Bend at the bottom of the hill. Now she is crying, loudly, and her nose is bleeding. She's done both her knees, they are flayed and scraped, and there is gravel embedded in her raw skin. She's alone in the world and her mother will slap her for ruining her summer sandals, which are all rubbed and scratched by the slide along the pavement. She cries hot wet tears. They run down her dirty face and mingle with blood and snot from her nose. She hasn't got a handkerchief.

She sits up slowly. She is nine. She is in a lot of trouble. More trouble, when she blows her nose on the hem of her frock. She sits for a while and no traffic comes. Her scooter wheel which spins round and round in the air comes to a slow halt. She pinches her nose to stop it bleeding. She is nine. Her mother is angry. She doesn't want to go home.

Rachel sits up slowly, listening to the woodland sounds around her. Scurrying birds in the undergrowth. Birdsong high overhead. A slight breeze. Rustling of leaves all around her. A robin comes to perch nearby, and watches her steadily.

'I'm in a lot of trouble,' she says aloud. The bird waits. She sighs and shifts position. The startled robin backs off and alights further away. She wriggles her toes, flexes her feet. Examines her hands. Soreness and grazing but nothing sprained. That's a blessing.

'Vonn, oh Vonn, I love you, I'm sorry,' she says to the woods around. 'Can you hear me back there by the car? I have to stop running away. I have to. I've been running all my life, it seems. Can I learn to trust you? Can I be trusted?

'I'm frightened. To flare so fast. To be so angry. To sink so low, to hit that bend on that scooter after only a few sentences. To come flying off.

'I see the red scooter there in the road, the wheel spinning, spinning. My anger spinning, spinning.

'I want this healed out of me. I want the dirt washed out of the blood. The gravel dug out of the raw skin, the flow of it stopped.

'I want to be angry with the things that matter, not with you. Not with you, Vonn, not with you. I know what I want to be angry about. Grandfathers who abuse our sisters. Fathers who beat their daughters. Mothers who don't put their own bodies in the way of the fathers who slap the daughters.

'Yes, I am angry with Truus. I have every right to be so. She abused me. She still does. Or would, if I let her.

'I need to let myself be angry with Truus. It's like toxins in my blood. So poisonous. The anger, so much of it. I need time, time to heal. Can you give me time? Can you? Can you?

'And you, Vonn, you. You are so angry deep inside you. It's real, it's real. Toxins inside you, poisoning you. Making you afraid and fearsome, at one and the same time. I see myself in you, yourself in me. Are we the same inside? Choking with desperate hurt and betrayal. And if so, can we find a way through? Can we, without drowning ourselves and each other in fear and despair? I hope so, Vonn. I hope so.

'Is that hope going to be enough to carry us through?'

Rachel slowly gets up from the grassy path. The knees of her jeans are stained green from the impact and she is shaken and bruised in different places, which reveal themselves to her as she stands looking around the leafy woodland. In a little while, the first drops of rain begin to fall, and their delicate sounds are at one and the same time annoying and musical. Strange notes of music, weird tonic intervals. Pattering of thin fingers on a soft drum. A flute somewhere. Another flute. Percussion.

This is all I need, she thinks: I wonder how Vonn is. She'll

170

be wondering where on earth I am. Perhaps she wonders if I am coming back or if I'd walk on to distant farm buildings, get a lift and make my way across the Lizard and down to West Penwith without her. Not that it would be easy, since all my money's in my wallet in the car. Maybe she's angry that I ran away and left her. Maybe she's remorseful too, that we let our anger hose each other, like the hoses of cold water they used to turn on the suffragettes in prison.

The rain intensifies. Soon, drenched through to the skin, Rachel begins to retrace her steps, slowly and steadily, up the soaking field of huddled sheep, where the Jersey cows have turned their backs against the weather and the donkey is miserable because donkeys loathe to get their hair wet.

It hurts to feel sharp rain on grazed skin: Rachel's bleeding hands are chafing in the open air, and she hopes that Vonn is waiting, sheltering in the car, and hasn't driven off somewhere.

Wincing, Rachel climbs the second of the five-barred gates and paces her steps along the farm track between the high Cornish hedges. She landed clumsily when she fell, so that her joints are hurting as she walks and a headache hovers with a dull thud.

There is no one in the wood, and the picnic is gone. It is raining hard now. All the paths are muddy and Rachel is chilled to the bone. But there, suddenly, on leaving the wood, there is the car, with a figure huddled under a picnic blanket.

Rapidly the car door opens, the figure leaps out and now it's not a figure, any figure, it's Vonn, life size and arms open.

Two women, tears streaming down their faces, calling one another's names, run headlong towards each other, arms open, hugging in tears and blood and rain and sorries.

* * *

Very early in the morning, on June 21st, Vonn and Rachel stagger out of bed, grab prepared sandwiches from the fridge, and set off for Bodmin Moor by car, with a copy of *The Diaries* on the back seat.

'We must be stark raving bonkers,' grumbles Rachel.

'Whose idea was this anyway?' Vonn's tone is light. She smiles in the dark.

'I know.' Rachel lets out a loud yawn. 'Reality's not so appealing.'

'It will be when we get there.'

'I hope so. Reward for all this effort, I hope.'

'Roads are clear, that's something. Good time of day.'

'Night.' Rachel yawns again. 'I quote: "To see the mid-summer sunrise over Stowe's Hill from Craddock stone circle." I bet she's watching us again.'

'Not if she's got any sense, she'll be fast asleep up there or wherever she is now.'

Another yawn escapes from Rachel. 'Too bloody right. I do get some stupid ideas sometimes. This takes the biscuit, this does.'

Vonn is laughing. 'You said it.'

'I'm allowed to. Don't you dare.'

They make fast time to Minions car park and presently, with the help of a strong torch and compass, they start the trek to Craddock stone circle. They walk uphill, over rough grass scattered with tiny potentillas caught in the torch beam like yellow stars, and small, dark shoots of new gorse cropped back to turf level by the Bodmin sheep that wander over the moor. The circle is ruined and the stones are almost flat, but Vonn knows the way, because she has done this walk several times.

'This is amazing, you know,' says Rachel, puffing slightly. 'To be miles from anywhere, just before dawn like this. Reclaim the night. I'd never have dreamt of doing such a thing till I met you and read *The Diaries*. It's quite light up here, isn't it? The stars are fading.'

'There's a bit of cloud too. Here, shine the torch, love, let me check the compass again. Good. Yes. This way.'

'Just a minute. I want to kiss you. Come here.'

Before dawn they are settled, on waterproof mats, their flasks and sandwiches spread around them.

It begins. A tell-tale smudge, brown sky awash with grey. In the distance is the rugged outline of Stowe's Hill, which means hill of hills, the central point for a wide network of stone circles, cairns, stone rows, tors and burial chambers here on the moor. They are aligned to one another and to the major sunrises, sunsets, moon-rises and moon-sets that the agricultural peoples knew and understood, following the wheel of the seasons, with Stowe's Hill at the hub of the wheel.

Behind the women, in the dark south-west, is Tregarrick Tor on a midwinter sunset alignment. Ahead of them, Stowe's Hill itself stands its ground between them and the midsummer sunrise, for which it waits with them now, facing the north-east, ready for the most northerly of all the sunrises of the year.

'Funny to think that this is the start of the descent into winter, isn't it?'

'I can't get my head around that, Rae. I never could, however many times Elizabeth told me. I understand the sun's at its zenith and the mechanics of it, on its way through the second half of the year, but it doesn't feel right – that it's going down when it's coming up at midsummer, if you get what I mean.'

'It's like when you're little and the summer term ends in July and that's summer, not this, isn't it?'

'Yes. Oh, oh I say. Isn't that hill dramatic against the sky? Oh yes, here it comes.'

'The first rays. Up and over. She was right. *The Diaries* are right. Oh, Vonn.'

Intuitively they now hold hands and stand up, watching as the sun itself, gleaming orange and deep pink, just tips the far hill and jumps off, and above and all around them yellow and beige and pink smudge and blend, shifting and pulsing.

Together, on the moor, they hear birdsong, and a lark whirls up round and round, then Bodmin Moor begins to shake herself awake, slowly, yawning as she stirs with her turf all tousled under the high, rounded tent of the sky.

They sit quietly for a while, watching the changing colours, the patterns of light and shade on the moors. Suddenly Rachel begins to speak. 'We never talked about Clare's mum, did we? But we both know her, me through Clare, you through Ben.'

'What brought her into your mind suddenly?' asks Vonn, imagining Eileen at home asleep in her small house in London, where the walls are adorned with pictures of Mary. There's even a shrine to Mary at the turn of the stairs, lit by an electric candle with a soft pink light, the colour of dawn, which flickers continuously.

Rachel shivers, and snuggles closer to Vonn in the cold dawn air, before answering hesitatingly, 'I don't really know. She just walked across my mind. People do sometimes. I don't know.'

'She'd love it here, she'd say it reminded her of the moors back home.'

'Perhaps that's it, the resonance, though it's not really a similar landscape, not to the one she was describing to me. Did she ever tell you about County Meath?'

'No, not really. We mainly talked shop, well, her being a nurse et cetera. She has some lovely pictures of the Wicklows, that's the moorland I was thinking of.'

'But it's not where she grew up. I used to ask her all about that and I suppose I'd not thought about it until this moment. It must come from being up here at dawn, I expect. Her favourite hill was the local one at Loughcrew: Sliabh Na Cailli. The guide books say the Hag's Hill or the Witch's Hill, but Eileen called it Old Woman. The old woman whose hill it was used to sit on a huge stone seat smoking her pipe. All the local people knew about it. Eileen used to be taken up there by her grandmother, from when she was a tiny girl. At midsummer and again at the autumn equinox.' Rachel pauses, shivers again from the cold, and watches the sunrise for a few moments before continuing.

'She told me that the Old Woman has cairns, and at the autumn equinox, when the sun rises about quarter past seven, thereabouts, the light beam shines along a passage into Cairn T and illuminates a series of carvings of the sun and spirals and squiggles at the far end. I s'pose *The Diaries*' reference to it should have alerted me to the comparisons, but it didn't, not until I arrived up here and saw this midsummer for myself.'

'We can be forgiven for not making all the connections straight away. Besides, we were concentrating on midsummer hereabouts. We'd have to go over to Fernacre for equinox. The sites on this part of the moor aren't aligned to the equinoxes, are they?'

'No, they seem to be missing the equinoxes just here. But I remember now so clearly, Eileen talking about Sliabh Na

Cailli at equinox. So misty, the hills of Carnbane East and West green and rising up above the cloud cover to let the sunrise in. She said it was so magical. She tried to make Clare understand, but Clare thought it was fairy stuff, and she didn't want it. You know what she's like. So resistant. You just can't get through.'

'Yes, it always surprises me. Ben is much more tuned in. He wants it all, he says. The mountains and the uprisings. Landscape and politics. Whereas Clare can't bear it if she thinks you're getting off on the land of Ireland. Like tourists . . .'

'But she's right,' interrupts Rachel. 'Misty mountains and lovely lakes – that's exactly what English imperialism has gone for.'

'Let's not argue, I know she's right. It just that sometimes she hits you with H-block and strip searches and Borstal Boy and the lot. Of course she is right to be angry, but . . .'

'But Ben can be a lot easier? I know what you're saying, Vonn. All of us women have such anger in us. When Clare's anger is triggered, woosh. Like mine, sometimes. We were very similar, she and I. I think it's part of the reason we didn't make it, you know. We were too inexperienced to deal with being so angry and so similar. I want to be different this time around, I really do. And it's not surprising you find Ben easier, is it? You've known him much more closely.'

'He saw me through a difficult time. He and David. Eileen was pretty good as well. We could always talk, she and I.'

'Yes. I love Eileen as well. When I said to her they shouldn't say "hag" but should say Old Wise Woman she nodded and agreed and it brought us close. She seems especially close right now. Gosh, I'm shivering. It's cold sitting here. Let's walk, shall we?'

They gather up their things and continue their discussion on the hoof. Rachel says, 'I'd like to do more of this with you – marking the changing seasons – connecting with these landscapes more like they would have been for the people who built them. It's what Eileen said – her grandmother taking her there, in modern times, because the places themselves have special meaning.'

'It's quite a change for us, Rae. To see these things together feels important, doesn't it?'

'Yes. I think this midsummer is significant for us. Being here. Holding the moment, sharing it.'

'I think of it as touching the land,' says Vonn. 'Come here, I'd like to touch you too. Don't look so worried, love, you can keep your clothes on.'

'Good. I'm happy to kiss you but that's the limit! I'm shivering.'

Presently, when they are walking again, Rachel says, 'So what we have in both places, I mean here and the whole cairn complex on Sliabh Na Cailli in County Meath, is a sacred landscape, is it not? If *The Diaries* are to be believed, sunrise and sunset alignments and cairns and stone circles were ritual centres, all carefully placed?'

'I think so. You don't wear a stone circle on your wrist. Or put up a cairn on the mantelpiece. You build a huge stone clock, all over your landscape, then you sing and live and farm inside it.'

Laughter is free in the sharp moorland air. The thin cloud remains patchy during the early morning, so the sky isn't clear, but, up here, as the women, talking again of Eileen, walk from Craddock Circle south-eastwards towards the Hurlers, it seems higher and wider than at West Penwith. Vast expanses of sky dip to blue hills around the edge of the moor, and the Hurlers feel strong and distinctive set in the bowl between Craddock Circle, Stowe's Hill and Caradon in the distance.

Of the three original Hurlers, only one circle is now intact. On this central circle, excavation and restoration has been carried out. The south and north circles are in ruins. Stones are missing or fallen, some lying half-buried by turf and gorse.

When Elizabeth Somerville was writing *The Diaries*, before she became ill with cancer of the spine, she often came here, and would imagine this central circle paved as it was originally, with white quartz shining in the sunlight, catching hold of the white light and bouncing it in every direction. Once at Samhain Eve, on the 31st of October, Elizabeth came and slept in a tent in this circle and from here she saw the Samhain sunrise over the first of a dozen or so cairns on the humpback of Caradon Hill. By the time of the winter solstice, the sunrise would have moved to the right to the last of the cairns, and then it would move back again. She knew the alignments so well. She wrote, *I long to understand fully the minds of ancient peoples who constructed a complex network of ritual centres here on Bodmin and who moved methodically from one to another according to the time of year, following the sun from rebirth at midwinter solstice through Imbolc on the 1st Feb; to spring equinox on March 21st; on to Beltane on May 1st; and thence to midsummer solstice on June 21st, at which time the sun reached its zenith. Then the days would shorten through Lughnasad (1st August) and autumn equinox back again to Samhain, which was of course the start of the Celtic year, marking a descent into the underworld where the sun slipped back inside the earth and she, Mother Earth, took a rest from fruitfulness.*

Today, as Vonn and Rachel touch the stones of the Hurlers and watch the far hill and check out the alignments, they marvel at the sheer accuracy of the astronomical knowledge held by ancient peoples. But on the other hand, it would be impossible not to observe seasonal changes in the sunrise and sunsets from a high and wild moorland like Bodmin. The sky is nearer up here and the blue touches the green land with the adept blending of a painter whose eye for colour and line is both intuitive and rational.

Today as they walk and talk, discussing *The Diaries* and their shared love of this landscape, Rachel says, 'It's this blend of reason and intuition that intrigues me.'

'Me too. And I love these discussions about it. I think that the archaeologists are just catching up with people like Elizabeth, who was ahead of her time in a way.'

'You mean about these being sacred centres, ceremonial, and so forth?'

'Yes, I do. They're now looking at the sacred uses, whereas before the focus was on land use and farming – field patterns visible on the surface of the moor. That sort of thing.'

'It's very cut about, though, what with tin coffens and stones being taken for farmers' walls.'

'People understand more now, as Elizabeth tried to insist

they should, that the moor was a very magical place – these centres were of deep significance to those who lived and worked here . . .'

'Mesolithic onwards?'

'So *The Diaries* say. Before the neolithic, certainly.'

'You can feel the magic in this circle. More so than Craddock, d'you think?'

'Maybe, but I love Craddock Circle. So bleak, with that tiny, solitary gorse bush just off centre. It's more special to me than the Hurlers, somehow. Perhaps because it needs more loving, you know?'

'You sound like *The Diaries*.'

'Maybe so. She was part of my life for a good while. She was my very good friend.'

They turn and hug each other, standing quietly in the central circle of the Hurlers for several minutes.

On the way up from the Hurlers to Stowe's Hill, Vonn and Rachel pass Rillaton Barrow and wonder, as did Elizabeth, whether this might have been an ancient processional route. Were the dead laid to rest here, in the full view of such sunrises? If so, it wasn't a straight line route, for to walk it today the women have to deviate from the straight line. They have to take a serpentine path. Was the route snake-like, similar to the routes at Avebury? Who knows? They did, those ancient people, but this information is lost now.

'Disjuncture and discontinuity,' mutters Rachel.

'But even so there are some things obvious to the naked eye, up here above the tourist places, above the tree line.'

They stand silently at Rillaton, looking around them, taking stock of everything they can feel and see and hear.

Afterwards they both say that they hear that music pours in the silences on the moor; and that the hill over there to the west is like a breast with a nipple; and that the moor feels especially female.

The eroticism of Bodmin Moor is extremely powerful. Her grass is soft like pubic hair, her belly slopes down to her inner thighs, where water seeps, hidden in the ferns, like a sleeping woman moist after making love.

This moor, beloved of twentieth-century artists and writers, was made world-famous by Daphne du Maurier, whose *Jamaica Inn* still sends shivers up her readers' spines. It was also much beloved in ancient times when the moor was Mother Earth herself. Her breasts, her thighs, her belly, her limbs, all were visualised here in this devastatingly shape-shifting place where Stowe's Hill – the hill of hills – and its famous Cheesewring stones shine over the whole area as the most special of all. Here, Vonn and Rachel climb and rest to eat their lunch.

Falling away from them in every direction are patchworks of fields and hamlets, valleys and pockets of trees. Here and there some mist clings to a gulley; now and then a bright mirror signifies water, catching and holding the sky in a time warp. Here the distant fields are blue, not green, and it's almost impossible on a slightly cloudy day like today to see which is the end of the land and which is the start of the sky. Are they clouds or hills, those distant blue shapes?

Here on Stowe's Hill rubble walls lie heaped in plentiful disarray where once the edge of the ritual area would have been. Some upright stones delineate the contours more sharply; elsewhere the natural rock shapes take over. Everywhere tiny pink sedums cling in the cracks, and ferns bend and arch to soften the hard, raw impact. This was never an easy place. This woman is difficult.

From here, north-west to Rough Tor, people would have watched the midsummer sunset. Beyond Rough Tor there lies the route to Tintagel.

Perhaps they lit fires here and danced to encourage the sun to stay longer. Perhaps they showed respect for the six-month journey of the sun back down into the body of Mother Earth, before rebirth at midwinter solstice.

However, midsummer would be a time for expansion and gladness, for the crops to ripen during a six-and-a-half week period of shared community and culture culminating in harvest. Time for both individual and group. There was no separation, then, in ancient times: everything was part of everything and all things were part of earth, and earth was female.

'Think I'll try and get some more photos,' says Vonn, unpacking her camera.

'Okay. I want to sit and watch the hills, you go ahead.'

Presently, Vonn disappears behind the stony outcrops.

Rachel leans back against a large rock, comfortable and relaxed, her eyes on the horizon, aware of the shadows coming and going on the moorland.

Someone is walking on one of the blue hills. An indistinct figure, a long way off.
An old figure, Rachel realises, a female figure.
An old woman.
The hill, the hill of the old woman.
Sliabh Na Cailli.
An old woman wearing an old green coat and gumboots.
She carries a staff of seasoned hawthorn.
She stops walking. Stands. Leans on her staff.
She is a long way away but gazes towards Rachel.
Go home.
Go home to the house on the dunes.
Warning. Warning.
Eileen. Eileen.
Go home. Go home to the house on the dunes.
She stands.
An old woman.
An old woman on her hillside.
Sliabh Na Cailli.
She wears an old green coat and gumboots and she carries a staff of seasoned hawthorn.
Warning.

Rachel screws up her eyes, peering into the distance.
An empty hillside. Blue. Green.

Her scream brings Vonn running.
'What, what's the matter? What's happened, why are you shaking?'
Rachel tells her.

* * *

Back at the house on the dunes, they hear a strange message on the answerphone. The voice belongs to Triss: 'It's Clare's mum, er, don't want to worry you but, er, we'll explain when you get here. Can you both come over, as soon as you can, please? I mean, er, thanks. Damn these things. Oh, anyway, thanks.'

'What's going on?' Vonn asks into the air.

'I dunno. Triss wouldn't ring if it wasn't urgent.'

'I'll ring them again. But why weren't they answering when we tried them from Minions?'

'I kept shivering up there at dawn. I thought it was the cold air. But I felt Eileen very close to me, didn't I?'

'Must be more serious than ill. It's an urgent-sounding message.'

'This sort of stuff's so spooky. I'm frightened, Vonn. Have I got powers?'

'We've all got powers. Ordinary women like us, we're not used to using them, that's all. You're opening up to your inner self. It's okay.' Pause. 'It's ringing. They're still not answering.'

'I suppose we'd better get on over there then. It's been a hell of a long day. Whatever can be going on?'

When they knock on Clare's door, no one replies. Rachel shares a worried glance with Vonn then tries her own key in the lock. Indoors, on the living-room table, they find a letter which leaves them in no mood for fun and breaks the bubble of freedom and happiness that had taken them to Bodmin Moor.

Clare writes:

Dear both,

We realised after Triss phoned and left the message that you'd been up early on Bodmin, so I know you must be a bit knackered. By now we'll be on the train to London to see Mum.

I had a terrible call from Ben while you were on the moor. You know we talked about Irish families in London being threatened because of the recent bombs? Well, it's all turned much too real . . . They're searching Irish households in Mum's area and this morning at dawn they raided her. Mum knows nothing, of course. But she has never felt safe in this Godforsaken country, plus her brothers used to be involved with all that stuff. Police hammered on her door. They didn't hurt her directly – she slipped during the kerfuffle and was terrified, so I suppose she wasn't watching where she was going. She fell and broke her hip.

Triss and me borrowed money off Triss's uncle in St Ives and he was wonderful and came and got us and took us to the train, and so when you get this note we'll be well on the way to London.

Please will you look after Floss and Suky? We can't take them because we'll be staying with Ben and David, and David's allergic to them.

We love you both lots. Very sorry this had to happen on summer solstice of all days. Dawn – must've been wonderful at dawn up there today. But not so wonderful for Mum – and there must be many others just as badly off. Multiple raids, so Ben says.

We love you both and it's wonderful to know we can trust you. There's precious few you can turn to when this sort of crisis happens.

Much love, Clare and Triss

'Shit a brick.' Vonn is shaking. 'Ben's Mum. Oh Eileen, why? Why?'

'Oh Eileen. Why her? She's never hurt anyone in her life.'

Vonn sits down as Floss and Suky make a fuss of her. 'This is awful.'

'All that pain. This is horrible. A broken hip's really bad pain. She is the gentlest, kindest woman. I love her house. I love her. She accepts Ben and David; she accepted me and Clare when we got together. I love her. How could they? How *could* they? She gives a lot of love – sit you down, sit you down, have a cup of tea, have a slice of pie. I never met a more hard-working woman. She just doesn't deserve this. She doesn't. She doesn't.'

'You're right, Rae. It's horrible. I'm so fond of her too. I can't bear to think of police invading her home. She'd be terrified. She knows what they're like.'

'What can we do to help? Apart from 'the girls', I mean?'

'We have to do something.' Vonn busies herself by putting the kettle on, all the while thinking fast. 'When she's convalescing we could offer for her to come and stay with us, couldn't we?'

'Oh, yes. I wonder if she'd want to – she knows us – it can be peaceful here. I wonder.' Rachel closes her eyes, imagining Eileen and the house of icons of Mary, Mother of God, and rapidly goes through a series of images of Eileen's friends in London, and which ones Eileen might prefer to stay with.

'Do you know what's in my mind? Silly, isn't it, how things come up? The icon of Mary at the turn of the stairs.'

'The little candle that never goes out?'

'Yes. It's right here,' Vonn points, 'in the front of my head. Flickering. Pale pink. Silly.'

'No, it's not silly. It's who Eileen is.'

'I hope we can help. She won't be able to be on her own for a while, with her hip in plaster. Ben could bring her. There's no room here, in Clare's place, is there?'

'No way – this place is barely big enough for Clare and Triss, let alone Eileen as well.'

'But there is at the house on the dunes. It was designed for disability, after all, and we're flat in off the road to the top of the house. That's why Elizabeth could live there. Besides, I know Eileen well. She was very kind to me on several occasions. I'm very fond of her.'

They hold each other close for a while and then, uncannily, the phone rings. Vonn picks it up.

'Vonn? Hello, it's Ben. Hoped I might get you. How are you?'

'Shocked. How is she?'

'Heavily sedated. She was in a bad state. It's a bad business, every which way you look at it. We've been down and given our statements.'

'When's Clare due there? And Triss?'

'Shortly. We're on our way to get them. Don't you worry now. Eileen will be all right. Mum's a toughie. She'll come through.'

'We were thinking. She could come to us. You could bring her. Though you'd have to hire something with a recliner, wouldn't you? She'll be on her back for a while?'

'Okay, Vonn, bless you. We need some time to think. Sort it out. Very sudden, you know?'

'We know. Love you all. Talk to you soon. Hang on a minute, Rae's saying something.' Pause. 'Oh, yes, you there, Ben? We'll sleep here tonight before we decide what to do next. I'm not working tonight, and tell Clare that Floss and Suky are fine with us. What's that?' Pause. 'Yes. That's right. Bye then.'

Two days pass, as Eileen works out what to do. On balance she feels she cannot make the long journey yet to Cornwall and she goes instead to a nursing friend of hers in Suffolk, where Ben and David can easily visit her. A week or so later, Clare and Triss return home and there follow long days and nights of reconnecting for the four women, all of whom are now very conscious of the Irish/Cornish reflection, representing for each of them, in individual ways, their respect for the resonance of every lived experience. There is no remaining possibility now for any of them of separating moment from sequence, incident from cycle, nor themselves from history.

* * *

It is the twentieth of July, early in the morning – Vonn's birthday with the new moon in Cancer. Vonn drives home from work but is not ready to sleep. Drawn like a crab to the sea, she parks the car at the house on the dunes, fills up her flask and packs her copy of *The Diaries*, then makes her way along the coast path until she reaches Pedn-mên-du, where she sits in a hollow looking towards Ireland and a rock known locally as The Irish Lady.

Here the tide is rolling in across the rocks while blue and white light plays into the green water in swirling ribbons of colour; and The Irish Lady, in her spreading cloak sits, ghost-like, remembering the shipwreck from which she was the only survivor. Watching the breakers recycling themselves far, far below her, Vonn rests, in this special place, where, with Elizabeth, she came every year on her birthday.

Immediately her thoughts turn towards the one other person in the universe who shared her first birthday and for whom one would expect this day also to be significant. This day should be unforgettable, but Vonn's mother doesn't even know what week it is, and barely what season of the year, let alone remember that today all those years ago she gave birth to a daughter.

Vonn's mother's madness is now changing, according to a letter from Aunty Molly which arrived yesterday with a birthday card and sponge bag. Every year Aunty Molly sends Vonn a new sponge bag for her birthday, so that Vonn, who hasn't much call for sponge bags, probably owns one of the finest collections of them in the West Country. You could keep hankies in them, freshly laundered; and tights or stockings; or assorted combs and make-up. But Vonn's are stuffed with other kinds of things, such as old letters from Frankie, darning wool in many shades, and dozens of pairs of thick socks. This year's version is a splendid shocking pink, red and orange stripey round bag with a drawstring, which Rachel says is like a Sennen sunset. So at the moment it has pride of place on the music room window ledge next to a mirror for double colour. Vonn thinks she might keep spare strings for her violin in it, since it also has a happy musical quality to it, like a children's song about the summer.

But not any of the happiness in the world can now touch her mother's madness, as if her mother has allowed the merry tunes of Vonn's and Jenny's childhoods to be silenced in the small central pocket of a drawstring bag which is never opened, and is lost, cast away to the back of an old cupboard in a council house in Brighton, or maybe thrown out with everything else when new tenants move in. Those tunes are too simple or too sweet to block the sound of crying from the childhood of Vonn's mother.

Vonn doesn't know what the sound of that crying was like, though she may guess, and she doesn't know how the rhythm of it was syncopated by slaps and screams. What kind of tune do you play, she asks, for that sort of anguish, little girl? And what kind of heart closure does it take when a mother does not know that in her own childhood she sobbed herself to sleep and listened to her own voice echoing No No? And when her heart finally opens to the knowledge, does not her mind sometimes close to the world of sound? What sort of chords clang that door shut in the mind of somebody's mum? So, a mother shuts the door to her mind and forgets that she once gave birth to a child called Vonn; and again to a child called Jenny. And when she finally closes her lungs and stops breathing, may this mother rest in peace, properly, for it will be the first rest she ever had a chance to experience, and may she catch up on the sleep she was entitled to as a little girl when her own bed was a nightmare of being kept awake.

Now, into Vonn's mind comes Eileen, Clare's mum, and her lovely book of Irish legends sent with a birthday letter.

Eileen, who is still in Suffolk, says that she would like to visit next spring in daffodil time. She still finds it difficult to sleep, and doesn't want to take pills, so she lies awake sometimes in the small hours, as if waiting for another fateful knock on the door. However, she is much better in herself nowadays, less jumpy, and her hip is healing well.

As she thinks of Eileen unable to sleep, Vonn's head fills with music, Irish music, with a haunting song by Christy Moore about the Birmingham Six. In the song, which is heart-wrenching and angry simultaneously, and written for the Six before they were freed, the singer says he would confess to anything, swear that black was white, after forty-eight hours of non-stop questions and glaring lights, if they'd just let him lie down and close his eyes.

Despite her broken hip, they had questioned Eileen for a long, long time. 'Oh Eileen,' says Vonn aloud, whilst watching a thick band of white cloud coming in off the Atlantic, 'I'm so glad you're going to be all right.'

Without realising she is doing so, Vonn runs her hands through her hair in a releasing gesture, and her sudden arm movement startles a couple of cormorants on a nearby rock. They streamline themselves back into the water fast, opening the sea with a sigh rather than a splash.

Vonn is aware of the swell of the sea, the depth here at Pedn-mên-du, the ruthless cruelty of the underwater boulders, the pull of the current: each year people are 'lost' from this coast for daring to disrespect the danger. The ocean has a remorseless appetite which is the reflection of her creative power. In *The Diaries*, everything comes from her and returns to her in the turning of the cosmic wheel.

Mindful of the ocean, watching the waves, Vonn notices

that the cormorants have reappeared far away, and are busy fishing. It would be so quick here to take control in one last moment of split-second timing and decision, before oblivion. So thorough, cleaving open the sea.

Vonn remembers backwards in time to Jenny who lived in fear of a knock on the night-time door. It was not cowardly, she thinks, to do as Jenny did. Jenny was always brave, even in extreme circumstances.

Then, whilst she recalls how despairing Jenny used to be at birthday time, Vonn suddenly realises that Rachel hasn't mentioned the possibility that for the first time in her life she might receive no recognition from her mother for her birthday in September. For women who were abused as children, and for whom contact with parents is now cut off, impaired or impossible, birthdays can be especially vivid reminders of anguish, thinks Vonn. Perhaps she and Rachel can together find a way to prepare.

Vonn's own situation isn't exactly like Rachel's, but it is, as Carol Belvedere helped her to discover, a reminder of loss, and a symbol of grief. That she was not herself abused like Jenny, nor like Rachel, carries with it a different circumstance, a different meaning, a different set of complexities and contradictions.

There is always such work to be done on her birthday, but for Vonn the chance for solitude and connection with the sea usually accomplishes a shift in the time warp from then to now, with a hope for love and creativity in the unfolding of the year.

So she usually comes to this place on this day, each year, in all kinds of weather and, in the mirror of the wheel's turn, she finds a growing, changing woman reflected back.

Today she sits and watches and listens for a good while as the waves break and shake themselves across the cliffs ready for the tide's turn. Everything changes, turns, begins again, thinks Vonn.

There is, of course, no card from Elizabeth Somerville, but each year Vonn sets out the cards she has kept from her, and puts flowers in the vase that Elizabeth once gave her, by way of thanks for the friendship that lingers on, in every part of the house on the dunes.

187

Sitting by the ocean, Vonn opens *The Diaries* at July, which was also Elizabeth's birth month.

Each of the entries for July has comments by Elizabeth on how she felt about the passing of another year. She would summarise these by reference to Anu, who was specifically the mother of Ireland, but was also represented in the Welsh Mabinogian in her triple form as Cerridwen of the cauldron, Ahrianrod of the silver wheel and Blodeuwedd, goddess of spring. These were the ancient mothers, and as such they understood the labyrinth of Time.

I think of Her, as both Anu and Danu, names which are sometimes separate and sometimes interchangeable.

She is mother of the Irish, but also the first astronomer, whom I call Grandmother Time, since she can connect all parts in this one moment, and holds together past, present and future in her imagination, beyond anything that scientists, even with all their new knowledge of the universe and chaos concepts, can possibly fathom.

Grandmother Time observes all the stars, the planets, the cycles of death and birth. She understands that time is not man-made and is not necessarily defined in mathematical pockets of now, then, gone and to become.

Time itself flows and grows inside itself. Indefinable. To Grandmother, puffs of smoke, and bird wings flying, thunder-storms forming and clouds moving are all significant in the labyrinth of time. For Grandmother Time it is easy to say that five hundred and twenty million years ago the Wicklow Hills are at the bottom of the sea; and that three hundred and eighty million years ago the Wicklow Hills are above the sea and form an arid desert; and that two million years ago the ice covers the mountains and shapes them female; and that in the time of Iseult the fair, some Irish people carve a maze on a rock near a village near a holy wood near a holy loch in the foothills.

She, Anu, watches the stars move across the dome of the sky, while the moon waxes and wanes, and the cailleach on her stone seat turns the earth to face the sun, and the ships of Irish voyagers find safe harbour in Bride's Bay in Wales, or arrive in the Camel Estuary in Dumnonia.

She, Anu, may be amused at the maze images being carved

*in a nearby valley as mirror reflections of the Holywood
original. She is the goddess of labyrinths, of the intricacies of
the passing of time. Thereafter, which to her is one and the
same time, she may reveal herself in the imaginations of
the poets and minstrels who sing for her and about her, maybe
creating images of her to watch over the hills and valleys,
where the moon waxes and wanes, and at the holy places of
the new country.*

*One such carving now guards St Anne's Well in North
Cornwall. Here at full moon I have come face to face with
myself one year older, a neurosurgeon, trying to comprehend
the anatomical maze of the human mind.*

Closing *The Diaries*, Vonn recalls how Elizabeth loved the
maze carvings in Rocky Valley, and how she challenged
the archaeological assertion that the carvings there dated
from the Bronze Age.

Vonn sits contentedly and watches the changing light on
the slope of the waves.

Elizabeth Somerville's lifetime has itself now ended. She
left *The Diaries* as her life thanksgiving. How did the mazes
happen, she asks? Only Anu herself knows, and she isn't
telling. Significant, perhaps, in the great scheme of things, if
there is one. To Grandmother Time, these things are not
coincidence, whilst Time itself is the touch of her finger on
the rim of the wheel.

Vonn sits for a long time connecting with the friendship
of Elizabeth. It is a consequence of Elizabeth's love for
Cornwall that Vonn comes to be sitting on these flat slabs
of granite at this very moment, on the twentieth of July. Like
Elizabeth, she thinks back over the past year, during which
she completed her science degree with the OU. She decides
that it was for herself and for her love of the earth that she
did that degree, not in order to change her work or make
more money.

Is she in some ways the same person now as she was when
she began nursing, a woman for whom making money isn't
the prime directive? She's lucky, she feels, to have enough
money. She'd like to travel a bit more, but she can do some
overtime for that and save up. To earn more she would have

to work full time and might even have to think of leaving Cornwall.

Such a thought would have made her shudder, even before this summer, and now, because she is in love with Rachel, the thought of leaving here appals her. So she dismisses it and thinks instead about everything that is good about her life, here, in this magical place, with an amazing new lover.

These thoughts bring her back from memories to equilibrium. She stands and stretches high up to the sky and yawns and then slowly retraces her steps to the house on the dunes for a good sleep.

* * *

Tristanne steps forward onward in and around, spinning lightly. To spin, to weave a tangled web, thoughts of the living and thoughts of the dead. Transformation. All is all and all is one. The end and beginning complete, not begun.

Into the centre the hub the vortex; into the self the one the many; time is around and inside and above. Into the centre the hub and the nub.

Here there are fields wide open and level, here there's a valley with sloping sides. Here there's a group of women who are chanting around the fire in the depth of the night. Pass around the women and one gives a candle pass around the women to the back of a cave. Here in the dark step forward and closer, enter the inner walls the place for the brave. Here the woman warrior faces the darkness inside the cavern the enclosure the spiral. Here the woman warrior sits on a stone seat raises the candle and looks around the walls. Paintings of creatures, some with antlers, paintings of spirals and circles and holes. Paintings of women with fat legs and bellies, whole and voluptuous, made to be known.

Blow out the candle, feel the warm darkness, the paintings are hidden now there is no light. The blackness is warm and the darkness inspiring, the circles, the spiral, the self, well known.

But there are changes now in the darkness. Why is there fear rising in the gloom? Where does it rise from, surrounding the woman? The warrior faces her fears all alone.

Here is the centre, the dark place the cold place the night

place the old place the one we know best. The place they carve for us in the hills of childhood the valleys of the shadows and the turmoil of death.

Death of the self in the hours of the darkness, death of the self when the people are at war. Here to this place comes the shaman or shamanka here to this place where the coldness is fear. Here to this place where the worst things can happen, all of them looming our demons at war.

Come to this place when the enemies are gathering. Enemies of freedom of women and of love. Come to this place when the search for love is hopeless. Come to this place when the soul longs for peace.

The worst fears are food for the deepest resolutions, the worst fears are food for the woman to use. The worst fears are those where the edge is the nearest, the worst fears are those that cannot get worse. Nothing is worse than the worst of this terror. Noting is worse than the demons of the dark.

These are the times when the soul is in torment. These are the times when ... the brightest spark ... kindles the fires in the coldness of hatred, kindles the fires in the loveless hours. Kindles the fires that make the finest music, kindles the fires that generate the heat ... that transforms this place into something to work with, that transforms this place into wells of hope. That transforms this place from demons into pictures that nurture the woman and give her back the life.

To enter this place is to find the woman warrior who battles with the self and the forces of decay. To enter this place is to find the real woman inside the anguished child that the world chased away.

The warmth of the fires begins from inside us; the warmth of the dark is from the inner strength. It is the same dark, but the warm one is friendly; it is the same dark but the warmth is alive.

It is the same dark; in the dark of transformation: it is the same dark and decisions live there.

They live there inside us, and create from the darkness, the things that delight and entrance and empower.

Tristanne stands in the darkness, breathing deeply. She is afraid of the barons, their weapons and their numbers. Afraid that King Mark will overcome her strength. He wants his wife and is determined to have her because she is the woman-land from whom he derives his power.

Tristanne breathes and breathes, calling up from inside her the deep warm fire she knows lives there. It rises like a snake from the depths of her being. It rises through her limbs and her belly and her neck. She opens her mouth as the snake yells inside her, rattling and hissing and calling and screeching. The noise reverberates around the enclosed dark space. She raises her arms and allows her fire power to flow to the roof of the place from the ends of her hands.

Turning, she flings the fire power around the cavern until the cavern pulses with the warmth that the fire power, from inside her, brings. She is the woman warrior and her fears are real. She is the woman warrior and she knows the man may win. She knows the barons want their power. She is under threat and she chooses life, to save her own life, to save her own life. She is singing now; they will not take away her desire to save her own life. She is the only one who can transform her own fears into this wonderful singing dancing pulsing rhythmic power, the power to be alive, the power to stay alive, the power to not give in, the power to not give it all away by letting the other ill wish her, the power to not give them power over her by making her afraid to state her wishes, name herself name herself.

She lets her hands drop.

She picks up the unlit candle, does not light it. She doesn't need to illuminate this dark; it is already illuminated while it is dark. It is the creative inner dark. She loves it, honours it, gives herself over to it. They may succeed against her but she will not give up herself without a fight.

She steps into the back of the first cave and ahead of her there are the women around a fire, chanting. Outward, from the centre outwards, spinning the weaving of a web, the network of the living. She is aware that the ancestors are watching as she completes her way through the circuit of the labyrinth of time and reveals her self once again to others who are wondering at the changes wrought there.

The living and the dead we are one we are one the dying and the living is the same thing the one thing; the one to do and be/the other to do and be: a decision in every moment.

* * *

Behind the market garden at Lou and Annie's place there is a south-facing field, surrounded by young trees, enclosed by tall ferns. A secluded field, with thick, soft meadow grass, undisturbed by machinery and not criss-crossed by electrical energy. You approach it from the house by a winding track under arching hazel trees and alders now about fifteen years old.

Clare, surprised at herself for agreeing to come along, since she doesn't know all the women here, and gets anxious when it comes to being in groups, sits comfortably in a wicker chair holding a box of tent pegs. She has come because Triss asked her to. Triss moved in a month ago and says she's in love with Clare and would like to stay. For the moment Clare is content to be sitting here in this quiet place miles from any sound of traffic or hint of benzene in the air. She isn't very well, and her legs aren't strong; it is going to take a long time to get her health back, but she is more hopeful nowadays. The women here are trying to include her, though they are all able-bodied and it needs the most flexible of minds to build disability into an event such as this. Clare's gaze encompasses all the activity going on around her.

Triss, Vonn and Rachel are poring over a book of diagrams which shows how to construct landscape mazes. Triss looks up from time to time to grin at Clare and check she is all right. Lou arrives with her friends, Kristina and Hazel from north Devon. They carry trays of breads and salad, summer fruits and summer wines, which they set down on a huge durrie laid on the grass nearby. At the perimeter of the field, Annie is collecting fruits and flowers from a mixed hedgerow of hawthorn, blackthorn, gorse, sorrel, wild roses, brambles, honeysuckle, nettles, herb robert, hawkweed and knapweed; other women with armfuls of barley and wheat from fields along the way are making a corn mother, amidst laughter at the enormity of her rosehip nipples.

'Hi, Clare, how're you doing?'

'Hi, Hilary. I'm much better, thanks. How's things?'

'Fine, thanks. But it's all green, this barley – we've searched everywhere. It's late this year – we need some really hot sunshine.'

'Sure do. Isn't this a lovely place?'

'Wild grasses, yes, it is. Are you and Triss coming back with us?'

'If that's okay? Yes, please. Did Lou mention it?'

'Yes, no problem.' Hilary looks up at the cloudy sky. 'No wind. Not moving much. Still, there's some blue. What you got there, tent pegs?'

'Yes, for the maze, but they'll tie some of it into the grass if we run out.'

'It's good to see you again, Clare. You are looking better.'

'Thanks. I'm feeling good.'

'Must be love,' says Hilary, glancing in the direction of Triss, whom she knows from her job at Age Concern. 'I've known Triss a good while. Sound as a bell.'

'She is. I'm lucky.'

They chat for a while about Hilary's husband and family, and the access course she's going to do at Helston in the autumn.

Meanwhile, the maze begins to take shape, strung along tent pegs rather like a spider's web without the initial warp threads. It is a seven-circuit labyrinth resembling the carvings found on a cliff face near the sea in north Cornwall. As the rope and pegs begin to superimpose the maze pattern on the grass, Vonn is thinking of Rocky Valley and of Elizabeth Somerville who wrote in *The Diaries* about ancient ways of maze-walking which are now being re-established throughout Cornwall by women at harvest time. Vonn also feels Rachel's nearness and a sense of sharing. She hopes the weather will hold out. The forecast says cloudy, mainly dry with a few scattered showers. The overhead clouds could drop rain just at the wrong time, and the wind isn't strong, so they aren't moving away as fast as Vonn would like.

Rachel is now busy pressing tent pegs into the grass as Triss plays out the rope and Vonn tries to translate from the diagram in the book to the thirty-foot area set aside for the purpose.

'Shall I try it out?' asks Triss. 'We don't want to get stuck halfway round.'

'Looks okay from here,' says Rachel.

'I'm not sure. I could roll up this bit of rope and walk it so far, see if it's clear.'

'Okay, you go first.'

Triss starts off but the centre bit is wonky, as she thought it might be. 'This bit's wrong here. Can I see the book?' She stands on one leg, turns to wave at Clare who is laughing at her, wobbles and says, 'Look, I should be able to put my other foot over here but the rope's in the way.'

Amidst laughter, Vonn calls, 'Annie. Can you sort this out? We're 'mazed.'

Annie puts down a pile of berries and rosehips. The red gleams on the grass. 'I see what's happened. The centre's not that bit. It's that bit over there, by Rachel.'

'What, and turn this one back on itself?' asks Rachel.

'Yes. That peg, that one there. Needs to go that way.'

'Oh yes. I get it,' says Rachel. 'Here. Now Triss, can you walk back out now?'

'Yep. Now we need another line inside there. All the way round.'

'Let me count them, from the outside,' says Vonn. She counts to the centre and out again. They place the rest of the rope on more pegs, where they think it should go. Then they all stand back to inspect the thirty-foot diameter maze. 'Someone should try it. See if we can get in and out this time.'

Vonn starts off. Gets to the centre. Turns and winds her way back out, walking between the strings marked out on the grass. A seven-circuit maze takes a few minutes, and now that the final strings have been laid, it takes her longer than it took Triss.

'It works. We did it.'

Meanwhile Sharon, Shona, and Ruth have arrived from Newquay; Josie and Fran from Cambourne; and Zoe and Sandra from Helston.

Some are Cornish, some are not. Some have husbands, some are single, some are mothers. Ruth, Kristina and Hazel are lesbians. Some of the women are musicians in their spare time – some have brought drums, shakers, and wooden flutes. Sharon and Zoe have tambourines.

For a number of years now Annie and Lou have offered their place in this way, though for this group maze-walking is a new activity.

Now that they are all here and the maze is ready, they form a circle sitting on mats laid out on thick polythene on the grass not far from the maze. The women go round the circle a couple of times, each saying her own name, and then Annie says, 'Welcome to our summer celebration, the beginning of harvest.'

Annie pauses, smiles at everyone and continues, 'Welcome to our Goldize, which means in Cornish, "Corn Feast." In Irish the month of August was named after the festival: Lughnasad. I'd like to start with part of Elizabeth Somerville's *Diaries* where she writes about mazes, and then Lou has offered to take us through a relaxation and meditation to help us prepare for our inner work of individual maze-walking. The idea behind this is that it's our inner harvest. So, while each of us walks the maze, the rest of us will drum for her, playing the instruments and chanting her name.

'We know some of you have to get back promptly after the feast but everyone's welcome to come indoors for a cup of tea and there's a fire there in case it turns cold.'

Annie opens her copy of *The Diaries*, shows the women a large photograph and reads:

The Troytown maze here is made from small stones on St Agnes in the Scillies. This is a landscape maze. It's a right-handed maze, which means that as we stand at the entrance our first circuit turns to the right.

The design of this maze is replicated all over the world. There have been mazes like this cut into the turf in other parts of Cornwall, and in England. Similar mazes can be found in Europe, especially Sweden, where fishermen used to walk the maze for luck before putting to sea.

The links between mazes and spirals are visually obvious. The concept of the spiral is of a journey inwards taking us to our quiet place, the centre, the hub of the wheel: the mirror spiral is the outward reflection – coming back again, ever

increasing circuits to the edge of the group, the edge of the
culture, the edge of the world.

This can be done over and over, inwards and outwards,
ever turning patterns of contract and expand, pulling in and
moving out, seedtime and harvest.

There is life at the centre and life at the edge. There is death
at the centre and death at the edge. The harvest of the self is
a letting go of the measurement of time; a transformation
which has a new self within the old self: joy and sorrow meet
as one.

Annie pauses, looks around the group and smiles, then reads:

In Cornwall the wise women carved mazes like this on small
stones which they could hold in the palm of their hand. A
wise woman might trace the shape with her forefingers into
the centre and out again. She might do this rhythmically,
perhaps humming or making an ohming sound to induce a
trance-like state. Then in that altered state of consciousness
she would be able to speak and channel her words by connect-
ing herself to the ancient stores of knowledge.

Then, closing the book and setting it aside, she continues,
'Our maze-walking today is a chance to connect with our
own inner wisdoms. When you get to the centre of the maze
you may want to place something there to symbolise your
own inner harvest, and for those who haven't done this
before, you need to take your own time there. You might
feel strange or changed. Some women leap about at the
centre, others kneel, others sit. You might want your eyes
open or closed. It doesn't matter. Be prepared that you might
cry. Or you might shout out. When you're ready to come
out of the maze just indicate this to us and we'll start up the
drumming for you again. Fast or slow, it's up to you. Also,
it has been known for some women to dash out right across
all the boundaries of the maze. They just leap out. Okay?'

The women are laughing now. The idea that you don't
have to stay in the maze is a comfort to Clare, who is not
sure why she feels so disturbed by this afternoon's process.

Now it's Lou's turn. 'I'd like you to lie down or sit down
on the mats and make yourselves comfortable.' She waits.

She says, 'I'd like you to slow your breathing. Listen to the breeze in the trees. The earth breathing. Breathe very slowly. I'd like you to feel the breeze on your skin. On your face. It's cloudy overhead but the daylight is bright here. Imagine your mind going up above the clouds. You can harvest the daylight from there. Bring it into your mind. Breathe slowly.' She waits.

The meditation through which Lou now guides the group is a simple, almost standard one, in which she creates a sense of harvesting daylight from above the clouds and dark earth energy from underground, allowing them both to blend inside the women's bodies whilst giving a long, slow time for the women to ground and relax after the busy turmoil of their lives.

She's thankful that a slight shower passes over. She can't ignore it, so she builds it into the meditation, but she would have been in trouble if it had started to rain properly.

After she has guided the women into the meditation, she says: 'Now, I want you to let your mind recall good images from the good aspects of your life during the past year. This is the time for harvest. Your lives have had changes since this time last year. Decisions, some choices, and turning points. Mistakes. More decisions. Let them flow and bring forward the good things that came through in the complex processes. Things weren't all simple this year. You may have had some difficult times, so think of the times that turned out well after complexities. For your lives are women's lives and they are usually not simple. Harvest now from those complexities. Dwell on the harvest, perhaps some things that were unexpected, and good for you. In a moment I'll stop talking and there will be a quiet time for the images and the outcomes to surface for you. Breathe very slowly through all this imaging. Let the images rise to the surface for you to harvest.'

There is an almost tangible silence as Lou's voice ceases. There is a sense of peace in the field. The maze is waiting, the trees are still, with their branches barely moving.

In the distance, the hills, blue-green and silent. Nearby, pairs of eyes, held steady, watching. Foxes. Rabbits. Badgers. Insects.

Thousands of slow sounds make this silence. No wind, in this the gentlest August. Gold ferns keep their leaves, branches unsnapped, spreading floating. Blood drips from bramble thorns, splashes on to old leaves, crimson wounds, notice me, I bleed though I am old.

Our first summer, thinks Lou, awake and silent whilst the women are deep in meditation, we pulled four thousand thistles from this acre, by hand, a hundred and fifty to a barrow into the barn, dried them, burned them. Two years of dormant seed, two more thistle harvests, then a third.

Now the wild grasses are long and soft and silky. Grass, close up, isn't only green.

The seed heads are purple and pink, apricot and russet. We have seen yellow, blue and beige in winter. But from a distance, if we were over on those far hills looking across to where we sit, we'd story-tell this field as green: a field in the making. I am here alive. My cancer cells learned how to die. That is one of the problems with cancer, she thinks. The cells only know how to proliferate, they have forgotten that they knew how to die as well. They are researching this these days. And every cell in every second makes a life or death decision, except for cancer cells, who have forgotten how to die. But you cannot harvest without cutting the corn. All is one and all is part of everything. I harvest my life for today. I am meant to be here. I am meant to be here with you all. Strong women. With a passion for truth.

Women are silent, eyes closed, relaxed in meditation, lying on the rugs on top of plastic mats so that they are warm and dry in the open air.

This is the hub of the harvest wheel. The centre. The place of rest. Occasionally someone moves an arm or leg. Some breathe with no sound, others with slow, quiet sounds. Each is in a different place, her own place, whilst sharing this place.

This is powerful and empowering. To be so alone but enclosed by the warmth of others. To be allowed. To give permission. For some women here in this harvest field, this is the only fifteen minutes of time for the self that the day will bring, the week will bring. Such is the crowded space they inhabit, in every sense.

For a couple of the women at least in this group, the only personal space is the six inches on the edge of their bed, between the bed and the bedside rug. Every other part of their household is full of people. For others, such as Clare, the amount of solitary space has sometimes been too much. Alone or in enforced solitude. So Lou's intention during the meditation is to create a sense of safety in a group situation.

Vonn lies on her rug, not far from Rachel, and feels the earth underneath her and the power of the daylight between herself and the cloud cover, blended now inside her. She finds herself clearing space in her own mind for *The Diaries* on the one hand, and on the other hand, for the poetry of Audre Lorde, whose *Cancer Journals* inspired the self-healing of so many, many women, and who herself then died from cancer. Whilst Lou was talking them through the meditation, Vonn could feel the healing power of Lou's own spirit, and she finds herself giving thanks to the universe for Lou's survival from cancer and for the summer celebration itself, because there was a time last autumn when none of Lou's nearest and dearest knew whether she would be with them this summer or not.

So, in her own inner harvest, Vonn finds herself over-whelmed with images of the women whose lives have touched her own, including of course Rachel, and giving thanks for the creative, empowering lives like Audre Lorde's, whose healing work sustains and challenges Vonn, touching her own healing powers very deeply at this moment.

Before this meditation, Vonn hadn't any prior knowledge of what images would surface nor what emotions might arise at the women's harvest. Now, lying on a rug in a field of wild grasses in a safe space created by Lou and Annie, she is filled with happiness, which eases the pain of her mother's anger, the loss of Jenny, the loss of Elizabeth, and the loss within the international lesbian community of the lives if not the voices of Audre Lorde and also Pat Parker, whose words are on one side of an LP which Vonn loves to listen to. Now, unexpectedly, these voices fill the air around Vonn, urging her to be happy, to go forward, alive and strong. She opens her eyes to find that Lou is sitting up, smiling at her.

Catching a sense of readiness from one another, the women begin to stir, change position and come out of the meditative state.

Clare moves back to her wicker chair near the maze and picks up a shaker. The others choose from the various instruments.

Annie takes her place at the entrance to the maze.

She says, 'I'll put these marigolds in the centre as my gift. I love them. They symbolise summer to me. My hope is for many more summer celebrations here with you all.'

They start to drum and chant her name. Annie. Annie. Annie.

They can make as much noise as they like. No one can see into the field.

For the next hour and a half they drum and dance around the maze, as each woman makes the journey, unwinding herself back out from the centre towards the group. Finally it is Rachel's turn.

Unlike Clare, Rachel has not been so much wary of maze-walking as curious as to its efficacy. How could it be that the simple twists and turns of a seven-circuit labyrinth could so alter the psyche as to effect shifts of consciousness, and accomplish inner changes? It sounds like one of those New Age quick-fix remedies to her.

She takes a deep breath at the entrance to the maze. She glances at Vonn, who winks and smiles in encouragement. She sets off and now the experience itself takes hold of her, takes over. She treads steadily, not hurrying, aware of her name echoing and the drumbeats picking up her own rhythm, different from the drumming for other names. How is it that each woman's name generates such a different set of sounds? When your name is echoing around a group like a mantra, then the sound is for you, in friendship, to support you. Is this why it is so powerful? Is it simply the group coherence that creates the change? Rachel. Rachel. Rachel. Rae. Rae. Rachel. Rachel. Rachel. Steadily she treads.

Steadily the beat builds up, rising and falling, rising, rising to a crescendo.

Silence.

She stands at the centre of the maze.

The efficacy? How does it work? Who knows? There is maze knowledge and there are maze traditions all over the earth, all of which are used to create altered states. No amount of cold analysis of such traditions is any substitute for the experience of winding into the centre amidst drumming and chanting.

Silence.

She stands. Eyes closed. Today she is conscious that something is calling her from this land, something very old, that she doesn't fully comprehend. She has had this feeling before and now, silent, at the centre of the maze, she feels the slipping away, down her back, down through her very still body, of a great weight of fear and apprehension, sliding away from her down through her feet into the grass and deeper into the soil under the grass. She has an image in her mind of the maze in Rocky Valley and its mirror image in the Wicklow Hills. Ireland. Cornwall.

She has had this feeling before, and now, connecting with her inner harvest, from the journeys of the past year, Rachel has a sense that she may be coming home, here with the women, in a magical protected place.

At the centre of the maze she feels a weird sensation that her feet are actually growing out of the land. She is like a plant, or a piece of rock with flowers growing on it, part of the earth, a piece of matter. Simply matter. She matters. She is inside the maze and inside the earth. She is standing in the air and is part of the air. She is crouching now, kneeling on the land, placing her hands on the wild grasses and every molecule of her body is alive and pulsing.

She lifts her hands from the grass, flings herself up to full height and with a great whoop, the loudest sound she must ever have made, she leaps high into the air. The women take this as her signal for the drumming to start once again and she leaps around the circuits, winding herself out in a great outpouring of abundant energy, whooping and laughing with her feet barely touching the ground. Loud drumming and hollering and shrieking accompanies her every move and there at the entrance are Lou and Vonn, who catch her as she flies out, amidst great huggings and laughter.

Clare and Triss have a lift home with Hilary and her friends. Clare is shining. She whispers to Triss, 'I'm so glad you asked me to come. I wouldn't have, otherwise. I thought I'd never be able to manage that maze-walking. But the drumming and the sense of all the women chanting for me, chanting my name, you know, just for me. It made me feel so strong. It went right into my bones. I thought it was wonderful.'

'You're going to get well, Clare. Give yourself enough time and you will get well. I love you.'

'I know you do, but it was me that wasn't sure. I was such a sick parrot, I didn't expect to find anyone, I'd given up any thought of it.'

'Well, it'd be an awful waste, that's all I can say.'

'How come you suddenly dropped out of the sky?'

'I didn't. I came on my bike, in the rain.'

Clare laughs and hugs Triss. 'I thought it was going to pour in that meditation. I thought, for sure, didn't I come with ME and now I'll get pneumonia as well.'

'Think positive.'

'I was trying to and there was Lou's voice going on about enjoying the rain on my skin. I was trying hard to concentrate, and I kept thinking, it's going to rain, it's going to rain.'

'Did it?'

'No.'

'Well, there you are then.'

'You're in charge of the weather as well now, are you?'

'Something like that.'

'I love you, Triss Martin. I'm very glad I came today.'

'So am I. Wouldn't have been the same without you.'

* * *

Along the banks of the wide river, as autumn colours tint the woodlands of the Kingdom of Dumnonia, the old willow trees weep golden leaves down into the flowing current which carries them on to the sea. The tallest branches stretch to the sky, lean over, arch across and hang themselves down again to touch the surface, but the roots of the willows pass deep into the underworld, asking what is going to happen to the young lovers now.

Red berries on the sacred Rowan trees gleam blood-like in the September sunshine, calling to the young women to eat them and find eternal youth, but the dark purple fruits of the elders are ripening only slowly and are bitter and sour to the taste.

Here on the wooded river bank, where the tall ash trees are already beginning to lose their leaves, the remains of a small camp can be found under a solitary oak tree, in whose trunk is carved a circle divided into four to protect it from lightning. Someone searching for Tristanne and Iseult might detect that here, at some time, they took shelter in the dark of night; but not very recently, because the cold embers are themselves scattered with unburned acorns which have fallen during the autumn winds.

Along a hidden path from the oak, past a glade of birch trees, their leaves shimmering gold in time for the autumn equinox, the hazel trees are now bearing fruit, though they do this only once in nine years, so this fruitfulness shows that some significant events are about to happen.

In a secluded clearing, not far from the swamp area known as Blancheland, Tristanne and Iseult light a small fire and into it they place two hazel nuts, to symbolise their friendship and love.

Then they wait, watching the central red part of the fire, and silently praying that the hazel nuts will burn quietly and evenly.

To their terrible consternation there is a sharp cracking sound when the nuts gain heat and suddenly one of them bursts, and in a second tiny explosion the other one splits open, cracks and disintegrates.

Holding hands, the lovers sink to their knees by the fire.

'It is not to be,' says Iseult. 'We are doomed.'

'Why? Oh, why this misfortune attending us so?'

'I see a terrible vision. You have been banished, but you fall ill and I am sent for. But I arrive too late to your side and find you dead. My heart breaks, and I die there beside you, in exile. But wait,' Iseult looks into the fire, 'there is more. Our bodies are brought home, here, and laid to rest side by side. From our grave, oh, oh yes, a shared grave, and from it there grow a hazel and a honeysuckle, mingling around it. We are souls in the other world, living on together, forever entwined.'

'But I am not yet banished, my love. Is there no hope for us both? Cannot we both live on here together?'

'I don't know, but I will try to claim more time. Perhaps the heart of the King will soften. Perhaps he will allow this love, or perhaps loosen the surveillance under which he threatens to keep us, so that we may meet and blend as one, sleeping here in the forest in one another's arms.'

'Come away with me, Iseult my love. Leave Dumnonia for ever. Let us both leave, then we do not have to wait for the next life before we shall be intertwined.'

'I cannot leave Dumnonia. I am wedded to this land. It is my fate.'

'I know this to be true, but forgive me pleading against it.'

'I shall do as the barons demand, my dearest. I shall stand trial by ordeal.'

'The hot iron is a terrible ordeal, Iseult my love. I cannot bear for you to undergo such a thing.'

'I shall use subterfuge, Tristanne. Listen carefully to me. I have a plan.'

So, now there are soldiers in groups, wearing Dumnonian garments and waiting in the sunshine on the river bank. Iseult has agreed to stand trial at the marshy place called Blancheland.

Unrecognisable to the soldiers, Iseult's lover Tristanne sits nearby, wearing leper's clothes and broken shoes. She carries a leper's crutch, a wooden bowl and bottle, and a clapper which all lepers use to warn everyone away.

The people begin to arrive to witness the trial of Iseult, and as they pass by Tristanne she proffers her leper's bowl and begs them to give contributions. 'Pity a poor leper. Take pity, lady, on a poor leper.' Many of them are dressed in royal finery.

Some of the barons arrive on horseback. Tristanne shivers, inside her disguise, but they do not attend to her. Tristanne, who hates them for their harassment of herself and Iseult, calls out to them. 'Pity a poor leper, fine sirs. Pity a poor leper. To your left, sirs, is the way to the ordeal. The Queen of Dumnonia shall meet her fate. To the left, sirs, is your path.' Thus she misdirects them and they go off the wrong way and begin floundering about in the marsh. Presently they are pulled out by soldiers with ropes. The barons have to change all their clothes in public because they are covered in mud and slime. Everyone is laughing at the sport of this, jeering and mocking at them.

The King's soldiers sound the trumpets and drums. To the sound of fine music Queen Iseult, Tristanne's lover, arrives. Iseult is dressed in a costly robe with fine soft pleats, made of silk from the markets of the Mount to which the traders come from the east.

Iseult's ordeal is that she must cross the marshland without wetting her feet. She dismounts, secures the reins and stirrups of her horse to the saddle and, giving the horse a sharp tap, she sends it by itself across planks which have been laid across the swamp.

She turns to the leper. 'You shall be my ass,' she says. 'You shall carry me across.'

Tristanne replies, 'I cannot, my lady. I am but a poor leper. I am not fit for this task.'

'I am Iseult, Queen of this land, wife of King Mark. You would dare to disobey me?'

Tristanne pretends to stumble, but agrees. Iseult settles herself piggyback, her legs held firmly by Tristanne's arms, and Tristanne, who is strong and lithe, carries her to safety on the other side.

To the King, Iseult claims, 'I am your true wife. No one has been between my legs save yourself and this poor leper.'

By this device does Iseult save her own life, and gain time for herself and Tristanne, until they can make more plans as to how to live and be together. For Iseult is being threatened by the barons with trial by fire if she lies to the King in any way.

Under constant surveillance the two young women find it difficult to be themselves. They are unvoiced in this land. They cannot name who they really are. They are controlled now by a king and his retinue. They live under his rules, in his castle. They live by his whims, his demands, his voice and his patterns.

At night Iseult is sometimes left alone, when the King is away. It is not possible for Tristanne to visit her. Outside the castle, the vine grows up the walls and bears its autumnal fruit. Inside the castle Iseult wears an amulet of the herb vervain to combat the curses of the barons. In the forest where Tristanne sometimes sleeps, so that she can keep the castle window always in her sight, she wears an amulet of vervain also, in her case to speed her upon her mission. Her quest: to free her lover from the demands of the King, to create a safe place where they both can live.

* * *

When Rachel wakes from this dream she has the sense of Iseult and Tristanne being very near her. Baffled by this feeling, and waking alone because Vonn is on duty, Rachel rises promptly, packs her saddlebags and cycles away from Sennen far up into the hills around Mulfra Quoit.

It is a wonderful autumn day, a few days before her birthday. Here the Cornish heath is fat and full with its purple bells clinging to the contours of the moors. Small compact gorse grows closely knit so that the ground is a mat of yellow flowers and dark green shoots, with purple swathes of colour. Here and there the lighter shades of purple ling make contrast with the heather. From here at Mulfra Rachel can see both sides of the peninsula.

She breathes deep in the clean air and then finds a sheltered spot by the great quoit and leans back having a late breakfast.

To her it seems that the dream was about patriarchal time, as much as patriarchal rules. To the barons, in the dream, the time had come for revenge. Iseult had done wrong. She must be scolded. She must bear witness publicly and if possible be shamed into confession. She must be parted from Tristanne and made to wait. But even then the King was not always consistent in his demands. His will could be done just as he liked, when he liked. Iseult must hang around, waiting on his needs, his pleasure, his timing.

In that situation, desperate as it was, Iseult seems not to have given up. Instead she comes up with a scheme to trick the man in charge, to give herself and Tristanne more time for their own plans. In doing so, she has help from her friend, ally and lover, Tristanne. They support each other and present a piece of teamwork that thwarts the barons temporarily.

Then, at night, Tristanne hides in the wood and keeps watch over the window where she knows Iseult is trying to sleep. To Rachel this feels like the attempt by both of them to keep one another safe in times of trial.

For her and Vonn it doesn't always work like this. Only in dreams do women lovers always behave well, forewarning one another of danger and getting the language right. In real life, hers and Vonn's, there are hiccups and inconsistencies that make interaction bumpy and rocky, but they are deeply in love and wanting to pull together and, with her birthday approaching, Rachel is profoundly grateful to Vonn for her willingness to take on board the pain and shifting realities that arise around her childhood memories of her father and his control of his castle, and her mother's bewilderment at the loss of self inside its modern walls.

* * *

On the evening before Rachel's birthday, the September moon rises over Mount's Bay, almost full, and curves a beautiful arch through patchy cloud in a sky which is deepening into thick blue twilight. Of course the sailors and astronomers are precisely accurate about the meanings of twilight, more so than so-called civilians such as Rachel, who simply like to 'stand and stare, begone dull care, be never so far from me,' to absorb floating moon-sky colours. Civil twilight begins as soon as the sun has set, and is a time when, as autumn becomes winter, people with jobs will hurry home from work, especially if they're in the city, as Rachel once was, working hard nine to five, hoping that the rush hour traffic won't be too snarled up this evening; and that the take-away or corner shop will still be open.

Rachel remembers all this as she stands holding her bicycle handlebars and steadying the basket of shopping in the supermarket car park, not quite ready to ride off with her back to the September moon. It takes her by surprise, because she's forgotten that it will be rising almost full here this evening, which is why she suddenly checks her watch.

The almost full moon rises just before sunset and, speeding

away westwards over the by-pass to Sennen, Rachel cycles as fast as she can in the hope of catching the sunset on the western side of the peninsula.

She's willing to admit that it's loony to be moonstruck like this, and to be timing her journeys around moonrise and sunset, but there is so much sky here that she finds herself wanting to take account of these phenomena. These days instead of knowing what time her train's due at Charing Cross, it's more natural to her to check her moon and sun almanacs, and to assess the tide times before walking on the long white beach.

An almanac, an almanac, find me moonshine!

So said Starveling the tailor in *A Midsummer Night's Dream*.

Now, as she cycles madly along the end of the land, Rachel recalls the moon rising into the roof of the open-air amphitheatre which hangs on the Cornish cliffs by Porthcurno.

A lovely moon, almost full, coming up right on cue. Magic.

She went to the Minack Theatre with Vonn and a whole bunch of women, armed with blankets and cushions, flasks, wine and food. The people in front of them had brought real knives and forks, plates and serviettes, ate off trays and drank from wine glasses and sat for an hour before the performance partaking in splendid dignity.

It was a fine production, starting at eight, before sunset, continuing through all the twilights, until, by the end, the sky was dark and clear for Titania's retinue to dance with candle lights.

It was a mill owner's daughter who built it. She fetched the sand herself from the beach, lugging it by the bucketful up the granite cliffs, to mix with cement, until her dream theatre was made to come true. Midsummer dreams: dreams in all senses, shifting realities, but under them the cliff is rock solid, holding up the dreams.

As Rachel cycles home, the holiday-makers have gone. Crowds have melted back to the cities, school children have begun their autumn terms, and the roads belong to the local people again. The Emmets – apt Cornish word for ants – have scuttled.

A blessing, thinks Rachel, reclaiming the road.

It's seven miles home so she pedals energetically, with the wind on her face. And there it is, the western sky, over the brow past Crows-an Wra, flaming and pulsing with the glow of sunset. It is spectacular tonight. Some patchy rain clouds that threaten imminent bad weather are illuminated from underneath by rose and apricot, inspiring Rachel to cycle even faster.

Signalling right, she turns finally into the road to the cove and stops on the very steep slope down into the village.

From where she is standing the sunset lasts longer than down in the cove, because of the angle over the horizon. A thin sliver of sharp red metal curves over the sea at the point of the sun's exit, and with a quick green flash, leaves.

Now the afterglow deepens, sending great flames of fire up into the sky, so that Rachel bends her head right back and stands, holding the bicycle, staring up at the overhead clouds, which look like scarlet leopards with furry black blotches. You could make out a complete Noah's ark of animals in the sky shapes if you had a mind to, but Rachel doesn't want to fix or predetermine any more of them, merely to absorb and enjoy them. She wouldn't swop this sky for a well-paid city job. Not now, not here, with so much to live for.

Back indoors, Rachel sorts out the fridge stuff and the rest of the shopping and then goes out into her two-strides-across garden and allows the rest of the twilight to happen around her. She recalls a passage from *The Diaries*.

Civil twilight is said to end when the sun is six degrees below the horizon, and nautical twilight begins. However, the sailors cannot use their sextants to measure the star altitudes relative to the horizon after the sun has dipped more than twelve degrees below. That is when the nautical twilight ends. But then the sun drops slowly through another six degrees, hidden from view, and that time is the time of astronomical twilight, the last phase of the dying of the light. Only after that can the sky be said to be truly dark.

You could call this the gathering dark, thinks Rachel, watching the red leopard skin fade away slowly until shades of blue-black begin to hint at themselves behind the last red and amber blurrings. This is earth time and sky time, time to be, and wait and feel. Feel the night coming on, feel the safety of it here now, and somewhere behind Rachel on the east side of the hill the almost full moon is climbing higher and higher.

The vocabulary of moon-rise and sunset has such lovely words, thinks Rachel, whose favourite is Azimuth. *The Azimuth is the angle measured clockwise around the horizon for the moonrise or moonset, sunrise or sunset.* When I get my new cat from Vonn for my birthday, Rachel tells herself, a great big fat tabby cat, who needs a good home, and whose name no one knows, I think I'd like to call her Azimuth. A wonderful word, which sounds like a sky goddess from ancient Libya, such as Neith, or a goddess of wisdom like Medusa or Minerva or Athene. I'll ask Vonn what she thinks of that.

Now, holding on to the garden wall and watching the stars begin to show in the dark sky, Rachel recalls the night, months ago, when she walked up the cliff path, watched the lights on the sea and thought of the ghost ships of childhood.

In order to peel away layers of the hidden self and come to terms with whatever else lurked there in those ghost ships, Rachel visited a woman healer, during the summer, a hypnotherapist who was recommended by Triss's friend the clairvoyant, also from St Ives. Vonn drove Rachel there on her days off, did some shopping during Rachel's sessions, and drove her home afterwards.

There were no other memories that surfaced during Rachel's healing process, beyond those that had already arrived in her own dreams. Much comforted by this, she now feels able to concentrate on what she knows rather than what might need to be known. What she knows, in relation to childhood, and what she experienced later as her parents' daughter, is enough for her to be working through, by itself.

Rachel swallows as she stands in the garden and watches the lighthouse beam of the invisible Pendeen lighthouse catch the top of the headlands to the north of Sennen cove. The other lighthouses aren't visible from Rachel's garden.

She would have to retrace her steps back up the cliff path, which she isn't inclined to do this evening.

As she prepares for her birthday, which this year falls on the end of September full moon – the famous blue moon of European skies – Rachel tries to shift the anger and distress from childhood into some kind of time perspective. She is aware that time flows and can flow in any direction. Measurement of time is a problem of theory. How you do it predetermines all the rest. Once you've set up the plan for measurement, it becomes a belief system. But it is only that, like any other belief system. It is not reality itself, not time itself. Any kind of measure of time is a belief system; even ones made by women for women based on moon and cycles. It is still not reality. That doesn't matter, so long as it is recognised for what it is.

But men like Rachel's father don't want to know this. The questioning of the theory of measurements is a challenge to them. The belief system is easily unfrocked. The structures of patriarchy then stand naked and visible. Men like Rachel's father find such vulnerability intolerable. Thus they restate their belief system and impose it as reality. Worse, thinks Rachel, they sustain it as unshakeable reality, and they do that with violence.

In such a way, there is no difference between John Markham, clockmaker of Salisbury, England; and Marcus Cunomorous, King of Dumnonia. That is the reflection.

Therefore the dreams of the memories become scenes in Act One of a family production. The interlude is followed by dreams of Tristanne and Iseult and dreams of love in the here and now. Taken as a whole, the dreams – both of memories and of archetypes – are the obsidian mirror's reflection of the child's and woman's reality. That is the reflection, also. Thus are the archetypes readily available to women for healing power. They are from within, which is where the healing also has its source. It is the only source.

This is so different from childhood, when sad little girls are led to believe that God comes from outside the Cathedral window: white light to constrain you; his time to contain you; in fifty-two names for Sunday.

Rachel is now trying to blend the child and woman into a whole where the child's needs are heard and cared for but not allowed to set all the mechanisms for the woman's timing. As a child she was hung up in the clock factory, by a velvet loop on the collar of her frock like a beautiful doll to look at: she was also Innana on a meat hook, naked in the underworld. Her anger oscillated to and fro with a pendulum swinging movement controlled by her parents when she was too young to comprehend.

There will be no birthday card from her father tomorrow because he is dead.

Preparing for her birthday, she wants to come to terms with the fact that her father, a clockmaker, ruled his family by patriarchal time. In her teens, she wanted him to admit that he was conscious of his place in society: that he could take for granted that there was family money, finance to fall back on; a safety net if he ever wobbled on the tightrope. But he wouldn't be drawn. So it was from his mother, her grandmother Markham, that Rachel teased out the story of who and what her father really was.

According to Gran, her youngest son, John, was usually a solitary child. He was very good with his hands; he was always taking things to bits and mending them; always making things. He also had a talent for languages which delighted his teachers.

Gran said that she was proud of all her sons. The eldest was Michael, who studied archaeology, went to work in the Andes, and wrote archaeology books. The middle one was Geoffrey, who studied history, gained a First and lived and worked in Singapore. Gran showed the photos of his wife and their swimming pool. The third and last was John, Rachel's father, who disappointed everyone with a lower-second degree in languages.

Gran's body language gave the game away. Rachel was sure, even as a very small girl, that John, her own father, was the deep favourite. Gran's tone and manner were especially soft when she came to talk of her youngest son.

'But he's a clockmaker, Gran. How come?'

'Well, you see, he wasn't very social. He didn't like living in halls in Oxford. He found lodgings in the town, and then he seemed happier, so we agreed that he could stay there to finish his degree. My dear Ralph, God rest his soul, wanted John to complete his education. Ralph was from a highly educated family. He couldn't bear the shame of John not finishing his degree. The men in the family all have degrees. That's part of Markham tradition.'

Rachel gulped. She wanted Gran to keep talking. Rachel was, herself, the apple of Gran's eye, now that they lived in England. She knew that it was Gran's wish that she, Rachel, would gain her A levels and be the first female of the family to go to university. John, her father, was odd boy out, in some senses. It endeared him to Rachel, who had to hear the rest of his story. She looked expectantly at Gran, and was silent, and smiled to encourage her to go on talking.

'Mr Lomax, with whom your father lodged, was a watch and clock repairer. Everyone who had a spare room took in students. It was an excellent way to make some easy money, especially if the student was quiet and obliging like my John. Now as I told you, Rachel, your father was always very clever with his hands. He became fascinated with Mr Lomax's tiny workshop and begged him to teach him the trade. Not that I knew of this until much later. All I knew of Mr Lomax was that he was a dear, kind man who was very good to my son. It was a clean, tidy place. Mrs Lomax had grown-up children nearby, and I think she was rather fond of John, in a motherly sort of way.

'Your father gave us many sleepless nights. We tried hard to discuss his future with him. However, he said it was quite secure. He would become a clock and watch repairer. I prefer to think of him as an horologist, naturally.'

The sound of her grandmother's voice is so strong in her head, as Rachel calls up images of Gran sitting there, being the family archive.

As Rachel recalls these stories from her teens, images arise from family photos: clear pictures of her mother, Truus.

Then, without speaking aloud, Rachel talks to her mother. What was it like for you being married to him? she asks silently. Did it sometimes seem as if our house, which happened to be called your home, was just an extension of my father's workshop?

Did it sometimes seem as if your present needs, past hurts and future dreams were all ticking clocks with wrong timing and unco-ordinated rhythms; some so soft you could hardly notice them until their alarms started ringing; others with crude, insistent loudness and chimes that did your head in?

Did some have the tendency to sound more important; did others need urgent attention, though they did not appear to from first appearance? And everything nineteen to the dozen and overwhelming, now and then, so that you longed for everything to stop for a precious period of uncharted time, so that we might all begin to laugh again, like we once did in Amsterdam?

It is now several months since the early intensity of the memories, which arose in the springtime. The images remain, but Rachel has begun a process of separating them from the emotional anguish which used to accompany them. Whenever she and Vonn talk about this it becomes clear to them that the Tristanne and Iseult dreams have been an integral part of a healing change, because as archetypes they have been mutually generated for the purpose of reflection. They assist in forming the question: what is reality?

Rachel looks up. Many stars, layers of beauty, revealed by the dark. Indoors there are long letters from Melloney and Oda, sending birthday wishes, and there is a beautiful card, showing the night sky in Africa, above the sleeping land. It's probably morning there already, and it occurs to Rachel that the stars still go on shining even when the sky is blue. It amuses her now to imagine this same sky with a pale blue daytime background and the same white fire constellations.

For some, the light is still travelling, but the fires went out long ago. Like Truus, thinks Rachel, sadly. Hidden all day. Who is she at night?

Truus, one generation: Triss, the next generation. Two women who happen to have similar-sounding names. Not reflections of one another, linked only by Rachel, yet both with Irish ancestry. Such realities occur frequently, the world over. As if the light from one sky/fire a million miles away just catches the edge of another, nearer sky/fire, and changes a millionth of a millionth of its energy. It happens all the time. The night sky is crowded. The air space dances with fire, exchange, exchange. She changes everything she touches, and everything she touches changes.

In Triss's tarot pack, Neith is the goddess of night, arching over the whole world, with stars on her body and Athene's chariot below her. In the book that accompanies the cards, which are round, Rachel had read that Medusa and Athene were once one and the same, and both represented wisdom with the night owl, Minerva. They aren't to be found in *The Diaries* because they aren't part of the Celtic tradition, which has its own goddesses of time and wisdom, but Rachel reads and studies and tries to put the pieces of a great cosmic time puzzle together.

Neith, Medusa, Athene: anagram; shape-shift to Azimuth, a woman's new name for a night creature; tabbycat: rescue; the night cat. Bast. The one who knows things.

Shape-shift from Neith/Medusa/Athene. Anagram. Azimuth. As if to reclaim Neith herself, an alternative form of reclaiming the night ... Rachel is now sure that it was night when her father would come into her room in the dark and sit by her bed, soothing her after another of her crying fits. But he himself had created her despair and her grief, her anger and her crying. How ominous seems this process now, to comfort a child whom you yourself have broken on the wheel of time. Stretched out by your ropes, your demands, your white light, your Cathedral window. And beyond to the patriarchal god of time: no capital letter; he is not worthy of it.

He is comforting her she is broken and weeping she has been rude to her mother his wife she is a sad and angry child howling when, semi-naked across his knee, being slappedslappedslapped on and on her skin is red her skin is sore she is a rude child ungrateful silly little cow she must learn to jump over the moon across the top of the grandfather clock when father god of the sky comes riding across the steppes on horseback he does not like to see the women and children laugh and play whenever they please.

As to her father, Rachel asks herself, what did time mean to a man like him? Was it simply that time meant money? He was a man whose death now splits her off from answers to her questions whilst simultaneously (which is itself a time word) it brings relief from confrontation. Strangely, thinks Rachel, whilst waiting for Vonn to arrive home from Truro, with the homeless tabby, there is a parallel between the ways in which I cannot ask my father, and the ways in which Vonn

216

cannot ask her mother. They are both gone, beyond the here and now, one through death, the other through dis-ease, and neither can help with healing. But in the case of Truus, there is still a possibility in the future of some bridge to new reality, and that is enough to know for now.

In *The Courage to Heal*, Rachel has read that some women try to reconnect, especially at birthday time, only to meet with more rejection, more anguish. She is in no hurry to create such scenarios, either in Truus or in herself. But the very fact of being in no hurry is itself a change which signifies stability, acceptance and, hopefully, compassion.

She notices that more stars are brightening up between patches of cloud, shivers, and returns indoors. Azimuth, if that's what she comes to be called, used to live in Truro, but was abandoned by her owners who moved up country. It was Consuela who told Vonn about the homeless tabby cat, who is being cared for by friends of hers.

However, since they are elderly women, with three cats of their own, one of whom does not like to have his territory invaded, he being a posh Persian pedigree called Lord Palmerston, Vonn and Rachel say they'll adopt the tabby. Vonn is on her way to Truro to fetch her, with a wicker basket borrowed from Lou and Annie.

Through help from Vonn, Rachel has had time to prepare for Truus's non-involvement with her birthday. She took the chance to write well ahead of time to Mieke and receive, also in good time, Mieke's loving reply. Their closeness isn't lost. She'd like to visit Rachel with the children next Easter, 'for a couple of weeks when Pete's away on business. Then we'll have some good time for each other, you and me.' It's a heart-warming letter. The thought of Mieke makes Rachel's belly feel warm.

But she bites her lip, thinking of Mieke's answer to a question she had posed. Indeed Rachel is right in thinking that Truus isn't going to mark Rachel's birthday. Truus is shocked at Rachel's behaviour, and, even now, refuses to accept that any of the Markhams who are unemployed are not simply workshy, an insult to the memory of John, her beloved self-employed husband, who worked up his clock business from nothing by the sweat of his brow and the skill of his hands. Everyone else should do likewise, according to Truus, unless of course the everyone else's are married women with homes to run and families to look after.

Rachel sighs, takes a deep breath, shakes herself until she is loose all over, then tidies up and gives Burn'ard, the aga, his dinner. He is now the au pair. They renamed him because they felt he should learn role reversal. He keeps the house warm, cooks the dinner on his forehead, dries the washing which hangs from his chin, and steam-irons it flat on huge silver plates on his head. It is hard to get a man to work like that, so Rachel is satisfied to employ him cheap for the winter season. He is up for review next April.

Perhaps, says Rachel to herself as she empties the ash pan and sets about making a meal for Vonn, separation may help me not to need Truus's approval any more. But that would take enormous strength, and who would want to put a time frame around that possibility?

* * *

Azimuth turns out to be very beautiful, though she never gets her full name. Usually she responds to Azzy, sometimes to Snazzy Azzy, a reference to her glorious appearance. She settles down well after being kept indoors until she reorient-ates to her new home, and after a little while, she shows much affection to both Vonn and Rachel, and a particularly strong liking for watching lesbian sex, from her favourite place on top of the chest of drawers.

'That cat,' says Rachel one evening, stretching luxuriously while the waves of pleasure continue to flow from her clit down her thighs and into her toes now limp with totality, 'that cat must have the loudest purr in the universe, whenever one of us is in this state of bliss.'

'One of us,' says Vonn, rolling her eyes in mock anxiety, 'who is this "one of us"?'

Rachel gathers all her limbs in from the edges where they seem to have floated off, rolls over, places her hand on Vonn's mound with an experienced touch, senses the urgent need that now rises in Vonn, and says amiably, 'Your turn'.

The fabulous tabby cat, who thought it was all over and had begun to groom her whiskers, sits up, peers over towards

218

the bed, settles down again, purrs approvingly, and for once turns her back discreetly.

* * *

Between the worlds two women sleep. Imagine this. Four arms four legs two bodies two heads. Dreaming into one another's dreaming. Dream. Image. Imagine.

A women enters. Who is she? Is she real? Is she spirit? Is she breathing? Another woman arrives, who remembers Carnac. They join hands and begin to swirl. Green grass, a ring of stones. They dance they dance a dance of bones.

Where are they now? Dans Maen. The dancing stones. Nineteen maidens in a trance, turned to stone, they dared, they dared to dance. Maidens merry, merry maids, they dance they swirl and twirl around they dance they dance on sacred ground.

Sacred grass, a ring of stones. How is this serpent dance of bones? Two figures turn and swing around a ritual dance on hallowed ground. A swirling serpent dance of night.

One of the sleepers stirs, surfaces slightly, turns in her sleep. The other responds, stirs, surfaces slightly, curls over, curls around her lover. Descend again to a ring of stones where dancers dance the dance of bones.

Two women dancers, holding hands, step and pause and point and step and skip and step once more, snaking in and out between the stones they dance they dance a dance of bones.

In the sky a thin-armed moon, silver sliver in the dome cradling a hidden shadow egg, dark egg dark shell a shadow shape, which holds inside its shell the tunes and all the words you ever need, a serpent song and a crescent arm, above the women dancing there. Dance they dance the crescent moon.

The moon is a serpent snake in the dome – the women dance they dance around, snaking the moon upon the ground, they dance they dance a dream a trance a serpent dance a thin-armed moon who holds a shape a shadow shape a cosmic egg a womb and eye. Image held in the dome of the sky, for ancient peoples used to know how the serpent moon would grow and dance her there with ritual sound and weave themselves on hallowed ground, dancing a serpent crescent moon, dancing the eggsnakewombeye tune.

The snake was the thin-armed moon in the sky, reflected from the sun at noon, and underground as spring and river, the serpent sacred flowed for ever with thread and blood and womb and loom, the snake was the earth and mirrored moon, and all was woman womb and tune.

The egg was the symbol shadow and dark holding the secrets of fire and spark and tune and words and women wise, in the dome of the sky when the moon was new, their feet they danced and sang and flew above the grass between the stones – they danced they danced a dance of bones.

Inside the egg inside the skull were written all the words of wise, at night in the dark in the thin-armed moon holding the secrets of blood and tune when music flowed between the stones as women danced the dance of bones.

Slip through time and land and sky between the worlds inside the womb and feel the pulse of woman tune. The words are old before the stones when people knew the dance of bones.

When women loved women and the earth was young and snake was sacred, and the old were wise and the shadow egg was the mother's eyes and blood was red and good and clean and thread was loom and snake and flow and people watched the new moon grow, reflecting all the noontide light they sang and drummed and tapped their feet and snaked the moon between the stones and danced and danced the dance of bones.

There was no rape no father right no child afraid to sleep at night, no girl to scorn nor vilify nor call her witch nor evil eye nor wife to beat nor daughter to sell no girl to bed against her will, when woman was moon and earth and sun and female was the sacred one, and people danced on ritual ground and twirled and sang and spun around; around the stones to the heartbeat drum spirals woven under the moon in drumbeat call and feet they flew above the stones as people danced the dance of bones.

And names of the mother were many and all when people heard the new moon call and some are written and some are forgotten and some are lost and some are torn and some are burned and some are raped and some are whipped around a stake and through the hearts of women broken some are gone and some are spoken. Some are harassed and vilified and some are tortured and denied. Some are hidden some rewritten and some are being rediscovered, danced and sung and some begun. Danced and tuned and newly worded, loved and hummed and re-recorded.

Know the names and know the call, know the names of one and all. All the mothers all the daughters, all the girls and all the babies, not forgotten lost in bones for we spiral dance the dancing stones. Under the noon and under the sky under the moon thin-armed and silver know the serpent know the call know the rivers freely flowing know the blood the new moon growing, know the woman's womb exploring know the woman's mind recording, know the body dreaming loving know the sleep the women sharing. Slow the dance the dance the caring sleep the women lovers daring. Slow the serpent, slow the rhythm, word the slowing. Open the books the new words making. Open the nights, the dream time taking. Careful lovers, bodies knowing. Fingers slow on nipples growing. Skin heat rising, slowly, slowly. Careful lovers bodies flowing. Women lovers, daring, knowing. Words from the moon, the night time sharing. Words from the egg, the pattern caring. Words from the womb, the new words, daring. Lesbian. Wisdom. Bodies. Sharing.

Slow the dance the night time sharing. Slow the snake the slither caring gentle stroking brushing sharing serpent waters rivers flowing the wet tongues wanting dragon breath. A dragon is a serpent with legs and arms the dragonwomen fired with life. The serpent lives and not on its belly. The Garden of Eden was not the first – the earth was there before the worst tales were told about Eve's evil. The dragon-women are living growing, the dragon breath is the serpent showing her form – out from under the sword of men; she will not stay where the men dismissed her. She will not obey the rules of them who kill and burn and tell their lies. The dragon breath will rise and rise and women dance and watch the moon and again shall learn the oldest tunes; and bones that once were turned to stone are living now and newly grown and serpentwoman sheds her skins and reads the words and then begins to dance and dance with loved ones knowing that she once more can make the tune that they danced they danced beneath the moon.

Between the worlds two women sleep. Imagine this. Four legs four arms two bodies two heads, dreaming into one another's minds. Time shifts and slips in the hours before dawn.

Deosil spiral into light. A dream, a dream a dance of night.

One of the sleepers stirs, surfaces slightly, her movements reflected by the other woman, who curls over, so they shift position without waking.

The dancers stop. One, who remembers Carnac, moves to the edge of the circle, picks up a harp, strums softly.

The other raises her arms to the sky, calling calling to the moon.

I am Iseult, daughter of Ireland.

I am the serpent dancer, I am the snake the dragon breath.

I call to the moon her sliver of light. In the dome of the sky. In the dark of night. I call to you the serpent moon, who holds in her arms a cosmic egg, dark, so dark we cannot make out her form. She is hidden from us but this we know. This egg you hold in silver arms contains the songs and words we need.

Release to us your music now, and write in the skulls of the women who sleep. Send your power send your songs send your dances send your words. Release release them now.

I am Iseult daughter of earth. I am the dancer snake and moon. I am reflection of the sun.

I know who I am and my name is woman. I know who I am and my name is earth. My beloved is a woman who strums this harp and we danced, we danced the dance of night.

Maidens dancing, dancing women, lovers with songs and fire and words. We are the dragons the serpents the snake power, gliding and sliding the waters of earth. We are life and love and words. We are songs and power and land.

I am Iseult daughter of Ireland. I am the serpent in the sky. My power reflected from the sun, the crescent shining thin-armed moon.

We danced. We danced a lovers' tune.

Iseult sways her outstretched arms, and changes her patterns of words, calling now to the sleeping women.

These are my healing powers, reflected from the sun. I am the solar power the lunar power a daughter from the oldest garden.

I am daughter of Danu, Anu, my ancestral mother, Mother of all Ireland.

Danu, my ancestral mother, is the old one; wise one; origin of all my people.

She is as old as Astarte, and a sister of Isis; sister of Libya, sister of Mawu; sister of Pele; sister of Kuan Yin; sister of Mahuea.

Danu is the land and I am her child. I am the land. I am the lover of a woman this woman whose fingers play the harp. We are the earth and all her gardens.

Know me now as Iseult the woman who comes with healing power. Know me now as Iseult, the dancer of the thin moon. For we are women we are land. We are the earth and she is us. When the earth dances, so do we dance; when the earth sighs so do we sigh. When the earth screams we scream with her. I was raped by a king. My garden harvested against my will. My garden older than the Garden of Eden. I call to you.

It is autumn now here in this land and time to me is unboundaried. I flow with the seasons and wax and wane with the moon, who is my healing power reflected.

Do not believe them when they tell you that first there was a garden with a woman called Eve who was bad and mad and sad. For it was not the first garden, and Eve was not wrong.

Do not allow them to name you as the devil's gateway.

I send to you both my healing power. You are the gateway of paradise.

Do not believe the hard cold men who are afraid of the serpent power.

The serpent is the land is the woman is the dragon breath. The dragon is the belly of the earth. Come now to a cave where the dragon sleeps and take upon you the serpent form.

Shed your old skin and emerge refreshed for the earth is the cave and a woman and a dwelling place. The earth is you and your belly, woman. In each woman there sleeps a curled dragon.

Time is unboundaried for me. I am Iseult, daughter of Danu. I was there in the early times when we danced the serpent dances. We watched the living sun, the woman sun, retreat into herself, down into her darkest depths where her healing powers live. Rest. Regenerate and shed a skin or two. The dragon is the serpent with legs of sunlight. She, the dragon, sleeps deep in her own bed. Earth in her mouth. Fire in a cave. Sunlight in the darkest dream. Woman who sleeps.

Women women sleeping women I call you in your dreams. I bring the healing power of the moon and the sun. The solar power the lunar power, the sky above and the earth beneath. The times of peace.

Do not believe them when they tell you war is the only way to be and has been always so. I was there before the wars and this I know. I call you now. My healing power shines at night above you and flows in the rivers and streams below you.

There is no woman in this land whose story I have not heard. I cannot save you all. Some will return refreshed renewed but, know this, there is no woman whose light will be extinguished for ever.

They will taunt me haunt me name me blame me. Call me sinful, selfish, evil. Call me the devil's gateway. Call me dyke and amazon. Call me dragon and snake in the grass.

They will put my name to scorn.

They will hound me harass me vilify me; hang me rape me burn me try me. They will torture me and dismember me; they will hide and deny me.

I will be homeless, birthing my children in the open air; I will be murdered in my bed; I will have my children ripped from me; and my eyes gouged out. Cold hands will freeze me; hard hands will harm me.

I am Iseult, daughter of Danu. I am the land, the orchard, the field, the valley, the hill, the forest and the garden.

Do not believe them when they tell you that Eve's was the first garden. I was there dancing the spiral dance, snake dance, dragon dance in the fields and hills of Ireland before men told lies about Eve. Do not believe them when they tell you that in my recent times I willingly lay under a king and let him have his route through my gateway into my garden. I was there and I know what happened.

Now I am here for you. I come and go as I please. I love whomsoever I choose. I choose this woman who plays this harp, while I call to you.

We emerge with dragon shouts and serpent songs. Our power rises from the depth of our bodies and we blend and join as one passing through our gateway to paradise and back to this grass where we dance our dance among the stones and write our music on your bones.

Do not believe them when they tell you that the dragon slayers are heroes. Frightened men who do not honour their mothers. Once there were serpent-dances in this land and then the people came to honour the sun's rest in the land, and watch her shed a skin or two and stand still. Sun stand still. Emerge again refreshed out of her woman self, a joyous birth from her womb of earth. So that if we pretended to slay the dragon we were only pretending, for what we wanted was to maybe touch a little of the old skin to know her power. We danced our dragon dances to welcome the sun and gladden her dance back from the cave and then to watch her dragon breath warm up the land again.

But the dragon-slaying men who came they wanted no share in our dances. Domination of their sisters was their aim and disrespect for their mothers.

They came with calls like conquer and fight; slay the dragon and rip out the tongue. Win and kill; with might and knight. They sought to own the sun.

The sun herself, the dragon breath the woman power reflected in the crescent moon who holds the egg the dark and hidden egg so safely in her silver arms. Those men murdered their mother the earth, to capture her dragon breath; men who raped the serpent and slayed her and turned the hallowed sacred names to terror. Dragon. Serpent. Lesbian. Snake. Names that once were sacred.

On thy belly shall thou go and woman shall be forever underneath.

Do not believe them when they tell you this was always

the way that things were done. I am Iseult, daughter of Danu. I and my woman lover were there and we know what happened.

Women, women, sleeping women dream on, and dream of us.

We dance for you. We are the snakes of the underground waters and we are the dragons of the magma of the earth.

We are the heat of the sun in the day and we are the rivers in the cool of night.

We are the serpent curled inside you ready to uncoil herself and release you to each other. Reach your hands to one another, touch the entrance to the dance. Together. Inside yourselves and visit the well-loved places. Open your throats and sing your dragon power. Open your hearts and know your snake power. Woman there is music for a serpent dance composed on the inside of your skull, enter yourselves and find this dance, find this serpent spiral trance.

I am the green of grass and the red of flame, the blue of water the yellow of bone. The orange of sunlight the purple of ling, the indigo of moonlight on the old quartz stone.

I am the green of heathland the red of tongue the blue of egg the yellow of gorse. The orange of rosehip the purple of sage the indigo of shadow in the season's turn.

I am woman and serpent one and the same; I am dragon and sunlight, the sky and the moon.

I am your lover, naked, in the afternoon.

I am the earth and nature egg and bird; I am the song and the singer the dancing word.

I said to the King: 'I am warning you. I am peaceful in the old times, polluted in the new. I shall pour my acid rain on you. I am rising and thunder and fire inside I am serpent and dragon and cannot be denied. I sleep now curled but watch me in the morning. I am woman and earth. You have had your warning. I am healing and hurting one and the same. I am wise I am young I cannot be tamed. Not for ever.

'I am dragon and serpent and amazon and dyke. I have this on my bone marrow. I have this in my blood. I have this in my breath. I am old and I am young. And you cannot have my tongue.'

I am Iseult. She, Tristanne. I am she and she is me. We are

both the daughters of this earth. We are the earth herself.

* * *

The wheel of the year turns from autumn equinox towards Samhain, the Celtic new year which starts on November the first, in the Kingdom of Dumnonia.

Nights draw in; lanes fill with dry leaves; skeletons of old hawthorns bend their backs against the windy sky; and the sun moves back down into the earth.

In an underground passage built deep into the womb of the great Mother, not far from the Merry Maidens' stone circle, on the south coast, Tristanne and Iseult lie in one another's arms, two nights before Samhain, knowing that the next day Tristanne will be banished from the Kingdom, and Iseult must return to King Mark or both of them will face certain death.

Sympathetic to their plight and not knowing that these are two women lovers about to share their last night together, a local farmer has given them straw and so they lie warm on the cold surface of the stones that line the fogou. Their last candles burn quietly in crevices in the granite blocks from which the fogou has been built.

Presently, Tristanne leaves the bed and creeps in the gathering twilight out of the passage and into the dim wood, to have a pee. Behind her in the west, the last rays of the late October sunset have faded. She tidies herself then turns to look down into the fogou and sees there the dark entrance now illuminated by the candle-light, a magical opening into another world. Here the ancient peoples came to meditate and chant; here the women gathered sometimes for a birth; here the shamans and shamankas prepared themselves for flights into the realm of spirits, there to find out what might happen in the future and how it may be divined through a communion with the past.

It is a beautiful, eerie and peaceful setting, in which the sounds are those of birds settling and roosting ready for the dark night.

Soon it will be Samhain, night of vigil for the spirits of the ancestors, flight of shamans and shamankas, bright dark space between the world of autumn and the world of winter, betwixt here and there, shifting this into that. Now and then.

Tristanne enters the fogou, bending slightly as there is only just enough room to stand. She steps carefully down the passage towards Iseult on the straw bed, thankful that the fogou is not inches deep in water as it can be sometimes, and grateful for those who built it down into the mother's womb so many centuries before.

She speaks. 'The day after tomorrow is the first day of winter. The first day of the rest of our lives, our first separation for all these months. I don't know how I am going to survive, my heart so grieving for you.'

'You are strong, a strong woman, you will survive and so shall I. You will find another, she who is also called Iseult. I have a premonition of such things. You will find warmth in her arms. Then you shall have the blessing of the triple Iseult: myself, herself and my mother, Queen Iseult of Ireland. Three in one and one in three. Here, take this lock of my dark hair and keep it in this tiny leather pouch. Then when you are sad you shall take it, feel it, hold it and remember I am with you in spirit though we are parted in reality.'

'In another woman's arms, you say? A premonition? How am I to make love with someone new when the one I long for is across the water from me, unsafe in the house of a king? We have not won against his armies, my love. We are not as powerful as he is, we are not able to direct our own lives here in this land and can find no home save this, a cave in the belly of the earth herself. How, then, am I to sleep at night, for anyone new will know that my heart stays here in Dumnonia, my soul lies always beside you?'

'In your dreams I will come to you, by night and by day,' replies Iseult. 'We are blended, you are my love, and I am Ireland, wedded for ever to Dumnonia, for this is the will of the fates. I accept my fate though it severs me from you. Tomorrow, the last day of autumn, we must part, so let us no more think of tomorrow but instead ask the blessing of the mother of winter to guide us through our time of despair and separation while I live for ever in the womb of night. Did not the great sailors who came to this coast tell us of Persephone? She who lived under the ground every winter, she who was separated from her mother, goddess of summer, she who became the queen of night, the queen of the underworld, the wife of Hades? Did I not have warning of this at the autumn equinox, when the trees began to weep their leaves for the sadness of the end of summer? There I scattered pins upon the waters and counted the bubbles and knew then that we had only half a season left together and that, with the onset of winter, I must lose you, my woman, my lover, and face the return of the sun into the body of the mother, face the extinguishing of the light that is our fire, our passion, and cannot become the fire of our hearth?'

'I know that what you say is true. It was so. The well waters do not lie.'

'For the omens did tell me that winter would part us. I am Iseult. But my name could have been Persephone. I am Iseult, daughter of Ireland, greening the land here in Dumnonia, for the King cannot get his power except by bedding with me, and it is my task, my duty, my fate if not my desire to be responsible for the vegetation here in this new country. This I must do. The fates decree it, the story must be concluded, and the loss of you shall call forth the dying of the land each autumn, every year, for the rest of time. When the trees weep, know me, that I weep for you, Tristanne. Your sadness shall be my sadness, your heartache shall be my heartache, your winter shall be mine also.'

Iseult touches Tristanne's face and continues, 'Now let us extinguish these candles and take control of the dark for ourselves, dedicating our love to the long nights of winter, for ever, in remembrance. Remember Carnac. Did not your foster mother, the wise Floreate, inform you that legends will grow up about us, this love we hold for one another? They will tell of a young man wise and strong who came to Dumnonia and was the one true love of the wife of the King of that new country. And as the winter nights unfold, so shall the cloak of darkness fall over us, and women only will know that we lay here, in this fogou, in the womb of the great mother, making love all night, two women whose bodies move as one, warm and wet and wanting, whose tears are the rain that make the crops grow in the spring, who bleed into the fertile soil so that every plant may thrive.'

'So be it, then, my love,' says Tristanne, voicing herself softly so that her words blend into pieces of dark which fold around the women on the straw. 'In the morning when we leave here, you for the castle and a life with Hades himself, though to the world he is known as Marcus Cunomorous, King of Dumnonia, and me for the sailing ship that will carry me across the waters, back home, from whence I came. In the morning, when we leave, the land here will carry the indentation of our two bodies, a warm shadow which we make here now, making love upon this earth, in this earth, carrying inside us the winter sunshine, in the mirrors of our souls. No impression could ever be warmer, left by two women lovers, in any land. They will tell of us for centuries to come.'

Then, in total darkness, Tristanne and Iseult invoke the spirits, make their promises, and rededicate their passion. When their rites are complete they bid the spirits farewell.

Then all night they blend and touch, murmuring sometimes, crying out sometimes, wet and soft, leaving no inch of one another's bodies unpassioned, their hands buried deep inside the warm wetness of their personal fogous, the passages that slide into their own bodies, taking them into the deepest caves inside one another, taking them into pulsing places that throb with raw loving, tempestuous and satisfied. This night must last them forever. There will never be another and with the certainty of separation, the dreaded power of fate, they carry themselves across oceans of want until satiated; they wrap themselves in one another and, in the spirit-filled darkness, hold each other gladly-sadly enfolded in the movement of the night.

'Iseult, my love, hear this. I predict, this night, the eve of winter's eve, that there will come a time, in the future, when women will visit this magical underground place, and they will hear the echo of our heartbeats, and they will feel, even in winter, the warmth of the sunshine, which is the passion we have for each other.

'In this land they will see the breasts that are our breasts; in this wood they will see that this fogou opens into the earth's body, which is a woman's body where we lie. Here we touch our fingers inside each other's fogou, loving here, finding our warm pulsing centre, our woman loving. We cannot lie here together for longer than this night, our last night, but they can. So, to the survival of their love we offer up the passion of our own.'

230

On the morning of 31st October, the eve of Samhain, in the early hours of dawn, Vonn reads from *The Diaries*.

This is my last Samhain – or to use the words of my Cornish ancestors, Cala Gwave, the Calends of Winter – in this life. I approach this transformation. I am afraid, of course I am. So this is my personal message, not my usual style here in these notebooks. But I am compelled to write in this way, this day, for death is near. She calls me now. It is appropriate, the timing. Samhain is the night of my ancestors. I prepare for them. I write urgently, with a sense of destiny.

Come. Come with me. To the place of night. To the place of beauty. To the cave of the great mother. The old one. The wise one. The Cailleach.

Come. Wear comfortable clothes. Bring something to rest on. Settle yourself. Be safe.

I have my journey to share with you.

Come.

You are in a beautiful inland valley. It is one of your favourite landscapes. The route is easy, in the night. White markers reflect in your torchlight beam.

Ahead you see a huge entrance to a cave. In front of the cave a group of women are seated, around a fire. They laugh. They are talking and eating.

You approach them. Recognise your friends. They greet you. One of them hands you a candle. You cup your hand around the flame. Then you pass by the group and continue on towards the entrance.

It is dark. Very dark. The soft floor is dry. You move slowly towards the back. The floor is soft but you can wheel your chair over it easily, if needs be.

There in the rocks to the left side is a much smaller entrance. It is flat to go in. There is just enough space for you to enter, with your chair, if needs be. A perfect size. You hold the candle low down. You enter.

It is small, unevenly shaped, with curving walls and roof. In the middle there is space for you to sit, and a stone to sit on, if you wish.

You sit. You place the candle down beside you.

It is dark, but not impossible to recognise the pictures painted all over the walls and roof. There are trees, plants, animals, women. There are many breasts. There are spirals and rings; cup marks and chevrons.

You absorb them, slowly, in your own time. There are leaves. Hands. More breasts.

You are safe. You reach down and extinguish the candle.

It is totally dark. The dark surrounds you. Holds you. Once before, you floated in the dark like this, inside your mother. You remember now. You swam.

You are safe. You survived that dark. You were born from it. You breathe the dark. Your eyes understand the dark.

But you were taught perhaps as a child to fear the dark. There are demons, maybe. You internalised external fear. Then when you were grown, you had your fears confirmed. You learned that the demons can be real. This is true. But you are here in this place because you have already survived them.

Now the demons return. Haunt you. Taunt you.

You are alone with them. They sometimes choose to visit this place.

They do not have the power to harm you now.

You have faced them before. Will do so again.

Your friends are by the fire at the entrance to the large cave.

Leave me, you say to the demons.

Dissolve now. Melt back into the dark.

Leave me now. I wish you no harm. I demand that you depart from here. You are not wanted here.

I face you now. Faced by me you must dissolve.

For I am strong. In here. This is my womb. My home.

My inner self. My own dark. Not yours. Mine.

Once you were real and I was not strong. You hurt me then. You are every ism that came from outside me. You are every human fear that has arisen to challenge me.

You are my demons. But you cannot harm me now. For now I am strong. I will stay strong. I have the power to face you. You were my worst demons. There can be no worse fear than you. And I have the inner strength to meet you. To challenge you. And I do so now. Here in this place where I am home.

You breathe slowly now. They slowly dissolve. Into the floor, into the walls, into the roof.

Your trust in this place is yours. It is the place of your inner dark. Your healing space.

Your own time. Your creative core.

You know that there are walls in here, but it is dark, dark in here. You put your hand in front of your face. You cannot tell where your hand is. You feel your hand move. Then you feel your imagination move. You move with it, into the walls, through the painted pictures which you know are there. And beyond.

There is no boundary.

You are beyond walls. Beyond boundaries.

Your spirit knows no limit. You are moving through the walls. The universe is vast now. Black. Your spirit moves into the vastness and the stars are infinite. You are yourself, inside; yourself, outside. You are unboundaried. Self and beyond self.

This is the obsidian mirror. The mirror of the creative inner dark.

Beyond your worst fears is your own dark. The dark is very beautiful here.

You were born from this place. You always hold this place inside you. And to know it, you will face the demons and dissolve them. They are every ism that came from without you: they are every human fear to challenge you.

Your spirit journeys between the stars in blackness, the deepest dark you have ever known; the place where your language begins; your pictures begin; your pots are made; your cloth is woven; your growth begins; your songs arise; your dances are formed; your every dream is seeded. The place where love begins and your every cell is born. Know this place. Make something from it.

You journey slowly now. In a long slow arc begin to return.

Back to the pictures on the walls where you sit. Through the pictures into the small, enclosed dark space. Floating there. Joining your body. Into your body. Seated on the stone. In the middle of this place.

You rest a while. You breathe the dark.
I am ready, you say into the darkness.

You pick up the candle. Your friends arrive at the entrance to the small cave. They bring you a flame. You light your candle.

You are aware, there, adjusting to the pictures which leap and dance now on the walls around you, in the unaccustomed candle-light.

Thank you, you say, to the place, to the walls, to the pictures, to the universe, to the origin.
You leave, slowly. Join your friends.
Move through the large cave with the dry soft floor.
There are greetings from the others, by the fire.
You rest there, then you sleep.
The caves will always wait for you, whenever you need the dark.

* * *

According to *The Diaries of Elizabeth Somerville*, Hecate stands at the crossroads on the night of the eve of Samhain. She is the old one, the wise one, the crone. In Irish Gaelic she is Cailleach, and her hill in County Meath is Sliabh Na Cailli.

In Triss's tarot set, comprised entirely of round cards, the crone wears a cloak of purple, the colour of night.

This winter, Clare is less afraid of her disability and is less sceptical about her own healing powers. When, in November, Triss does a reading for the coming months, Clare finds herself face to face with Hecate, a major arcana card, centrally placed.

Hecate is the significator, the 'who am I?' question. She brings challenge with her, because there are three ways at the crossroads and it is up to Clare to work out what they are or which one to take. Hecate carries a lantern, as if to remind everyone that once there was another old wise woman who sent a message to them all – a woman called Warning who lives on a hillside and has a staff of seasoned hawthorn. Months ago, in Rachel's dream, Warning was wearing an old green coat and gumboots. She was lighting fires instead of carrying a lantern.

Clare and Rachel talk this through one November evening, while Triss is visiting Consuela in the nursing home.

'What do you think Hecate means in the reading?' asks Clare, sitting in the firelight with Enya's *Shepherd Moons* playing on the deck in the corner of the cottage.

'It's what you think that matters, the reading is for you.'

'It usually means a period of solitude. But Triss and I are in love, and she shows no sign of wanting to move back out.'

'But you're not together every minute, are you? She's out and about a lot, isn't she?'

'She's very busy. And to be honest, Rae, I couldn't be doing with her here all the time, I still need to rest and be very quiet. I'm happier with that now. I feel as if I'm actively waiting, does that make sense?'

'What d'you mean exactly?'

'I don't think I'm so passive now. I'm getting better, even if it's going to take a while. If I want to do something I wait a week and then try it, but I do at least try it. I managed to go back to London when Mum broke her hip, and I built in my rest times, and I got through it. I pattern it much better and I don't sink back into despair like I did. But the solitude thing in the tarot was a bit scary.'

'Well, I don't know, I'm no expert on tarot, but you don't seem so frightened of everything these days, more like your old self.'

'Yes. My confidence is coming back. Sometimes I need the wheelchair, sometimes not, which confuses local people who, like most other local people, wherever they are, have stereotypes about people with disabilities. Either you need a wheelchair or you don't.' Clare pauses, then adds, 'I'm more resilient now, and I don't care so much what people think. If I need my chair I use it, if not it stays folded in the lobby, ready and waiting. The chair might be passively waiting, but I'm not. I'm waiting actively.'

'So the solitude isn't so huge, not so threatening?'

'True. That's interesting. Besides, I can walk a lot more and do the garden. Hecate's herbs are nettles. The witches' herbs from All Hallows. So when the garden was cleared we burned them and it felt like a new start.'

'In *The Diaries*, Samhain – All Hallows – is a new start. The Celtic Year starts on the first of November.'

'Funny to think of winter as a new start. I like it.'

'Oh, so do I. I haven't had a chance to tell you, but my dreams don't feature Iseult any longer. Not since Samhain. But they do contain a young girl. It's me. I'm in my own dreams now. Feels good.'

'Time for new growth, for all of us? I hope. But the three roads confuses me a bit.'

'It's whatever you want it to be. It can't tell you anything. It can only be a tool to guide you.'

'Triss thinks it's not her way or my way; it's about finding a third way, our way, you know, working out who we are together. I quite liked her saying that. I trusted that.'

'Maybe that's the key. It's what you feel and trust that'll be right for you.'

'Do you have all these kinds of questions, Rae? I mean about ways forward?'

'Yards of them. Especially about anger. Finding a way to let it out without attacking anyone, mainly Vonn, of course. She's there, so she's the one who gets it. And vice versa.'

'Are you frightened of anger? I am.'

'I was last summer. When we had the row at Iseult's Ford. Well, we never did find the ford, but you know what I mean.'

'So what's changed?'

Rachel searches for words. 'It's not easy to explain, but I'll try. If I was hurting about something, I used to feel I was under attack. I'm fairly sure it comes from me and Mum. There was a lot of attack, so if ever I was hurting when I was little it was glued to a feeling of being attacked. I didn't have any words for it. I'd be very distressed, terribly angry and yelling my head off.'

'Go on.'

'We – you and me – had a good few rows when we were at college, if you remember?' (Clare nods and they both smile at the timespan. College seems so far away from their present friendship.) 'Well, with Vonn this summer and through the autumn we've been looking at how to pull apart the bits of the situation, process, whatever, melt the glue. So now if I'm hurting about something I don't automatically assume I'm being attacked by her. I'm beginning to trust that she isn't intending to attack me. And mostly she isn't actually attacking me, though she sometimes does and that's hard.'

'Go on.'

'Sure?' (Clare nods again and so Rachel continues.) 'Well, it used to be a sort of straight line process. Hurt. Therefore I am under attack. Therefore she is attacking me. Defence. I am being attacked so I must attack back. Followed by swift attack by me. And of course I was verbally vicious because that was all I could be as a child.'

'Oh, Rae. That's a lot of stuff. But, when it's happening, how does it get stopped?'

'It doesn't always, and that's dangerous. I have to be careful. So does Vonn. The main un-gluing is between feeling hurt and going into attack.'

'But we have to let out our anger. Anger makes women really ill.'

'I know. So we're trying to learn how to say that something is hurting us or to listen when the other one is hurting. Not feel attacked when one of us says she's hurting.'

'So if Vonn is saying she is hurting you'd have to manage to stay very calm so you could listen to her?'

'Yes. Jump back and take a deep breath rather than what I used to do, which was jump in all guns flashing.'

'Sounds very difficult.'

'It is. Because our mothers are huge there, in our psyches, having a go at us, or in Vonn's case, withdrawn into cold anger that is body language as well. There's quite a complex mental image. Vonn's saying she's hurting and I'm taking a step back and trying to separate the image of her and my mother stuck like Siamese twins in my head and they're both speaking at once; and I have to separate them every time it happens. But once I'd done it a few times it was quicker after that and didn't seem so violent. But it really was like a Siamese thing. I mean, I wanted them independent and both surviving. I didn't want my mother to die in the process because then I'd be guilty and it'd be worse.'

'So while you're trying to keep them both alive, Vonn's still talking?'

'Yes, but she knows now that I will listen to her, so she can afford to take a deep breath as well, sort of step back and take her time to tell me.'

'You must love each other an awful lot to give it this effort.'

'It was make or break for a while back in the summer. I had a strong sense of Iseult at the time, a very powerful presence. Holding me, coming through in dreams, and I thought, Now you look here, Rachel Markham, this is a big one! Don't mess this one up.'

Rachel starts to laugh at herself and Clare joins in, thinking of the past and present. It seems to them both a long time since they were lovers and students, but they know each other well and there's a gladness for each other that is real.

'Are you less angry nowadays?' asks Clare.

'It's hard. There's an awful lot of anger inside. Some of it's mine from childhood; but some of it's more of a cosmic rage on behalf of all women everywhere, and all the little girls who are abused, many of them at this very moment.'

'Yes. Justifiable. It's all tangled up at the bottom of the pond and if you get a stick you can easily stir up the whole mess.'

'You've got anger around disability?'

'Hell-bent on destruction sometimes. Triss goes out. I think the Hecate card might be for those times, you know, when I need to scream and throw things without anyone around. Just because Hecate's the crone doesn't mean she has to stop screaming. It might be wise to scream. Does the solitary woman have to be smiling and benign? Surely we have plenty of strong images of screaming witches, harpies, furies. I could go for that.' Clare is pleased by the thought of allowing herself to scream the walls down, and no one daring to stop her from making all that racket. She adds, 'Sounds nearly as good for me as orgasm, and I make enough noise then!'

Rachel laughs too, then says, 'When I'm angry I go to the edge of the sea, and I pound up and down by the waves, sometimes screaming, sometimes just muttering like a mad woman. No one can hear. In London I used to scream in the car with the windows closed, driving around, d'you remember?'

'Get me a padded cell, quick.'

'Me too.' They share laughter, that's hard-edged, sharp and pointed. They need to scream with good reason.

'I'll fetch the coal and get us a cuppa, d'you want one, Clare?'

Presently, from the kitchen, Rachel calls, 'What does Triss do with her anger, then?'

Clare calls back, 'She digs, till the sweat pours off her. Garden's coming on a treat.' When Rachel returns with the tea, Clare says, 'It's very interesting, Rae. I mean, before I met Triss I'd have never looked at tarot or anything like that. You've been doing all this Tristanne and Iseult stuff and somehow here in this place, you and me, we're beginning to find what we need to get ourselves sorted. Hurt or anger or dis-ease. All that stuff. I think it was wise to come here, even if it is a terrible challenge. It brings you face to face with yourself, it makes you do the work. Healing, I mean, though I never used such words before. I just got sick and it wasn't until my body said, "Stop, no more", that I began to listen. My body knew, because it kept on telling me, but I didn't do anything about it.'

'I don't agree with that, Clare. You knew you had to move and that's why you came here. At a very deep level you already knew that.'

'I accept that. Oh, it is good to see you, Rae. We haven't had a talk like this for ages. Being in love, I suppose. It crowds everything and everyone out.

'This tarot thing intrigues me, because Hecate is goddess of winter, and of the dark. I think back to Lughnasad, and the imagery of the meditation. It was the first I'd ever been to. I wouldn't have gone but for Triss. But it meant a lot to her, so I went. Now I think a bit about the dark days, and how happy I am, and how I plant seeds in the dark, and cover them with paper, to encourage them. The light would burn them when they're just starting off. I was thinking about that yesterday.'

'It is only in New Age thinking,' Rachel says, 'that the light is all-important. It puts too much emphasis on the healing power of light.'

'The seeds would burn,' Clare repeats. 'There's such a thing as too much light. People who worked in Stalin's salt mines went blind from the dazzle of white light on their retinas. The light killed them. And governments have known for a long while that if you keep prisoners in an all-white room with no other relief from colour they become rapidly disorientated and descend into madness. The British Government denies the use of white light of course.' Clare shrugs with one of her characteristic angry shrugs, reminding Rachel of the Clare of their student days, and all the Brits Out of Ireland campaigns. She adds, 'So why this obsession with light itself?'

Afterwards, back in Melloney's cottage, Rachel sits and rocks by the aga, thinking that the gift of winter in a granite cottage with small windows is the gift of a cave, a fogou, but more comfortable because this is a warm, dry little house, not a passage down into the earth. In this enclosed dark place you can come face to face with your deep centre, the place of the most fear, the place of the brightest creative dark. It is the same place, inside a woman, thinks Rachel, who hears Vonn's voice in her mind: 'The dark phase of the moon. You have to trust she will return.'

Vonn is working, so Rachel goes to bed alone. Falling asleep, she imagines Warning, the crone, the Cailleach, becoming fused with night and the goddess of winter, representing the wisdom of a woman who is no longer menstruating, whose wise blood is held, now, inside her, and from which she derives the energy of creativity. She remembers the myths and legends she has read of the old wise women all over the world. Spider Grandmother, who spins a web of destiny. Copper Woman, whose daughters carry her knowledge down the generations. Cailleach who sits on an old stone seat, on her own mountain, in Ireland, smoking a pipe and turning the earth to face the sunrise. Mawu, and Pele and Mahuea; Kuan Yin, and all the faces of wisdom.

As Rachel falls asleep, she remembers that Iseult has gone, and that if there is a young girl in her dreams tonight, it is she herself, a child called Rachel.

* * *

It is winter and in an open boat a girl is sleeping. The sea is dark bluish-green under a new moon. The tide is low, flat and steady as the boat runs aground. From a hillside an old woman wearing an old green coat and gumboots, carrying a staff made of seasoned hawthorn, makes her way down to the sandy shore.

The girl wakes up and cries, feeling abandoned, cold, hungry, and frightened, but the old woman has a kind face. The girl steps up on to the edge of the boat and clambers down on to the shore. She walks with the old woman to the hillside and enters the old woman's house.

It is a safe place. There is food and a warm fire. In the corner of the room there is a clarinet. The old woman plays many wonderful tunes which make the girl want to dance.

She has never before heard such evocative music, and the sounds fill every part of her body. She dances and dances until she becomes the music. There is no separation. She is the music and the music is her. She feels as if she is a plant in a garden, filled with growing. She is a tree whose branches move in the wind. She is a bird flying high, its throat wide, singing and singing. She is a girl dancing and she is all these things and still the old woman plays the clarinet and the notes fill every part of the house, through the windows out into the open air, flowing down the hillside, along the sloping path, down the lane to the long white beach . . .

* * *

So now there begins from Samhain onwards a period of intense music for Rachel. She comes alive with enthusiasm, composing with Vonn, whose idea for an opera based on Tristanne and Iseult becomes transformed into a musical piece of theatre, in which several of the local women begin to be involved. Rachel calls forth from a hidden place inside herself the music of Iseult, in melodies and rhythms that delight the others. Never before has she given so much time to her music. She fills hours of each day and begins a long process of using her creative inner dark in harmony with the dark of winter, when it is literally dark, to pour out her ideas on sheets of music, composing for scenes and characters as the idea begins to take hold.

Clare and Triss both play the guitar, and Annie, having

given up her career as a journalist, finds that she wants to write again, so begins to juggle with scripts and publicity. Lou likes drumming, but has no formal training, and has only ever drummed for celebrations like the maze-walking, but she has a beautiful mellow bodhran and a small wooden drum and begins to play with Celtic rhythms to accompany some of the Tristanne and Iseult scenes.

The laughter and networking begun at Lughnasad are being extended and there are cross-currents of interest and experiment.

Rachel, who used to hate winter, and dreaded the sun setting at four in the afternoon, now finds an excitement about the landscape and the relationship between light and dark that is famous to artists of the Newlyn School and the St Ives School in all the artistic records of the peninsula. However, to Rachel, the reflection is through music rather than paint, so that her question to herself is: how can she turn the colours into sounds so that when people hear the sounds they see the colours that she sees initially?

She is so fascinated by this question that days become nights become days and suddenly it is December and she has been so busy that time itself has become a liveable balance of reality and dream, music and silence.

And this brings her full circle to a stone circle, Boscawen-Un where she met Triss Martin.

Alone there in early December, she holds on to the quartz stone and lets the music flow in and out of the stones, into and out of her body, inside and outside her mind. She is entering her own creative centre and this is not what she thinks of as winter.

Winter, in her past, is cold and heavy and to be struggled through. But here, though the mist hangs low today over the breast hills of Chapel Carn Brea and Bartinney in the distance, and cobwebs string themselves along the gorse bushes and the grass is soaked with last night's rain and the air is chilly, the circle is filled with light and sound and with echoes from the sixth century into which the dream characters have disappeared, back into the mist.

Since's Vonn's fogou dream, the sixth-century women lovers have departed. So it is their memory that is being kept alive by the musical theatre piece which Vonn and

Rachel are composing about them. This winter, thinks Rachel, is a winter of deep contentment and creative challenge that any artist would be grateful to be faced with. When the music pours from the gorse bushes in through the gaps in the stones and you are standing there holding on to the quartz stone and the other eighteen stones are maidens dancing, poised for the notes from your clarinet, poised for the rhythm of your drums, then you are brimming with a sense of good fortune, because you are journeying to the centre of yourself.

* * *

The days grow shorter. By the end of the first week of December, dawn doesn't begin until after seven in the morning and sunrise doesn't happen till after eight o'clock. By half past four the sun has set again, but in this period of long winter evenings neither Vonn nor Rachel feels any sign of depression, this year, because of everything that they are reaching out for.

Sometimes, in the late afternoon, they walk together on the beach at low tide watching the reflections of the house lights from the cove in the long, shallow flat mirrors of water now sliding slowly on the wet sand, and it seems much more than four seasons since they met and fell in love.

At about four o'clock the red winter sun touches the horizon, melting into the sea, spreading its colour through the water and shimmering the whole surface with vermillion and scarlet, like red metallic paint that floats on the surface and swirls around the rocks and Longships lighthouse. Sometimes the coastline is blurred by mist and sometimes there is no sunset to speak of, just a soft, furry smudge where the sun should have been.

'I was thinking about last night's dream,' says Rachel as they walk at a very low tide. 'You know I said it was about the Cailleach, but now I think she may have been fused with a much older version of Iseult. Their faces were so similar, but I didn't think of it when I first woke up.'

Vonn replies, 'Versions of the same woman? Young and old, the essential healing power? It's interesting that we don't dream directly of Tristanne and Iseult now.'

'D'you think that's because they finished passing on their messages?' says Rachel.

'Perhaps their story is told. I don't know. They might come back.'

'It doesn't feel as if they will. I'm not sure, either.'

'It's more peaceful without those dreams. I wake up refreshed.'

'A bit of a relief?'

'Yes, a relief. It's been very intense this year, hasn't it?'

'You can say that again. I love you, Vonn. We're doing all right, aren't we?'

'We are. I love you so much, Rae, and the music is soaring.'

'Takes me right back to the start, you noticing my clarinet with the light catching the edge of the music stand.'

'Sharing it – it's beyond words.'

'Literally.'

Their laughter is light and bubbly, and they link arms walking along the shore. 'Yes. I'm glad.'

They walk the full length of the beach and clamber down over the rocks to the place where they first met. There they sit watching the low, low tide and the fast-fading twilight. Here by the rocks the sea darkens to deep grey-green and is bluish-brown in places where the angle of the last rays can't reflect in the water, although there is slow white foam which bounces the light along the edge of the tide. They listen to the lapping sounds, and they feel a breeze gathering strength as it starts to catch the foam and flip it backwards.

Presently Vonn says that, despite the relief of the dreams having gone, she also misses the contact from her dream characters and that she has a sense of loss and some bewilderment.

Rachel has her arm round Vonn as she replies, sitting beside Vonn on a huge boulder that protects them from the tide, which is just beginning to turn. 'D'you mean because in the original legend it didn't end with Tristan's banishment to Brittany?'

'Yes, exactly. All through the spring and summer after we met, we dreamed into each other's unconscious minds, we lived ate and slept with Tristanne and Iseult. They seemed real to us and we neither of us really knew how that happened or why it did. We woke each other up at night just from the power of the dreams, and talked it all through all the time. We went to Iseult's Ford . . .'

'Which we never found – though we did in a way because we waded through some awful stuff and we're still together . . .'

'Exactly. Then we came to winter. Here we are on our beach, on our stones, but Tristanne and Iseult aren't here any longer . . . it's so strange, even though it's a relief.'

'Unfinished business?' Rachel watches the incoming tide for a while and looks at the horizon which is now unevenly dark, with an indigo line separating the sea and sky. 'We could say goodbye to them, if you like.'

'How so?'

'We take a last look at the legend in *The Diaries*, and then we close *The Diaries* for a while and light a candle and say goodbye to Tristanne and Iseult, sort of properly, after dinner. Or we could take ourselves in the dark to Alsia and say goodbye to them at the well, something like that. They did that kind of thing in their century all the time and I know we're not into ceremonies like they were, but maybe we could finish this business, before winter solstice. I think so. A feeling of it came just now.'

'Why not? Can I think about it on the way home? We could go all the way back along the edge of the waves in the dark. The cove lights are lovely back there in the shallows. I'd like to be quiet, let the idea take hold, if that's okay?'

'Fine by me. I love walking with you. I can listen to the waves.'

* * * *

On the night of dark moon, Vonn and Rachel make their way to the hidden magical well of Alsia in the heartland of West Penwith.

Over the rise of the first field they trudge, carrying a torch and wearing wellingtons and warm clothes. The dew is heavy on the dark ground. Down the sloping wet field they make their way, bearing to the right, until they reach the stream and curve of hawthorn trees whose grey-blue lichen gleams grey-silver in the torchlight beam.

At the gate to the enclosed area they pause and hug tight. Then silently they open the gate. Once inside, they light candles which they float in the water of the low shallow well. Above the well a single hawthorn with a woman-shaped trunk and old appearance hangs like the Cailleach, witnessing and attending.

On the bank, near the stream, they place a sprig of honeysuckle entwined around a branch of hazel. Quietly they say goodbye to Tristanne and Iseult, and touch each other's faces with water from the well. They do not incant, or chant, or sing or dance.

'Goodbye,' they whisper. 'Thank you.'

They hold hands and watch the reflections of the flickering candles in the water of the well. Around them the night is dark, the stars hidden behind a thin cover of cloud. This is the most gentle of the wells of West Penwith, the hardest to find – you have to know where it is, to be shown this place by someone who already knows it. Next spring the thin trickle of sound of the water leaving the well and running into the stream will be one of many sounds when the sheep give birth and the bleating echoes around the valley here. But now, tonight, on the night of dark moon, with only a few days to winter solstice, on a still night with no wind, the only sound is that of the water. It is enough. For although this well is the gentlest, the most hidden and apparently the sweetest, it is known to be a powerful place, where people have come since long before the Celts for divination and healing. It works, and no one knows how, on a time lapse. Be careful what you ask for at this well. You are likely to get it.

This they know. The Cailleach tree, she of the winter's night, the dark moon, the three ways, the inner strength, she holds her branches steady, like arms with hands, over this place.

They light a dish of dried sage and nettles. They walk around the enclosure allowing the smoke to waft freely.

'To the women of the past, be peaceful.'

'To the women of the present, be named.'

'To the women of the future, be whole.'

* * *

246

Woman. Vonn. Woman. Rachel. Side by side. Warm bodies under a duvet. Arms legs thighs entwined. Celtic image. Imagine this.

Woman. Vonn. Woman. Rachel. Lips touching mouths open, tongues warm exploring. Eyes open. Twilight. Warm room. Low light. Candles.

Woman. Vonn. Woman. Rachel. Shift position shape-shift. Woman is owl flying. Woman is raven calling. Woman is recreated from flowers in the spring. Woman is the warm dark twilight blending to mysterious night. Shape-shifting. Hold this moment. Smile. Create statue women lovers arms enclosing. Dissolve the moment, move together, stroking touching. Mouth on mouth and feel the changes.

Woman you are the raven soaring. You are the cloud above the trees. You are route to the earth beneath. Root of the earth. You are the earth.

You are air and fire and earth and water. Wanting, wanting more.

The four directions cannot contain you. You are more, much more, the fifth place. Woman you are the centre of this place. Centre.

East is air the spring the dawning. South is fire our heat at noon. West is water love juice flowing. North is earth our cunning knowing. Shape-shift woman lovers moving. Slide is five new love-words forming. Tempo shape-shift music blend. Five our centre calling. Slide is five and blend and touch. Belly is five and slope of a hill. Woman's hand on a woman's belly sliding down her sloping hillside to a glade where ferns are moist where woman earth and music blend.

Woman. Vonn. Woman. Rachel. There are many words for love. Music and earth and touch and slide. Slide down down a hand moves, the earth moves, women lovers shape-shift ourselves bodies blend. Woman touch on woman skin. Woman hand on woman belly. Down down the slope of the earth. Your hand slides down down this slope.

So walk your fingers twilight parting ferns the entrance to her cave. Here is her fogou calling you. Five-letter word for woman cave. Five is her fogou, she is cunning. This is knowledge woman wording.

Walk your fingers to her place. Space. Enter now her other world. Time slip into woman space. Between the world of you and her. Which is witch we cannot tell. Between our worlds where joy and sorrow birth and death day and night meet as one.

Blend. Time slip. Slip your fingers where her fogou place is dark. Alive. Warm. She wants you. Slowly inwards to her centre. You are outside she is inside. She is outside you are inside. Which is witch we cannot tell. Dark in here. Beyond twilight. Moist and pulsing.

Finger touch along her fogou. Woman walls of woman place. Move so easily. Welcome now. Love so easily in this place. Her cave, her centre, fogou space.

She is the cunning woman wise. She is the Kennet river deep. She flows with warmth and pleasure sounds. West is woman wise and wet. East is air her sounds are soaring. Fogou wise and good and loving.

Five-letter words for woman loving, they are earth and south and north. South is fire and heat and passion. North is land and cave and woman. Four directions and much more – fogou is a cave inside us all.

Finger walk along the walls. She is a cave washed by a spring. She is a way towards this dream. Feel her ridges. Feel her smoothness. Feel her moisture. Know her sounds.

Dips and rises, dips and rises. She is calling rising falling. Sounds are music, music making. Touch. Touch. She is the cave washed by the spring.

Dark this fogou. Good this loving. Woman, woman place. Know us in this woman space.

* * *

On the shortest day of the year, there are several women carrying wood to the field behind the market garden at Lou and Annie's place near Porthallow.

It is a misty night, and you cannot see any stars. Suddenly into the night the flames leap high and the figures are silhouetted against the light. A silhouette: a woman seated on a chair. Other figures moving. Moving round, changing. Whirling. Touching.

Whooping and shouting, some figures can be seen now dancing around the fire, whirling and leaping, high-energy dancing, and joined by the sound of a drum. Faster the drumbeats, faster the feet leap, faster the figures whirl and circle.

Solstice solstice sun stand still.

Solstice solstice sun stand still.

Wait for the morning, wait for the dawning, wait for the birth of the child from the earth.

Days will grow longer, sun will shine higher, welcome the sun from the womb of the earth.

The earth the air the fire the water,

Return return return return;

The earth the air the fire the water return return return.

She changes everything she touches and everything she touches changes. She changes everything she touches and everything she touches changes.

Touch me. Woman woman touch me.

Change me Woman woman change me.